Praise for the Stranje House

"It's speculative historical fiction, with a trace of steampunk inventiveness. . . . Swoony moments also abound; after all, this is a romance as well. Yet gender stereotypes are turned upside down as the women, who each have an unusual talent, plan a daring spy mission."
—*The New York Times Book Review* on
A School for Unusual Girls

"The richly detailed setting and intriguing alternate history are well crafted, but the characters are what stand out. Narrator Tess is headstrong, melodramatic, and awkward, but she is also brave, bright, and completely real."
—*Kirkus Reviews* on *Exile for Dreamers*

"A tale of daring, conspiracy, adventure, and romance set against the tumultuous backdrop of war-torn Europe in 1814 . . . This alternative history series will appeal to fans of Gail Carriger's works and the Cecelia and Kate novels by Patricia C. Wrede and Caroline Stevermer."
—*School Library Journal* on *A School for Unusual Girls*

"Baldwin has crafted a Regency romance that celebrates smart, strong young women who, while careful to embrace many of society's mores, hold their own with the men they encounter, oftentimes besting them both intellectually and physically."
—*Booklist* on *A School for Unusual Girls*

"Think *Gallagher Girls*, but written by Georgette Heyer."
—*VOYA* on *A School for Unusual Girls*

Also by Kathleen Baldwin

A School for Unusual Girls
Exile for Dreamers
Refuge for Masterminds

EXILE
FOR
DREAMERS

A Stranje House Novel

KATHLEEN BALDWIN

**TOR
TEEN**

A TOM DOHERTY ASSOCIATES BOOK
New York

EXILE FOR DREAMERS

Copyright © 2016 by Kathleen Baldwin

Refuge for Masterminds excerpt copyright © 2016 by Kathleen Baldwin

Reading and Activity Guide copyright © 2016 by Tor Books

All rights reserved.

A Tor Teen Book
Published by Tom Doherty Associates
175 Fifth Avenue
New York, NY 10010

www.tor-forge.com

Tor® is a registered trademark of Macmillan Publishing Group, LLC.

The Library of Congress has cataloged the hardcover edition as follows:

Baldwin, Kathleen, author.
 Exile for dreamers / Kathleen Baldwin.—1st ed.
  p. cm.
 "A Tom Doherty Associates Book."
 ISBN 978-0-7653-7602-2 (hardcover)
 ISBN 978-1-4668-4928-0 (e-book)
1. Napoleonic Wars (1800–1815) 2. 1800–1837 3. Dreams—Juvenile
fiction. 4. Napoleonic Wars, 1800–1815—Juvenile fiction. 5. Boarding
schools—Juvenile fiction. 6. Boarding schools. 7. Dreams. 8. Great
Britain—History—1800–1837—Juvenile fiction. 9. Great Britain—
Juvenile fiction. 10. Great Britain.
 [Fic]—dc23

2016288117

ISBN 978-0-7653-7603-9 (trade paperback)

Our books may be purchased in bulk for promotional, educational, or business use. Please contact your local bookseller or the Macmillan Corporate and Premium Sales Department at 1-800-221-7945, extension 5442, or by e-mail at MacmillanSpecialMarkets@macmillan.com.

First Edition: May 2016
First Trade Paperback Edition: May 2017

Printed in the United States of America

0 9 8 7 6 5 4 3 2 1

To the beloved men in my life who taught me to run, swim, hunt, ride the rapids, ski powder, hang glide, and rock climb—back when girls did not do that sort of thing. To Kathy Redwing for showing me how to talk to horses and gallop without a saddle. To my dad for teaching me to box at a time when it was considered sacrilegious to strap a pair of boxing gloves on a little girl. You all made my life richer, and I will be grateful to you forever.

And to Susan.
Thank you for your extraordinary skills as an editor.
You always make the story better.

Contents

CONTENTS

EXILE
FOR
DREAMERS

One

⊤ESS

~Stranje House, British Coast, May 11, 1814~

I run to escape my dreams. *Dreams* are my curse. Every night they haunt me, every morning I outrun them, and every evening they catch me again. One day they will devour my soul.

But not today.

Not this hour. I ran with Phobos and Tromos, the half wolves, half dogs who guard Stranje House. We raced into the cleansing wind. What is the pace of forgetfulness? How fast must one go?

"Tess! Wait!" Georgiana's gasps cut through the peace of the predawn air and broke my rhythm.

I slowed to a stop and turned. A moment later, Phobos broke stride, too, and trotted back beside me. He issued a low, almost imperceptible growl, impatient to return to our race. Georgie leaned forward, breathing hard. Her red hair hung in wet ringlets, dampened from the sea spray that had bathed us as we ran along the cliffs. But we were inland now, headed for the woods between Stranje House and Ravencross Manor, and except for the misty ghostlike vapors swirling about us, the air was much easier to take in.

Winded, she gulped greedily for more. "I have to stop. My side hurts."

Tromos trotted behind her and nipped at Georgie's heels.

"Ouch!" She jerked her boot away. "Stop that."

"She wants you to keep running."

"I'm trying." Tromos tried to nip her again, but Georgie swatted at her. "Back!"

The dog growled in warning and Georgie withdrew.

"Tromos," I scolded.

She tilted her head at me, tail wagging, and shook droplets of moisture out of her black fur, quizzical as to why I'd called her off. After all, she was only doing what was best for her pack, training the young one to run faster.

"Walk." I looped my arm through Georgie's and tugged her forward, needing to get Georgie moving before Tromos took to nipping again. "Ever since that night on the beach, when she kept you warm, Tromos considers you one of her pack. She's practicing for when she becomes a mother in a few weeks"

Georgie's eyes opened wider. "Is that really why she nudges me with her nose so often? She thinks I'm one of her pack?"

"In a sense. Yes." It was true, but I had to stifle a smile.

Georgie was such an unlikely creature of the forest, especially clad in that bright white cotton dress. It was one of the absurdly frothy concoctions her mother had sent with her to Stranje House. Georgie had ripped the flounce off so that it was short enough to run in, but the fierce white only served to make her

appear more flamelike. Georgie is a burst of fire, a blazing beacon in the early morning gray.

Unlike me.

I am part forest. Wearing this brown dress, I blend with the
woods. My eyes are green as leaves, my hair is dark as shadows
on bark, and my skin is as pale as frost. I am Welsh, a daughter
of the earth. My mother used to tell me that the spirit of these
things, the soil and trees, the rocks and beasts, they call to us.
"We are part of this land," she would say. Only now, my mother
lies silent, cloaked in the very earth she spoke of with such love.

I shook away those thoughts.

"Are you well?" Georgie asked. "You went pale for a moment."

I refuse to speak of my mother's death, so I ignored her
question and mumbled, "Tromos also nudges to show affection." I pulled Georgie into a faster walk. "Today she's prodding
you to make you keep running, so you'll learn to go faster and
longer. If you don't want to—"

"I do. I simply can't. My legs won't go any farther this morning."

"Strength is not found in the legs. It's in the mind." I run
because I fancy I'll escape my wretched dreams, but with Georgie,
it is a different matter. "Why did you want to come running
with me this morning anyway?"

Her chest heaved. "You know why."

I had my guesses, but I wanted her to say it, so I kept mum.

"If I'd been faster that night in London . . ." She gasped for
more air and didn't finish speaking.

I knew she was thinking of Lord Wyatt, the young diplomatic
attaché who had paid a painful price because of her mistakes.
But he'd made mistakes, too. Sebastian had known better than
to fall in love in his line of work and yet he'd let Georgie steal
his heart. She could not be held accountable for that.

I hated to see guilt clawing at her mind. "Stop blaming yourself for what happened in London and Calais. It wasn't your fault."

Georgie had been at Stranje House for less than a fortnight when Lady Daneska captured her as part of a plot to put Napoleon back on the throne of France. Nor was it Georgie's fault that Lord Wyatt was kidnapped when he attempted to rescue her. He couldn't very well have left her to Lady Daneska's mercy. Daneska has none. It would've meant a cruel and painful death.

Poor Georgie, she'd been sent away to Stranje House innocently believing the scandalous rumors about it being a school that employed brutal methods to reform the manners of troublesome young ladies to make them ready for the marriage mart. And why shouldn't she? All of England's high society thought the very same thing.

Only a handful of people in the entire world knew the truth, that Miss Stranje secretly trained gifted young women to serve England as spies. And we'd dared not tell Georgie until we were certain of her loyalty. We knew the price of trusting too easily. After all, Lady Daneska had been one of us, an outcast, a student at Stranje House, and my closest friend. And yet she'd betrayed us, betrayed Britain. She'd run away and aligned herself with Napoleon's secret Order of the Iron Crown.

"If I'd been faster I might've caught up to Daneska, and—"

"No!" I tugged her forward. "You don't know her like I do. If you'd been faster that night, Lady Daneska would've captured you, too. Then she would've delivered two hostages to the Iron Crown instead of one."

"You don't know that." She yanked her arm away. "I might've been able to lead Captain Grey to them. Or perhaps, if I could've stopped their wagon and freed Seb—" She squeezed her eyes closed and trailed off, unwilling to say Sebastian's name out loud.

I knew she was remembering him as he was in Calais, the day when we rescued him from the Iron Crown's stronghold. She was seeing the wounds on his chest and back, proof of the torture he'd endured.

I bit my bottom lip to keep from blurting out the fact that if she had caught up to them in London, without a doubt both she and Lord Wyatt would be dead. "Lord Wyatt recovered, Georgie. He's alive and well, and that's thanks to you." I pointed east toward Europe. "Because of you Sebastian is over there with Captain Grey, serving king and country, doing his very best to stop Napoleon."

But my words failed to console her. She stared off at the pink rim of dawn on the horizon. "It was my fault he was captured in the first place. If I'd caught up to them, maybe I could've bested Lady Daneska and spared him all that suffering." She said it with soft uncertainty, as if her words slid down an oily strand of false hope.

"That's too many *ifs* and *maybes*. Daneska is fast and skilled with a blade. I should know, I sparred with her and lost often enough. You'd had no training yet. I don't see how—"

"That's the point, isn't it?" Her chin jutted out like it always does when she musters her courage. "Madame Cho is training me now, teaching me defensive arts. I'm improving with both the dagger and my fists. But I want to be able to run faster in case . . . in case someone's life depends upon it.

"That's why I insisted on running with you." She shoved a handful of curls defiantly away from her face. "And now, if you will excuse me, I'm going back to the house. I would rather not be around when you meet up with Lord Ravencross. We're nearing the spot." She waved her hand at the opening in the trees, as if I'd forgotten where we were.

Lord Ravencross.

The sound of his name on her lips made my foolish heart tumble as if it had lost its footing.

I stared at the clearing up ahead and caught my lip. Except for this gap, thick stands of trees separated his estate from Stranje House's grounds. This glade was where I usually cut through to run on his pasture. The ground fell more evenly there, or so I told myself. This juncture was also where he liked to exercise his horse, Zeus. It was the place where he used to pretend he didn't plan to meet me. The place where he'd had the audacity to kiss me several weeks ago.

But things were different now.

"He won't be there." My words whirled through the air and came back to me, landing hard, like stones dropping on my chest from a great height.

Georgie denied them with a shake of her head. "Surely, he will—"

"No." I drew in a deep breath, and made myself face facts squarely. That's what I try to do, always face the truth. There's no sense lying to oneself. "He hasn't come out riding in the early morning, not once since that night in London when I abandoned him on the dock."

Georgie stepped closer as if to comfort me. "Perhaps he doesn't know we've returned from France."

I moved back. "Don't be absurd. It's been two weeks."

"Only thirteen days," she corrected, always accurate, always exact. "He may not have observed . . ."

Fortunately, she dropped that foolish line of defense, except the pity that took over her expression made things worse.

I wanted to run again. Instead I did something I never do with Georgie. I argued. "You like to put a favorable construction on things, don't you? Well, in this case, you are just plain wrong."

I didn't intend for it to sound that harsh, but I couldn't let her sympathy weaken me.

In less strident tones I added, "He's taken a dislike of me. And why shouldn't he? What sort of a young lady takes a running leap off the end of a pier and grabs hold of a moving ship?"

"But you *had* to." The loudness of her declaration startled the dogs. Georgie caught her bottom lip and lowered her gaze to the grass and bare patches of dirt between us. "You knew I would need your help in Calais. I was terribly glad you did," she mumbled. "Lord Ravencross is bound to have understood."

I doubted that.

I recalled his alarm when I'd slid down from the back of his horse. "What in heaven's name?" He'd called after me even louder when I'd hitched up my ballgown and dashed down the length of the wharf. "Tess, stop!" But I'd kept running, and as Captain Grey's ship sailed past the end of the pier, I'd launched myself off the dock. Midair, during those breathless seconds before slamming into the ship, I'd heard Ravencross's unmistakable roar. I hadn't known what that awful cry had meant. Had it been fear that I would miss the mark? Shock? Anger? Disbelief?

Whatever it meant, I was fairly certain he would never forgive me for putting him through the turmoil of that night.

I narrowed my gaze at Georgie. "You think he understood, but when you hoisted me aboard you must have seen his face. Did you think he looked pleased that I'd left him in that manner?"

She didn't answer right away. I didn't need her to. I could envision his scowl. "Well, no. He looked startled. He probably didn't realize you knew how to swim. Very few young ladies do. He was worried, I'm sure . . ." She kicked at a pebble.

With a resigned sigh I said, "And there you have it. The high and mighty Lord Ravencross has turned his heart back into stone. And when it comes to any thought of me, he will have ground my memory to dust."

A thin wisp of vapor snaked across our path and blew apart as if a blast of wind exploded it. Phobos, his ears peaked and alert, trotted a short distance up ahead and halted.

Something was not right.

The woods were too quiet. Morning larks, who every night tried to hurry sunrise with their song, had hushed. Rabbits, who loved to suckle on grass covered in morning dew, ought to have scampered into the underbrush at our approach, but they were already hiding.

Still as the birds around me, I strained to hear. A breeze blew through the woods in broken patterns. Leaves rustled in stops and starts, disturbed by some intruding presence. I closed my eyes and heard a whicker in the distance, stamping hooves. Horses in the woods. Impatient. Pawing. A snort, followed by the clacking of a metal bit against thick teeth. Horses held at a standstill, not allowed to graze.

Georgie touched my sleeve. "What is it?"

"Hush," I whispered. Both dogs came silently to my side. I drew the knife from the sheath on my calf.

Phobos and Tromos crouched into hunting position, their shoulders slunk low as we crept forward. I heard a twig break in the distant underbrush and pebbles click under horseshoes as one of the animals moved through the thick stand of trees at the north corner of the field.

In that instant, images flashed through my mind. Blinding splotches of color tumbled and spun in my head. I could no longer see the field or woods. Instead, I was overcome by a burst of black and then an explosion of white. Georgie's dress? It shimmered away, and in its place I saw Tromos tearing at a man's leg. Blood. Knives slashing. Lord Ravencross's face. A searing pain struck my chest. The blast of a gunshot startled me out of the vision.

I gasped and clutched my upper chest to stop the bleeding. Except there was no blood. No wound. It had only been a phantom pain. I opened my eyes wide and stared at the stillness in the predawn field. There were no frightened birds winging away in the sky. Nothing had disturbed the dewy gray-green grass. No shot had been fired, and yet I shook as if it had truly happened.

It had only been a dream.

Not real.

A useless, indecipherable vision. It was *nothing*, I told myself. Only a cursed waking dream, like the ones that drove my mother—and her mother before her—to their graves.

I forced myself to breathe slow and even, quieting my heart so I could listen more closely to what was actually happening. One horse moved through the undergrowth in the woods up ahead, and yet I still heard others. Why were they staying back?

A lone rider emerged from the trees and rode toward us. He touched the rim of his felt hat and called out a greeting. "Good day, *mam'selles*."

Phobos bared his teeth and growled. I didn't like the man either. Menace wafted off him like stink from a chamber pot. His eyes landed on Georgie and brightened with a vicious sort of glee, and I knew—they had come for her.

We would never be able to outrun his horse. But the wolves and I could fend him off while she escaped. "Georgie." I spoke low. "Run," I urged through gritted teeth. "Go. I'll hold him off. Get help. Bring weapons."

She hesitated. "I can't leave you."

That was all it took. The blackguard saw her alarm, issued a shrill whistle, and kicked his horse.

"Run!" I ordered, this time in a voice she couldn't argue with. She took off and, tired or not, she tore for the house as if her life depended upon it. And it did.

Georgie had the presence of mind to scream, a shrill, throaty shriek that sliced through the early morning peace like a bolt of lightning, and she kept at it, yelling for help, loud enough to awaken half the countryside.

Phobos and Tromos streaked toward the horseman.

The man cursed in French and dug in his spurs. Except his mare was no warhorse seasoned for battle. This was a skittish rented hack, wide-eyed with terror at the wolves charging her. She wheeled sideways and reared, snorting and shying to ward them off. Their snarling, snapping jaws gave her no quarter. Phobos circled behind her. The horse kicked, spun, and reared again, throwing her rider to the ground.

Just then, three more horsemen charged out from the underbrush.

Three.

Knife in my hand, I took a stance, ready to stop whoever came at us first, the men on horseback, or the fallen rider struggling to escape Tromos, whose teeth were buried in the scoundrel's leg. I caught a glimpse of another rider galloping across the neighboring field. He was only a speck in the distance, but I would recognize him from a hundred miles away.

Lord Ravencross!

Gabriel had ridden out this morning, after all. Surely he could hear Georgie's screams. But even if he did, Lord Ravencross would arrive too late to save her. And what would he use to fend off the brigands? His bare hands? No, it fell to me.

Phobos and Tromos left off attacking the fallen man and raced to face the three new riders. One of the henchmen was able to steer wide and galloped past them. He ran to the fallen man and dismounted to help, but the injured man shoved him away and pointed in my direction. "*Idiot.* Leave me. Get her."

The new arrival squinted at me from under the brim of his sailor's cap. "That 'un? Nah. When Herself arrived in England, I heared her clear as day. We was to nab the redhead. That 'un ain't red." He swiped an arm across his mouth. "An' she has a knife."

I glanced over my shoulder at Georgie. She was still too far away from the house. Still too easily caught. The wolves held the other two riders at bay, but how long would that last?

"*Imbécile! La fille rousse* is halfway to the house. *La comtesse* also promised extra francs if we did in the Marquis from next door. But I don't see a lord strolling by, do you?"

His cohort glanced toward Ravencross Manor as if he was actually expected to answer the question. Had they not seen Lord Ravencross galloping in our direction? Perhaps not, since he was riding along the north field beyond the trees. But if they should turn and look behind them . . . My stomach knotted even tighter. There was no time to consider what might happen if they did. I stepped back, placing myself in a better position to block these scoundrels' path to Georgie.

The injured man spit on the ground at his companion's feet. "Think, you sorry excuse for a dog's bottom. There'll be no silver for us, and hell to pay if we come back empty-handed. Are you afraid of a little girl?"

"Hoi!" the other man objected. "That's no little girl—not holding a dagger like that, she's not."

I continued edging back, trying to gain some distance.

The one giving the orders cursed under his breath and limped to his companion's saddlebag. He drew out a pistol and thrust it at the other man. "Take it. Go! Bring one of those girls back alive. I don't care which."

The lackey advanced on me, a burlap sack tucked in his belt and the pistol waving unsteadily in front of him.

Tromos yipped as one of the riders lashed at her with his riding crop and shouted to the other rider, who was struggling with his rearing mount. "Cut 'em down."

"Leave her be," I shouted. *She was pregnant.* My pulse quickened and my free hand fisted in anger. I wanted to protect Tromos, but I couldn't. My focus snapped back to the man fast approaching me.

"Y-you . . ." He swallowed and his Adam's apple bobbed up and down nervously. "Put down that knife."

Perhaps I should've called the dogs to help me, but that would have freed the two riders to run down Georgie and all would be lost. I couldn't let them take her, not knowing how Lady Daneska enjoyed torturing her captives. I had to stop them. I wasn't precisely certain how I would do it, but I knew from my training that every move I made now would count toward her life or death.

Time did a peculiar thing. All the clocks in the world must have stopped as I shifted the knife in my palm and changed my hold in preparation to throw.

The gunman striding toward me seemed to slow down. Birds stopped flapping their wings and hung flightless in the air. The wolves' deep guttural barks and snarls faded to nothing. Even the horses' fearful neighing and rearing stopped. Their tails lay stretched out and frozen on the wind. It was as if I possessed all the time in the world to aim and send the blade speeding to its mark.

I threw. The knife streaked in a blaze of silver through the gray morning air and plunged into the gunman's chest. I lunged to the left in case his gun went off. It didn't. He glanced down at his chest, stunned, staring at the hilt of my dagger as if a bee had stung him rather than six inches of steel.

"*Mon Dieu*," he said, dragging out each vowel, and then he dropped the gun. It tumbled slowly from his fingers, struck the grass, bounced, and fired.

The blast of his pistol awakened the world and set time spinning again. The sun peeked up from the horizon, a crimson fireball trying to burn through the morning haze.

The wolves turned to see what had happened. The other riders fought with their frightened horses, who shied and kicked in a desperate attempt to retreat to the woods.

Across the park, Ravencross bent over Zeus's neck and broke into so swift a gallop it was as if he were racing God himself.

Everything was going to go very wrong in the next few seconds if I didn't do something quickly. I needed my knife. I rushed to the fallen gunman, kicked the pistol farther away from him, and wrenched my dagger out of his chest. His eyes opened wide when the blade slid free.

"I'm sorry," I whispered. He wouldn't die, surely not from that one wound. Or so I thought, until blood spurted out of the vacant gash, and when his mouth moved in a wordless plea, thick wine-colored liquid bubbled out.

I winced, swallowing back the sickness rising in my own throat.

With shaking hands, I wiped the blade on the grass. There was no time for the paralyzing horror to what I'd done. It was nothing new, I told myself. How many deaths had I lived through in my dreams? *Hundreds.* And yet this felt different. Vastly different. Always in my dreams, I was the one who died, experiencing deaths yet to come, or deaths that might be. But this man was real. He wasn't an elusive dream. He lay dying because of me, his blood seeping into the ground because of me. My dagger had cut his life in two.

I heard hooves pounding the earth, coming in my direction. I heard Phobos and Tromos leap back into action. I even heard the leader's limping gait as he ran toward me, shouting in French, telling his men to grab me. Even so, I couldn't stop wiping the death stain from my dagger.

I began to shake. At least, I think I did. I remember a shudder coursing through me until I heard Gabriel call my name.

"Tess!" His voice seemed to echo to me from far across the field, as if we were in one of the smugglers' caves that riddled the coastline beneath Stranje House. "Tess!" It rang so forcefully in my ears that it seemed to reach in and shake my very soul. I glanced up just in time to see Gabriel leap Zeus over one of the hedgerows in the north field.

He was coming.

I blinked slowly, letting the sound of him calling my name wash over me. He shouted again, this time with such urgency I realized that if we were to save Georgiana, it was time for me to stand and prepare for another fight.

The roiling sickness inside me ebbed and I tried to stand. But as I rose, a grain sack descended over my head and shoulders. I struggled, swinging my fist and thrusting my blade out, but struck only air.

Something hard cracked against my skull. A roar exploded in my ears.

This was no dream. No vision. No nightmare from which I would suddenly awaken. This time, the bursts of light spinning in my head were real. And the devouring blackness would not wait.

Two

ALIVE

I awoke from that dark oblivion to the unbearable certainty that I'd failed.

There was little doubt that by now the men on horseback would have run Georgie down and captured her. And Lord Ravencross—

I swallowed against the dread swelling in my throat. What chance had he stood? One man against three. Three men with weapons. The curs will have killed or wounded him. The tightness in my throat swelled into a dry, prickly knot.

I was barely able to wheeze air into and out of my lungs. My skull throbbed as if the demons of hell were hammering against it. I'd been slung across the front of a saddle with the gunnysack still cinched over my head, and we were galloping hard. My arms dangled against the side of the horse, and I fought an overwhelming urge to retch.

My thoughts whirled from despair to rage and circled back again, to stomach-churning anguish. I couldn't stop picturing

Georgie captured by Daneska's brigands and Lord Ravencross wounded or dead. And I hung there like useless baggage, unable to help either of them. How could I help them now, when I didn't even know where I was? What could I do?

Nothing.

Nothing, except surrender to Miss Stranje's training.

I squeezed my eyes closed and tried to slam my mind shut against the terrifying thoughts of what might be happening to Georgie and Ravencross. If there was even a remote chance left for me to help them, I needed to think clearly. I could almost hear Madame Cho barking at me to *regulate my breathing,* and Miss Stranje instructing the five of us girls. *"In a sticky situation remain calm."* She would clap her hands marking each point. *"Order your thoughts. Assess the situation. Once you know the wisest course, take swift and sure action."* She'd repeated that litany to us so many times it had almost become a song in my head.

There was nothing left to do—except obey. So I made a cold, unfeeling list of my circumstances and weighed the options.

My first inclination was to yank the stinking burlap sack off my head so I could see more than this reedy view of road and horse. Except that would alert the rider that I was awake, and in so doing I could expect another whack on my head.

Next, I considered shoving myself off the horse. Although falling from this angle, while galloping this fast, would most likely pull me directly under the horse's hooves. I might be able to grab my abductor's leg and yank him out of the saddle with me. Then we would both tumble under the horse, but at least that would injure him, too, and I might get free.

The horse.

I should've thought of that sooner.

"Arhosiadau," I whispered, which meant "halt" in the old language. She tensed, lurched, and took a quick misstep before

regaining her gait. Skittish. This was another rented horse, uneasy and fearful. I thought of a way to spook her, except at that very moment I heard a shout accompanied by the steadily increasing rhythm of another horse galloping not far behind us.

"Stop, or I'll shoot!"

That voice froze me in place. *Ravencross?*

No. It couldn't be him.

He shouted again. It *was* him. Giving chase. Like the skittish mare, my pulse pitched forward and took several missteps before regaining her gait. How? How had Gabriel escaped the other men?

My kidnapper did not stop. Instead, he whipped our horse into an even faster run. I doubted Lord Ravencross would shoot. I wished to heaven he would, but he wouldn't. Not at this bruising pace. He'd figure the bullet might stray and hit me, or the horse. Even if he shot my captor, he'd assume, and rightly so, that the riderless horse would bolt with me slung over the saddle.

Time to act.

My hand dangled near the sensitive area where the horse's neck met her chest. I dug in my fingernails, moving them like tiny claws. The horse, thinking it was a rat or some other vermin that might bite her, shied and nearly threw us. I slipped my other hand under the girth strap and held tight, thrusting my nails into her neck again.

A gunshot startled me and the horse. Ravencross must have fired after all. The terrified mare reared, stood on her hind legs, and pawed the air. I prayed to God she wouldn't fall backward.

With me draped across the front on the saddle, the rider had no pommel to grab, nothing to hold. I felt him scrabbling and clutching at my back, except I soared up with him. But I had flung both arms around the horse's neck and hung on for dear life, kicking my feet back. The saddle jerked as the rider flew off.

My legs airborne, I scissored them so that when we crashed back to earth I landed straddling the saddle. My frightened steed took off in a frantic gallop. I clung to her neck, the bag still over my head.

The poor animal smelled of fear—sugary sweat and urine. "*Tawelu*," I called to her in the ancient Welsh tongue. I wrapped my arms around her neck and spoke calming words to silence her fear. "*Gwroldeb. Areulder.*" She still ran, but not quite as fast.

I heard Ravencross and Zeus gaining on us. Blind inside the sack, no stirrups, barely able to stay astride, I remained hunched over the pommel, holding on to her neck. The reins whipped useless in the wind. All I had were words. Melodic old words of peace. *Tangnefedd.* Ancient word songs about brave horses. She slowed to a jarring trot and snorted in answer.

"Good girl," I crooned. "*Boddhaus.* I'm proud of you." She tossed her head and allowed Zeus to come alongside.

An arm encircled my waist. I didn't need eyes to know his touch, to recognize his gentle strength. *Ravencross.* I let go, trusted him to swoop me away. As soon as he pulled me onto his saddle, I yanked that stinking hood off my head. We circled away from the runaway horse and slowed to a stop. He lowered me to the ground and dismounted.

"Tess," he murmured, his hands scouring my head and shoulders as if he couldn't believe I was in one piece. "Tess," he said again, this time with a sigh, as if saying it relieved some great strain. Then he frowned. "You've a lump the size of London on your head. You could've been killed."

"What of you, my lord? You're bleeding." The fabric just below his collarbone had been sliced clean through, and a gaping wound was staining his white shirt a rich scarlet.

He kept staring at me. "It's nothing."

Nothing?

I shuddered, remembering the pain of that wound, having felt it earlier that morning. *Nothing?* It had been as if someone shoved a red-hot torch into my chest. That's what the dreams often do, they make me live through another's pain for a short time. For what reason or to what purpose I cannot fathom. I know only that the firstborn women in my family must bear this curse. Perhaps we are being punished.

I clutched his sleeve, in sudden terror of what else may have come to pass in that waking dream. "Georgie? Did they capture her?"

He squinted as if he didn't understand. "That's what they were after, then? *Her.*"

"Yes. Yes. Is she safe? Did she make it to the house?"

"Aye. I believe so. I saw her running toward Miss Stranje. Your headmistress came out of the house brandishing a pistol. She managed to shoot one of the blighters and reload. That's how I came by this." He glanced down at the now empty gun tucked into his belt.

"You fought with them, didn't you? And they stabbed you. How did you get away?" I wanted to lay my hand over the wound and somehow make all the pain he must be feeling disappear. If only I were magic.

"How did I—" He ignored my question and raked back his dark curls. "You baffle me, Tess. In London, you fought beside me, but not like any girl I've ever known. And then, when you leapt onto Captain Grey's ship, I didn't know if you would . . ." Gabriel clamped his lips tight and took a step back.

"If I would what?"

He shook his head and looked annoyed. But I could see the hurt beneath it.

"I had to do it. I had to jump." I parroted the words Georgie had used to console me earlier. They didn't seem to comfort him any more than they had me. And that raised my ire. Not that my ire isn't usually pretty close to the surface. "Aside from that, I had nothing to fear by trying. Had I missed my mark I would've simply swum to shore. I am a perfectly able swimmer."

"Of course. You would be, wouldn't you," he muttered.

"I'm sorry if that displeases you, my lord."

"No, what displeases me is that without a thought for your-self, or a care for what I might fe—" He stopped short and rammed his fingers in his hair as he always does when he is com-pletely flustered.

I'd hurt him that night. It grieved me to think it, but there was no denying what was plainly written in his face.

Part of what I liked about Ravencross was that, at least to me, he often seemed more beast than man. Never more so than he did that morning. He reminded me of our huge wolf-dogs, proud, strong, and magnificent. Even his hair was dark and wild like theirs. Yet, despite his powerful build, he remained guarded and cautious and wary as a wolf.

"It's highly irregular, that's what it is." His boyish confusion vanished, and he flexed his jaw. "And now this." He gestured at the runaway mare, as if I ought to have done something differ-ent. "I don't know what to think about you."

If he were Phobos or Tromos, I would have ruffled his hair and challenged him to a race to goad him out of his wariness. Instead, I tilted my head to the side as if accepting a pretty com-pliment. "It's enough to know you think of me, my lord."

His brows drew together in a frown, but I saw the corners of his eyes soften, hinting that underneath he was pleased that I'd flirted with him. "*Vixen*," he said, as if that would humble me. "What I *think* is that you are the most troublesome female in all of Christendom."

"Such flattery, my lord. You'll turn my head."

He paled, and I realized he'd lost too much blood.

"Gabriel?" I took hold of his arm.

He looked down at my fingers on his sleeve and his lips curved in the merest suggestion of a smile. Except it wasn't a smile I liked. It was weary, too weary, and reeked of relief and surrender.

He looked at me oddly, the way a lover might if he were bidding farewell. "I'm tempted to kiss you and ruin your reputation altogether."

He was teasing. The almighty unsmiling Lord Ravencross was teasing.

A distraction.

My heart faltered. It tumbled weightless through the air as surely as if I'd been thrown from the horse. Gabriel would tease in such a way only if his wounds were worse than he let on.

Much worse.

I tugged him toward his mount. "Get on Zeus. Now."

"You first. We can both . . ." Without another word he gave up arguing and raised his foot into the stirrup, almost too spent to heave himself into the saddle, but he managed. Short of breath, he held out his good arm. "I'll pull you up."

He sounded so weak, so un-Gabriel-like. I fought back the tears that were stupidly trying to water my eyes. There was no time for that. Instead, I took the hand he bravely offered and swung up behind him, clasping his blood-soaked waist. Thick wetness seeped through my fingers. So much blood. Too much. The coppery smell of it stung my nostrils. I regretted every second I'd wasted talking. We needed to hurry. I clucked my tongue and nudged Zeus forward.

Gabriel did not kick Zeus into a gallop, another testament to the truth of his condition. It meant he wasn't certain he could keep his seat in a gallop. We did an easy canter past my abductor. The wretch lay unconscious or dead in the road. I didn't care which. I had only one thought—get Gabriel home and tend to his wounds.

"Tell MacDougal . . . to collect that"—Gabriel drooped in the saddle—"that rubbish."

"My lord?" He didn't respond. I reached around him, cradling his hands in mine, holding the reins with him. "Gabriel, wake up." I had to keep him talking, so that he would remain alert enough that he didn't fall off the saddle. I held my arms more firmly against his sides. "How did you escape the attackers?" When he didn't respond, I spoke louder and jostled him lightly. "You were outnumbered. Tell me."

He groaned. "Saw that cur hit you."

"Yes, but obviously one of them stabbed you. How did you get away?"

"Couldn't let them take you."

He had escaped for my sake. "Oh." I drew in a shivering breath and, for just a moment, pressed my cheek against his back.

He straightened a bit. "When he hit you—it lit a fire in my veins." I felt his muscles tense. "Could've killed ten men." He slumped again. "But now . . ."

"No. No," I pleaded. "Gabriel, don't give up now."

He tried to sit taller. I felt his muscles tighten and then falter again.

"Stay with me. *Please.* Your manor is up ahead. There. See it?" I held him and kicked Zeus faster. *Don't die,* I begged silently. "We're almost home. Please."

Lord Ravencross swayed in the saddle, barely conscious, making short unbidden sounds every time Zeus jarred him. Not full moans, and yet each utterance stabbed my heart as surely as any blackguard's knife. I told myself that at least those groans meant Gabriel was still with me, still conscious, *still alive.*

We neared the place where the road split between the two manors. "Georgie!" I screamed. "Miss Stranje! Anyone! Help!" Someone *please* help us.

I was about to veer toward Stranje House when, in the distance, I thought I saw Miss Stranje and several others standing in the drive at Ravencross Manor. They appeared to be circled around what looked like a dead man sprawled on the gravel. I shouted again and strained to see who was there. That's when I spotted Georgie. She was alive. *Safe.*

It was Seraphina who noticed us first, long before any of them heard my cries. She dashed toward us, running faster than I'd ever seen her go. Her bonnet flipped back and her white-blond hair flew in the wind as if she were an angel on God's errand. Georgie took off right after her, and a burly Scotsman followed hard on their heels. He must surely be MacDougal, Lord Ravencross's man-of-all-work. Miss Stranje scurried behind them, her black skirts flapping like a raven in the wind.

When Sera reached us, she hollered back to the others, "He's hurt." She took hold of Zeus's bridle to steady the horse.

Breathless, Georgie ran straight to my side. "Thank goodness he caught up to you—*oh.*" She took one look at Gabriel and blanched. "How bad is it?"

There was no time to answer her question. MacDougal came huffing and puffing up to us and let go with a guttural cry when he saw Lord Ravencross bloodied and drooping. "Aww, laddie, not again."

He must've been remembering when Gabriel got wounded in the war. We stopped on the drive, and he helped me and Georgie ease Lord Ravencross off the horse. Gabriel was conscious enough to drape his uninjured arm across his servant's shoulder. They stumbled and limped toward the manor. I got hold of his other side to help, and glanced over my shoulder at the ribbon of blood trailing behind Gabriel. How much could he lose and still live? Georgie would know, but I couldn't bear to ask.

"Mrs. Evans!" MacDougal's shout echoed across the drive with enough force to have awakened everyone in the county. "Where are ye, woman?"

A plump woman in a cook's apron stood in the manor doorway crossing herself as she stared at the gristly tableau before her, a circle of neighbors surrounding a dead man on the drive and MacDougal half carrying their employer, who was covered in blood. "Merciful heavens!" Her hands flew to cover her mouth.

"Look lively, woman! The master's hurt."

As we approached with Lord Ravencross, she shuffled back against the doorframe about as helpful as a trout flopping on a riverbank.

We half dragged, half carried Lord Ravencross into the entry hall. MacDougal stopped to catch his breath and looked up the length of the staircase. He heaved a deep sigh. "He's not going up all them stairs, I can tell ye that much."

Mrs. Evans grimaced at the dripping wound. "Aye, poor lad, it's a fine mess he's made of his shoulder. My rooms are closer. Take him down the hall to my bed."

MacDougal renewed his grip in preparation for their journey down the hall, which was too narrow for me to assist them. Lord Ravencross groaned as they started down.

"Careful," I warned.

Miss Stranje pushed between us and herded me back, out of the manor, onto the front step. She leaned close and spoke so softly that only the two of us could hear. "Tess, I must ask you to remain outside."

"What?" I jerked back, astonished. "No." How could she expect me to abandon him? "He needs me."

Her face hardened. Our headmistress is like a hawk. Miss Stranje sees all, and watches over the young in her care, but when it is time to go in for the kill, her eyes darken, and what may have been mistaken for soft feathers turns into steel-plated armor.

In a cold, unwavering voice she laid down the law. "You will stay out, Miss Aubreyson. This is no place for a young lady with your delicate sensibilities. It would be highly improper."

Had she lost her wits? "My delicate sensi—"

"Highly improper," she repeated in a low tone coupled with a flash of indignation. It was as if she thought I was the one being thickheaded. "Particularly with onlookers present."

She bristled up, a veritable wall of black bombazine barring my entrance into the manor. With brusque finality she motioned for Lady Jane. Somehow Jane managed to glide across the gravel drive with the grace of a queen crossing a ballroom. She reminds me of an elegant doe, the way she walks and the way her porcelain complexion sets off her soft brown hair. She is everything I am not, a perfect young lady.

Miss Stranje leaned forward to give Jane instructions, and although she sounded calm a marked urgency punched each word. "Lady Jane, you must hurry to Stranje House and fetch my treatment kit. You know the one—it contains my remedies and bandages."

Jane left without hesitation.

Miss Stranje crooked her finger and issued another order, this time to Maya. "I need you to attend to Tess. She appears to be injured and overwrought."

Maya is small and looks almost childlike. Perhaps it is because her eyes are so large. But there is nothing of the child in Maya. She seems to carry the collective wisdom of her entire village in India with her wherever she goes. Normally when she looks at me it's as if her mother, her grandmothers, her aunts, and cousins are staring out at me. Today her eyes were filled with concern for me. *Pity.*

I didn't need sympathy. Not now. Not ever. What I needed was for Miss Stranje to listen to me.

"I am not overwrought. I'm perfectly fine." Lord Ravencross needed me. He was in pain, and like any wounded beast, he would be more unruly than ever. Who else would be able to calm him? "I'm certainly well enough to assist you."

Miss Stranje's ferocious frown silenced my protest. "Nonsense. Look at you. There's blood in your hair and on your clothes. You are pale and shaking." She glanced past my shoulder as if something of concern stood just beyond me. "You will do as I say." With a sharp toss of her chin, she spun around and headed down the hall.

"Let me help," I rasped pathetically. "*Please.*"

But her shoulders stiffened and she did not even glance back. Mrs. Evans took one look at our formidable headmistress and stepped aside.

"Bring warm water and towels. Quickly." Miss Stranje sent the housekeeper scurrying off to do her bidding and continued marching down the hall. "Mr. MacDougal, as soon as we have situated Lord Ravencross, you must ride with all haste to fetch the doctor."

They all disappeared into the housekeeper's rooms, and I remained standing on the front step, staring into the empty hallway, helpless, prevented from entering as surely as if our headmistress stood guarding the way with a flaming sword.

Three

INNOCENTS

In all the confusion, someone rushed up behind me. It wasn't Sera or Jane. Although I vaguely heard Sera warn, "No. Not now. You mustn't—"

A stranger's voice startled me. "You there, miss—"

That was all I heard before a hand rested on my shoulder and tried to turn me. I'd had enough of strangers grabbing me that morning. I stepped back, clamped hold of the offending paw, dipped forward, and yanked whoever it was over my shoulder.

The maneuver worked as efficiently as it always did in practice with Madame Cho.

My assailant flipped over my shoulder and smacked down on his back in the gravel by the front step.

The young gentleman on the ground appeared to be surprisingly well dressed. His hat had toppled off, revealing honey-colored cherubic hair and eyes blue as an afternoon sky. And although he was trying desperately to catch the wind back into his lungs, his expression was brimming with innocence and inquisitiveness. If he were an animal, I would've instantly liked him. But he wasn't one, and what's more, he'd had the audacity to lay a hand on me.

Where most men would have turned angry at being tossed on his backside, this fellow remained astonished. "I must say—" He gasped hard, gathering in more breath. "That was unexpected." He looked somewhat pleased.

Sera stooped beside him. "I did try to warn you. Are you injured?"

"Not at all." He grinned at her. "Quite all right." And with no heed for the fabric of his coat, he propped himself up on his elbows. "Astounded, mind you, but otherwise undamaged. Only thing bruised is my ego at having been taught my manners."

He stopped beaming at Sera, who had lowered her lashes and blushed a ridiculous shade of red, and turned to me. "My apologies, miss. I should not have startled you. I'd only meant to ask about the man you killed." He seemed in no hurry to move from his position on the ground.

Regardless of how good-natured he might be, I had no interest in his cheeky question. "If you are referring to the man I stopped from abducting Miss Fitzwilliam, I don't see what business it is of yours."

"*Tess.*" Georgie hissed my name and her eyes widened in warning.

"What?" I snapped.

"I don't believe you have been properly introduced," she proceeded, with an oddly formal air. "Miss Aubreyson, this gentleman is Mr. Chadwick. His father, our local justice of the peace, dispatched him to see what all the shooting was about. Apparently neighbors sent word to him after they were awakened by the screams and gunfire. If I understand the situation clearly, until his father and the coroner arrive, it is

Mr. Chadwick's duty to maintain the scene of the crime and collect evidence related to the . . . uh . . ."

She hesitated, obviously avoiding the word "killings" for fear of its effect on me. Her worried expression flittered self-consciously to the place out in the field where we'd been attacked, where he was, the man I'd killed.

". . . the deaths," she finished.

Meanwhile, Sera still knelt beside the overturned magistrate's son, blushing pinker than boiled shrimp. She was unbearably shy and normally withdrew to the edges of most gatherings, watching, and noting anything of importance. But today she remained squarely in the middle, looking completely flustered.

Maya gently urged Sera up and extended a hand to our fallen guest to assist him to his feet. "Our deepest apologies, Mr. Chadwick. As you can see, it has been a most trying morning." Maya's voice flowed smooth and sweet. Her lilting Indian cadence was intoxicating, and her words melted over our ears like warm butterscotch. "Miss Aubreyson's nerves must surely be frayed after having been abducted so roughly, and now . . ." Her hand fluttered gracefully toward the trail of blood. "With Lord Ravencross wounded. I'm sure you can sympathize with her fragile state of mind."

Fragile?

Me?

I tried to shake myself loose from the soothing strains of her voice. It was an absurd thing for her to say. I'm not fragile. Not in the least. Quite the opposite. I journey through hell and back nearly every night, and yet here I am. Why would she say such a thing? I can't risk being fragile.

Before I could object, Chadwick, that impertinent whelp, chimed in. "I understand completely. No one can blame her for being overset. It is not my intention to distress her with these questions. I'm sure this is a difficult situation for all of you genteel young ladies." Mr. Chadwick dusted off his hands and straightened his rumpled coat. He took a second look at my coarse running garb, perhaps reassessing his remark about our gentility. "My father and the coroner will arrive shortly to take matters in hand. But in the interim, Miss Aubreyson, at the risk of troubling you further, I must ask if I might have a word with you while the events are still fresh in your mind—"

"You may have all the words you like, Mr. Chadwick, at another time. At the moment, I am far too concerned with Lord Ravencross's welfare." I stepped around him, hoping to catch a word about Gabriel's condition from MacDougal, who had just charged out of Ravencross Manor. But he swung up onto Zeus and dashed off to get the doctor so fast that I missed my opportunity.

"Ah, I see." Chadwick brushed specks of gravel from his hat. "Then, am I to assume you are his betrothed?"

That stopped me. "Don't be daft." I turned back to him. "The man can scarcely stand to be in the same room with me."

He tilted his head as if trying to cipher it all out. Sera, the wretch, had the temerity to press her lips together, suppressing a smile. They all assumed there was something more than mere acquaintance between Lord Ravencross and me. I don't know what Georgie had told the other girls about that kiss she had witnessed a few weeks ago. But it meant nothing. A moment of weakness on his part, that's all it was. I'd goaded him and he fell prey to my taunts. Nothing more.

Except now they were all hiding smirks.

Enough!

Pushed to my limit, I waved my hand at Georgie. "I suggest you ask Miss Fitzwilliam about the morning's events. She was there. She saw everything. Or quiz Miss Wyndham here." I pulled

Seraphina forward. "Given the fact that she has perfect recall, I'm certain she can give you a complete accounting of anything she may have seen or heard. And knowing my fellow students"—I glared at the pack of them, even Maya—"they will have seen a great deal from their windows."

After all, we attended an establishment for young ladies that trained us to do exactly that, to make detailed observations while pretending we hadn't seen a thing.

His attention whipped to Sera. "Perfect recall?"

I tromped back to the open door and called down the hall. "How is he?"

The housekeeper pattered across it into the bedroom, carrying a bowl of water and fresh linens tucked under her arm. She returned empty-handed and headed straight for me. "Miss Stranje says you're to keep a civil tongue in your head when speaking to the justice of the peace's son, and I'm to close the door."

"No! Wait." I held it open. "You must tell me how he is."

She shook her head. "Wish I knew, miss. It don't look good. That's all I know." Then she shut the door with a click that echoed as loudly as the gunshot had earlier that morning.

I may have thumped my fists against the heavy oak and let out a roar of frustration. I confess, I don't know for certain. Young ladies are not supposed to do such things. I do remember hearing Tromos from clear across the park let out an answering howl.

The sound of it preyed even further on my mind. I felt as if I might explode.

"Very well." I whirled on the justice of the peace's son. "What is it you would like to know?"

He offered me a puppyish smile. "You're injured. Perhaps if you sit down, I might ask you a few simple questions to speed my father's inquiry along." He indicated a bench off to the side of the drive.

I declined his offer and kept pacing. I was too agitated to sit. If I sat down, I felt as if I would slide off and collapse in a puddle.

"And, of course, the law requires us to confiscate your weapon."

My knife. He wanted my knife. The one with a stranger's blood all over it. "Help yourself." I pointed brusquely at the tall grass across the park in Miss Stranje's back field. "My dagger is out there somewhere. You'll have to pardon me for not knowing the exact location. They forced a sack over my head."

For the first time I became acutely aware of the body lying in the gravel on the other side of the drive. "What happened to that man?"

I wanted Georgie or Sera to answer, not him, not the interfering Mr. Chadwick. But he responded first. "Your headmistress shot him in an attempt to protect Miss Fitzwilliam and rescue you." He indicated a spot across the park near Stranje House's garden door. "From there. Quite a distance. I wouldn't have expected a spinster schoolteacher to manage a shot like that at a moving target."

Hackles raised, Georgie huffed. "What does her being a spinster have to do with anything?"

Sera interceded with a slightly less quarrelsome approach. "Surely, you are not assuming that Miss Stranje's aim would be less accurate because she is unmarried? One thing has nothing to do with the other."

"Not at all." He raised his hands, warding them off. "You misunderstand me."

"Hmm." Georgie crossed her arms. "If not, then you must be suggesting a woman cannot fire a gun as accurately as a man. Which is a preposterous notion—"

"Heavens no." He backed up under her onslaught. "My own mother is an excellent shot. Outshoots my father on almost every hunt. No, I simply meant that in her profession, as a headmistress at a finishing school, one would not expect Miss Stranje to have acquired any skill with firearms."

"*Oh.*" Georgie's arms dropped to her sides. "I suppose that is a fairly logical deduction." She fidgeted. Georgie is unable to lie without displaying a great deal of discomfort. "Yes, I see why you might have drawn that conclusion. But it is quite possible Miss Stranje learned how to handle firearms while hunting with her father." She smiled, pleased with the explanation she'd concocted.

It was clever, and I hoped it would throw him off the scent. What Georgie didn't know is that she had just told the plain truth of the matter. Miss Stranje's father had indeed taught her how to handle a gun. Mr. Chadwick need not be told that Miss Stranje's father had been one of England's finest spymasters and that he trained his daughter to follow in his footsteps. We had to guard the true nature of Miss Stranje's school at all costs.

He bowed his head to the side, seeming to accept her explanation.

Seraphina usually speaks with a gentleness that matches her angelic appearance, as if she empathizes with everyone. But that day Sera frowned at Chadwick. No, she well and truly scowled at him. I hadn't thought it possible for her.

In fact, she chided him in a tone so prickly that it sounded completely foreign coming from her. "I'm surprised at you, Mr. Chadwick. It is a dangerous thing to make assumptions without ascertaining the facts first. Particularly when you are here in service to your father's office."

My mouth opened in shock. It was not like Sera to deliver a scold to anyone, and she wasn't finished. "Why *are* you here? Shouldn't you be off studying at Cambridge or Oxford?"

"I . . . well . . . er . . . no." The young gentleman flushed, adjusted his collar, and looked considerably more rattled than he had when I'd yanked him over my shoulder. He took a deep breath before continuing.

"If you must know, and I'm not saying it's of any importance to the matters at hand, but as things stand I didn't, well, you see . . ."

Odd. He'd been such a talkative fellow, and now he stumbled over his words.

His back went rigid, and he did not address any one of us in particular. Except he did glance sidewise in Sera's direction. "Very well, if you insist on the facts of the matter—I surpassed what might be gained at Cambridge at a fairly young age. That's why I am here. My father hired tutors to educate me. Excellent tutors." He turned several shades of pink while explaining. He looked away, smoothed the nap of his top hat with care, and replaced it snugly on his head as if that signified an end to the matter.

So agitated was he at having told us about not going to university that he failed to notice Sera withdrawing even more. She closed in on herself as she so often does. It is impossible for Sera to hide her feelings. A sad gray pall settled over her.

She studied the gravel and quietly said, "You are fortunate to have such understanding parents."

Ah, so that was it.

I understood then what was vexing her, and my heart ached on her account. Mr. Chadwick had been given approval and granted the opportunity to learn. Whereas Sera's peculiar gifts of memory and intellect had been treated with distrust and suspicion. He'd been rewarded for his extraordinary mind with tutors. She'd been locked away in the attic until her family finally sent her to Stranje House, hoping Miss Stranje would force their daughter to be more normal.

Uneasy with the silence that fell between them, I glanced over to where Georgie stood studying the dead man. I took a closer look and drew in a sharp breath.

Mr. Chadwick leapt to attention at my gasp. "You recognize him?"

Despite the sizable hole in his skull, I knew this was the man who'd lashed Tromos with his riding crop.

In a sudden panic, I whirled to Georgie. "Where's Tromos? Did they—is she hurt?"

"She's alive and well." Georgie grasped my shoulders and frowned. "But Miss Stranje is right, you're trembling. You mustn't worry. Both dogs are fine. Agitated, of course, but unharmed. Jane fed them and took them to the kennels."

I nodded with relief and she let go.

Chadwick renewed his question. "So you recognize the dead man?"

"Only that he whipped our dogs because they were trying to protect us. Other than that, no. I don't know him." I backed away from the gruesome specter of his remains, stumbling in the gravel.

I never stumble.

I'm not squeamish. Not a bit, and yet gooseflesh raised on my arms and I shivered.

Mr. Chadwick closed in on my weakness. "Miss Wyndham saw this fellow lift you onto the horse. Do you remember anything else about them? I'm sorry to put these questions to you, but even the slightest detail might help us identify who they were and ascertain their purpose."

"Their purpose?" My hand flew to the lump on my head. "They clubbed me and bagged me! As if I was an animal to be slaughtered." Dizzy with rage, my voice flew up in pitch. "I know nothing of their purpose. How could I?"

He had the decency to flinch.

Georgie reached for my hand. Normally, I would never have taken it. I stand alone. Every night I face carnage and suffering—*alone*. Always alone. I cannot rely on the strength of others. But that morning, I let her clasp my hand in hers, and I am forced to admit it helped calm me.

Chadwick leaned in sympathetically. "My sincerest condolences, miss. They were villains of the first order."

"*Condolences?* Are you pitying me? I'm not the one who is dead. Those men were nothing to me."

He stepped back. "No, miss, but they put you in the monstrous position of having to take a life in order to protect yourself and someone you care about." He shook his head and squared his shoulders. And for just a minute it felt as if his chief concern was my welfare. Except his voice regained its inquisitive bent and he flung one more horrid question at me. "Do you have any idea why they would try to abduct you rather than simply leave you unconscious in the field?"

I pressed my lips together, willing myself to silence, and shot Georgie a desperate glance, remembering exactly what the cutthroats had said. It was supposed to be *her* in that bag, not me. The command had originated from a female leader, and that could mean only one person: Lady Daneska.

What could I tell this prying son of a justice of the peace? *The truth?*

We are actually young ladies with highly specialized talents. Miss Stranje is training us to work with spies and diplomats in service to our country. But we have been betrayed. One of our number ran away and joined Napoleon's Order of the Iron Crown.

Should I tell him that I had simply been an inconvenient substitute? That the traitor, Lady Daneska, in her vicious desire for revenge, planned to abduct Georgie and torture her in order to extract her formula for invisible ink and obtain the current location of several key spies, in particular Captain Grey and Lord Wyatt.

Out of the question. I couldn't say any of that.

So I shrugged weakly.

"It's all so very puzzling." He rubbed his thumb across the faint stubble on his chin. "My father will have a number of questions before we can put this matter to rest. In all likelihood, he will suggest that Miss Stranje hire a Bow Street Runner to investigate. In my opinion, that sort of investigator would be of little use. They've no access to the higher circles of society, and I suspect there is something larger at work here. You're certain you have no idea who these culprits are? Or what connection they might have to yourselves or the school?"

"Of course not." I swallowed against the lie that turned my mouth dry as sand. "Why would I?"

His hat shaded dangerously intelligent eyes. Nevertheless, I could read the signs—in the skeptical tilt of his head, his cheek muscles flinching, and his eyebrows raised a millimeter too high. He didn't believe me.

"How very perplexing." He pursed his lips.

Sera wrapped her arm around my waist. "They were murderers and thieves. They must have assumed Miss Aubreyson came from a wealthy family and planned to extract a ransom."

"That is possible." He continued to appraise me far too astutely. "Although, given her mode of dress, I find that unlikely. Why *are* you wearing a dress of that sort?" He also noted the ragged hem on Georgie's dress. "What brought the two of you outside so early in the morning?"

"A walk," I said tersely and rubbed my arms to keep warm.

"Precisely," Georgie piped up. "We like to take a brisk walk in the cool of the morning before weeding the garden. You wouldn't expect us to wear our Sunday best for that, now would you?"

"I suppose not. But if that's the case, we must assume these men had been watching the house. How often is it your habit to perform these early morning activities, and . . ." Chadwick rattled off a string of questions, but my head throbbed and I found I could no longer listen. All I could see was the dead man with his skull blown half off.

It surprised me when Mr. Chadwick finally quieted for just a moment. He, too, stared at the dead man. "I still think it was a lucky thing your Miss Stranje was able to make that shot."

Lucky?

I turned to stare out at the field where it had all begun. There was another man lying out there with a fatal wound in his chest. *My dagger having done the deed.* Lucky? There was nothing lucky in all this. I hated the word. It tasted like poison on my tongue. The pounding in my head grew nearly unbearable. I reached up to check the bump and was rewarded with a handful of matted hair and blood.

"Let me have a look at that." Sera tugged my shoulder down so she and Maya could inspect the goose egg about to hatch on my skull.

"She needs rest," Maya murmured to Sera. "The shock has been too much."

Sera nodded and turned to my inquisitor. "Mr. Chadwick, look at how pale she is. She must lie down soon, or I'm afraid she'll collapse right here on the drive. We must excuse ourselves and take Miss Aubreyson home straightaway."

"Yes, certainly. My apologies. I should've noticed she's worse off than she let on. I'll help you—"

"Wait." I turned and pointed down the lane. "There may be another man, back there, lying in the road. I don't know if he's dead or not. When Lord Ravencross fired his pistol, the horse reared and threw the rider. We couldn't stop to check. Lord

Ravencross's injuries were too . . ." I stared down the length of my arm. Wine-colored streaks stained my sleeve. Gabriel's blood was everywhere. Crusted and drying. I gaped at my outstretched arm. "Too severe."

Shivers changed to quaking. I'm not the missish sort. Truly, I'm not. Nor do I have a weak stomach. Nevertheless, I felt as if I would vomit at any minute.

"I'm cold." My plea sounded puny and weak even to my ears.

Mr. Chadwick whipped off his coat and draped it over my shoulders. He turned to Sera. "I'll help you get her home."

Sera brushed him away. "Thank you, no. We can manage." Maya put a supporting arm around me on the other side.

Georgie wedged herself between us and him. "You've done quite enough for one morning, Mr. Chadwick. At any rate, aren't you are obligated to stay here to meet your father and the coroner?"

"Yes, but . . ." He stood there looking more bewildered than ever as we trudged down the drive and started across the lawn toward Stranje House. Apparently, those excellent tutors of his had not taught him how to deal with young ladies.

Four

SECRETS

Mr. Chadwick called after us, "I didn't mean to distress you. I hope you feel better tomorrow, Miss Aubreyson. We'll call on you then, and perhaps you'll be able to give us a more thorough account."

Georgie took the lead as we pushed through the grass heading back to Stranje House.

"He asks too many questions," I mumbled to Sera.

"Mmm," she agreed, and glanced back over her shoulder. "He's too curious by half. And unless I miss my guess, he'll be like a dog with a bone until he solves this puzzle. We must come up with some suitably engaging answers."

Jane met us where the two properties bordered as she was coming back from Stranje House. Philip, our footman, trailed behind her, carrying Miss Stranje's doctoring bag and a stack of extra linens from our bandage closet. Immediately, she added the ewer and basin she carried to the footman's stack and rushed to us. "What's happened?"

Sera kept hold of my arm as she explained, "The blow to Tess's head is worse than we thought. We're taking her home."

"Wait. I'll help you." Jane instructed the footman to hurry on to Ravencross Manor and take the equipment directly to Miss Stranje.

He left us and we continued on our way, but when we passed the undergrowth on Stranje House's park, I stopped walking. "We may be making a mistake." Something was gnawing at me. I needed to reconsider our hasty departure. "Sera, I think you ought to go back. Return Mr. Chadwick's coat to him. Try to convince him that he needn't come back tomorrow. You'll think of something to say." I pulled off his coat and held it out to her. "Please. I can't bear any more of his questions. Besides, you can tell his father everything you saw without having to lie."

"Tess has a point." Georgie agreed with me for once. "Sera, you could help guide them as they investigate the scene. One of us really ought to be there to throw them off the scent. And it was obvious he respected you the most."

"I don't know." She glanced back at the young man pacing on the drive. "What if he sees through me?"

I shivered without the warmth of his coat. "He won't. You're a girl. He'll underestimate you. They always do."

"That's right." Jane patted Sera's arm. "You'll think of something to keep them from looking too closely at what goes on at Stranje House. You're the best of us at strategy."

"I'm not as convinced as you are that he'll underestimate me. And Jane, everyone knows you're better at strategy than I am. You're just trying to convince me to go stick my neck out."

Jane didn't argue. She simply glanced to her feet and shifted uncomfortably. "Perhaps, but you're definitely better at pointing out details they might not notice, or knowing which of those clues might be to our advantage if they didn't notice."

Sera sighed. "Very well, I'll do my best." With a determined nod, she snatched the coat from me, turned, and marched back to Ravencross Manor like a soldier bravely headed off to war.

Jane pushed aside the branches of a scrub oak and we pressed on to Stranje House. Georgie took Sera's place, and I leaned closer to her. "You do realize it was you they were after?"

Her eyes squeezed tight for a minute as if she could keep the truth out that way.

She needed to face it. "I heard them say so. They'd been told to nab the girl with the red hair, and the person who gave them their orders was female. *La comtesse.*"

Georgie caught her breath. "A countess, then—"

"Daneska!" Jane finished for her.

"Undoubtedly," I said. "She'd also told them she'd pay extra if they killed Lord Ravencross." I shivered even more violently, but this time not from feeling cold. "Why would she want him killed?"

Worry flashed between Georgie and Jane, followed by a conspiratorial expression that set warning bells clanging almost as loud as the drumming in my head. *They were hiding something.*

"What is it?" I demanded. But they remained buttoned up tighter than clams out of water. It didn't matter, I would fish it out of them eventually.

Jane tried to smooth over the uncomfortable silence. "You *know* why. She's hated him ever since Möckern, when he . . ." She trailed off.

Möckern.

The battlefield where Lord Ravencross was wounded the first time.

The day Lady Daneska's paramour died.

I'd lived it in a dream. No, not a dream, a recurring nightmare that haunted me long before I'd actually met Ravencross. Three times

I'd dreamt of that ghastly humid battlefield in Möckern. I could still see the insides of the ramshackle farmhouse where they fought. Could still smell it. That house stank of rot, mold, and the coming storm. Three times I lived through that sword fight between the brothers. Two men on opposite sides of the war, one loyal to England, and the other, leader of the Iron Crown, Napoleon's secret order of knights.

Gabriel's older brother almost killed him that day. Sliced his leg nearly in two. An injury he still carries. Anyone else would have died.

Not him.

Gabriel does not die easily. I prayed that today it would remain true.

His brother, Lucien, had moved in for the death blow. Instead of giving up, Gabriel swung his sword around and delivered one last protective thrust. Lucien collapsed like a toppled tree. His cheek struck the splintered floorboards, and his mouth gaped open in bloody surprise, his eyes fixed in a wide death stare.

I could still see Lucien's lifeless face. Could still feel Gabriel's desolation. Three times I have awakened to a scream that still shreds my peace. Gabriel's cry of anguish. Not for his own pain, but for having killed his only brother.

Of course, Daneska hated Ravencross for killing her lover. But I could tell Jane and Georgie were still holding something back, something that had to do with him, with Ravencross. "What are you hiding? Tell me."

I glared at them, annoyed that they would try to keep a secret from me. I would wiggle it out of them in time. Not today, though. Today I was weary, and my head hammered like a blacksmith reworking a bent horseshoe.

"We must concentrate on the matter at hand." Georgie's ploys are transparent. Obviously, she sought to distract me. "Think hard," she wheedled. "Did you notice anything about your kidnappers that might lend us a clue?"

"I'm not Sera," I grumbled. "I don't remember details."

"Try."

We crossed through Miss Stranje's gardens. A tangled mass of roses left to grow wild created a maze of thorns, calculated to discourage visitors from arriving in that direction. Georgie persisted with her questions. "There must be something you recall. Did they say anything else that might help us? Perhaps you noticed an accent?"

She needled as much as Mr. Chadwick, except now that I thought of it, she was right. I *had* noticed something. "The one with the injured leg had a thick French accent. But the other one, the man who came at me, the one . . ." *The one I killed.* I bit my lip before continuing. "His vowels were mixed up. It sounded as if he might've been from East Sussex."

Then I remembered the worst of it. "He said she'd given him their orders when she arrived in England."

"Ohhh." Georgie blew air through her lips. Her brow pinched up and her freckles paled. "That means she's here. Lady Daneska is back in England."

Jane and Maya both stopped cold. We all did. Jane turned around, her lips pressed tight. "Then we must assume they traveled here from somewhere along our coast. Close by."

"I could be wrong. Perhaps the blow to my head has muddled things," I said, hoping to ease their minds, except I could still hear those blackguards talking in my head.

Georgie rubbed her ear as if that might change the facts she'd heard. "This is not good. Not good at all."

"Come on, let's get you into the house." Jane put her arm around my waist and urged me forward.

Georgie stomped along behind us, grumbling about Daneska's brazenness at returning to England. "Doesn't she know she could go to the gallows for her treachery?"

Maya answered with a quiet but troubling truth. "I believe Lady Daneska fears very little."

"She's an irrational creature." Georgie's hands balled into fists. "No better than a common viper."

A *common* viper?

No, there was nothing *common* about Daneska. Oh, Dani was poisonous, all right, but she was more like an exotic cobra. Beautiful. Mesmerizing. Deadly.

And twice as crafty.

After all, she'd fooled me from the very beginning. The two of us had lost our mothers, so I'd mistakenly thought our grief bonded us.

When I first arrived at Stranje House there had been two older girls at the school, but soon after they both made advantageous marriages, marriages that strategically placed them in key foreign courts. That left me a lone student at Stranje House until Lady Daneska appeared at our door. After her mother died, Daneska's father, one of Napoleon's newly minted dukes, sent her to live out of harm's way with her maternal aunt, Lady Pinswary, one of Miss Stranje's neighbors. Lady Daneska had complained that her aunt and cousin nearly suffocated her with boredom and that rumors about the school sparked her curiosity. But after all that's happened, I wonder if getting into Stranje House had been her objective all along.

She told me she'd badgered her aunt into sending her to Stranje House and even offered to pay the tuition herself. Lady Pinswary finally relented, but only after issuing numerous warnings about Stranje House's notorious discipline chamber and the reputed cruelty of our headmistress.

I admit I'd been exceedingly glad of Daneska's company. In no time we were thick as thieves, competing against each other in defensive arts, playing tricks on Madame Cho and Miss Stranje. I'm still not certain why she befriended me. When Lady Jane, an earl's daughter, came to the school five months later I would've thought her a much more suitable connection. But Daneska had no interest in Lady Jane, nor in Seraphina, who joined our ranks a few weeks later. From the start Daneska had been intrigued by my dreams, and I'd thought she understood me as no one else had ever done. When in truth, the traitor had merely been learning how to best take advantage of my friendship.

I realized later, she had never felt the loss of her mother as I did. Her grief had been a pretense, a cobra's mesmerizing dance.

The only loss Daneska mourned was being a countess in her father's court.

Georgie slapped a twig out of her way. "If Lady Daneska had a lick of sense she would be afraid, because if I ever get my hands on her scrawny neck there'll be no need for a hangman. She must be made to answer for what she did to Sebastian."

"And for her betrayal," added Jane.

As we climbed the back steps, the garden door flew open and Madame Cho rushed out. Clearly, she'd been watching from the window. She nudged Jane and Maya out of the way and marched me into the house. The minute we were inside, she began sizing up the lump on my head. I winced as she inspected it, while evaluating me with her coal-black eyes.

"Come." She tugged me down the hall to the small sitting room where we usually studied geography and language. "Sit." She wrapped an afghan around me, washed the blood from my hands and face with a ewer and cloth. By the time she finished, the water in the basin had turned a sickening red. She peered closely into each of my eyes, first one and then the other.

Madame Cho clicked her tongue, rattled off something in irritated Chinese, and then told me what I already knew. "You have a bad bump. Very bad."

"I'll mend. I just need to rest." I leaned back against the sofa and closed my eyes.

Madame Cho yanked on the bellpull, and Alice, our parlor maid, hurried in. "Bring tea."

Alice had no sooner left than Greaves, our butler, appeared in the doorway and cleared his throat. "Pardon me, ladies, but we have a visitor."

Madame Cho looked up, suddenly wary. I think it was because of the way Greaves said the word "visitor," as if it wasn't simply Lady Somebody-or-Other from the village.

"We've no time for visitors today." Jane took charge, as she is inclined to do. Not that Jane is domineering. It's simply that she excels at managing. "You may tell whoever it is that we are not at home today."

"Begging your pardon, miss, but this one claims he carries a message."

When Jane makes up her mind, she won't budge for anything less than an artillery shell. "Tell him to leave his message and go."

"But—"

Georgie exhaled loudly. "Don't you see, Tess is injured. We've bodies in the field, a nosy magistrate's son, and Lady Da—" She stopped short and caught herself before sputtering all of her worries out on poor Greaves. "Not today. We simply can't allow vis—"

Greaves never interrupts, but he did that day. "A message from Lord Wyatt."

Georgie paled and stood, staring at Greaves. Her frustration drained entirely away. Quiet as a breath, Lord Wyatt's given name escaped her lips. "Sebastian."

"Yes, miss." Despite the hump on his back, Greaves stood as rigid as the king's guard and solemn as an undertaker.

"I'll go with you." Jane took Georgie's arm. "Greaves, you may show the messenger to the upstairs parlor. Thank you."

"Wait!" I leaned forward to stand up. "I'm going with you, too. I'll not have any more secrets."

"No. You will not." Madame Cho clamped an iron hand on my shoulder and pressed me back down. "You must stay still. No stairs. Not yet."

"Very well, if you're that worried about it, we'll all stay together." Jane acted as if, in Miss Stranje's absence, she were the matriarch of Stranje House even though she was younger than me, and Madame Cho really ought to be giving the orders. But she has that air of command about her, and everyone just seems to fall in line. She guided Georgie back to the divan and issued more instructions. "You may show this messenger in here, Greaves."

"Here?" Georgie looked about the room strewn with books and maps.

Madame Cho grumbled about it not being proper. She probably would have objected further except Alice hurried into the room with a teapot and tea tray.

Greaves hoisted his nose higher in the air, obviously disapproving of the decision. Before he could leave the room, Philip burst in, hunched over and panting as if he'd run all the way from Ravencross Manor.

Greaves raised one gloved hand and delivered a disciplinary smack to the center of his footman's back. "I will not have you bolting into a room huffing and puffing as if you have just finished a race. Not in front of the ladies."

"No, sir." Philip stiffened to soldierlike attention. "Begging your pardon, ladies. I was given orders to run straight here with a message from Miss Stranje, in particular for you, Miss Aubrey-son. I'm to tell you to stop fretting. The doctor has arrived, Lord Ravencross is being well cared for, and it looks as if he is going to live. She also said for Madame Cho to make certain you rest, so that you may do the same." He gathered in another breath. "*Live*, that is."

"Hmph." Greaves clamped Philips by the shoulder, turned on his heel, and guided his first footman out of the room.

For the first time all morning I took a deep breath of relief. Then I got to thinking. His message had been worded so carefully. "She said to '*tell me*,' but does that mean it's really true?" I looked to Jane or Maya for confirmation or denial. Jane glanced down at the worn Turkish carpet and chewed her lip. She didn't answer, none of them did, because we all knew our headmistress was prone to setting down the truth in ways that most benefited her purposes.

Maya broke the silence. "The doctor is tending to him. Of that much we can be certain." It wasn't much comfort.

Georgie's hands were clasped tight and her attention fixed on the doorway, awaiting the good news or bad that would arrive at any minute.

Madame Cho handed me a cup and saucer. "Drink your tea."

I'd barely taken a second sip when Greaves returned and ushered in our guest. I looked up expecting to see someone who would ordinarily carry a message for King and country, someone like Mr. Digby, or one of the other soldier-like men we had met while working with Captain Grey in Calais. My expectations were as wide off the mark as snow in July.

When the visitor stepped into our workroom, I nearly dropped my teacup.

Five

MESSENGER

M r. Alexander Sinclair." Greaves enunciated our guest's name oddly, straining to pronounce each syllable care-fully. "From the *Colonies*," he added, in a tone that indicated our guest's origins caused our aged butler a bellyache.

"United States," the visitor corrected and bowed stiffly from the waist. Clearly, he wasn't accustomed to bowing.

We all stared at the young man whose golden curls were tou-sled and looked as if they hadn't seen the useful side of a comb in several days. His ill-fitting tailcoat was dusty and hung open, revealing a waistcoat of blue and purple stripes that did not mix well with the brown of his trousers. Not only that, but it appeared to be buttoned incorrectly. He must have borrowed the trousers, or else he'd grown since purchasing them, because they were em-barrassingly short. His buckle shoes were so scuffed and worn they looked as if they hailed from a previous decade. One of his stockings had slithered down from its moorings and collected around his ankle.

Madame Cho took in his appearance and sucked disapproving air through her teeth. Jane uttered an audible gasp. Georgie took a deep, steadying breath. On the other hand, I found his disastrous appearance both amusing and interesting. For a moment I forgot about my pounding headache.

Who had we allowed into our midst?

"Welcome, Mr. Sinclair." Georgie extended her hand to him. "We were told you carry a message for us."

He took her hand and, rather than bowing elegantly over it, he gave it a firm shake. More and more intriguing, this unruly pup from the Americas. "Yes, miss. I've a letter from Lord Wyatt to be delivered to Miss Fitzwilliam. From his description, I take it you are she?"

Her hand flew out of his and up to her distinctive red hair and self-consciously to her cheek covered with equally distinctive freckles. Then she took a deep breath and regained her confidence. "Yes, I am she."

Mr. Sinclair reached into his coat and produced a sealed letter. "Lord Wyatt said you'd know what to do with it."

Georgie's hands shook as she took it and broke the seal. "You must excuse me for a moment. Would you care to be seated, Mr. Sinclair?"

"Thank you kindly, but no. Feels as though I've been sitting for a fortnight. A man needs to stretch his legs now and again or the muscles freeze up like a waterwheel in January." He demonstrated his need to loosen his muscles by shaking out first one long leg and then the other rather vigorously.

Madame Cho hissed again.

I will admit we stared openly at our peculiar guest. It was rude, but none of us looked away. Me, fascinated. Jane appalled that he would mention legs and muscles, and then proceed to shake said legs as if he had fleas. It's a lucky thing for Mr. Sinclair that

Madame Cho didn't have her bamboo cane in hand, because her natural inclination would've been to wallop him for his appalling manners.

Undaunted, Mr. Sinclair continued to regale us with the intimate details of his arduous journey from Paris to England. Much of his tale is not fit to recite in polite company. Although, given his American dialect, I may not have comprehended all of it. It was a bit difficult to decipher his odd accent and phraseology, made all the more challenging because his overly vivid descriptions were frequently interrupted by Jane gasping and Madame Cho hissing like a Madagascar cockroach.

Georgie had excused herself from the room, no doubt so she could apply a developing solution to the invisible ink on Lord Wyatt's letter. She returned to us, studying the contents of the letter. At last, she handed it over to me, Maya, and Jane. We abandoned our study of the peculiar Mr. Sinclair to read it silently:

May 9, 1814
Dear Miss Fitzwilliam,

I am sending you a gift by way of this gentleman. You will need to apply some effort in order to open it properly.

Meanwhile, I am desirous of knowing how you fare. Are you in good health? How fares our Miss Stranje? Is she as determined as ever to transform you into a proper young lady? Please extend to her my sincerest best wishes in the endeavor. Captain Grey also sends his warmest regards and asks if she would please look in at his cottage now and again, to make sure the servants are diligently tending to their tasks. Our business on the continent has met with a few setbacks as you might imagine with Napoleon sitting on the throne of France.

Yr humble servant,
Lord Wyatt

The real letter, the letter that had been written in invisible ink, now lay exposed between those innocuous lines.

My dearest Georgiana,

This fellow, Mr. Alexander Sinclair, like yourself is something of an inventor and engineer. I discovered he was being held prisoner by the Iron Crown in a house outside of Paris. We took the liberty of slipping him out from under their care and are sending him to you for safekeeping.

He is the nephew of a remarkable engineer and artist, Mr. Robert Fulton, of the Colonies. He assisted Fulton in France on the construction of an extraordinary underwater ship. The French were disappointed, but if the flaws were corrected, we might use an underwater vessel to great advantage against our enemy. Not only that, but Sinclair has ideas to improve upon Fulton's design of an underwater bomb called a torpedo. Sinclair also carries by memory the plans for Fulton's warship powered by steam. You will immediately grasp the value of such a ship. I trust you will aid him in his work as he will need to build a prototype. I'm certain that between you and Lady Jane you can harness his faculties and put them to good use.

Although our government originally rejected plans for the warship, with Napoleon back on the throne of France, Lord Castlereagh feels certain there may be a change of mind on the matter. He is desirous of having drawings and a small working model of the warship to present to the council at Whitehall as soon as it can be arranged.

Georgie, my dearest, a word or two of caution: there must be no late-night collaborations. Remember my previous warning about not tempting gentlemen beyond their ability to resist. If poor, unsuspecting Mr. Sinclair should behave toward you in an overly friendly manner, I would have to call him out and beat him senseless. Thus, the world would be robbed of his brilliant mind. Apart from that, I ask that you listen to him with respect and that you and Lady Jane assist him in his work.

Beseech our beloved Miss Stranje to house and keep him from danger. We must not let him fall into our enemies' hands. I rest easy knowing that at least he is at Stranje House and away from the reach of the Iron Crown, for now.

Yours with deepest affection,
Sebastian

Mr. Sinclair shifted uncomfortably from one foot to the other. Madame Cho folded her arms and narrowed her dark eyes at him, so that I'm sure the poor fellow felt as if he were under guard.

Georgie leaned over our shoulders while Jane, Maya, and I read the letter. When we finished, she frantically whispered, *"For now?* What do you think he meant by that? Something is wrong. I know it. And Mr. Sinclair isn't safe here. Not with Daneska back in England."

Before I could respond to Georgie's question, Jane sprang up to confront our guest.

"This is impossible." She waved the letter at him, shaking it as if she could not believe the contents. "What kind of game are you playing at, Mr. Sinclair? You cannot possibly be an engineer. *You?* Robert Fulton's assistant?" She looked him up and down, bristling more by the minute. "Impossible. Robert Fulton is one of the finest minds of our"—Jane almost stuttered—"and you . . . you're . . . you're an *American*." She drew out "American" as if it meant he'd been born on the wrong side of the blanket rather than the other side of the ocean.

"Yes, miss. Born in Lancaster, Pennsylvania." Mr. Sinclair doffed an imaginary hat. "As was my uncle."

Jane gathered her wits and proceeded more calmly. "That's not what I meant. I meant to say that I am familiar with Mr. Fulton's work. I studied the locks he made for the Duke of Bridgewater's canals. I've read all about the steamship he is building in New York. But this underwater vessel . . . there you have gone too far. You would've been a mere child when Mr. Fulton constructed the *Nautilus* for Napoleon."

"Yes, miss." He answered her warily. "I was a lad of twelve when I served my uncle in France."

"I am not a *miss*." Jane corrected him with a surprisingly indignant tone. Although, to be fair, it was the second time he'd addressed her as a commoner. "I am Lady Jane Moore." She pursed her lips and skimmed the letter again.

"A thousand apologies, *my lady*. I'm honored, to be sure." He made a great show of bowing. Too great a show, and I felt sure that wry curve of his lips indicated a bit of covert mockery.

Jane studied the letter as if the answers must still be hidden in the text. "That is preposterous. Why would a man of his intellect bring a twelve-year-old boy to France?"

Mr. Sinclair took a long, slow breath and his easy manner turned as cold as that frozen waterwheel he'd mentioned earlier. "Begging your pardon, *my lady*, but despite all those fine papers you may have read, you don't know beans about my uncle. He is the best of men, kind, generous, and he loves his family. He took notice of how I liked tinkering. He and my ma decided I should benefit by serving as his apprentice. And so, I did. Twelve being the accepted age to begin an apprenticeship."

She glanced up from the letter, blinked, and looked momentarily chastised. That's something for Jane.

His voice lost some of the stern edge. "I was with Uncle Robert when the *Nautilus* made her maiden voyage on the Seine in July of 1800. If you read the account, you will know that there were four men inside the *Nautilus* that day. It ought to have reported three men and a boy. But to be fair, I was tall for my age."

He added this last remark about his height with a jaunty grin that seemed to completely unsettle our Jane. She pruned up and refused to look at him.

Mr. Sinclair relaxed then and itched absently at his snarled hair. "A leaky tub, that *Nautilus*. We took her down twenty-five feet. Water pressed against the copper hull, dripping in around the seams, and she creaked so loud I thought she would burst her buttons any second. But we kept her under for seventeen minutes." He watched Jane for a reaction. When none came, he repeated, "*Seventeen* minutes." Then as if Jane might be a little slow-witted he added, "underwater."

She sniffed and straightened her back gracefully.

"Folks watching along the banks were amazed, I can tell you that. They reckoned we had all drowned until we bobbed up and, pretty as you please, steered back to shore as if we hadn't just sailed nearly four hundred feet downriver."

I watched him, this insolent apprentice engineer from America. He wasn't quite the dunderheaded fool he appeared. There was a spark of mischief in his manner, but he lost interest in Jane when one of our maps caught his attention. Without dismissing himself, he strolled over to our worktable. "Is that . . . are those the new European borders?"

"No." Madame Cho snatched up the maps and rolled them. "History lessons. Old maps. Nothing to concern you."

He looked confused. "But I saw—"

"No. They are old. Not new." Madame Cho waved him away, gathering up all of our papers and maps. "You go back over there."

Georgie took him by the arm and guided him over for a look at the tea tray. "Surely you would enjoy some tea to refresh you after your long journey."

"I . . . well . . . yes. If you say so. Thank you, I suppose that might be just the thing."

She deposited him in a seat and he managed to convince his long gangly legs to cooperate. In the diminutive lady's chair, his knees stuck up too high and the rumpled stocking was even more apparent than before.

Jane seated herself beside me and squeezed her eyes shut for a moment, in an effort, I'm sure, to block out the sight of his hairy leg exposed by the droopy stocking. She grimaced when he tucked a kipper inside a cucumber sandwich and consumed it with puppyish enthusiasm. Then he smeared two heaping spoonfuls of quince jam on a warm bun with a spoonful of curried egg topped off with a slice of Stilton cheese. Jane blinked in disbelief at this concoction.

For someone like Jane, who valued order above all things, whose gowns hung in the wardrobe in graduated colors, whose hair ribbons were meticulously rolled, and who kept neatly penned planting records to account for *which* type of wheat ought to be planted in *what* field in order to yield the most abundant harvest, I could see how a man like Mr. Alexander Sinclair might cause her to grind her teeth.

As she was doing now.

I, on the other hand, found him amiable company, refreshingly guileless and yet clever. He reminded me of an otter. Except less tidy.

It wasn't until we watched him consume half the tray of food Cook had sent down that I remembered none of us had eaten breakfast that morning. Georgie finally helped herself to jam and bread, and Jane selected a delicate bacon and cheese finger sandwich while carefully avoiding eye contact with Mr. Alexander Sinclair.

I found it difficult to concentrate when across the park I was certain Lord Ravencross must be gritting his teeth in severe pain. Real pain. Never mind what the footman had been told to tell me, it was the kind of pain that could steal one's life away. I stared unseeing at my cup of murky tea, into which Madame Cho had stirred some excessively bitter herbs. I nibbled absently at a biscuit, but it promptly turned to dry cotton wadding in my mouth.

Despite the pounding in my head, I wanted to run back to Ravencross Manor and demand to be admitted. It was foolishness to sit here sipping repugnant tea when he was suffering.

Jane reached over and laid her hand over mine to stop me from shredding my biscuit to crumbs. "I know you are worried, but there would be nothing you could do for him."

Maybe not, but I could be there. I could annoy him just enough that giving up would not be an option.

Georgie fretted, too, but for other reasons. She turned her plate of bread and jam round and round in her lap. "Mr. Sinclair, would you mind telling us how you left our friends, Lord Wyatt and Captain Grey? Are they well?"

Usually Georgie asks a hundred questions where one will do. Today it was the opposite. I knew what she really wanted to ask, but couldn't. The yearning in her small query made me wince for her. She wanted to ask so much more. She ached to know if the man she loved was safe. *Were Lord Wyatt's wounds healed? How much danger was he in? Were he and the captain on the run from the Iron Crown? Or were they the ones doing the chasing?* Most of all, Georgie wanted the answer to one gut-twisting question: *When would Sebastian return home to her?*

Our guest finished chewing before responding. "Lord Wyatt said you would ask after him. He instructed me to tell you he is in fine fettle."

Georgie's lips pursed for a moment. "*Instructed you.* Does that mean he is well or not?"

"Yes, miss. Both men are hale and hearty. A daring lad, your Lord Wyatt. I'm under strict orders not to recite the details of our escape from France, but I can tell you this, he and the captain are men to be reckoned with." Mr. Sinclair stopped speaking abruptly and made short work of a sausage roll.

Georgie blanched. I could well imagine the scenarios she must be conjuring in her imagination. "Tell me frankly, Mr. Sinclair. Is he unharmed or not? No new injuries?"

"Nothing to speak of. A scratch here and there. The man is a first-rate swordsman." Mr. Sinclair reached for a salted egg, and I wanted to slap his hand for terrifying poor Georgie. I was beginning to think the rude American was as deceptive as Miss Stranje.

"You needn't worry, Georgie. He has the right of it. Lord Wyatt is an excellent hand with both sword and gun." I spoke with a firmness meant to settle her fears.

Out of the corner of my eye, I saw Miss Stranje and Sera in the doorway. I jumped to my feet, nearly toppling my plate to the floor, catching it just in the nick of time. "What news?" I'd risen so suddenly the room began to whirl, so I slumped back into my seat and gripped the arms of my chair.

Miss Stranje looked grim, grimmer than her earlier report warranted.

"What's happened?" My voice cracked and sounded odd even to my own ears.

She answered me directly, no hedging this time. "Lord Ravencross is doing as well as can be expected." She looked drained and weary, and she absently rubbed her palms on the side of her dress. "The doctor stitched him up and gave him laudanum. They've moved him upstairs to his own rooms, where he seems to be resting more comfortably than he was in Mrs. Evans's small bed."

"*Seems to be?*" I asked.

"We'll know more by tomorrow morning." Miss Stranje straightened and gave me a shrewd once-over. "And you should be resting as well."

I waved her reprimand away. "He isn't safe. Not in his condition. They might come back. I overheard—"

"Not now." With a stern look, she held up a hand, forestalling my outburst, and turned to our guest. Our odd Mr. Sinclair had the presence of mind to stand when Miss Stranje and Sera had entered. He stood quietly watching her, alert, reacting to every nuance of her speech precisely the way a curious otter might.

Georgie introduced him. "He arrived with a message from Lord Wyatt."

"Welcome to Stranje House, Mr. Sinclair." Miss Stranje extended her hand and, as he had done to Georgie's, he pumped her hand up and down as if it were the handle of a water spigot.

Jane thrust the letter of introduction at Miss Stranje.

Miss Stranje ignored Jane's interruption, even though I knew she must have a mad itch to look at that letter. Nor did she let on that she noticed anything objectionable in Mr. Sinclair's appearance. She treated him with the same respect she would have given a peer of the realm, graciously gesturing for Mr. Sinclair to take a chair. "Please be seated. You mustn't let me interrupt your tea. You've had a long journey I'm sure."

Only after he took his seat did she accept the letter from Jane, who was fairly frothing at the bit for her to read it.

I clutched the arm of the settee because suddenly the room began to swim before me. The lump on my head must be worse than I thought. But then I glanced at my teacup on the table and remembered the bitter herbs. "You gave me a sleeping draught?"

Madame Cho had been watching me. With a curt nod, she stood. "Come. We must take you to your bed."

The very last thing I wanted to do was sleep, but what choice did I have? If I didn't go with her to the dormitorium, I would collapse. Before accepting Cho's help, I leaned over and whispered sternly in Jane's ear, applying enough grim warning that she knew better than to refuse, "Wake me at nightfall."

Six

SHADOWS

Jane jostled my shoulder and awakened me from a remarkably dreamless sleep. "I hope you appreciate us disobeying orders. We were told to leave you sleeping." All four of them stood next to the bed, surrounding me in the dark.

Wary. Worried.

Sera thrust a crusty roll stuffed with meat and cheese at me. "Ham and cheddar. It was all I could slip into my pocket."

Maya laid an offering of grapes in my lap.

"Thank you." My throat was dry, so it came out sounding garbled and croaky.

Georgie handed me a glass of lemon water. "You're planning something. What is it?"

I gulped down the contents. "It's best if you don't know."

Jane crossed her arms. "Tell us anyway."

"It's something I must do alone."

Georgie took the glass from me, refilled it from a pitcher, and set it down with a firm *plunk*. "We work together. Remember?"

Even in the dark, I could see worry dampening the fire in her features, and it needled me worse than anything she might say.

"Explain your plan, so that we may help." Maya's soothing voice almost lulled me into confiding.

"Don't use your tricks on me, Maya. Not tonight." I took a bite of the sandwich, hoping food would help awaken my groggy limbs. "Go to bed, all of you."

Sera sat down on the covers beside me. "You intend to check on him, don't you?"

"Perhaps. Someone has to protect him. Daneska's men could come back." I took another bite, chewing vigorously to hide my defensiveness.

Hands on hips, Jane gave an exasperated huff. "If they dared return, and I'm not saying they would . . ." She straightened to her full height as if towering over my bed might lend her more authority. "But if they *were* foolhardy enough to come back, what makes you think they wouldn't attempt to kidnap Georgie again?"

I took another drink of water before explaining. "Because, as you say, they *aren't* foolhardy. Georgie is here. Safe inside Stranje House. And they've already lost one of their number to Miss Stranje's prowess with a gun. I don't think they would be so daring, not with servants and all of us to protect her. But Lord Ravencross is a different matter. They need only put a bullet in him to get paid, and he has one lone servant to protect him, MacDougal."

Jane countered feebly, "You're forgetting Mrs. Evans."

"*Phfft.*" I popped a grape into my mouth. They all stayed quiet for a moment, mulling over my reasoning.

Jane bristled. "Well, I don't like it. What do you intend to do, roam the perimeter of Ravencross Manor all night watching for murderers?"

"No. There are too many ways someone could sneak past." I took the ham out of the bread and ate that.

Georgie rubbed her arm, thinking. "What if each of us took a section of the grounds to guard?"

Jane whirled on her. "*You're* not going anywhere out of the house. Not after what happened this morning. You heard Tess. You're safest inside."

Sera shifted uneasily. "Besides, if we all went out, Miss Stranje would be bound to notice. Sometimes I feel as if she has invisible bells tied around our necks. She always seems to know."

"Or she has clever ways of discovering it." Maya didn't credit our headmistress with being as all-knowing as the rest of us did. "We have the additional problem that in the darkness, if only four of us are walking the grounds, a skilled assassin could easily slip through our net."

I wiped the crumbs from my mouth and took another sip. "There's an easier way."

"Oh!" Georgie blurted too loudly. "I know what you're planning to do. You'll—"

We heard footsteps outside the door. *Madame Cho.* Everyone scattered to their beds. I quickly stuffed the remaining food beneath the covers and scooted down, head on my pillow.

The door cracked open and Madame Cho shuffled partway in. We had practiced pretending to sleep often enough that we knew to keep our breathing slow, loud, and rhythmic. She came to my bedside and gently brushed hair away from my face.

Checking.

I imagined her squinting at me, worried, silently scrutinizing her patient. The others don't like Cho as much as I do. She is a mystery, strong as sword steel and yet she has the touch of a grandmother. A grandmother I never had. I am her favorite, or so I tell myself.

Grandmother or no. Tonight I had to deceive her.

I stirred as if in restless slumber, shifted and turned away, sinking deeper into the pillow. Satisfied, Madame Cho tucked the covers around my shoulder and glided quietly out of the room, shutting the door behind her. But she is tricky, crafty as an old cat, and so we waited, counting our breaths, knowing she continued listening at the door. At last we heard her soft footsteps drift down the hall.

Georgie was the first to come padding back. "You'll climb into the manor, won't you?" She guessed this because of that night in London when I'd thought we needed to enter Lord Castlereagh's town house by stealth and I'd told her that I would climb the wall, enter through a window, and then pull her up. Someday I would tell her about the first time I had to climb a wall. But not tonight.

"What?" Jane's whisper blew hot in my ear, and carried all the urgency of a scream. "Climb through his window? Are you mad? You can't do that. You could get shot. Or worse, caught. Then you'd be ruined."

"It doesn't matter. I have to protect him. You know what Daneska is like. She won't let her assassins' failure today deter her. If anything, she'll hire better, more skillful killers. If you truly care about me, you'll help me sneak out of Stranje House without Madame Cho noticing."

Sera stood at the end of my bed. "Through the passageway?" I nodded.

In silence, I donned my dark blue running dress. I would blend with the night just as I'd blended with the woods that morning. Georgie handed me her knife to replace the one I'd lost in the field. I checked the balance; it would have to do. "Sharpened."

"Of course. Just as you taught me."

I strapped a sheath to my calf and slid the blade into it. Jane went to the oak paneling along our back wall and pressed the latch that led to a secret passage. As soon as the panel opened, my two pet rats scampered out and danced around my feet. I tossed Punch and Judy a morsel of bread. They snatched it up, stuffed the bread in their cheeks, and scurried into my outstretched palms. I handed them to Sera. "Keep hold of them, will you? I don't want them following me outside."

She nodded.

Jane blocked the secret passage. "Mark me. If you're not back by sunup we're coming after you."

Circled around me, they all nodded, looking stern, except I sensed the worry beneath their bravado. I had the uncomfortable urge to hug them, but of course I would never do such a thing. If I had, it would've alarmed them even more. They know I am not by nature demonstrative. "If anything goes wrong, you'll hear me. You know how loud I can be."

"Like a roaring wind," Maya said, with more admiration than I deserved.

I turned away from them and ducked into the pitch dark of the secret passage. I knew every bend and turn through the thick walls of Stranje House by heart. Instead of going up to our secret room in the attic, I took the narrow stairs down. The first turning to the left was difficult to catch; I ran my fingers lightly along the crumbling plaster until I found the slender opening. I slipped through and from there I headed along the back of the house until the passage behind the first-floor gallery opened up.

Once, not so very long ago, Miss Stranje had said that I knew these passages better than she did. I doubt that. She was born here and ran through them as a child. But I do know them well. In those dark days when I first came to Stranje House, these passages had been my sanctuary. It had made me feel safe knowing

I had a hiding place and, more important, that I had a way out, *an escape.*

Cool air seeped around a slender hatch at the bottom of the steps. I pressed the spring lock, ducked my head, and wriggled through the narrow opening.

Night.

I breathed in deep. The air was fragrant from all the blooms of May, and I could taste salt and moisture from the sea. In the distance, I heard the surf crashing against the rocks. A waning half-moon rode on smoky gray clouds, casting a silver light on the world.

Our shadow dogs, Phobos and Tromos, trotted up silently and greeted me, blacker than night itself, the pair of them. Georgie was right—they were more wolves than dogs. And they loved to run as much as I did. I gave them a soft whistle, no more than a night wren's call, and we were off. Racing across the park. They led the way as if the three of us were a pack, running on the hunt.

I stopped at the edge of Stranje House's property and crouched. *"Distewi,"* I warned Phobos and Tromos in a hushed voice. They sat on their haunches beside me, panting, as I searched for signs of intruders and listened for anything that didn't seem right. High above us, a hawk's high-pitched skree meant a mouse or mole was about to meet its doom. Natterjack toads burbled and drummed unworried in the underbrush. Cicadas buzzed undisturbed. Those reassuring sounds meant no intruders were in these woods or fields. *Yet.*

"Trigo," I commanded. *Stay.* The two of them sat, a matched pair of dark sentinels, waiting, watching, as I leapt up and dashed across the Ravencross lawns.

I circled his manor house, keeping a watchful eye on the shrubbery and trees, searching for any hints of light. There was none on the first floor. But on the second floor I spotted the tell-tale flicker of a candle. That could mean only one thing. That was his bedroom. The candle had given his location away, and if I could figure that out, so could a murderer. Precisely the reason I had to come. Ravencross was too vulnerable.

I made quick work of scaling the wall, finding ready toeholds and fingerholds between the stones. I'd learned to climb even before I'd come to Stranje House. I had to learn the day I'd fled from my uncle by way of an attic window and a three-story wall, but I'd continued learning under Madame Cho's tutelage. I was becoming so adept at scaling walls that should my current profession fail me, and if I'd had the disposition for it, I might've made a capable thief.

The casement creaked only slightly as I pushed open the window and slipped over the sill into his room. The candle fluttered with the influx of air, but still no one stirred.

All my stealth was for naught, I could've come in whistling a tune. Neither of them heard me. MacDougal's rhythmic snores were so loud I'd heard them long before I opened the window, and as Miss Stranje said, the doctor had dosed Ravencross with laudanum to ease his pain. I saw the bottle sitting on his bedside table.

I tiptoed along the edge of the wall, wanting to have a closer look at Gabriel just to satisfy myself that he was indeed breathing and still alive.

Sheeting covered him only to the waist, leaving his chest bare except for the bandages wrapping the left side, bandages ripe with bloodstains. Taking in the bloodstains and his nakedness, I drew in a sharp breath. For modesty's sake, I should've looked away. But I didn't. Apart from the bandages, Gabriel had a magnificent chest, smooth and muscled. More important, he was alive. *Alive.* Why should I look away from so gratifying a sight?

His eyes were closed, and he looked so peaceful. *Beautiful in sleep,* his face was at rest, and not nearly as tense as it usually was. I resisted the urge to smooth my hand over his cheek. The one with the scar.

"What are you doing here, Tess?" He spoke without opening his eyes.

"I . . ." I didn't finish answering. He had to be dreaming, talking in his sleep. He couldn't possibly know I was here. He'd had laudanum. I hadn't touched him, and I'd been quiet as a church mouse. Quieter. A winging bird makes more noise.

I stepped back silently.

His eyes flashed open. "I will only ask once more. *What* are you doing here?"

"Guarding you." I was so startled, I could scarcely speak in a whisper, the words squeaked out of me. I glanced sideways at MacDougal, who shifted in his chair and snorted as if something had disturbed his slumber.

"Don't be absurd," he growled.

And for an instant, I felt absurd, but then I remembered the man I'd slain that morning and his bloodthirsty companions. I inched closer. "Someone wants to kill you, my lord. Someone very dangerous."

"No more dangerous than you, I think." He closed his eyes again as if drowsy. "I already have a nursemaid. Go home."

Lady Daneska was far more dangerous than I. Pressing my lips together, I glared down at him with all the severity I could muster. "Oh, yes, and a marvelous watchdog he is."

MacDougal underscored my words with a gurgling snore loud enough to rattle the paintings on the walls. I bent close to Ravencross's ear. "If I can climb through your window with such ease, so can an assassin. I will stay and guard you until MacDougal has caught up on his beauty sleep."

He motioned for me to lean closer but rewarded me with a rather snappish tone. "You needn't have worried. Do you think me a fool? MacDougal might need his rest. I, on the other hand, have been forced to lie in this confounded bed ever since our morning's escapades. More to the point, I heard you coming long before you crept through my window." With his good hand, Gabriel slid a gun out from under the covers. He gestured for me to back away. "Luckily, I guessed it might be you. Now, if you will be so kind as to shut the window on your way out."

I didn't back away. I found it quite pleasurable looking at him up close in the candlelight. The amber glow turned his skin a delicious creamy bronze. I had the absurd urge to kiss his forehead, and the scar on his cheek, and most especially his divine mouth. Which, at that very moment, was puckering up with irritation.

Instead of kisses, I bestowed upon him several words that I plucked solely for the purpose of vexing him. "You're going to make me climb down? How very ungentlemanly of you. Climbing down is much harder than climbing up. I might fall. Aren't you worried I'll fall?"

He exhaled, heavy and hard with exasperation. "Woman, you worry me in a hundred ways. *Falling* isn't one of them. Given all the other things I've seen you do, I'm certain you'll manage." He said all this while studying my lips with an intensity that made blood crash through my veins like a flash flood. Then he closed his eyes and bit down on his bottom lip.

"You're in pain." I leaned across him, checking the bandage for new evidence of blood.

"For pity's sake, Tess. Get out of here before your reputation is completely in tatters."

I drew back. "I don't give a fig about my reputation."

"Well, maybe I care about it." He grabbed the front of my

dress and pulled me close, close enough that I could taste his scent and feel the heat rolling off him. Surely, he had a fever.

"You don't look right," I said sternly. "Your color is too high. Shall I call for the doctor?"

"No." He grimaced. "I want you to . . ." He didn't finish. His voice faltered, but his grip on me tightened. His pupils widened, so hungry and dark I feared they might swallow me up and trap me there forever.

Words passed over my lips, more of a breath than a whisper. "You're not well, my lord."

"I want you to leave." He let go and sagged back against the pillow. "I can't rest with you here. Get out."

I stepped back, hurt that he would send me away so callously. "Must you always lie?" I said it to myself, so softly he couldn't possibly have heard. MacDougal's snores grew noisier and more rhythmic.

He couldn't cast me out that easily. I neared him once more, stooping next to Gabriel's ear. "I will settle into that corner, in the shadows. You won't even know I am here."

"Have your wits gone begging, Tess? Don't you understand? Even if I were half dead, drugged to the gills, deaf, dumb, and blind, I would know you were here. How can you expect me to rest when you arouse such madness in me?"

Madness.

I nearly laughed. "I know all about madness, my lord. You have my sympathy. However, in view of the fact that I refuse to leave you untended and unguarded, you will simply have to cope, as I must." Having said my piece, I left him and eased into the dark corner across from his bed. Smiling. Because there had been a declaration of some kind in his words.

A declaration made all the sweeter by the fact that he had *not* wanted to make it.

We had no future, this lone hungry wolf and I. I could not bear the idea of destroying his life by entangling his with mine. *Madness, indeed. What did he know of madness?* I would spare him the suffering of my father and grandfather. I would shield him from the very real madness that would someday overtake me.

But for now, for this one night, I might watch over him, stand guard in his den and pretend that things might be different. I would never be the doting wife who wiped his brow and smoothed back the wild curls from his fevered brow. But tonight, *tonight*, I could do this one thing, I could watch over him while he was wounded. I could wait in the shadows with my blade at the ready. And even if Daneska herself came, I would cut her heart out to protect him.

I would keep him alive.

"Irksome female."

"If you mean to chase me off, you will have to do better than that."

"Witch," he muttered and shifted in the bed, trying to find a comfortable position.

It stung, for him to name me a *witch,* as he knew it would. But only a little. I was used to that one. So I said nothing in retort. He needed his sleep. Timing my movements with MacDougal's snores, I tiptoed to the window, tightened down the latch, and took up my vigil in the shadows. I sank onto my haunches with my back propped against the wall. I would feel a vibration should anyone try to open the window or tread on the floorboards.

I checked the knife blade. Sharp as a dragon's tooth.

Twice the doctor came and went, checking on his patient, and not once did he notice me sitting vigil in the dark recesses of my corner. In the early morning hours, MacDougal's snores finally changed key to the gurgle of a lighter sleep. He would wake soon. I left the shadows and stood next to the bed. Gabriel was wrong. He *had* slept—well and deep. His arms were spread wide and relaxed, his hands flung recklessly atop the covers, nowhere near the hidden gun.

Farewell.

His innocent black curls tempted me. I had no right to touch him. No right at all. And yet I dared to gently smooth them back from his forehead. They were softer than I had imagined. He slept so peacefully that he didn't even stir. My fingers drifted feather light down the scar on his cheek, scarcely touching the jagged ridge. His breath caught, broke rhythm. I yanked my hand away and fell back into the shadows.

Foolish girl.

Time to leave.

I slipped out of Lord Ravencross's bedroom the same way I'd come, scrambling down the wall with ease. My muscles, having crouched all night, were glad of the exercise. The moon was still out, and although the sun would not crest for another two hours, the world was bathed in a smoky gray. It reminded me of yester-morning and the chaos that had nearly taken him from me.

It seemed a hundred years ago.

I dashed home through the dewy grass. My tracks might be mistaken for those of a deer springing joyfully through the glade.

Seven

CAUGHT

It surprised me that Phobos and Tromos were not waiting where I'd left them. But I supposed even wolf-dogs must sleep now and again. I leapt over the low brush between Stranje House and Ravencross's park, wove through the trees, navigated the maze of wild roses, loped past the kitchen gardens, and wriggled around the archery targets tucked away between a towering hedgerow and the side of Stranje House. Targets we also used for long-range knife-throwing practice. There is a reason Miss Stranje keeps the landscape *au naturel*. From there it was only a short dash to the small trapdoor.

I stopped short.

My joy vaporized into a gasp.

Miss Stranje leaned against the wall, Phobos and Tromos pacing on either side of her. "Good evening, Tess. Or should I say good morrow? I gather you are feeling better?"

Caught.

I swallowed in answer.

"And how is our patient?" she asked, as if simply making polite conversation, nothing more.

Devil take it! There was nothing I could do except face my punishment. Still panting from running so hard, I bent to catch my breath. "Resting."

She stood relaxed, at ease, as if we'd simply happened upon one another at a dressmaker's shop. That's how I knew to keep my guard up. Miss Stranje was always more dangerous when she was relaxed.

"You do realize these passageways exist so that if Stranje House is ever attacked and overrun by an enemy we might be able to make our escape." When I did not answer, she took a step closer. "They were *not* designed so that young ladies might sneak out in the dead of night and climb into a neighboring lord's bedchamber."

That set my nerves thumping. "Put like that, it sounds rather sordid."

"So it does."

"You know perfectly well why I went. There was nothing unseemly about it. He needed protecting."

Miss Stranje waited as unmoved as a monolith in the moonlight.

"How did you know I'd gone?" I straightened and crossed my arms, shoring up against the peal she would surely ring over my head.

"Madame Cho went to check on you in the middle of the night. Imagine her dismay to find you missing from your bed."

To this, I could only dip my head, shamefaced.

Miss Stranje understood my attachment to Madame Cho, an attachment she shared, which gave her all the more reason to scold me. "She came to me in considerable distress."

I was sorry to have worried Madame Cho, but I would still have gone. Someone had to keep him safe from Daneska's murderers. Defiant, I looked up and collided with her hooded-hangman expression.

"Madame worried you had wandered off in a stupor. We live near some rather treacherous cliffs."

"And yet . . ." I jutted my chin higher. "You didn't sound the alarm. Why is that?" I kept my shoulders back, square, as rigid and unyielding as hers.

She took a deep breath, calculating whether to admit the truth. "You know why." Something akin to pride tempered her expression.

"You guessed where I'd gone."

"It didn't require much conjecture on my part." She exhaled and clicked her tongue as if I was being childish. "It did, however, bring into question my trust in you."

"For that I am sorry. And for alarming Madame Cho. But I do not regret that I went. Daneska hired assassins—"

"Yes, I know." She waved away my protest. "Sera and Jane explained it all to me. Nevertheless, *you* must understand *my* position. It was not so very long ago that Lady Daneska snuck out at night to rendezvous with the former Lord Ravencross. I should not like to see history repeat itself."

She might as well have slapped me.

"How can you say that?" I jumped back, throwing my hands wide. "I would never! *He* would never. How can you even suggest such a thing?" Tromos yipped softly and nuzzled my hand in an effort to calm me.

"Because, my dear, I hadn't expected it from Lady Daneska either. At least, I hadn't suspected the extent of her treachery."

"But I am nothing like her." I thumped my palm against my

chest. "*Nothing!* Daneska is an evil, vicious, conniving . . ." I could not find the right expletive. Georgie's words from the previous morning came back to me. "Vipers are more trustworthy."

Miss Stranje's shoulders pinched up. She looked away from me, out across the park to where Ravencross Manor stood, still a dark silhouette at this gloomy hour before dawn. She stared. Silent. Remembering.

I remembered, too.

The night she left us, Daneska told me the truth about Lucien.

It had been cold the night Daneska left, having snowed the day before. I'd awakened an hour after midnight to find her bed empty and the panel to our secret passage slightly ajar. I'd caught up to her as she was headed out through this same hidden door. She was carrying a satchel, and I knew my best friend was not simply sneaking off for another assignation. But she wouldn't tell me what she was doing, not until she swore me to secrecy.

Once she'd obtained my promise, she confided that they were fleeing the country because Lucien had aligned himself with France. He was obsessed with Napoleon's ideologies and had even gone so far as to join the Order of the Iron Crown. I could still hear her laughing at me for not understanding why she, too, intended to side with France. She and Lucien were convinced Napoleon was destined to win the war and that he would one day unite all of Europe. With her chin at a haughty angle, hoisted well above the white fur of her ermine collar, she'd said, "And then Lucien and I will rule at his side."

I'd begged her to reconsider. When, in desperation, I'd asked if loyalty meant nothing to her, she mocked me. "*Loyalty?* Do not be so naïve, Tessie. I have no country. No king. My father's duchy has been laid waste by British armies. I owe my allegiance to no one, not you, not Miss Stranje, and certainly not your fat

English prince. I am loyal only to myself." Even though we were the same age, she'd patted her glove against my cheek as if I were a toddler she pitied. "Not even to Lucien. Like all men, he is merely a means to an end."

She'd grinned wickedly, as if it pleased her to admit that even Lord Ravencross had no hold over her. "I'm not like him," she'd said proudly. "I have no interest in democracies and lofty ideals. But I do have a keen interest in being on the winning side."

She'd laughed then and slipped through the door. "Power, Tessie, that is what matters. Money and power."

I'd followed her out and stood in my nightgown and bare feet watching her traipse across the snow. Ice crystals blew in soft sparkling swirls as she turned and pressed a lone gloved finger to her lips, reminding me of my promise not to tell until morning. She knew that where she had no use for loyalty, I prized it. Though it ate at me like a green sickness, she knew I would keep my word. With another laugh, she ran away. The sound caught on the wind and turned to breaking glass. I kept standing there, my feet going numb, watching as she faded into the night, leaving dark, coffin-shaped footprints in the snow.

It had taken me a long time that night before I'd ducked back into the passage and slammed it shut behind me, and even longer to trudge back up to the dormitorium. Daneska's betrayal angered me more than it could ever vex Miss Stranje.

It still gnawed at my stomach, a churning ball of spiked fury. I wanted to cough it out and forget Daneska had ever been my friend, forget she had ever existed.

Some wounds take longer to heal.

With a quick intake of breath, Miss Stranje spun back to me, herself once again. "You're right. You're not like her, Tess. Not in the least."

She meant it. I saw it in the softening of her features.

The dogs paced between us, looking first to her, then to me, gauging our words, whimpering at our harsh exchanges, unsure how to protect against this kind of trouble in their pack. I felt bad for them. And for her. I lowered my pretense of pride. "I'm sorry I worried you and Madame Cho."

She nodded and put an arm around my shoulders. "It might surprise you to know I did not wait out here at this hour to scold you. To warn you, perhaps, but not to scold. I do understand why you went." She swallowed, and hesitated, as if the worst was yet to come. "I waited for you so that we might have a private word."

Private.

Twelve kinds of trouble dripped like poison from that word.

Phobos tilted his head suspiciously, and I expect I may have done the same thing. "Private?"

She dropped her arm and resumed her normal headmistress-like self. All business. Except her tone was too stiff. Too formal. "I'm concerned, you see." She took a deep breath before going on. "Matters are going rather badly on the continent. With Napoleon back on the throne, making sweeping advances to the north, Wellington's troops have been forced to retreat. Bonaparte has driven them all the way up to Hanover. The House of Lords and several of our military advisers are recommending our troops return home to protect British soil against his inevitable attack. But it is extremely difficult to transport more than a few troops at a time, especially when the nearest port is even farther north, in Hamburg."

All this I already knew. Last week Georgie had been desperate for news of Lord Wyatt. She was frantic to find anything that might tell her where Sebastian was or even if he was alive. The two of us decided to put our training to use. We crept into our headmistress's office and searched for correspondence about the war.

"Although I suspect you already knew this much."

I caught my breath and turned to scratch Phobos behind the ears, afraid to meet Miss Stranje's gaze for fear of giving away our duplicity. "I may have read something of the sort in the newspapers, and I'd heard—"

"Come now. Did you think I wouldn't notice that my papers had been disturbed?" Her tone lightened. She wasn't angry. But I was.

Caught again.

It rankled. I exhaled loudly. "How did you know? We were so careful to put everything back exactly as it was. We replaced the stack of books atop the papers at precisely the same angle."

The corner of her mouth turned up in amusement. "You may not have noticed the small broken nib I left sitting on the lower left corner of the papers."

"A spent nib?"

"Yes." She tsked, as if I'd suggested something silly. "You don't think I would be so sloppy as to leave a cut-off nib on my papers for no reason. I also left a small corner of felt midway through the stack."

"You were testing us." I growled and kicked at the grass, dislodging a sleeping grasshopper. Tromos bounded after it.

She merely inclined her head in answer.

"And we failed."

"Not entirely. You entered and left my study without being seen."

"Unlike tonight," I said, suddenly feeling weary and not nearly so light of foot as I had earlier. "What is it you wanted of me?"

She caught her lip and for an instant looked worried. Miss Emma Stranje is nothing if not intrepid. Where she might bite her lip in consternation, the rest of the world would quake in their boots. If she was worried, matters must indeed be grave.

She rallied her air of authority. "It is about your gift, your dreams. You haven't mentioned them of late."

I glanced sideways at her. *What was she getting at?* "I hadn't thought them important."

She blinked as if she thought I was being obtuse. "Whyever not? They were instrumental in helping Georgie with the ink, and without them, who knows what lives might've been lost."

"That one time, perhaps. But most of the time my dreams are inscrutable—a roiling mess of sadness and pain. Of what use it that?" *Apart from causing my mind to break.*

Miss Stranje spoke to me as if I was still a young girl in her classroom. "The fact that they are sometimes predictive—surely you see the benefit of that?"

I retreated a step or two, trying to hide the low growl climbing up my throat. "I'm no prophet."

"Of course not . . ." She waved my dispute away. "But if it weren't for you and your dreams, Sebastian might be dead, and who knows what would've happened to the diplomats in Vienna. You must admit that much."

I exhaled loudly, trying to breathe out the confusion she was stirring up. "Except things have gotten worse, not better. Worse! Napoleon is back in power." I shook my head, trying to escape this debate. Nothing she could say would convince me anyway. "None of this matters. We've no way to know what would have happened had I not interfered."

She sighed. "I suppose there's not much use in mere mortals pondering such things."

"Then let us leave it, shall we. What is it you wanted?"

She sniffed, haughty, defensive, very *unlike* Miss Emma Stranje. "Well, as a matter of fact, I would like to know if you've had any other dreams. In particular, any dreams about the situation on the continent. Or the war—"

"You want to know if I've seen anything pertaining to Captain Grey?" I asked, not intending to be cruel, simply wishing to get to the point a bit quicker.

She caught my arm. "He is not the only reason for my asking." She let go and turned back into the sharp-eyed hawk. "Naturally, it's frustrating not knowing. If we'd had some small word, *anything*. You know how I dislike being kept in the dark. The diplomatic office has had no word either. So, yes, among other things I would like to know if he and Lord Wyatt are . . ." She pursed her lips.

"Alive?"

"If they are *well*." She seemed annoyed that I spoke her fear out loud. "Have you seen either of them? A glimpse, perhaps? Anything at all?"

"No. Nothing of them."

Her shoulders sagged a fraction of an inch lower than her normal soldierly posture. "I thought as much."

I felt sadness fall upon her like a cold fog. Phobos whimpered and rubbed his head against her leg. Miss Stranje stared down at the dark pool of grass surrounding us. Wind rippled across the ebony blades. The moon had abandoned us, leaving the world still shrouded in the funeral clothes of night. Morning larks had not yet begun to sing and nightingales had long since fallen silent. In the stillness that lay between night and morning, one last star glittered just above the treetops, a small beacon of hope in the darkness engulfing us.

"Shall we go in through the garden door?" she asked.

With the wolf-dogs at our heels, we walked silently through the predawn fog. As we neared the back steps, she said, "If you should happen to dream about Captain Grey or Lord Wyatt—"

"It doesn't work like that." I spoke too harshly, but I knew what she wanted. "I cannot *try* to have a dream. I don't control them. They fly at me without warning. It's like being shoved off a cliff into the pit of hell. *Into madness.* Each dream, each vision, carries me closer to that abyss that devoured my mother—"

"Tess! Stop." She grasped my shoulders. "I would never ask that of you. You mustn't even think such a thing." She forced a calming breath and leaned close, so that we were almost nose to nose. "I know you can't control these visions of yours. And I'm fully aware of how much they upset you. I would never *ask* you to dream. Only that, *if you do,* you would come to me and tell me what you've seen so that we might try to decipher it."

"Oh." I swallowed and my heart slowed its thundering gallop.

She let go of me, still standing near enough that I saw the sad soft curve of her lips.

We climbed the steps and she opened the garden door, but neither of us went in. I bowed my head, embarrassed about my outburst. "Then you're not going to lecture me about how we must all make sacrifices?"

"Heavens no, child." She held the door open wider. "I'm not willing to sacrifice your sanity, Tess. That is too great a price to ask of anyone."

secure his silence. I did give the fellow credit for being straight-forward enough to give an honest answer.

"You can't go prowling around the house, prying into our private papers. It simply isn't done. Miss Stranje wouldn't like it."

He rubbed the back of his neck, appearing at least a little cha-grined. "I suppose that other one wouldn't like it much either—the Chinese lady."

"No. She would not. I daresay Madame Cho would come after you with a bamboo cane and give you a well-deserved thrashing."

"A well-deserved thrashing, is that what you think? What do you have against me, *my lady?*" He said "my lady" in that hard American twang of his as if her title was something repugnant he wanted to scrape off of his shoe.

Jane's voice lifted a bit too high, a bit too strident. "I . . . Against you? What, *indeed.* Where should I start . . ."

"Spit it out." Even from where I hid, I could hear the smirk in his tone.

"See. There it is. *Spit.* That is just the sort of uncivilized thing you are wont to say, isn't it?"

I peeked around the corner. His arms were crossed and he towered over her like an imperious king, albeit a rather gangly and ill-dressed imperious king. "Afraid to tell the truth, my lady? Or is it that you don't have a reason worth spouting?"

"Hah!" Jane huffed. "Oh, I have reasons. Several perfectly rational reasons. I meant to spare you, but since you ask—"

"Spare me? Ha!" He rocked back on his heels. "*Tsk, tsk,* my lady, you mustn't soil yourself with lies. The truth is you haven't meant to spare me since I walked through the door. Are you too lily-livered to speak your mind?"

"*Lily-livered?* How dare you."

Now he'd done it. I knew Jane well. That up-and-down heaving of her shoulders, the gasps and starts, the way she balled her fists—these signs did not bode well for Mr. Sinclair.

"If you want the truth, Mr. Sinclair, I shall be delighted to deliver it." She ground out his name. "I find it difficult to believe that any engineer worth his salt can't figure out how to tie a cravat properly. Or wouldn't know how to button his waistcoat properly. I ask you, what kind of engineer can't manage his own buttons?"

"The kind of man who doesn't give a two-headed nickel about what's on the outside, because he's far more concerned about what's on the inside." Mr. Sinclair's arms remained crossed, and he stared down at her from his great height as if she were a toadying magpie. "*Lady Jane.*"

"I have found," she answered with cold, queenly dignity, "that the outside is a fairly clear indication of what is on the inside."

She stretched her chin up, standing on her toes in a vain attempt to match his height. "If one is a careful, meticulous sort, as most engineers are, one polishes one's shoes so that they might last more than one winter." She glanced down at his scuffed footwear with disdain.

He tilted his head and I saw that expression, the one I'd noted yesterday, the one that gave me the impression he found life amusing, and that even Jane's harsh diatribe entertained him.

He answered her in a calm, clear tone, like one might use with a child. "I know a great many engineers, my lady, and their dressing habits vary as much as feathers do on birds. What's more, if one must steal the shoes off the feet of one's unconscious prison guard or else traipse barefoot halfway across France, one might not have much to say about the treatment those shoes received prior to his acquiring them."

"Oh." Jane drew back, her fingers covering her mouth. "I hadn't thought—"

"No, my lady. You hadn't."

She inched toward the workroom. "That still doesn't give you a right to go poking through our maps in the wee hours of the morning."

"Are you suggesting I might do it later in the day?"

"No," she squeaked. "You know perfectly well what I mean."

He scratched his head, looking puppyish and befuddled. "No, Lady Jane, I confess you are something of a riddle. I see now how you counted my wardrobe, my shoes, and my error in addressing you on the negative side of the slate. That still doesn't explain why you come at me with a temper hotter than a badger."

"A badger." Her voice lifted again. If she didn't get it under control soon, the entire population of Stranje House would be awakened and joining us in the hall.

Her agitation seemed to ignite his tongue even more. "You know what a badger is like, don't you?"

"No, I'm not personally acquainted with any badgers, but I can tell you this—"

"Oh, well, let me explain. It's a fine fierce little critter. Looks something like a skunk. Black and white. Only about this big." He held out his hands showing her the approximate size. "But, *oh*, you must watch your step around her, *my lady*. She has a mouthful of vicious teeth and a growl that will melt bones."

"A skunk." The depth of insult twisting on Jane's features nearly made me laugh aloud.

"That's right, a skunk with fearsome teeth. And I've seen one of those furry little gals take on a bear just for strolling too close to her den."

Jane didn't move away from him, even though he was clearly

making sport of her. In fact, they both stood excessively close to one another.

He leaned in to have a better look at her. "And that is what you're doing, Lady Jane. Taking on a bear, and you don't even know it."

"Ha." She lifted her palm, and I swear I thought she might slap him into the next county.

He laughed. "See what I mean. The way you're sputtering and carrying on, anyone would think I'd stepped on your gouty big toe."

She backed away, scalded. "Oh, now you're just being rude. You know perfectly well I don't have gout."

"Begging your pardon, my lady. I thought all you English aristocrats had trouble with gout. On account of being so plump and drinking more wine than water—"

"Mr. Sinclair!" Jane's hands fisted and she seethed like a teapot boiling over. "*I. Am. Not. Plump,*" she said in a menacingly low voice. "Nor do I overindulge in spirits. As for you daring to publicly comment on the state . . . the shape . . . the weight of my . . . my person . . ." She practically choked on each word. "There is nothing more to say than that your manners, sir, are atrocious!"

"Aye, that they are, *my lady*. Disgraceful manners." He chuckled and held up his hands in surrender. "I have eyes, Lady Jane. I can see that you're no plumper than you should be. And if it weren't for that spicy temper of yours, a fellow might find your proportions somewhat pleasing." He gave her a roguish grin. "Although I have to admit, it was worth the breach of etiquette to watch you color up like red flannel and flap about like a flustered banty hen."

"A banty hen!" Jane made a gurgling, stuttering noise that

I supposed was her version of a growl. A very un-Jane-like noise. Jane never growls.

"Yes, my lady. It's a small fussy hen—"

"I know what it is," she said through gritted teeth. "You're impossible! The rudest, most exasperating, insulting—" She waved him away, shaking her head. "Insufferable! I don't see how we can be expected to assist you with your inventions and prototypes. Not only that, but why we should put our lives at risk protecting you, when you are clearly the most obnoxious—"

He grabbed her shoulders. "Hold on there. No one asked you to protect me."

"Oh, yes. Yes, they did. Lord Wyatt did exactly that in his letter." She glanced down at his hand on her shoulder.

He instantly let go. It was his turn to shake his head and step back. "Begging your pardon, my lady, but that's stuff and nonsense. More of your fancy lies. Lord Wyatt is a perfectly rational fellow, and there's no way he would expect a passel of females in a girls' school to protect me from the likes of the Iron Crown. That would be pure foolishness. I reckon he sent me here because this place is so unlikely, so far removed from anywhere the Iron Crown might expect me to be housed, that it is one of the last places in England they would look."

"That's where you're wrong. *Dead wrong.*" Jane crossed her arms and cocked her head, having finally caught him in an error. "This is one of the very first places they'll look."

"I don't believe you." He shook his head. "No. Lord Wyatt would no more expect a little mite like you to protect me than he would expect a horse to do math."

"I am not a little mite, Mr. Sinclair. I'm taller than most women, and it might surprise you to learn that I could flip you over my shoulder and break your arm in three places before you had a chance to say *begging your pardon, my lady*, in that ear-scraping American brogue of yours."

Jane couldn't really do that. Not yet. She was out and out bragging. If our practice sessions were anything to go by, she might be able to tug him over her shoulder. *Maybe.* Jane had skills, but combat wasn't one of them.

Mr. Sinclair shared my skepticism. "Care to place a wager on that?"

Fortunately, she was spared answering. Miss Stranje burst through the garden door at the end of the hall and strode toward them.

Mr. Sinclair greeted her with an almost passable bow.

"Ah. I see you are both getting an early start. Good. Lady Jane, please show Mr. Sinclair the workroom, where the paper is kept, the ink, the drawing instruments, and so on." Miss Stranje briskly opened the workroom door for them. "Madame Cho will be along shortly to chaperone. Mr. Sinclair, should you need to mix chemicals, we have a well-stocked stillroom just down the hall. Miss Fitzwilliam will assist you there later. However, for obvious reasons, I would ask that if you mix explosives, you do so out of doors—well away from the house." She marched past them with a curt nod. "Breakfast will be served at nine."

She strode down the corridor and headed upstairs. I remained hidden, holding my breath, lest she might turn and see me sneaking about the house, eavesdropping instead of sleeping.

I gave up on the idea of sitting with Jane and returned to the dormitorium thinking I might rest for an hour or so before breakfast. Not sleep. Not that. I'd stay awake and simply rest my head.

"You're back." Georgiana sat up in bed, yawning and stretching, her red curls a tangled but charming mess.

Sera leaned up, propping herself on one elbow. "How is Lord Ravencross?"

"Healing." I remembered the peace on his face as he slept and smiled to myself. "Barring an infection, he should recover."

"Good." She flopped against her pillow. "We were just about to come find you."

"So you say, sleepyhead. Jane beat you to it."

"Jane?" Georgie's gaze shot to Jane's empty bed. "Where is she?"

"Downstairs. I think you might want to hurry to the work-room. When last I saw her, she was threatening to break Mr. Sinclair's arm in three places."

"What? Why? Besides, Jane is no good at hand to hand—"

"I'm well aware of Jane's combat limitations. Unfortunately, Mr. Sinclair provokes her so thoroughly that I think she might give it a go."

Georgiana threw back the covers. "I wouldn't want to miss that."

I chuckled. "I rather think it is your job to keep that from hap-pening. Lord Wyatt asked you to protect our guest, did he not?"

"Fiddlesticks! What sport is there in that?" She grinned at me and hurried toward the water closet.

Sera was already pulling on her morning dress. I helped her tie her tapes. "I'm tired. I need to rest for a few minutes," I admitted.

She pointed to the sleeping draught. "Madame Cho left that for you. She was furious with us for letting you go last night. I imagine we will pay for that in our lessons today."

"I expect you will. I'm sorry for that. I don't want to rest for long. Rouse me for breakfast, if you would? I'm famished."

She agreed and hurried off. I removed my shoes, propped my feet up on the bed, and leaned back against the headboard. Punch and Judy scampered across the covers and leapt into my arms. Chittering and sniffing, their little whiskers tickled my cheeks. "I've no food for you today. No, not even a morsel."

Clever little devils, their pink ears perked up as if they understood what I'd said. Judy gave me a whiskery kiss of forgiveness, but Punch jumped onto my shoulder and poked about behind my neck and into my hair, checking to see if I might be holding out on him. I shooed him down, and they tumbled and wrestled in my lap for a moment, then coiled up next to me to sleep.

"You rascals needn't settle in. I'm not going to sleep."

Punch stuck his pink nose in the air. His whiskers twitched as he scrutinized me intently. Then, with a cynical little pip, he curled up next to my thigh.

"Scamp."

He swung his tail and gave me a light swat in answer.

"I suppose I might close my eyes. Not to sleep, mind you. Not that. Only to rest for a moment."

Only a moment.

I would not sleep.

Nor would I dream.

Yet even as my eyelids drooped, the world shifted. I knew, as it spun and whirled me into the void, that this would be one of those dreams—not so very unpleasant at first, but dangerous later.

Nine

ghosts

I found myself plunged into a sea of swirling images, some of which I understood. Others were too outlandish. *Impossible.* Then the dream whirled me to a place I knew.

The dungeons of Stranje House. I recognized the smell of mold and dampness that pervades that place. Thick darkness nearly suffocated me. I heard someone crying. It struck me that Lady Daneska might have captured Georgie. The sound of weeping echoed through the dark corridors of my dreamworld, but no matter how hard I tried to find her, she eluded me. I ran as fast as I could in the tangled underbelly of the house, and yet her sobbing only got weaker and more desperate.

Chasing the sound through the murky fog, I raced around a corner and collided with Lucien, Lord Ravencross's older brother. He looked as shocked to see me as I was to see him. His expression flashed from alarm to violence. He aimed a pistol at me. I've no idea why he didn't fire. In a blink, he vanished into the darkness.

Often in dreams, a scream is a wispy desperate cry that no one hears.

I awoke in a panic, gasping, a hoarse shriek trapped in my throat as if there had been many screams proceeding it. My heart thumped like a terrified rabbit, and Georgie's cries still rang in my ears.

Except it couldn't be. Georgie was here, shaking my shoulders. "Wake up!" I recognized her voice. "Tess, you must wake up."

Slowly, she came into focus, her red hair glowing like fire in the sunlight that poured in from the dormitorium's windows.

It had been a dream. Only a dream.

And yet she looked frightened. She signaled frantically for Alice, our housemaid. "Go get Miss Stranje. Hurry! Run!" Then she called to Maya. "Do something. She can't breathe. Look, she's turning gray."

Maya moved Georgie aside and blew softly on my face. "Tess, you must listen to me. Breathe."

All I could do was gasp.

"It's over. You are safe now." When Maya spoke, it was low and resonant, it sounded almost as if she purred. "Let the air out. You have taken in too much." She exhaled slowly, showing me exactly what she wanted me to do. I tried to follow. "Yes, that is the way. Very good. Slow, even breaths." It was then that I finally understood Maya was like a cat, a silken exotic cat. One of us and yet not. After that, I trusted her more. At least as much as anyone can trust a cat.

"Thank heavens." Georgie sank onto the end of the bed and sighed. "Her color is returning. She'll be all right, now."

But she would not.

"Georgie, get behind me." I surged forward. "Hide. They're here—"

"Who? Who's here?" Jane leaned in from the other side and

pressed me back against the pillows. Her brows pinched up with worry. "There's no one here but us."

"What is it?" Miss Stranje rushed into the dormitorium. "What did she see?"

Thank goodness she was here. Now someone would listen to me. "Daneska! She's here. Or she will be. She and her henchmen." I looked at all of their faces to make sure they understood the threat. "And Lord Ravencross's brother, Lucien. Except, no—" I shook my head, trying to clear it. "That can't be. He's dead. I never dream about the dead. The *dying*, yes. But not someone who has already passed."

Yet I felt certain it had been him. He had looked different somehow, older maybe. But that was impossible.

Maya stood and edged away from me, slipping quietly behind the others. Georgie and Jane glanced at one another, exchanging the same worried look they had earlier. *More secrets? Or the same secret?*

Sera sat beside me and clasped my hand, even though I had tightened it into a fist gripping my bedcovers.

"You know that we have the deepest respect for your dreams. But it sounds to me as if this one might have been nothing more than an ordinary nightmare, the kind any of us might have after the awful events of yesterday. You knew Daneska was behind the attempt to kidnap Georgie. Could it be that what you saw this time was simply your worries emerging in your dreams?"

"*Ordinary*," I repeated, astonished at the thought, so much so I very nearly laughed.

If only it were true.

Perhaps it was. I wondered if anyone else would welcome an ordinary nightmare with such open arms.

"What other explanation can there be?" Sera asked softly.

"We know Lucien is dead. Lord Ravencross killed him at Möckern."

"Yes," I said, and my heart stopped beating quite so fast. My fists began to relax. "That could be it."

But then I noticed Georgie and Jane had said nothing. Under normal circumstances, Georgie would have offered an opinion. So would Jane. Instead, both of them kept their eyes averted, looking anywhere but at me. That's how I knew that whatever it was they were hiding, it had something to do with Lucien. My stranglehold on the sheets tightened again.

Miss Stranje stood at the foot of my bed like a captain steering a ship. "What else did you see?"

"Nothing of any consequence. No Captain Grey. No Lord Wyatt. It was another worthless jumble. Explosions. Smoke. Water. Napoleon—"

"Napoleon?" She tilted her head, narrowing in on me.

"It was of no consequence."

"Perhaps not. Indulge me."

"I saw myself in a prison of some kind, except I was surrounded by soft cushions and had grapes to eat. I was dressed in fine silk, and yet I was chained and there were bars on the door. So you see, it makes no sense. And then Napoleon came in carrying an ornate silver bowl filled with swirling mystical green water. He told me to drink. When I refused, he grabbed my head and thrust me face-first into the bowl. It felt as if I was drowning, except then the dream changed and suddenly I found myself in the dungeons beneath Stranje House."

"Hmm." Our headmistress scrutinized me as if I were an errant pupil. "You're quite certain it was Napoleon you saw? How did you know?"

I refused to meet her gaze, carefully folding the edge of the sheet over the top of the coverlet. "He wore the emperor's gold laurel leaves on his head and yet he was dressed like a general." My stubbornness returned and I looked up defiantly. "I *knew*."

"Yes, of course." Miss Stranje placed her hand on the spindle of my bed. "A most curious dream."

"That part of it can't possibly mean anything. It was absurd. Perhaps Sera is right, maybe it was an ordinary nightmare, I don't know. What I do know is that I saw Daneska here. Inside Stranje House. And that part felt real." I thumped the feather ticking with my fist. That portion of the dream unsettled me most. Some childish part of me liked to think of Stranje House as impenetrable, my personal fortress. And the thought that I couldn't protect one of my friends from her vicious schemes twisted my insides until I felt like a wrung-out rag.

"Mystical water in a silver bowl?" Sera quizzed. "What do you suppose that means?"

I had no answers, nothing more than a hair-hanging shake of my head. I sat forward, suddenly struck by a hopeful notion. "What if it wasn't Georgie I heard crying out after all—maybe it was Daneska?"

Jane snorted derisively. "I doubt it. Daneska doesn't cry. She doesn't have it in her. "

"No, of course not." My heart sank again and I peeked up at her, wincing, wishing the wretched dream would evaporate. "Then it must have been Georgie screaming for help."

Jane crossed her arms. "It could've been your own screams you were hearing. They were loud enough."

I pressed my face into my hands, hiding my turmoil from them. But in so doing I saw Lucien's face again, as I had in the dream, coming at me from the darkness and then vanishing around a corner. It didn't make sense.

I'd had enough mysteries for one day, for one lifetime. "Enough games. What is it about Lucien you aren't telling me?"

Georgie sat on the end of the bed, pensively tracing her finger over the embroidery on the coverlet. She cast a scowl up at Miss Stranje. "I told you she'd find out."

"Find out what?" I demanded.

They all stayed mum.

"I swear, if you don't tell me what's going on this very instant, I will never tell you another thing about my dreams. Not a word. I don't care if they predict the assassination of Prince George, or if Napoleon himself appears to me in one of them."

Sera jumped up at the violence of my demand. My outburst seemed to convince her that Jane and Georgie were hiding something from me. *From us.* Because, clearly, Sera didn't know either.

She scoured each of their faces, hunting for clues. "Whatever it is. We've a right to know." The hurt vibrating through her words seemed to land on them with more force than my anger.

Without a sound, Maya retreated deeper into the shadows. Jane, on the other hand, looked squarely to Miss Stranje for guidance.

So our illustrious headmistress and even Maya had a part in this tight-lipped conspiracy. I couldn't blame them for their silence, not entirely. Everyone has secrets. I have mine. Besides, secrets were our stock-in-trade. But I meant to bite my teeth into this one and drag it out into the open.

Now.

I met Miss Stranje's hawklike stare with a white-hot blaze of my own.

"Hmph." She did not look displeased with me. It was rather more as if I had passed some sort of test. She abruptly turned and dismissed Alice, our maid, with instructions to tell Greaves that we would be down to breakfast a few minutes late and to go ahead and serve our guest.

Our headmistress gave Jane a curt nod of permission.

Jane exhaled. "Thank goodness. We—"

"I wanted to tell you right away." Georgie quickly scooted closer to me. "And a hundred times since. But we—" She glanced over her shoulder at Miss Stranje. "The thought was that it would be better if you didn't have to keep a secret this important from *him*, from Gabriel. Because if we tell you, you *will* have to keep this from him. Do you still want to know?"

"Of course, I want to know. It isn't as if we're betrothed." I emphasized my point with a great deal of heat. "Why should it be difficult? Lord Ravencross and I are no more than neighbors to one another. Mere acquaintances. Not even friends. Not really. If you must know, he finds me irksome. He said so himself only last night. Despite what you may think, Georgiana, I have no future with him. For that matter, no future with anyone, least of all him."

During this rather forceful protestation, Miss Stranje pressed her lips into a thin exasperated line and cast her gaze to the ceiling.

I didn't care if she believed me or not. It was nothing less than the truth. Nevertheless, I brought my strident pitch under control. "What I intended to say is that I care about him, of course, but I would not wish to make him suffer because of my dreams, not the way my father and grandfather did."

"Very well, then, I'll tell you." Georgie caught her lip, as if she was loath to spring the truth from its hiding place.

Miss Stranje rolled her hand, indicating that Georgie should get on with it.

"The fact of the matter is . . . well, you see, Lord Ravencross didn't actually kill his brother."

I shook my head. "But—"

Jane cut me off. "He thought he did. *Everyone* thought he had. But somehow Lucien survived."

Georgie gave a somber recitation of the facts. "Captain Grey and Lord Wyatt waited outside the farmhouse the day Gabriel went in to convince his brother to come back to Britain's side of the war before it was too late. The exchange between Gabriel and Lucien quickly turned into a heated argument. When Captain Grey and Lord Wyatt heard steel ringing against steel they rushed inside. But it was too late. They found the brothers collapsed in pools of blood. They had fled before the enemy discovered them and only narrowly managed to escape with Gabriel and carry him to safety. Captain Grey and Lord Wyatt were both absolutely certain Lucien was dead."

Georgie stopped and shook her head. "Who knows what happened. The French surgeons are reputed to be the best in the world. Lucien was a leader in Napoleon's Iron Crown, they must've moved heaven and earth to save him."

"But I saw it all in a dream," I reminded her. "He fell down dead. There was no bringing him back from that."

"You're right, and we don't actually know *how* the man survived, only that he did. Like you, Sebastian believed Lucien was dead. He saw no breath signs and there was enough blood on the floor to warrant that conclusion. Although how much of that blood actually belonged to Gabriel rather than Lucien, we will never know."

"I saw his eyes. They were lifeless," I muttered.

"Yes." She took a deep breath and pressed on. "But I assure you he is very much alive. We saw him. Jane, Maya, and I, we all saw him the day we rescued Lord Wyatt from the Iron Crown's stronghold. The former Lord of Ravencross was very much alive."

I could scarcely breathe. "If this is true, it means that Gabriel is not . . ."

Jane completed my worrisome conclusion. "Strictly speaking, you are correct. He is not rightfully Lord of Ravencross."

"Gabriel must be told," I said with flat finality. "He would want to know."

"Would he?" Miss Stranje's icy tone silenced everyone in the room. "What do you suppose he will do once he knows?"

I didn't answer. It was one of her traps.

Georgie responded for me. "He would report it to Whitehall."

He would. He would feel it was his duty.

Jane finished closing the door on the trap. "And then the title, his lands, and his family honor would be stripped away. Not to mention the disgrace that would be brought down on his head given the fact that his brother is now quite aptly named—"

"No!" I sucked air. "*Ghost.*"

My stomach shot straight through the feather ticking and crashed against the floorboards.

It fit.

Lucien had come back to life as Ghost, the elusive shadow leader of the Iron Crown. Ruthless. Brutal. And extremely efficient in his treachery. I closed my eyes, cringing as I considered the shame this would heap upon Gabriel.

When I could breathe again, I made a feeble protest. "But he's miserable because he thinks he killed his brother."

Miss Stranje shifted to her instructive mannerisms and voice. "And so you must ask yourself, would he be less miserable knowing the truth?"

"That his brother is England's most notorious traitor." Sera stared out the window. "Gabriel's loyalties would even come into question."

His own brother, leader of the Iron Crown? It couldn't be. Yet it made perfect sense. Naturally Daneska would have allied herself with a murderous traitor. The gnawing betrayal I'd felt because of her, Gabriel would feel a hundredfold.

His own brother.

Gabriel's brother hid behind the mantle of Ghost. I would make an honest man of him and turn him into a real ghost.

I would kill Lucien.

Georgie was right. "Gabriel must never find out." The words echoed from my throat, hard and commanding. My soul turned into that of an assassin, dark as midnight and as calculating as sharp steel. "No one outside of this room must ever know."

Georgie looked at me, suddenly guarded. "But someday, won't he . . ." She hesitated, wary of the hardness in me.

"I will stop Daneska and Ghost before they come."

"We," she said, her voice shaking. "*We* will stop them."

We?

No. I shook my head. Georgie was too good and kind. I would never let death stain her as it had me.

"Perhaps he ought to know." Sera turned from the window. "Do we really have a right to hide this from him? I'm not so certain."

Yes. No. Who was I to decide his fate?

"I don't know." I collapsed into my hands again, burying my face, uncertain of either path. But they were all waiting for some kind of decision. I had no right to decide.

Suddenly I felt angry again. No, I *wanted* to be angry. I chose to be angry. I wanted a distraction. I needed the heat of rage to wrest the icy misery settling into my veins.

"Why is it that I haven't dreamed this? *Why?* What good are these infuriating visions of the future if they don't even reveal something as important as that?"

Miss Stranje, still playing at being our teacher, cocked one brow imperiously. "I believe you just did, don't you think?"

"Hardly," I grumbled.

Then, out of nowhere, a wry thought occurred to me, and I smirked as aptly as I am able to smirk, which isn't much at all.

It is Jane and Miss Stranje who can successfully pull off irony. Nevertheless, I took a stab at it. "And here I'd thought Lady Daneska had taken up with someone new."

Jane was the only one who thought it funny.

Georgie slumped and propped her chin in her hand. She seemed to be pondering something in a completely different direction. "You said you dreamed of fire and water. Do you suppose that means they might have gotten the plans for the warship out of Mr. Sinclair?"

"It's quite possible." Jane's jaw tensed. "For all we know, he could be in league with them." She started to pace. "What do we really know of Mr. Sinclair other than the fact that he is vulgar and ill-mannered?"

Georgie shot up. "We know that Sebastian thought him worth rescuing."

Miss Stranje intervened. "Ladies, we must not leap to conclusions one way or the other. Let us simply discover what information he gave them before he was rescued and proceed from there. The Iron Crown may have forced his hand. We are all too familiar with the cruelty they are capable of inflicting upon their prisoners."

Jane stood very stiff and guarded. "How can we find out without tipping our hand? He's more clever than he lets on. Too clever by half. It is quite possible he was never a prisoner at all. That he is one of them, sent here to infiltrate our ranks."

Georgie fumed at her. "Don't be ridiculous."

"I'm not. France allied with the Yanks when they fought us for independence. Have you forgotten, the Americans declared war on Britain in 1812? Last year they burned York to the ground."

Georgie rushed to his defense. "Yes, but attacking Canada was not a popular action in his country. Many of his countrymen rioted against the war. He may not sympathize with—"

"We're still at war." Jane stiffened and elevated her chin. "He is our enemy. And don't forget it. Mr. Sinclair has far more reason to swear his allegiance to France than to England."

"Yes, but it is highly unlikely." Sera stood to the side, watching and observing as she always does. "He appears to be straightforward to a fault."

"Oh, yes. He's excessively straightforward when it suits him. Rude, I should say." Jane bristled. "Being blunt does not make him honest. Nor does it mean he's on our side. He's still an American. Who knows where his loyalties lie. He might very well be a spy."

"That's preposterous." Georgie propped her fists on her hips, and I rather expected she would stand by him to the death, because in so doing she defended Lord Wyatt's decision to send the engineer's apprentice to us. "His uncle has not taken either side in the war with Napoleon. Fulton offered his inventions to both sides. Surely Mr. Sinclair is as neutral as his uncle."

"There is nothing neutral about him," Jane grumbled.

Maya stood back by the curtains and laughed softly. I love Maya's rare waves of laughter. They bubble up from a place of complete contentment and it warms the soul to hear them.

Miss Stranje moved between Jane and Georgie and clapped her hands together, ending their debate. "I suggest we go down to breakfast and ask him. If he is as straightforward as Sera believes, he will tell us exactly what plans he did or did not give the Iron Crown. *However*, a word of caution. There must be absolutely no mention of Lady Daneska or Ghost until we are completely certain of this young man's loyalty. Agreed?"

We all nodded in response, but our headmistress turned and singled out Jane with a stern expression pinching her face. "Lady Jane?"

"Me?" Jane's hand flew to her chest. "Why would you doubt

me? I'm not the one. It's Georgie who trusts him. Not I. If it were up to me, I would never speak another word to the man." She sniffed and stuck her chin higher. "For any reason."

"Very well. You may all go. But wait to question him. Tess and I will join you shortly." She dismissed them and turned to me. "I'll help you change into a morning gown. But first I would like to hear your answer. Do you intend to tell Gabriel about his brother, or not?"

I looked down at my bare toes, and with a deep sigh, answered, "It's not my place."

"Hmm. I wonder."

We were a few minutes late to breakfast. As it turned out, it might have been better to skip it altogether.

Ten

QUESTIONS

The breakfast room is my second-favorite room at Stranje House. It always smells of bacon and toasted muffins. The walls are painted butter yellow and, no matter the season, light drifts through the broad windows and warms the soul. There is a secret passage through the cupboards along the south wall. I often sneak in here at other times of the day just to breathe in the homey scents and bask in its lovely warmth. I'm like a cat that way. I prowl and roam where I will. But today the breakfast room felt decidedly sullen, and it had nothing to do with the light.

We found it filled with silent, brooding occupants. Maya was the only one who didn't look disgruntled. She hummed to herself and cheerfully peeled an orange. Jane looked as if she planned to cut off someone's head, and not the one belonging to the hapless fish under her knife. Georgie stirred the contents of her plate into an unrecognizable smear. Sera studied everyone at the table with nervous intensity.

Upon our entering, Mr. Sinclair hopped up out of his chair, almost knocking it over. Miss Stranje greeted him and asked how he was getting on with his morning's work.

He bowed his head before answering and proceeded with cautiously chosen words. "I thank you for your hospitality, Miss Stranje. Your accommodations are generous and comfortable." Then, rather more coldly, he added, "Lady Jane tells me you have some questions for me."

Miss Stranje sent a wordless scold in Jane's direction.

"He goaded me," Jane sputtered with indignation. "Tell her." She nudged Georgie. "Tell her how he tricked me into saying something."

Georgie shrugged at Jane's outburst and appealed to the two of us. "They are like fire and oil."

Sera leaned across the table. "I think you might mean like fire and water. Opposites."

"No. If that were true, they wouldn't keep bursting into flames, now would they?" Georgie turned to the food on her plate and began slicing a kipper.

"You may be seated." Miss Stranje nodded to Mr. Sinclair and took her place at the head of the table as she always does. A footman presented her with a silver tray containing the day's notes and letters. She didn't go through them right away as she usually does. Instead, she clasped her hands in her lap and addressed our guest. "Jane is right, Mr. Sinclair. I do have a few questions about your sojourn in France, if you would be so good as to indulge my curiosity?"

"At your service, Miss Stranje. Ask away."

"I appreciate your candor." She motioned for the footman to bring her a boiled egg. This she dealt with as she always does. A swift swipe of her knife, and the egg, shell and all, was split cleanly in two. She scooped out each half with a spoon and pressed it atop her buttered toast. *I have attempted her method and sent my egg flying halfway across the room.*

She dispatched egg and toast, wiped her mouth, and turned to Mr. Sinclair. "I would like to know exactly what information you gave the French."

"Ah. So that's it, is it?" Mr. Sinclair nodded, and his normally amicable expression turned serious. "They asked me a great many questions about my uncle's steamships. I found it odd, considering Uncle Robert presented the idea to Napoleon himself and had been turned down flat."

He warmed to his subject and forgot for a moment his indignation at being questioned. "If I remember correctly, the high and mighty emperor said something along these lines, 'Fire is the great fear of all sailors, Mr. Fulton, and yet you would make a ship sail against the winds and currents by lighting a bonfire under her decks? I have no time for such nonsense.'" Mr. Sinclair forked a sliced potato and drew it through the egg yolk on his plate, scrawling something before continuing with his story. "And yet here come a half dozen of Napoleon's finest engineers with a flurry of questions for me about how to connect the paddle wheel to the steam engine and the like."

"And did you tell them how to do it, Mr. Sinclair?"

He set his fork down with a plunk. "No, Miss Stranje, I did not. And it isn't because I fancied myself a great friend of Britain at the time. Because I'm not. I'm sure I need not remind you that we are at war with your fine country." He held up his long tapered fingers, forestalling her reaction. "Before you sound the alarm and have me arrested, let me assure you I am no longer a friend of the French either. I am, however, loyal to my uncle. If I had given Napoleon's engineer patented information about the steamship mechanisms, I would be robbing Uncle Robert of the price he asked Napoleon to pay. That would make me worse than a thief. Whatever else you may think of me, and I gather from some of your students that the general opinion of me here is rather low—"

"Jane does not speak for all of us," Georgie fumed.

"Whatever the case," continued Mr. Sinclair, "I would not do such a disservice to my uncle. A more generous man does not exist. Uncle Robert bought my mother a farm and handed the deed over to her and my da without strings of any sort. He did the same for my grandmother and aunts. He undertook my education and brought me to work alongside him as if I were his own son. I would not betray him." He picked up his fork and gave the potato on the end a shake. "Not even at the cost of my life."

Miss Stranje acknowledged his devotion to his uncle with a squaring of her shoulders and one of her rare expressions of respect. Mr. Sinclair's speech pleased her, but she pressed on. Her voice held no inflection that might indicate her deep concern, no current of condemnation or approval. "When you refused to help their engineers, what happened then?"

Mr. Sinclair's countenance fell. His lips pressed together and he stared at the fork as if he'd like to stab it into something besides a potato. "They hauled me off to that house outside of Paris. The one where your friend, Lord Wyatt, found me."

Despite his sudden dark mood, our relentless headmistress gave him no quarter. "And is that all?"

He stared at her as if she had all the diplomacy of a wide-mouthed cannon. "No, Miss Stranje, that is not all. They tried to persuade me." He abandoned his fork for a swig of apple juice. "Here's where I'm faced with a dilemma." He raised the glass as if to toast us. "I was given to understand you all found my con- versation coarse and unfit for the drawing room. Begging your pardon, I meant to say unfit for your *workroom*. So you can understand why I hesitate to regale you at your breakfast table with the details of my torture."

He lowered the goblet and tugged down his cuff, just enough that we could see a scabbed line of cuts and the purple bruises marking where he'd worn heavy irons on his wrists.

Georgie set her spoon down with a decided plunk and glared at Jane, who turned white with shame and stared at her plate.

Miss Stranje nodded and said, "I apologize, Mr. Sinclair. You must forgive me for having asked these questions. I would not have intentionally stirred such unhappy memories. You need not say more. We know firsthand the sort of cruelty one may expect from Napoleon's secret order of knights. The Iron Crown is—"

Loud pounding at the main door startled us.

The thumping got louder and more insistent until Greaves scraped the door open. After which, we were treated to a booming Scottish brogue ordering our butler to "Stand aside, man, afore we chop ye down."

An even louder and more agitated voice, belonging to Lord Ravencross, carried into our breakfast room. "I don't care if they are in the middle of tea with the Queen, you'll let me in. Where are they?"

"Not that way, yer lordship," MacDougal called after his master and sniffed loudly. "Unless m' nose deceives me, they'll be at breakfast. I smell sausage and it's straight down this way."

Greaves is sturdy as a pike, but he is an old man and no match for MacDougal and Ravencross. Greaves shuffled after them, maintaining a dignified tone despite repeating numerous times, "I'm warning you, my lord. I shall summon a footman."

Our only footman, Philip, was already trailing along behind Greaves, no match for the burly Scot and Lord Ravencross, who was a great bear of a man, even though he was down to the use of only one arm, the other being in a sling.

At that point, Lord Ravencross had already charged like a bull into our breakfast room.

Philip and Greaves made a desperate lunge to apprehend him.

I stood abruptly and shouted, "Leave him be." They turned to me in alarm. Miss Stranje rose and nodded permission for her servants to stand down.

After that, my wits went begging and all I could do was gape at Lord Ravencross like a foolish besotted schoolgirl. He was still rumpled from sleep. He wore a simple cambric work shirt, which hung open at the throat, buckskin trousers, and riding boots. This was not a social call.

Miss Stranje indicated a chair. "Lord Ravencross, perhaps you would care for some breakfast?"

"No. No, I . . ." His eyes did not leave my face. He appeared to be completely astounded to see me standing there looking back at him.

The breakfast table was lined with spectators, but Lord Ravencross didn't give them even a cursory glance. "I . . . I thought you were hurt . . . that is to say . . . I heard a scream. Several screams."

Miss Stranje sighed heavily and muttered, "I must remember to make certain those upstairs windows are shut tight."

Georgie squinted up studiously. "I don't see how he could've heard—"

Miss Stranje cleared her throat and, in a tone that demanded attention, she said, "My lord, clearly, you've not had your breakfast yet. Won't you please have a seat?"

MacDougal spoke up in place of his tongue-tied master. "Right you are, miss. He hasn't had a bite to eat since yesterday. Even then, it weren't no more than weak broth. Not near enough by my way of thinkin'. Came roaring up from his bed as if the devil were jabbing 'im wi' a pitchfork. Shoutin' and carryin' on, saying as how the young lady must be in trouble. On account of he could hear 'er screaming, y'see?" MacDougal scratched at his side-whiskers. "Tried to calm him, miss. I did. Me and the doctor held 'im down for as long as we could manage. Told 'im as how I'd been awake the whole time an' not heard a peep, save the cock crowing. But it weren't no good. He fought us and flung the covers at me, demanding his clothes and boots. And here we are." He gestured at me as if I was the source of all the commotion. "And there she is wi' not a scratch on 'er just as I promised."

A blush climbed up Ravencross's neck. He rubbed at his forearm, the shoulder still wrapped in bloody bandages. "I feel a fool."

"No, my lord. You were concerned, and rightly so." Miss Stranje sounded surprisingly conciliatory. "Miss Aubreyson did, indeed, scream this morning because of a particularly bad nightmare. The sound alarmed me as well. As you know, I am not easily alarmed." She gestured to a chair at the end of the table. "Won't you please sit down? Miss Aubreyson will explain it all to you after you've eaten. You, too, Mr. MacDougal."

The burly Scot backed away, waving his hands. "No, miss, couldn't do that. T'wouldn't be proper fer the likes of me to sit at yer table, what wi' me being his lordship's servant an' all." He eyed the warming pan full of crispy fish on the side table. "But I wouldn't say no to takin' one of these kippers with me to the kitchen. I'll just wait for you there, shall I, sir?"

Sir. Lordship. MacDougal's wobbly forms of address would leave the listener confused as to whether Lord Ravencross was a duke or a baronet. Miss Stranje waved her fingers, and the footman took the hungry Scot away to the kitchen with a heaping plate dressed with fried fish and potatoes.

Lord Ravencross remained standing where he was. "I wouldn't want to impose."

"Sit, my lord. You are more than welcome at our table."

He continued to stare at me, as if staring reassured him that I was truly alive and well. "You're all right, then?"

I nodded, still astonished.

"It was just a bad dream?"

"Yes."

Jane muttered under her breath as I took my seat. "*We are nothing to each other.*"

Her sly remark jarred me from my stupor.

"*No more than neighbors,*" she mocked, only loud enough for me to hear.

"Enough." I pinched her as she sat down. A trick I'd learned from Daneska, how to pinch while pretending to smile and be polite.

Had I'd truly screamed so loud he heard it all the way across both parks? I shook the idea away. It seemed impossible. Or had he dreamt of me? Perhaps he'd had a worry nightmare like the one Sera accused me of having. Was he worried about me just as I was about Georgie? I felt absurdly pleased at the prospect. I shouldn't be happy that he'd had a nightmare, and yet the thought that I might be that much in his thoughts made my blood gallop and my heart dance.

The footman brought him a plate heaped with food. Lord Ravencross glanced with little interest at the bacon, curried eggs, sliced oranges, and toast. He looked around the table, moving from face to face until he landed with a jarring thud on the personage of Mr. Sinclair.

"Who the devil are you?" Lord Ravencross did not say this with the gentility one might expect from a guest. His tone made it clear he expected a prompt answer. He issued his demand with the force of a man having discovered a gentleman caller in his wife's bedchamber instead of finding a perfectly civil male visitor seated across the breakfast table in a girls' school.

"Apparently, I am the fox in this henhouse."

Jane groaned and rolled her eyes. Miss Stranje performed the introductions, but Lord Ravencross continued to frown at Mr. Sinclair.

We concentrated on our breakfast, eating in silence, save the scraping of forks and clicking of spoons.

In the relative quiet, Miss Stranje perused her morning post. She squinted at the address of one of the letters, flipped it over, and broke the seal. If it had been a letter from the captain or someone in the diplomatic affairs office, she would have slipped it into her pocket and read it later. I watched with curiosity as her pallor increased and she pinched the bridge of her nose as if the contents pained her.

At length, she held the missive out to me. "From your aunt Lydia," she said cryptically.

My knife clattered to my plate, the marmalade meant for my toast splattered. In all these four years, there had been only a handful of letters from my aunt, and those were usually short. By the grievous look on Miss Stranje's face, this lengthy missive could mean only that my uncle had succumbed to his injuries and died.

Injuries that were my fault.

I closed my eyes tight against the memory of my tumble from grace, willing it away.

But it would not go.

The sound still thundered through my head of my uncle stomping up the stairs to my attic bedroom, cursing my name. "Tess, you worthless she-demon. I know what you've done. You've turned my horse against me."

Willful child that I was, I had slammed my door and shoved the bureau in front of it. Admittedly, it hadn't been a very clever way to escape a whipping. I had trapped myself. Except there *was* the window.

That day was when I first learned to scale walls. I'd thrown open the window and crawled out, planning to climb down and escape to woods. *Or fall.* But at thirteen I had little care for caution. I'd hung from the moldy sill, dangling three stories above the ground, my skirts flapping madly in the wind as I struggled to find a foothold.

Finally, I was able to wedge my toes into the narrow mortar grooves between the stones. I'd clutched the window frame and scrambled my fingers across the rough limestone, searching for a protrusion to hold. I found a thin lip on a stone beneath the window, but my leg trembled stupidly as I lowered myself down onto the wall. I remember taking a deep, steadying breath and telling myself, *don't look down.*

Concentrate.

Breathe.

The cold, reliable certainty of rock beneath my fingertips helped calm me. Stone walls and falling—these things I'd understood. They were dependable truths. Fall, *die.* Hold on, *live.*

Simple.

Understandable.

Unlike my uncle. He'd baffled me. Why would my riding Orion without a bit upset him so much? And anyway, why had he insisted on using such a cruel type of bit on an animal as obliging as Orion? Didn't he see that the thing was tearing up his horse's mouth? If his beast revolted against that, it was his fault, not mine. But Uncle Martin had liked to be in charge. He'd kept my aunt completely under his thumb. Back then, I used to wonder if perhaps I was more wild animal than human. I had always been able to figure out horses and dogs, all manner of creatures, even the elusive foxes that hid in our woods behaved in ways I'd readily understood. But my aunt and uncle had been impossible to comprehend.

So I'd climbed to freedom—one handhold, one toehold at a time, down the side of the house.

He leaned out of my window and hurled the tin water pitcher at me. It clanged off the stones above my head. "First, you spoil my horse. Now, a broken door. You'll pay for what you've done!"

The ground lay more than a story away, but his scarlet rage made the distance seem short. I'd dropped and tumbled down-hill, away from the house, rolling and rolling, skirts flopping, until I stopped, scrambled up from the wet grass, and took off in a dead run.

Uncle Martin came after me.

I had been fast even back then. *Very fast.* On foot, he never would have caught me, not even if he had a hundred lifetimes in which to give chase. But Uncle Martin was crafty. He came after me on horseback.

His stallion's hooves thudded against the soft soil, flinging clods of earth, thundering behind me, louder and louder. I pushed harder and faster. My lungs burned and I prayed the wind would lift me up and sail me on its current. But I'd had no wings, only frightened rabbit feet. So I'd raced for the woods.

In the forest I would've had a chance. The trees would've hid-den me. After all, hadn't my mother taught me I was part of the forest? Almost to the woods, I'd glanced over my shoulder. He rode at a mad dog pace, whipping Orion into a lather. What a fool I was to have looked back. I stumbled. A hole hidden in the grass. Ironic. Me, the rabbit, tripped up by a rabbit's lair.

Stupid! It had been a stupid mistake. I should never have looked back. My ankle snapped. Pain, hot and sharp, shot up my leg and brought me down in a crumpled heap. I drew up my knees and clutched my ankle.

Uncle Martin jerked Orion to a sudden stop, leapt off, and marched toward me, slapping his riding crop across his hand. "Not so high and mighty now, eh, you little witch?"

I remember shaking my head and scooting backward, uncertain how to ward him off. He'd slapped the whip again, this time against his thigh. Orion shied. Martin should've known better than to threaten me in front of that horse. It was because of that very stallion that my uncle hated me with such passion. He should've known. How could he have not known what would happen?

He raised the crop, intending to thrash me. Orion reared. My uncle turned.

There were three screams that day.

Mine.

My uncle's.

And Orion's. Right before his hooves struck my uncle's head.

A stallion's scream blots out all reason. The sound plunges the hearer into a dark, echoing cave of fear. When I'd regained my senses, the big brown horse stood beside me, snorting, stamping, and shying like a confused child. My uncle lay unconscious on the ground a few feet away from me.

"Shhhhh," I'd crooned, beckoning Orion to me. "It's all right, boy." He tossed his head, agitated, afraid. "You didn't mean it. I know you didn't. You were just trying to protect me."

Even as I said it, I knew the sad truth. When Uncle Martin awakened, he would shoot Orion for his actions that day. It wouldn't matter that the horse was a superb hunting mount and a valuable breeding stallion. I'd struggled to my feet somehow and limped to the agitated horse, smoothing my hand down his neck to quiet him, leaning my head against his withers. I'd murmured words from the ancient Welsh language my mother had taught me, telling him how much I loved him for trying to save me.

My guardian still hadn't roused. "Uncle Martin?" I edged toward him. Any second, I'd expected his hand to flash out, snare me, and I would've been in for the beating of my life.

Only he didn't move. Apart from the wind ruffling his hair and neckcloth, he lay completely still. His mouth gaped open, a silent echo of the scream he'd uttered before Orion kicked him. I saw then how his head rested at an odd angle against a small boulder.

Suddenly dizzy, my stomach spun through empty air, falling like a baby bird from the nest. "No," I whispered. "No. Don't let him be dead. Please. Not dead."

I knelt beside him. "Uncle Martin?" Blood had pooled at the base of the rock, a thick burgundy ooze, staining grass and soil. "Uncle Martin, wake up!" His chest lifted ever so slightly. He was alive.

Barely.

I ripped a strip of cloth from the bottom of my underdress and wrapped his head to slow the bleeding. Then I'd hobbled back to the grazing stallion and heaved myself onto his back.

"Run, Orion," I'd shouted. The stallion's ears flicked up sharp. "*Rhedeg*," I'd said in the old tongue, and he took off, racing for the house, galloping across the field so fast that half the time his feet scarcely touched the ground.

"Lydia!" I cried out for my mother's sister, praying she would hear my call for help.

As soon as I'd explained, she'd sent servants to unhinge a door and they'd used it to carry him back to the house. Martin still breathed, but the doctors could not wake him. "Any day," the doctor had said, and then he'd shown Lydia how to squeeze broth from a cloth and let it drip down my uncle's throat. But as the days passed, the doctor's expression had grown more solemn. His words "any day" had changed to a death watch.

My uncle's family had arrived already wearing black. It was not long after that they exiled me to Stranje House. Not Aunt Lydia; she'd wept when they carted me away with my hands bound. It was Uncle Martin's prune-faced sister and his fat sweating father's doing. They'd sent me here to be punished, to be beaten into submission, to learn to conduct myself in a manner befitting a proper young lady. Beneath their fine words and stiff speech, it was as if they had thought I truly was a demon child. And Miss Stranje had the perfect reputation for being able to exorcise the devil from unmanageable girls like me.

Or so they had thought.

I glanced at the headmistress I'd come to respect and with shaking hands reached for my aunt's letter. I had no desire to read it, but just as traitors must face a firing squad, I knew I must face the sad truth that another death would be laid at my door.

Lydia's handwriting is challenging under the best of circumstances, as it is small and fraught with a great many decorative flourishes. Add to that the dread and guilt blurring my sight, and as a consequence I stumbled along, scarcely able to make out the words on the page. Upon the second reading, my disbelief settled, and here is what it said:

My dear Niece,
I have news.
My husband's family has given up hope that Martin will ever recover. What black thoughts his people have. They persist in ignoring the fact that he is greatly improved. I was not sorry to see them pack up their belongings last month and leave. They have gone home to Middlesbrough, saying they

will not return until Martin's funeral. The good Lord willing, that occasion shall not take place for a great many years.

Now that a month has passed, I believe they are well and truly gone. That means you may return here without fear of being locked in a closet, tied to a bedpost, or anything else. I feel simply wretched about all the horrid thrashings they wrought upon your person. You must understand, it is just their way. They are rather stern folk.

I confess, it has been duller than old porridge and twice as sticky having them so frequently underfoot during the past few years. Especially his sour-tempered sister. They have been constantly in and out, arriving unannounced, staying for weeks on end, and bringing all manner of physicians with vile treatments to inflict upon poor Martin.

His father's parting words were unbearably cruel. He lamented that there is nothing left of his son save a sniveling, useless child. He refused to even kiss Martin farewell. "My son is dead," says he.

It isn't true.

In point of fact, I find my husband's company quite pleasant these days. What does it matter if I must wipe spittle from his chin now and again? Martin no longer yells, nor does he drink too much, and he no longer broods. It is miraculous how he seems to delight in the simplest things. He will sit for hours in the yard playing with the kittens. He would never have been content to do so in the past. In my opinion, he is vastly improved. You will see for yourself when you return home.

There are a few minor problems, which I must explain. For instance, I cannot allow him to go near the stables. He seems to have forgotten which end of the horse is most likely to kick. Sometimes even the sight of a horse will throw him into a terror *and we find him cowering in a corner. We must also watch that he doesn't wander off into the woods. These problems are not usually burdensome because most days his legs will not support his weight as they ought. I had a bath chair constructed for him so that we might roll him around with ease. Martin quite enjoys riding in his chair.*

After another week or two I think we can be fairly confident his family will not return unexpectedly. At that time it will be safe for you to return to my house. Surely you are longing for release from that horrible school to which his sister exiled you. Nor have I forgotten my promise to your dear mother that I would take care of you 'til the end. I mean to keep my word.

Aside from that, Martin's father has decided he will not send any more funds for your tuition at Miss Stranje's establishment. So, as it stands, there is no alternative but for you to return here to Tidenham.

I will arrange with Miss Stranje for your transportation.

Fond regards,

Lydia

My chest felt heavy. I couldn't sort my thoughts. They tumbled and rolled and collapsed in a chaotic heap. *Martin was alive.* Not dead. That much filled me with relief. Lydia was making the best of it, but my uncle had been reduced to a helpless child because of me.

My fault. That turned my relief to remorse.

Lydia had promised my mother to take care of me *'til the end.*

I knew what she meant. She would take care of me until the madness swallowed me up and I died. My mother had known that would be my end, just as she had known it would be hers.

Lydia wrote of my death. Not Martin's. I was to return home until I died. Remorse changed to fury.

Home.

That had never been my home. The forests of Wye Valley, maybe. The trees and brooks where I'd played as a child. But not the manor. Not really. Not now. It belonged to my uncle now. I had no home except Stranje House. My stomach lurched, fisting up around breakfast.

I dropped the letter on the table as if it burned my fingers. They were all watching me. All of them. Gabriel, too. I needed to run. I wanted to spring up that instant and dash out of the room.

If I run fast enough none of this will catch me. Instead, I choked out an answer to their unasked question. "There's no more money. I am to return to Tidenham." *To await my death.*

"You can't go!" Georgie surged up from her seat.

Sera snatched the letter from my plate and was reading it.

"Georgie's right. We need you." Jane reached for my arm, but I pulled away. She whirled on Miss Stranje. "You have to stop her."

"Sit down, Lady Jane. You, too, Georgie. You will *all* control yourselves at my table." She lowered her voice, but I did not miss the fact that she continued on with a small uncharacteristic tremor strangling her words. "Miss Aubreyson must be allowed to make this decision for herself. It is not our place to make demands."

"It isn't as if I have a choice in the matter. My uncle's family will no longer pay for my room and board."

Miss Stranje sat very straight and stiff in her chair. In a cold *no-nonsense* voice, she said, "There are always choices." She adjusted the table linen beside her plate. "Always."

She looked up at us, and the room got deadly still, as if we were all afraid to breathe. "Tess has been invited back to her home. This ought to be a moment of celebration for her. You will not harry her. Or get maudlin. Nor will you put undue . . ." She caught her lip. It took a moment for her to gather herself, but she flexed her jaw and stood with backbone befitting a queen. "Tess, after you have had time to consider your aunt's offer, if you would like to discuss it, I will be in my office. Now if you will excuse me, I will join all of you in the small parlor in two hours' time to discuss the matter of a possible attack."

"Attack? From whom? Napoleon?" Mr. Sinclair shoved back from the table.

Both he and Lord Ravencross rose, as gentlemen must do when the lady of the house leaves the room, but long after she hurried away both men remained standing.

Lord Ravencross looked limp and white faced, as if he'd just found himself standing on a gallows facing a noose.

Eleven

ᴅEATH AWAITS

G abriel turned to me with a devastated expression twisting his features. It ripped what remained of my composure to shreds. I couldn't think. All I could do was rush out of the breakfast room, skirts flying.

"Wait!" He strode after me and caught my arm in the hall.

"Go away." I jerked free. "I need to run. If I don't, I'll lose my mind."

Not the obedient sort, he didn't go away. "Very well, if you need to run, I'll run alongside you."

"You can't."

"Don't let my lame leg fool you. I can keep up as well as any man."

It wasn't the old wound in his leg I was concerned about. "Not without tearing open the stitches in your shoulder."

His posture stiffened. "I'm willing to take that chance."

"Well, I'm not." I backed against the paneled wall and pressed my hands over my face, roaring in frustration. He would've done the same if matters were reversed. I flung my hands down. "If you insist on accompanying me, my lord, I suppose I will have to settle for a brisk walk."

"Gabriel," he said. "For pity's sake, call me Gabriel." He motioned for me to lead the way. "You've been in my bedroom. I believe we can dispense with the formalities of my title, don't you?"

I groaned. "I was there serving as your watchman, not your lover. So, no, my lord, I believe the formalities are still very much in play."

We left the house by way of the garden.

"You *will* call me Gabriel." He said this with a firmness that brooked no argument. "I never wanted the blasted title in the first place. Such things belong to men like my father. Men born to rule. It suited my brother. Not me."

His words evoked memories for both of us. Gruesome images of the last time he saw his brother alive. And undoubtedly their violent duel. The secret haunted me then. It was harder than I thought not to relieve his pain. Except that would only bring a new torment. So I changed the subject and walked faster. "Perhaps you should sit here on this chair beside the garden and rest. It's too soon for you to be walking after losing all that blood."

"I find I am much improved this morning. I was surprised to find that I rested quite well last night despite having so many people in my room."

He was baiting me, but I could not joust with him. Not today, not when my future was crumbling faster than I could run. I chose a path on the opposite side of the property, as far from Ravencross Manor as possible. We walked in silence until we were well away from the house. My thoughts fluttered about like frantic geese being chased by a dog.

When he finally broke the silence, it startled me. "Why were you screaming this morning?"

My scream? That's what he chose to discuss? *Not,* what is all this talk of an attack?

Or, when will you leave?

Or, please don't go.

"It was a bad dream. That's all."

"But your scream sounded real. Not like, well, not like something from a dream."

"I've no idea how you heard it, all the way from your house." I glanced over my shoulder across the distance to Ravencross Manor, trying to sound casual.

"Yes, that is peculiar. At times, sound carries oddly along the cliffs."

"I suppose." *Why didn't he ask about my leaving?*

"What did you dream about that upset you so badly?"

"It isn't important."

"Important enough to send me tearing over here like a complete fool."

"I apologize, my lord. You should've stayed in your bed. I shall endeavor to scream more quietly in the future."

"Are you going to tell me or not?"

"Not."

"And if I insist?"

"I'm told I can be rather obstinate."

"I can attest to that. But I would like to know what upset you. You are not the screaming sort."

"If you must know, it was Lady Daneska."

He stopped walking, suddenly quiet.

I turned and waited for him to catch up. "I dreamt she was here, at Stranje House, with her band of assassins, and that she had captured Georgie."

"Then do you mean to say it was she who was behind the attack yesterday?"

I wasn't sure how to answer him without revealing too much. "Who else could it have been?"

"This is a very odd girls' school." He rubbed at the stubble on his jaw. At length he glanced at me, and I saw in his eyes that he was leaping to all sorts of dangerous conclusions.

"It was just a bad dream." I lengthened my stride.

He matched mine. "And because of this dream of yours, you and Miss Stranje think Lady Daneska is actually coming here again? Is that the attack she mentioned? Surely not."

I didn't want to discuss this now. Not when I faced having to leave Stranje House and abandoning Georgie and him to deal with Daneska's murderous intentions. I came to an irritated halt and balled my fists at my sides. *Why didn't he have the decency to ask about me leaving? He could at least act as if it troubled him.* But no, he must bring up Daneska and the dreams.

I didn't know what to say, or how to say it. After numerous false starts, I blurted, "I can't leave. Not now. Not when you . . . when they . . ." I pointed back at Stranje House, at Georgie and the others. "You're all in danger."

"Do you *want* to leave?" Gabriel gently took hold of my elbow, squinting at me, trying to decipher my muddled speech. "If it weren't for all this other trouble, Tess, would you want go home to your aunt?"

"Don't make me answer that." I folded my arms and huddled over them. "What difference does it make? I've no choice in the matter."

He let go and I wished he hadn't. "It makes a difference to me."

"There are far more important things to consider at the moment, my lord, than whether or not I want to go back to Tiden-

ham. Georgie is not the only one in danger. You are, as well."
It was all I could do to keep from shouting. "I tried to tell you
last night. Daneska sent those men to abduct Georgie, but she
offered to pay them extra if they killed you."

He nodded and strolled ahead as if I'd said nothing of importance.

I hurried up beside him. "And after that dream, I am convinced you are in far more danger than I thought." For reasons
I couldn't tell him. Even though I itched to know why his brother
hated him so much. Surely Lucien hadn't tried to kill him that
day in Möckern simply because they were on opposite sides of
the war. "This was no idle whim on Lady Daneska's part." *At least
I didn't think it was; with Daneska, one could never be too sure.*
"I don't see how I can leave in the middle of—"

"Hold!" Gabriel stopped in his tracks, his eyes widened and
his nostrils flared. "Am I to understand that you actually think
you must stay here to protect *me?*" His eyes slowly narrowed until
the dark slits resembled glinting daggers.

I swallowed, suddenly very sure I should not answer that question. I slid my foot back, preparing to skate away.

"Tess?"

A low warning rumble from deep in his chest made gooseflesh rise on my arms, but I stood my ground and didn't bolt.

With a disgusted growl, he said, "I can take care of myself."

It was the way he said it that made me mad, as if I was a
foolish girl to have even thought such things. "Oh, yes. How
silly of me. Of course, I should've known you are used to deal-
ing with murderous henchmen. It's an everyday thing for you,
I suppose?"

"I should think I've a great deal more experience with it than
you."

There he was sadly and quite utterly mistaken. But I couldn't correct him, not without revealing Miss Stranje's school for what it really was. So I scoffed wordlessly.

He exhaled in a frustrated burst, filling his chest with stern bravado. His face became an unyielding mask, and it brought to mind the paintings of his father I'd seen hanging on his staircase wall, grim and cold. "You're impossible. Besides, all of this is conjecture. You can't know Lady Daneska is going to return here for certain."

I said nothing.

"You dreamt it. Dreams can be false."

I sighed. "Not mine."

"You took a blow to the head. A bad one. More than likely, this is nothing more than wild imaginings brought on by your injury."

Wild imaginings.

"I wish it were so, my lord." *I refused to call him Gabriel. We were no longer friends. My dreams were many things. Frustrating. Horrifying most of the time. Wretchedly inscrutable usually. But they were not wild imaginings.* "You may think what you wish. But my dreams are not the ordinary variety."

Ordinary. If only they were. What must that be like?

Perhaps it was the sadness in my voice that made him lean in as if he was trying to understand. "How is it they differ?"

I bowed my head, not wishing to watch his face as I unwound the ugly truth. "Like my mother, and her mother before her, I am the firstborn daughter. In our family, the eldest daughters are cursed with dreams of things yet to happen. It has been so for generations, clear back to when the druids inhabited the forests in my part of the country. We are inflicted with confusing visions, flashes of the future, inscrutable bits and pieces of terrible things, deaths and horrors. All of which I would give anything not to experience night after night."

When I dared look up at him, I saw by his eyes my words had troubled him. "These things you see, do they . . ." He hesitated before answering. "Do they come to pass?"

"Often enough." I sighed heavily. "Eventually, many of the fragments, these little bits and pieces of the future, prove true."

Doubt lingered on him, plaguing me.

I could have told him about seeing the fight between him and his brother. But I couldn't do that without bringing up things I would have to hide. So I flung down my last card. "That's the reason we went to London. I'd dreamt about what would happen if we didn't take Georgie's new ink to Lord Wyatt. He would die. You helped us because you believed me. And you saw what happened there."

"You told me only that Lord Wyatt's life was in danger. That's why we went. I didn't know we were going because of a dream."

"If I'd told you, would you have taken us?"

All of Gabriel's beautiful golden color drained away. He turned ashen white.

"You've done too much, my lord. You must sit." I checked for telltale bleeding coming through his bandages, but there were no fresh stains. Even so, I tugged him to a large overturned log.

"Do you mean you actually saw Lord Wyatt die in a dream?"

"No, my lord, that's not how it works. I lived it. It was as if I died with him." *I could've told him that, once upon a time, I'd nearly died with him, too. But I didn't.*

"Good Lord." He rested his head in his hands. A few moments later, he looked up to the cloudless sky and then back to me. "If what you say is true, if Lady Daneska is coming here bent on murder and kidnapping, then you must go home to your aunt. You'll be safer there."

He would send me away? Away from him? Away from my friends?

I shoved my fists against my hips. "I'm touched, my lord, that you are so eager to be rid of me."

He snared my arm and jerked me onto the log beside him. "Rid of you? Are you daft?" He held me close, and I watched his pupils widen into dark chasms. "You told me once you could *see* how I felt about you. Have you suddenly gone blind?"

No, his hunger was still plain to see. But there was something else, something bricking up in his heart.

I decided to try chiseling it free with the sharp edge of my tongue. "As I recall, for my honesty on that occasion, you called me a witch."

"I did." His voice dropped to a low whisper. "Because you were right."

My lungs filled in a jubilant rush.

His grip on me softened. He stared at his fingers wrapped around my arm and loosened them so that his hand barely grazed my skin. "Truth is, to keep you here, I'd drop to my knees this instant and beg for your hand. That is, if I could stomach being that cruel to you. I want you, Tess, but you deserve a better man than me. A man with some semblance of a heart left. A man who would coddle you and treat you as you deserve. Not someone as worthless, and lame, and scarred—"

"Stop! Stop saying such things about yourself. You are worth ten of any other man I know."

He let go of me and the absence of his hand made me feel unnerved, as if an important article of clothing had been stripped away and I sat there half naked. But I could hardly grab his hand and slap it back on my arm. So I settled on words. "Do you think so little of me? Can you honestly believe I have my sights set on a man who would coddle me? What do I care about fine jewels, or carriages, or trips to the theater? Look at me. Am I a china doll to be petted and cosseted?"

I waited, but he didn't answer.

"Now who is blind?" I asked.

He stared at me, his lips parted as if he meant to say something, and then he closed them.

Lost.

Gabriel is normally a powerful man. Even though he bears a limp from the wound his brother gave him, it only proves his strength. He is a man who could not be cut down, even by a death blow. But all this—his height, his bearing, the powerful muscles in his shoulders and arms—only made that *lost* expression on his face all the more heartbreaking. I ached to throw my arms around him.

Instead, I clasped my palms together as if praying at an altar. "You can't truly believe your scars bother me. How can you? When, God help me, I yearn to trace each and every one with my lips."

Color returned to his face in a blazing crimson flood. He looked away as if my declaration pained him.

I stood, careful to keep my gaze from his, ashamed of my boldness but not yet finished with my confession. "Here is the saddest truth of all, my lord. My feelings are of no consequence. We have no future, Gabriel. Because there is only death ahead of me."

I gave his cheek a sorrow-drenched kiss and ran.

Ran away, back to Stranje House. I didn't run elegantly like a deer, or fierce like a wolf, or even like a frightened rabbit. I ran with no grace at all. Like a lost girl. A stupid, foolish lost girl. Half blind with wild thoughts, I stumbled on the stairs.

I never stumble.

Only death ahead of me.

I slammed through the garden door and practically flew through the corridors, up the staircase, down the hall, and flung wide the doors to the ballroom. She was there, as I knew she would be.

Madame Cho.

Waiting. Sitting beside the mats where we practice grappling and throwing one another.

The ballroom is the best of all the rooms in Stranje House. Better than even the dark maze of secret passages and deep hiding places. This is my favorite room. *My haven.* A climbing rope dangles from the two-story ceiling. Miss Stranje had it installed especially for me. I knew every knot intimately. Off to the side stood a full-size cloth man stuffed with sand and wadding, built so that we could learn to throw our punches and kicks more accurately. I remembered the day Sera inked a moustache and face on him. I passed the case of sabers, a pile of bamboo swords, the throwing knives, and the rack of foils we used for fencing lessons.

Only death lay ahead of me.

I clenched my fists. I didn't want to leave Stranje House. And I didn't want to die. Not because death frightened me. It didn't. Not anymore. I'd died a hundred times in dreams and visions. Death had lost its mystery long ago. No, I wanted the one thing I could never have—a life with Ravencross.

I wanted to live.

My teacher sat, calm as sunlight, waiting for me, watching, as if her ancient dark eyes saw centuries beyond my pain. In a desperate childish rush, I ran and threw myself into Madame Cho's lap. Dry choking sounds came from my heaving chest. I wasn't crying.

I never cry.

Twelve

FIGHT

Once my outburst subsided, Cho lifted my shoulders, and although there was kindness in her eyes, I saw no pity. "You must fight."

With that she dumped me off her knees and stood.

I don't know how old Cho is. There's no way to tell. She has only a few gray hairs, but there is an ancientness about her that stretches beyond the years she may or may not have. She may be old, but there is still a formidable hardness about her that speaks of youth. There is no weakness in her. I can tell she has been hardened by too many difficulties, but where some women might have broken, Madame Cho's difficulties have turned her as sinewy and tough as dried leather.

She picked up her bamboo staff and struck the mat with it. "Practice."

I blinked away whatever water remained in my eyes, knowing from experience that if I did not get up, I would soon feel that bamboo on my backside. She tossed me a staff of equal length and gave me time to tuck my skirts up. "I don't feel like fighting."

"Yes, you do. You have been fighting since you came out of the womb." She swung her stick, and I met it in the air. The clash of wood against wood awakened the heat inside me. I whirled and swung a sweeping arc where she stood. She leapt over my stick as if she were a girl of twelve and brought hers down over my head. I dodged, but it grazed my arm, and the sting made me grit my teeth.

"See," she said triumphantly, and swung around for another blow. "Practice clears the mind."

I barely deflected it with my staff. "No. It only makes me angry."

"Too bad." She shifted her pole to parry my strike. Our weapons collided with a ripple that I felt all the way up my arm. She whirled and hooked her foot around my ankle, sending me sprawling across the mat on my back. "Anger is not good. It makes—"

"I like being angry." I raised my staff in the nick of time to stop hers from chopping down on me.

"It feels like power, but it makes you reckless. Sloppy," she said, backing off for a minute. "Anger shifts the balance. Makes you forget who you are."

I rolled to my feet and brought my staff up with me in a jarring clash against hers. "Maybe I *want* to forget."

"Forgetting is not possible." She flipped the pole around her shoulder. "You must concentrate on something else." She caught the bamboo with her left hand and rapped me on my shoulder so hard that I dropped my weapon. "Like how to block my attack."

She stood patiently, waiting for me to collect myself.

"Where did you learn to fight like this? Who taught you?" I dared ask my oft-repeated question, expecting the same answer she had always given me over the years, a sharp rap with one weapon or another.

She stared at me, contemplating, and a whisker of sadness flitted through her dark eyes. Without answering, she picked up my staff that had rolled to the edge of the mat.

"I learned this in my village, near where the Xi and Tan Rivers meet." I saw pride in the set of her chin and an ache for something lost. "My father taught me."

She tossed the bamboo to me, and I knew that our time for speaking had come to an end. And so we fought. Again and again, until I was red faced, tired, and bruised, and the turmoil in my heart was no longer the only thing I could feel.

Thirteen

S℮HEMES

A half hour later, I slipped into the small parlor to meet with Miss Stranje and the others at the appointed time. I arrived late. They were all there. Somehow Madame Cho had gotten there before me. Even Lord Ravencross was there. *Why had Miss Stranje allowed him in?* He did not look at me at first, even though I know he saw me come in. He'd probably taken a disgust of me after my brazen declaration.

Good. Now that he knew the truth, he would pull back from me and guard his heart. *How very wise of him.*

"Ah, there you are." Miss Stranje did not scold me for being late as she would normally have done. *Because she knows I'm leaving and that she will no longer be training me.*

In the time it takes to snap one's fingers, the churning tempest returned to my heart.

I looked around at the inhabitants of Stranje House, at the people I cared about, storing up each movement, each word for the long, dreary years I would spend without them. Lady Jane leaned over the table, watching Georgie sketch a diagram of Stranje House and our grounds. Sera pointed out the location of a copse of trees on the drawing that required correcting.

Jane trailed the handle of a watercolor brush over a section of the map. "I doubt Lady Daneska will bother coming in by the main gate. We ought to post sentries here, here, and here." She tapped the brush on the garden door, the servants' entrance, and the underground passage through the sea cave.

"What of the secret exit on the side?" Georgie asked, and placed another X on the drawing.

Mr. Sinclair glanced over Jane's shoulder. "It might be easier and more efficient to batten down those sneaky entrances and make them inaccessible." When Jane turned and glared at him, he added, "Temporarily, of course."

She acted as if he had insulted her personally. "What do you mean, *sneaky* entrances?"

"Well, that's what they are, aren't they? Entrances for sneaking in and sneaking out."

"Of course not." Jane practically vibrated at his callous assessment of her beloved Stranje House. It didn't matter that he was right. "And what's more, I'm not at all certain *you* should even be allowed to *look* at this map."

He had the audacity to grin at her. "Don't fret yourself, Lady Jane. Your precious diagram is safe with me." He jabbed at his temple as if the information was stored there. "Like a bear trap. Besides, I already know my way around the house fairly well. And I knocked on enough walls to figure out there might be a hidden staircase or two."

"Ladies and gentlemen." Miss Stranje clapped her hands softly. "We must return to the matter at hand. How might we best protect ourselves against possible intruders?"

Maya hummed quietly and looked on.

This might've been any other afternoon in our workroom. Except there were two men here working among us, and this wasn't simply a fictitious strategy problem our teacher challenged us with today. This was a painfully real discussion about Lady Daneska stealing into Stranje House with her band of French assassins.

Sera stood up abruptly and glanced self-consciously about the room, avoiding the men who were present, but her shyness did not deter her from speaking. "Before we can settle on the best way to protect ourselves, it seems to me we must first figure out exactly what Lady Daneska *and* . . ." She caught her lip, glancing nervously at Lord Ravencross. "And the *other* members of the Iron Crown are after."

"Georgie's ink, of course," Jane blurted.

I frowned. I knew Daneska better than they did. "I think it is more than that. Lady Daneska does not like to have anything taken from her. She wants revenge."

Lord Ravencross rumbled. "That would explain why she wanted me killed as well. Retribution for my brother's life."

No one said anything. Even Mr. Sinclair, who knew nothing of Ghost, kept respectfully quiet.

Maya broke through the awkwardness. "It is understandable that she wants revenge. We have stolen her valued prizes, Georgie's formula and the information Lord Wyatt would have given her. Surely, she will want them back. Does that not place Georgiana in great peril? She knows the formula and could also be used as a pawn to lure Lord Wyatt."

"Yes," Sera agreed. "But we must not forget about Mr. Sinclair and whatever inventions they wanted from him."

We all turned to stare at our American inventor.

"Tess and Maya make valid points. The attack yesterday reeked of vengeance." Miss Stranje pressed her knuckles against the edge of our worktable. "Lady Daneska's hand was all over it, although it certainly wasn't one of her more organized schemes."

Almost as if she intended for it to fail. But there was no room for me to make that observation. Everyone started talking at once.

Georgie rose. "The men were poorly trained. Some were French, some English, it's as if they'd been thrown together on the spur of the moment."

Sera shook her head. "I don't know. Mr. Chadwick is convinced they must've been watching the house for days. Otherwise how would they have known exactly when you usually go for your run, er, your brisk walk?"

"It's the Iron Crown," Georgie defended her point. "Surely they always have someone watching the house."

Mr. Sinclair shot an alarmed look at Lady Jane. Under his breath he muttered, "You were right, they *will* be looking here first."

Jane responded with a cocky lift of her eyebrows, clearly saying, *I told you as much.*

"That can't be true!" I burst into the fray. I am not good at arguing points. I lowered my voice to a more respectful pitch and attempted to make my case. "About them watching the house, I mean. I'd have known if someone had been in the woods. I would've seen them. At the very least, I would've sensed their presence." Judging by their skeptical expressions I could tell they were not persuaded. I exhaled with considerable irritation. "Oh, for pity's sake, Phobos and Tromos would've warned me if anyone was hiding nearby."

Upon my mentioning the dogs, they all nodded, convinced. *A fine thing that is.*

They doubted me but immediately conceded the dogs would have known. Perhaps it was just as well I was leaving. At least at home they would have believed me. They wouldn't have been comfortable about it, they might've accused me of being a witch, but they would've believed me.

Jane's face screwed up as if she'd bitten down on a lemon. "That means they came by that information some other way. But how?"

We looked about the room at each other, shifting from foot to foot, and I felt distrust creeping into all of our minds. After Lady Daneska's betrayal, the possibility of treachery was never far from our minds.

Miss Stranje put a hasty end to our suspicions. "They could've gleaned that information any number of ways. It could even have come from one of our neighbors. Perhaps, Lady Pinswary. She is forever spying on us from her upstairs window."

We knew for a fact, because we'd observed her through our telescope standing at her window with a pair of opera glasses trained on Stranje House. Although from clear across the fields I wasn't sure how much she could've observed at that hour in the morning.

Miss Stranje mumbled under her breath, "I've been meaning to plant some tall growing trees on that side of the grounds."

Georgie brightened, relieved that she didn't have to think one of us had betrayed her. "For that matter, Lady Daneska could've observed it herself last month when she stayed with Lady Pinswary."

"Lady Daneska could've gathered that intelligence any number of ways," Miss Stranje concluded with a cluck of her tongue. "Given Tess's dream this morning, I think we must expect the Iron Crown will be more involved in the next attempt. That being the case, we should expect a far more organized approach."

Lord Ravencross raked a hand through his hair and pushed forward. "We ought to contact the authorities. I'll send a note to Lord Castlereagh and explain the situation."

Miss Stranje smiled politely at his remark. "And tell them what, my lord? That based on the dreams of a seventeen-year-old girl we have reason to believe a band of ruthless cutthroats may try to gain entrance to our house? What do you suppose they would do? Send a troop to stand guard?"

"Might do." Georgie remained bent studiously over her drawing. "After all, France went to war over Joan of Arc's dreams."

"Don't be ridiculous." Jane flicked Georgie's arm. "No one in Britain would move troops on the say-so of a dream." Jane had her back to me. When she saw the others glancing worriedly past her shoulder at me, she flushed a guilty pink and turned. "I didn't mean that as it sounded, Tess. You know I have complete confidence in your visions. I am merely being practical."

Ravencross stared in my direction. There was sureness in his gaze, a steadiness, and a warmth that made heat race into my cheeks.

No. He mustn't do that. Hadn't he listened to me? We had no future. I looked away. Down. Sideways. Anywhere but at him.

Lord Ravencross would not relinquish the idea that we needed outside help. "What about contacting Captain Grey? Or Lord Wyatt? Surely they would come to your—"

"Yes." Miss Stranje rarely interrupts anyone, but there was a sideways fist in her even tone. "I intend to send word as soon as possible. But we have not heard directly from either of them for a number of weeks. Mr. Sinclair's arrival was the first inkling we've had that they are even alive."

Georgie's sharp intake of breath hushed all of us.

"As matters stand," Miss Stranje continued in a much softer tone, "we must conclude that we are on our own."

A pall fell over us. Even Maya stilled, not so much as even the whisper of a hum. I fancied I could even hear the clock tick in the main hall. Georgie scratched the graphite in shading lines indicating the ocean on her diagram.

Jane cleared her throat. "Very well, we are on our own. It won't be the first time." She said it proudly, and with a catch in her voice that forced us all to remember who we were.

We were the same five girls who'd crossed the channel and dared breach the Iron Crown's stronghold. We'd freed Lord Wyatt from his chains and set the place on fire. Miss Stranje squared her shoulders and smiled at her pupils.

Jane rallied us further with a clarion call. "This only means it is even more important that we determine exactly what the Iron Crown wants. And how they might try to get it." She sat down with a fresh sheet of foolscap and her quill. "Shall we begin the list with Georgiana and her ink?"

Sera looked round the room at us, paler than normal; the seriousness on her elfin features seemed so out of place. "You all realize, of course, that we are not the only ones in danger."

She lifted Georgie's drawing and set it aside. It had lain atop a map of England and France, which outlined the new borders on the European continent—borders Napoleon had recently established. This was the very map Mr. Sinclair had been so eager to see, and now he viewed it with a grave expression.

"There is a larger problem at work here." Sera pressed forward, forgetting her shyness for a moment. She set a tin cup filled with sticks of graphite on the map near Hanover. "The bulk of our army is cornered here. What troops do we have left to guard Britain's coast? A battalion stationed in Chatham at Fort Amherst? Another at Dover? Five hundred men? Six hundred? What would happen if Napoleon decided to invade next week?"

Jane gasped. "They would be slaughtered." Mr. Sinclair cast an anxious look in her direction. I tried to swallow my trepidation, but it left a dry lump in my throat.

"And then what?" Sera is normally kindness itself. But today, even though she spoke gently, her matter-of-fact tone chilled the air. "Would they send the Yeomen to the coast and leave the monarchy defenseless? No, they might try to raise the Fencibles again, and call out the volunteer militia. Perhaps Wales and Ireland might send troops. But all these measures would take time. I have it on good authority that Whitehall is trying to transport our troops home for this very reason." She caught herself, recalling how we'd searched Miss Stranje's papers to glean this authoritative tidbit, and turned a guilty sheep face to Miss Stranje.

I waved away her concern. "She already knows."

"Go on," Miss Stranje urged.

Sera's alarm faded and she continued. "At best it would take several weeks, more than likely a month or more, to transport enough of our troops from Hanover, especially given the fact that most of our ships are engaged in the conflict across the Atlantic, four or five weeks away." She glanced apologetically at Mr. Sinclair, who merely nodded his understanding that she meant the war the Americans had brought against us in 1812.

She picked up several of the small buttons that we normally used to symbolize ships. "We must face facts. Napoleon is no fool. At this very moment England sits at her most vulnerable. Helpless." She placed the ships in the channel between Britain and France. "I believe the Iron Crown may be paving the way for an invasion of England. With that in mind, yes, Georgie's ink would be a prize worth taking. But assuming he told us the truth at breakfast and that he has not already given them plans for his uncle's warship, I believe they will be hunting most ardently for Mr. Sinclair."

We turned as one to our American guest. It was the first time I'd seen Mr. Sinclair without even a trace of humor on his sunny features. His lips blanched and formed a round, soundless whistle. He jammed his fingers into his mess of golden curls. "Looks as if I'm in a bit of a pickle."

None of us argued the point. Jane looked particularly pensive.

"Yes sir-ee." He thrust both hands into his coat pockets. "If I were a betting man, I'd say I'm done for."

Miss Stranje straightened and tried to reassure him. "Nothing of the kind, Mr. Sinclair. We've been in far worse fixes than this."

"You may have been in tighter squeezes, Miss Stranje, but not I. I'm a tinkerer, pure and simple." He turned to Jane. "And regardless of what you may think of me, my lady, I'm a darned fine engineer." He edged back from the table. Apparently the map he'd been so eager to look at no longer held any appeal. "What I'm not, is a soldier. Oh, I know which end of a gun to hold when it comes down to it, but I'm not the killing and fighting sort."

No, he was an otter. Playful and smart.

"Do you want to make a run for it, then?" Georgie tilted her head, taking his measure. "You could make your way to a port town. I'm sure if you're willing to work for your passage . . ."

"The thought did occur to me," he admitted.

"Run if you like." Jane sniffed. "Of course, with impressments being as rampant as they are, it is more than likely you'd be put in service, and then it would be a handful of years before you'd make it back to your home in the Colonies."

"United States," he corrected reflexively.

"She's right, you know." This came from Lord Ravencross. "I'll take you to a port myself, if you wish. But chances are, you will get thrown straightway into a crew. Then, whether you like it or not, you'll find yourself in the middle of a battle at sea."

"Aye, I'd figured as much." Sinclair scuffed at the Turkish carpet with the toe of one of his borrowed shoes. "A piece of bad luck, this. I'm caught between a grizzly bear and a rattlesnake."

"Take heart, Mr. Sinclair," Georgie chirped, just as if her life weren't in as much danger as his. "There's an alternative. In Lord Wyatt's letter, he explained that our foreign Secretary, Lord Castlereagh, believes he can get approval for funding for your uncle's steam-powered warship if you will but create a drawing and working model. We could help you in this endeavor. If we move with all haste, you and your plans will be safe with White-hall, and if you succeed, you will be doing both your uncle and us a great service."

Miss Stranje faced him squarely, without any discernible emotion. "It is, of course, your decision, Mr. Sinclair. But should you chose to stay with us, I assure you, we will protect you with our very lives until such time as we can guarantee your safe passage home. That is no small promise."

"Indeed. You should see her with a pistol." Georgie nodded vigorously. "And if your warship or one of your other inventions proves useful, I'm sure the government will conduct you safely to your home. The war between our countries can't last much longer."

"Then I suppose we'd best get to it." Mr. Sinclair sat at the table, picked up a pencil and Georgie's protractor, and began sketching a diagram of a steam-powered warship. Georgie leaned over the table, watching with interest. Jane stood between them, arms crossed, watching him draw.

I envied this boldfaced American. It was quite possible the Iron Crown would capture him when they attacked and torture his uncle's secrets out of him, but unlike me, at least he would be staying here with the people who mattered most to me in all the world.

Some things were worth the risk.

Fourteen

INQUISITION

While Jane, Georgie, and Mr. Sinclair worked on his warship plans, the rest of us tackled the problem of how to fortify Stranje House against intruders. Mr. Sinclair's suggestion to seal up the sneaky entrances met with mixed opinions.

Miss Stranje wasn't fond of the idea. "We can't seal the underground door. If Captain Grey and Lord Wyatt return by way of the sea cave and find their normal passage into the house blocked, they'll be forced to use the path up the cliffs to gain entrance. At night it is too hazardous a climb."

I'd been up and down those cliffs a number of times and not by the narrow path that wound up the side. "They're more than up to that task," I tried to reassure her.

She remained unconvinced. "Not if one of them is injured. I don't like it."

I didn't either, but for other reasons. It made me furious to think of my fortress being invaded by Daneska and her murderous thugs. But the thought of our escape hatches being boarded up made my palms sweat. When I remembered the fact that I would not be here, I'd probably be halfway to Wales when they tried to sneak in, I panicked even worse. "God forbid, if Lady Daneska and her men are successful getting into the house, how will you flee if all your secret escape routes are blocked off?"

Lord Ravencross suggested we might secure the secret doors by using barricades that could easily be removed from the inside. His idea set us to working on a list of what must be done to fortify Stranje House. We worked for more than an hour.

Miss Stranje stood and perused the progress Jane, Georgie, and Mr. Sinclair were making on his warship plans. "I'll send Philip to town first thing to purchase the supplies you will need," she said, studying the diagrams. "Although some of these items you might find in my storeroom. There is copper piping in Miss Fitzwilliam's laboratory that might work." She tapped his drawing, thinking, and turned to Jane. "Don't we have an extra copper tub stored in the garret? I'm certain I've seen one. I'll check."

The garret Miss Stranje referred to was the long, narrow storage attic above our dormitorium, where the five of us often liked to gather at night long after we were supposed to be sleeping. It was our secret meeting place. It has lovely windows that extend out over the roof. Our spyglass comes in very handy in the garret. That's where, through our spyglass, we'd caught our first glimpses of Lord Ravencross after he'd come home wounded from the wars.

"Yes, I believe I saw just such a tub last time I went up to retrieve something out of my trunk." Jane jumped up. "You needn't trouble yourself. Georgie and I will fetch it for you." Jane knew exactly where that copper bath was. We all did, because we'd flipped it over to use as a table in our secret room. Our makeshift lantern sat atop it.

"Thank you," Miss Stranje said, and I thought she hid a smirk.

"I must attend to other matters now, but later today we will consider what other safety measures must be taken." Miss Stranje tapped me on the shoulder. "A word with you, Tess, in my office."

I nodded silently, unable to answer because my throat felt as if someone was squeezing it shut. *This was it.* She would arrange my travel, and just like that I would be dismissed and sent out of their lives, back to Tidenham where my aunt would await my death.

Just when I thought my legs might fail, Greaves entered the workroom.

"Your pardon, miss. But you've several *more* visitors." He cast a disparaging look at the two men in our workroom as he addressed Miss Stranje. "Mr. Chadwick senior and junior, and a Mr. Griswold, whom I gather is coroner for the crown. They asked specifically if they might speak with Miss Aubreyson. I have situated the gentlemen in the blue parlor."

I whirled to Sera. "I thought you told him not to come?"

She flushed oddly. "I did my best. He is exceedingly difficult to manage."

"Sera, I think you ought to accompany us to the drawing room." Miss Stranje took me by the arm. "It will be all right. Stick with short answers as close to the truth as possible. You might try being a bit shy. That is always excused in young ladies."

"I'm coming, too." Jane hurried to my side. "That Chadwick fellow is too sharp for his own good."

"I'll come with you as well." Lord Ravencross was deaf to my protestations that he should stay here. "I'm coming. That's my final word on the matter."

Mr. Sinclair blew frustration through his lips. "Then I shall join you as well and see for myself what manner of man this

Chadwick is that he would distract you all from so grave a purpose."

"No!" Jane and I blurted as one.

"I see." Mr. Sinclair adjusted his coat and sleeves. "You think I'm not a fine enough gentleman for such exalted company."

"That's not it at all," Georgie insisted.

"Please, try to view it from our position," Sera gently explained. "We're concerned that the local justice of the peace and his son might find it a bit odd that a young man is staying as a guest in a school for young ladies. Add to that, the fact that you are an American, and do you not think it might make them even more suspicious?"

"Put like that, I see where my presence might be a bit sticky to explain." Sinclair raked a hand over his clean-shaven jaw. "But what is it you think he'll be suspicious of, exactly?"

"Nothing in particular," Jane said brusquely. "But with the attempted kidnapping and all, it will be difficult enough for us to explain what happened yesterday. And Lord Ravencross being here complicates matters. But then, he is a neighbor, and that is a bit more expected. Perhaps it will distract—"

Lord Ravencross interrupted Jane with an exasperated breath. "We ought to just tell them the truth about the entire matter."

"The truth?" Georgie stared at him as if he'd just asked us to paint London Tower pink. "You mean that we suspect the attempt to kidnap me might have something to do with Bonaparte's secret organization and his plan to attack Britain? That truth?"

"Yes." He grimaced and adjusted the bandages on his wounded shoulder.

Sera didn't like opposing him. She stared at the floor and said, "Rather a lot for them to take in, wouldn't you say?"

Even Maya offered up an opinion. "Do you not think they will question why such things are occurring at a young ladies' finishing school?"

Jane crossed her arms. "Yes, and if a handful of young women at a finishing school were the first to bring the Iron Crown to their attention, what conclusions do you suppose they would draw about Miss Stranje's establishment?"

"The obvious." Ravencross glanced at me. "That you are not ordinary young ladies."

Mr. Sinclair pounced upon these observations. "You see, that's the real fly in this particular ointment, isn't it? You are a rather *peculiar* lot. Not exactly a typical finishing school, is it?"

The five of us turned to him in alarm. He couldn't possibly have deduced the whole truth. Not this quickly.

"Don't look so surprised." He chuckled. "I just witnessed a roomful of girls strategizing about how they might best divert an attack from one of the world's most sinister organizations. Do you think I'm a complete idiot? Did you really think I wouldn't notice that you're studying more than dance steps and embroidery at this *school?*"

We all stepped back. I pressed my lips together, waiting for him to reveal exactly what he had guessed.

"Not only that, but this morning when I was making my way down to the workroom, I happened upon your ballroom. Such rooms are usually the showcase of grand old houses like this. I merely intended to have a gander at the architecture, but . . ."

I sucked in my breath and held it, fearing the worst.

"Not the usual fare for a girls' school, is it?" He watched our expressions carefully. "Now that I think on it, I doubt you use that mannequin with the roguish mustache for dancing practice, do you? Not with that impressive assortment of cutlery lining the walls, and his stuffing coming loose in key places. And then there's Lady Jane here . . ." He winked at Jane as if she was in on the joke. "Only this morning, she threatened to toss me over her shoulder and break my arm in several places. It all begins to add up rather curiously."

Jane groaned.

Georgie cursed under her breath.

Maya began to hum.

Sera shot a look of pure desperation at me, turned to the wall, and surreptitiously studied a rather gruesome oil painting of a dead pheasant atop a table beside a bowl of pears and a silver goblet of wine.

"You practice on a mannequin?" Ravencross stared at me.

I decided I might have to kill Mr. Sinclair after all. He'd trespassed into my private sanctum. With gritted teeth, I said, "Jane, be so good as to take your meddling American elsewhere while the Chadwicks are here."

"He's not *my* meddling American—"

"I don't care," I warned. "Take him and go. He must not appear anywhere near the justice of the peace. While you're at it, explain to our guest that if he ever steps foot in my ballroom again, I will be forced to use some of that *cutlery* on his throat."

He should've had the good grace to be frightened, but he wasn't. He bowed. "*Pax*, Miss Aubreyson. You needn't fear. Your secret is safe with me."

"I doubt it."

Jane scowled at him. "Audacious rogue."

"Guilty as charged." He tried to disarm us with that teasing grin of his.

I was immune. "That's the problem, Mr. Sinclair. I am the only person here at Stranje House allowed to be audacious." I turned to Jane. "Take him for a walk on the grounds, if you must. But for pity's sake keep him away from any windows that look out from the blue parlor. Maya and Georgie, you'd best go with them and keep our overly inquisitive house guest from getting into any more trouble." I dismissed the four of them with a flick of my hand.

"Well done," Miss Stranje said quietly, and patted my arm. Then she and Sera headed for the blue parlor. Reluctant to face the justice of the peace and his son, I trailed behind with Lord Ravencross. I indicated his wound. "How is it feeling?"

"Like the very fires of hell are burning in my chest. Thank you for asking." But still he held out his arm to conduct me down the hall as he would any proper young lady.

I rested my fingers possessively on his forearm. Bold, I know, but it felt good to touch him, and all too soon I would be leaving him. "I'm concerned about your welfare tonight, my lord—"

"You need not scale my wall tonight. I have the matter in hand. I've sent MacDougal to see if he can hire a man from among my tenants to stand guard in your place."

"Oh. Very good."

It was good. Wasn't it? I should feel comforted that he would be safe. *Yes.* And yet part of me felt robbed of the duty. I would miss it. *Miss him.* I pulled my hand from his arm, but he covered my fingers with his and moved them to the crook of his arm to continue escorting me. "Shall we go?"

I stopped and extracted my hand from him. "I wish I didn't have to."

I didn't want to speak with *anyone* just then, least of all men who intended to riddle me with questions about yesterday's carnage. I wanted to stay here with him. Or else dash back to my ballroom and make certain it was untouched, unsullied by outsiders. I needed to punch something, and the mustache dummy would do. Except I couldn't run off like that, duty tugged at me as if I were a dog on a chain. So I stalked toward the parlor in a mood to bite.

Ravencross matched me stride for stride. I warned him, "You may accompany me, my lord, if you choose. Although I don't see why you would want to subject yourself to this inquisition." There, I'd said it aloud—inquisition.

"I want to make certain that *charming* Chadwick rascal keeps his distance."

"Don't be ridiculous. He asks too many questions to be charming."

He growled. "I am not the ridiculous sort."

"You're not the jealous sort either."

He grumbled something unintelligible and then answered crisply, "You could do worse than young Chadwick."

"You can't have it both ways, Gabriel. You can't play the jealous suitor and then sing his praises. Aside from that, I have no interest in Mr. Chadwick. You're worth a dozen of him."

His posture swelled at that, and I cautioned myself to stop putting his ego to the bloom. It wouldn't do. So I tried to counteract my hasty words. "That wasn't meant as a compliment."

"It wasn't taken as one," he said gruffly. Then, with a sideways smirk, he added, "A *dozen*, eh? So many. Poor fellow. Mr. Chadwick must hold a painfully low position in your esteem. I'll wager earthworms have a higher status."

"Not quite that low, my lord." I was surprised at Lord Ravencross. Normally he snarls like a wolf at everyone, and yet here he was, trying to coax *me* out of my temper. "I think of Mr. Chadwick more along the lines of a squirrel—clever, overly inquisitive, but a pest all the same."

"Ah, a *squirrel*. I see." He sounded excessively grim. "Then it is a lucky thing I came along with you. Squirrels can be criminally endearing."

I almost smiled despite my mood. "Have a care, my lord. I'll not have you shooting any rodents in the blue parlor today."

"Then it is also a lucky thing I left my pistols at home."

I was not used to him making light of anything. It both pleased and baffled me. "I suppose the real reason you are accompanying me is that you know they'll be knocking at your door directly after they finish here?"

"I suppose they would," he said as we entered the blue parlor.

The younger Mr. Chadwick was amazed to see Lord Ravencross enter our drawing room. He bowed dutifully and inquired after Ravencross's health. "You were so badly wounded yesterday, my lord. It surprises me to see you have left your sickbed this soon."

"*He's not squirrel-like at all,*" Lord Ravencross said under his breath to me, and his good humor seemed to have flown. He answered Mr. Chadwick with all the warmth of a statue in winter. "I heal quickly."

It was true, although I'd seen Gabriel moving gingerly earlier in the day and guessed he must still be in considerable pain.

"There was a great deal of blood, my lord. I'd just assumed . . ."

Ravencross took in the curiosity on Chadwick's face and realized he was not entirely believed. "If you must know, my doctor was not pleased about my getting out of bed either. But yesterday I witnessed one of those brutes strike Miss Aubreyson over the head with a cudgel." He drew up to *charming* Chadwick like a wolf with his teeth bared in warning. "I'm sure *even you* can understand why I could not rest comfortably until I was satisfied she was not gravely injured."

Mr. Chadwick's father took up the reins of the conversation.

"Yes, yes, quite understandable, my lord. Good lad. Would've done the same myself." He slapped the arms of his chair. "A horrible business—those ruffians. Bad business, indeed. What do you suppose they were after?"

We all took our seats, and Gabriel said, matter-of-factly, "It seems to me they were intent upon abducting one of these young ladies, and after I interrupted their plan, upon killing me."

The justice of the peace unconsciously combed his fingers through his bushy side-whiskers. "Then I take it they didn't ask for your purse? No stand-and-deliver sort of speech?"

"Nary a word." Lord Ravencross adjusted the bandages beneath his coat and sling. "Of course, I didn't give them much of a chance for speeches. I saw the brigands accosting Miss Aubreyson and flew into action."

Mr. Griswold, the coroner, was a painfully thin middle-aged man. He wore a vivid apple-green silk coat and breeches like those of a Georgian dandy from the previous decade. At Gabriel's statement, he drew back, aghast. "You saw you were outnumbered three to one and yet you rode straight into their midst? *Alone?*"

"Yes." Gabriel frowned at him. "What would you have me do? Abandon the young lady to her fate?"

"No, but it was a brash choice, to be sure," muttered the coroner. "Foolhardy, some might say."

It looked as if Lord Ravencross was biting his tongue to keep from bashing the fellow. At any rate, the muscles of his jaw tensed before he answered. "To be fair, I thought there were only two men. I didn't see the others until I rode past the trees." His jaw flexed again and his hand balled into a fist atop the arm of his chair. "But it would've made no difference."

"Of course not." The elder Chadwick harrumphed and cast a disapproving frown at the fastidious coroner. "Would've done the same myself. You're a military man. Been an officer in his majesty's service. It's only natural you would've thought you could settle accounts with a handful of misbegotten thugs."

"Miss Aubreyson." Young Mr. Chadwick slipped into the conversation when his father took a breath. "Miss Fitzwilliam mentioned yesterday that as soon as you saw the first man come riding out of the trees, you immediately told her to run back to the house, to safety?" The question sounded casual enough, and yet I sensed he put more stock in its relevance than he let on.

I nodded and did my best to pretend I was shy.

"Why did you not run with her?"

This I could answer without hesitation. "It was the way he looked at her. I guessed he was after her, not me. And then the others came out of the woods. Obviously, we wouldn't have been able to outrun men on horseback. I hoped I might be able to block their path. Or at least slow them down so that Miss Fitzwilliam would have time to escape."

The justice of the peace slapped his palms together. "Brave girl! Well done." He magnanimously congratulated all of us. "You are all to be commended."

Sera smiled politely but kept a keen watch on his shrewd son.

"As you say, Miss Aubreyson put herself in harm's way to protect her friend." Although Lord Ravencross spoke to the room at large, he gazed steadily at me. "There is no greater love than that."

And Gabriel had done the same for me.

I turned color. I know I did, because I felt heat scald my cheeks.

Mr. Chadwick spoiled it all with another question. "Why do you think they chased after Miss Fitzwilliam and not you?"

"Who can say why a man picks one woman over another?" I shrugged.

"Hmm." He was not pleased with my answer. "I was told you

became aware of the men in the trees before they showed themselves. Is that so?"

I couldn't tell them about being overcome by a daydream or a vision, not unless I wanted to be hauled off to a madhouse. Miss Stranje says when one must conceal facts it always best to stick to as much truth as possible. My own philosophy is that it is much better to run away rather than to talk. Right then I would've preferred to do exactly that, *run*. But I couldn't. So I settled on something close to the truth.

"I realized something must be wrong, because the insects and birds were too quiet."

"Remarkable observation." His father slapped his thigh emphasizing the point. "Astonishing. Not many gels would've noticed so subtle a clue."

What could I say to that? "I daresay, you would've noticed, too, sir, as you must be familiar with the woods here about." I hoped flattery would divert them from their questions.

The justice of the peace preened a bit and then waved the compliment aside. "Yes, of course. But one doesn't expect a young lady to pay attention to such things." He was like a great tame bull, used to being king of his little pasture. I smiled. The Chadwicks were a good lot. I would not like to see Napoleon's soldiers force them to kneel in submission. *But for just a minute that very image flashed before my eyes in all of its ugly truth. The father refusing to comply. The mother running for her hunting musket. And the son . . .*

No! I closed my eyes to it.

No visions of death. Not now. Not here.

"Miss Aubreyson?" Young Chadwick was snapping his fingers in front of my face. "Miss Aubreyson, are you all right?"

Lord Ravencross sprang up and shoved him out of the way. "She's not well. Leave her be."

"No, I'm quite all right." But my voice sounded shakier than I would've liked. "Truly, I am." I held up my hands blocking their attentions. "I'm sorry. I don't know what came over me. For a moment, I—"

"It's the trauma," droned the coroner, straightening the lace at the cuffs of his green silk coat. "Oversets the ladies every time."

Young Mr. Chadwick scooted his chair closer to mine but well out of Lord Ravencross's reach. "Did you remember something just now? Something about the men who seized you?"

"No," I blurted.

Miss Stranje called them to order. "Gentlemen, I beg you to proceed gently. Miss Aubreyson received a severe blow to the head. Is it any wonder she doesn't recall the incident?"

I studied my hands in my lap. "I'm sorry. Most of that dreadful morning seems to be completely blotted out." I tossed up my fingers as if they were the ashes of my memory. "I simply can't remember much of anything."

Except for the horrific bits.

And everything in between.

"A pity." Young Chadwick was not easily deterred. "I can understand your memories being affected *after* such a blow. But before that, when the men first emerged from the woods, did you happen to overhear them speaking?"

I maintained a studied look of ignorance on my face. "I may have. It's all so very fuzzy."

The coroner sighed. "I warned you, gentlemen. This is a waste of our time. Young women are never useful as witnesses."

Sera broke her silence to protest. "That can't be true."

Young Chadwick held up his finger, calling for more forbearance on the coroner's part.

"What about before you threw the knife at the man coming

to assault you? Do you think perhaps they might've been speaking French?"

"French?" I blinked, lowering my lashes, trying my best to look innocent and probably failing miserably.

Must have, because the nosy squirrel did not tumble to my ploy. Mr. Chadwick sat back and squinted at me. "Excellent throw, by the way. We have determined you saved Miss Fitzwilliam from a most unpleasant ordeal. But I'm curious as to why you would carry a knife with you on a morning walk. I daresay, it isn't a common practice among the young ladies of my acquaintance."

More vexatious than ten squirrels.

I tried to bite my tongue. Truly, I did, but I couldn't stop myself. "And are you acquainted with a great many young ladies, Mr. Chadwick?"

A laugh burst from Sera.

His father joined in with a hearty guffaw. "A bit of an elbow to the ribs there, eh, Quinton, m' boy."

Poor Mr. Chadwick, his skin flushed to a vibrant shade of rose, and he turned a sideways glance at Sera. She brushed the smile from her lips.

I took mercy on him. Besides, I'd finally figured out how I might answer. "It is my habit to carry a knife with me always. I was raised in the north, sir. The forests there are far more treacherous than these tame woods you have along the coast. And before you ask, yes, I was trained to throw the knife as well."

In a booming voice, his father congratulated me. "Thank providence! For it may have saved your life, young lady. Or from a fate worse than death."

Chadwick ignored this and yanked me back to his questions. "You're certain you didn't hear them speaking a foreign language of any kind?"

I lowered my eyes, not wanting to hold back the truth. "I may have overheard a word or two. As I said, it is all so hazy."

His father scooted to the edge of his chair, leaning in to the conversation. "My son is only asking because we've determined two of the killers were Frenchmen. Their clothing caused us to suspect such might be the case. Upon closer inspection of the . . . er . . . the remains—" He ran a finger around his collar and looked apologetically at Miss Stranje. "Pardon my indelicacy, ladies. Mr. Griswold found that the dead men bore identifying marks. Both men had tattoos from a French prison."

"Oh, dear," I said, feigning alarm but not doing a very good job of it. "What do you make of that?"

I'll wager they couldn't possibly guess those were Lady Daneska's henchmen, hired by Napoleon's Order of the Iron Crown.

The justice of the peace, a large man, obviously unaccustomed to sitting in one place for longer than three or four minutes, sprang up and paced to the center of the room. "We don't know what to think, yet. Suspicious doings. No question about it. Trouble is, we can't assume that just because they bore the prison marks they were French. Could've been English fellows locked up for a time in a French prison. Now, if you'd heard them speaking French, it would be a different matter."

I tried again to appease them. "There *may* have been an accent or a word here and there. If only I could remember." Then, with the intention of distracting them, and nursing the wild hope that they might offer some support after I left Stranje House, I stepped cautiously into new waters. "Your honor," I pleaded, "what if those awful men return? I'm terribly frightened they might come back."

Miss Stranje cleared her throat, as a warning to me that I'd gone too far.

"You needn't worry, miss." The justice of the peace strode to the fireplace and placed an arm on the mantel. "We've no reason to think they will return. The coroner believes it was a random act. Don't you Mr. Griswold? A handful of criminals in search of a young woman they might sell into, er . . ." He stopped, nervous about how to phrase his indelicate assumption.

Mr. Griswold nodded sagely. "Just so."

Meanwhile, the younger Mr. Chadwick frowned at the carpet and muttered, "I'm not so sure."

His father paid no heed. "Searching for a young lady they might sell into trade. Yes, that's it. Take my word for it, those cads won't be back. Have no fear. You and Miss Stranje put paid to that." He slammed his fist into his palm. "Well done, ladies. And, by the bye, that was a fine piece of shooting."

Miss Stranje inclined her head, accepting his compliment.

I massaged my forehead and said, "I'm beginning to recall little snippets here and there. Perhaps in a day or two, when my head feels better, I might remember more."

"We can only hope." Mr. Chadwick nodded thoughtfully. "The fellow you dispatched, Miss Aubreyson, had tattoos and a gold earring."

"Which proves he was a sailor." Mr. Griswold sat forward and smoothed his shiny green lapel. "Gold earring is an old tradition, worn by sailors to cover burial costs. As for his tattoos, they were from countries known for French trade." He preened, smoothing back his thin hair and adjusting his brocade waistcoat. "I've made an extensive study of tattoos. It comes in handy when the odd body floats ashore, which happens more often than one might think."

Instead of being appalled at this impolite topic of conversation, Miss Stranje praised Mr. Griswold on being so thorough and committed to his esteemed profession.

Thus with his feathers fluffed up, the coroner treated us to a history of how these ink markings came into being, complete with a narrative of the coroner's visit to London to meet first-hand Captain Cook's famed tattooed Tahitian warrior, Omai.

Young Chadwick lost patience with this lecture and drew the conversation back to his interrogation. "We have additional evidence. My lord, the knife we found in the blood—*begging your pardon, ladies*—where you engaged in a struggle for your life, is of French craftsmanship."

Lord Ravencross forgot his dislike of young Chadwick for a moment. "How in heaven's name could you tell where the knife came from?"

"Ah." Sera perked up, keenly interested in this new evidence. "You found the knife maker's mark, didn't you?"

"Exactly." Quinton Chadwick beamed at her. "How did you guess?"

"I didn't *guess*." Sera was offended at first, then she lowered her eyes, suddenly shy but still not willing to let him think she had merely guessed. "A knife of any consequence bears the stamp of its maker. A small mark near the base of the handle that can be traced to its origin."

"Just so." The justice of the peace's son should've been impressed with Sera's knowledge. Instead, I watched his eager expression turn from solving one puzzle to intense curiosity about another. She'd said too much. Our Sera, who is normally so shy that one must coax her to speak, had given him too intriguing a glimpse into the workings of her mind. And that would lead to more curiosity about her and in turn about Miss Stranje's school.

This interview needed to end before he cracked open too many of our secrets.

Fifteen

PROMISES

I sighed loudly. "My apologies, gentlemen. But unfortunately my head is throbbing abominably. I'm far too tired to discuss this dreadful subject any further. I pray you will excuse me."

All of the gentlemen stood. Mr. Chadwick bowed with precision. "Yes miss, of course. We can come back in a few days when you're feeling more the thing."

No! I screamed in my head. *Don't come back ever.*

I calmly tilted my head. "I'm afraid that won't be possible. You see, I will be leaving Stranje House—"

The stricken look on Miss Stranje's face made me stop mid-sentence.

"Then you've decided," she said, as if I'd stabbed her.

What choice did I have?

"I'm afraid it's a matter of necessity," I answered weakly, wondering why she should have thought anything else.

Lord Ravencross strode behind my chair and placed a hand

on my shoulder. "What Miss Aubreyson is trying to say, gentle-men, is that she has, this very day, agreed to a betrothal."

Betrothal?

"To me," he announced grandly.

My mouth dropped open, but words failed me.

He's gone mad.

I finally stumbled upon something to say. "I did no such thing!"

"She's just being modest." He patted my shoulder as if I was a child of twelve. "She did."

I sprang up from the chair and turned, astounded that Gabriel would say such a thing. My mouth gaped open, and I floundered with unintelligible utterances.

The justice of the peace cleared his throat and interrupted my stuttering. "I, um, that is to say, felicitations to you both."

"No." I reeled back to them, blinking. "No, there's no need for felicitations. I assure you I didn't, we aren't . . ."

"We ought to be leaving." Young Chadwick's face was a study in discomfort. He edged toward the door.

"Yes," his father agreed emphatically. "Just so. Must be going. A pleasure, Miss Stranje. Lovely to see you again." He nudged the coroner. "Time we took our leave."

"Must we?" The coroner remained standing in front of his chair enthralled with Lord Ravencross's astonishing performance and my bewilderment. "Finally getting interesting."

"Aye. We must!" The justice of the peace gave Mr. Griswold a pointed frown with his great bushy eyebrows. "Past time. Come along, then." The coroner reluctantly accepted his hat from Greaves, and my three inquisitors left the room escorted by Miss Stranje. Sera slipped out behind them.

"*Betrothed?*" I whirled on Gabriel. "What possessed you to say such a thing?"

"I was explaining to our magistrate that you would be leaving Stranje House to become my wife. I see nothing extraordinary in that."

"*Extraordinary?* It is a complete and utter lie. The laudanum must be playing tricks on you, my lord, or else pain has twisted your reasoning, for I agreed to no such thing. In fact, I clearly told you the very opposite. That we have no future—"

"Ahem." Miss Stranje had returned and stood in the doorway.

Gabriel turned very stiff and formal. "You must be overtired, my dear. I distinctly heard you consent to become my wife. Surely you remember telling me that you did not find my scars at all repugnant. In fact, I can recall your exact words. You said—"

"Aaargh!" I roared, to stop him from talking and flung myself in the chair. "He's gone completely mad."

"What is all this, then?" Miss Stranje did not sound angry, but she did not sound pleased either. "Lord Ravencross, did you propose to Miss Aubreyson or not?"

"He did not." I smacked my hand down on the arm of the chair and whipped my attention back and forth between the two of them. "You didn't! And even if he had, which you most certainly did not do, there are at least a dozen reasons why I could not accept."

"Only a dozen?" Gabriel made a pretense of incredulity. "*So few.* I had thought you would say a hundred or a thousand." He turned gravely serious. "You wish to stay at Stranje House, do you not? I have just delivered the means by which you may do so." He turned to my headmistress. "Miss Stranje, as her fiancé, I will gladly pay whatever outstanding tuition she might owe. And when the next bill comes due, you may send it directly to me."

For the second time in the last three minutes, my mouth dropped open. Then it closed because I thought I finally glimpsed an explanation for this absurd charade. "That's why you said—"

"Not entirely," he snapped. "But it'll have to do, until you come to your senses."

Miss Stranje intervened. "That will not be necessary, my lord. If Miss Aubreyson wishes to stay, I will find the means to keep her here."

Again, I gaped, but this time at Miss Stranje. *She would?*

"Excellent." He winced and opened the flap of his coat to check his wound. "Nevertheless, my offer stands. Do whatever you must to keep her here. And now, if you will excuse me? I believe my bandage is beginning to leak."

There was, indeed, a scarlet bloom spreading on his shirt.

"You've overexerted yourself, my lord. Pray, sit down. I'll send for my kit and change that dressing." Miss Stranje hurried to the wall and yanked on the bellpull. "Philip!"

But Lord Ravencross did not sit. He yanked a handkerchief out of his pocket and stuffed it between his shirt and his coat. "Nonsense. You needn't fuss. The sawbones is waiting at my house. He can attend to it. I'm paying him well enough to do so." He was almost out of the room when Philip rushed in.

Miss Stranje issued orders to her footman with the steely authority of a field marshal. "You will accompany Lord Ravencross home. All the way home, mind you, and make certain he is in the hands of his physician before you return."

Philip pulled on his forelock, signaling obedience, and dashed after Lord Ravencross, who was already striding down the hall.

I stood. My instinct was to run after them, to make certain Gabriel made it home to the doctor, but for the first time in my life I found my legs would not move. I was frozen in place, still stunned by what he'd said. It occurred to me I might be in the midst of another dream. I stood, blinking.

"Sit down, Tess." Miss Stranje's sharp command brought me back to reality with a thud.

She pulled a chair next to mine and sank into it, hands folded calmly in her lap. "Now then, what is all this business about marriage?"

I groaned. "Then he really did say all those things? I'd thought I must be daydreaming. The betrothal?"

"Most assuredly. And he did so quite publicly."

"Oh, dear."

"I take it you are not pleased," she said flatly.

Pleased?

Was I?

Suddenly, I grinned. Not only that, I could not keep from grinning. I tried to stop, because I never grin. I don't. I really, truly don't.

I put a hand over my mouth and tried to wipe the silly thing off my face, but it simply wouldn't budge. I felt wickedly and enthusiastically happy. Truth be told, despite it being dreadfully wrong of me, *I was pleased.*

Excessively pleased.

"Hmm." She crossed her arms and contemplated me. "I see."

"No. No, you don't." I shook my head, ignoring the discomfort this brought because of the bump, which was now truly beginning to throb. "I'm not pleased. Not really. Oh, I suppose some stupid part of me feels absurdly happy that he would do such a kind thing for me, but—"

"I sincerely doubt kindness had much to do with it."

My foolish grin vanished and I sat back. "Then why?"

"You know why."

The lightness of being I'd felt a moment ago disappeared entirely. In its place a millstone thudded down atop my chest. "No," I gasped. "He *can't* be. He *mustn't* be. Surely, he isn't in love with me? There's no future in it."

She didn't argue with me. No, Miss Stranje is far too clever for that. She never argues a thing directly. She always goes around the corner from an obstacle and attacks it from the side.

"If you say so," she said with a dismissive flick of her eyelashes, as if it were something as unimportant as the weather we'd been discussing. "Let us turn to the matter of your aunt. If you wish to stay at Stranje House, and I gather now that you would prefer to stay here rather than going back to Tidenham. Although for what reason, I'm not certain . . ."

She waited, letting her half-spoken question hang in the air, and I sank deeper into the chair without answering.

"We can always find a position for you here. I'm certain your assistance with diplomatic matters will, of course, prove extremely valuable to your country in the coming years."

She meant spying. Even in private she rarely used that term.

"If, on the other hand, for various reasons you would prefer to stay nearby—" Miss Stranje paused again, but being met with only silence from me, she pressed on. "Madame Cho believes your fighting skills are excellent enough that you might help instruct the other girls."

I took a deep breath and let it out. "Thank you. I cannot tell you what a relief that is. I did not think my aunt was actually looking forward to my return."

"Agreed. I sensed reluctance in her letter as well. Although I'm certain she desires your company, I believe her reticence has more to do with that cryptic promise she made your mother. The promise that she would watch over you until—"

"*The end,*" I murmured.

Miss Stranje probed artfully. "Yes. What a very odd thing for her to say."

Not really.

"Tess, you've been here for how long?" She was coming at me sideways again. Emma Stranje is not the prying sort, she respects secrets more than most, but when she decides to find out something she goes at it like the hawk that she is. She circles her prey until the exact right time to dive down for the kill.

So I hesitantly answered her question, wary of where it would lead. "In October I will have been here four years."

"Four years. Hmm. And in all that time with me, you've never once spoken about what happened to your mother."

For good reason.

I try every day not to remember.

"No, I haven't." It came out soft as a whisper.

"I believe it's time you told me." She didn't say it as if I were a field mouse caught in her claws. There was softness, and a directness, that spoke only of concern. When I searched her eyes, I nearly cried at what I saw there. I thought only mothers looked at their children that way. I bowed my head.

It was time.

"For generations in my family, the oldest daughter has been afflicted with the dreams. The dreams took my grandmother early. They tormented my mother so badly that she stopped sleeping. Fear of the dreams kept her awake. Days she would go without eating or resting, wide-eyed, talking incessantly. Then the visions started coming even when she was awake. With each passing day, they got worse. Until one afternoon, moaning and crying, she bolted from the house and ran barefoot into the woods. We thought she'd come back. She always came back.

"Three days we hunted for her. All of us searched, Lydia, Uncle Martin, my grandfather, our servants, even me."

Especially me.

"I was nine at the time, but I knew my mother's forest haunts better than anyone else. My grandfather tried using the hounds to track her, but they lost the scent. We combed the nearby woods. Hunted through the forests. Scoured the riverbanks. All of us did."

Especially me.

I couldn't bring myself to tell Miss Stranje how panicked I'd been. How I'd searched with the frantic desperation only a child knows. Grief from my father's death two years earlier had still pressed heavily on me. I couldn't bear to lose my mother, too. I needed her. I had to find her.

"On the third night after she went missing, I had my first dream. I saw her death."

"No." Miss Stranje pressed her lips tight and covered her mouth with her hand. The lone sound had come out of her mouth like a breath, a feary wisp of anguish for the girl I'd once been.

I swallowed hard and tried to tell her the rest as best I could. She might as well hear it all.

"I'd hoped that dream was a simple nightmare. Except it wasn't. I'd seen flashes of the place. My mother falling. Just glimpses. But it was enough. I'd recognized that ravine and led my grandfather and uncle there. We saw her lying at the bottom. My grandfather shouted at me to stop, to not go down. 'Come away, child!' he'd shouted."

"But you went down, didn't you."

I nodded. "I had to. I scrambled down the steep incline and crumpled to my knees beside her. I think I knew she was dead. But my foolish child's mind thought surely she would awaken to her daughter's plea. I begged her to wake up."

Miss Stranje murmured, "Oh Tess, I'm so sorry."

I shook away her pity and took a deep, shuddering breath. I stared at my hand gripping the arm of the chair and remembered how my fingers had trembled that day when I'd reached out to brush decaying leaves from my mother's hair and cheek. I'd touched her pale brow, it had been smooth as ice. I remembered noticing that her fearful creases were gone. A rare softness curved her lips. That's when I knew she'd truly left me. Her eyes were finally closed.

Asleep.

"She finally found peace," I said a bit too loudly and looked squarely at Miss Stranje, as if it wasn't ripping me up inside to remember all this. "And she left me to deal with her nightmares."

Alone.

Miss Stranje probably wondered why I was able to tell her this story without crying. Perhaps I should've explained to her that I never cry. My last tears fell beside my mother's body, lost forever among the withered leaves in that ravine.

I have not cried since.

Not until today.

Except that didn't really count as crying.

She rubbed her chin, studying me. "That's why you told Lord Ravencross no, isn't it? You believe you will suffer the same fate as your mother. And clearly, so does your aunt."

"Yes. I mean, no. That is to say, Lord Ravencross didn't actually ask me to marry him. Not really. But yes, my aunt and I have discussed this at length. We both want the dreams to end with me. The idea of my marrying *anyone* is out of the question."

"I see." But her face remained pinched up as if she was still scrutinizing the matter.

"What's more important, I am committed to the work we do here. It gives what's left of my life purpose. Besides, what sort of wife would I make, scaling walls and throwing knives?"

The small lines beside her eyes crinkled up. "A very dangerous sort, I should think."

Sixteen

DANGEROUS

A very dangerous sort.

"Precisely," I said.

"Very well. Since you would rather stay here—"

"I would. Except what will you do with me when the dreams get bad and turn my mind?"

"That is still a very long way off. Let us tackle that problem closer to the time, shall we? At present, we must deal with your aunt. I shall write to her and explain that her very generous father-in-law covered your tuition for another year and a half—"

"He did?"

"Oh, my dear, I always overcharge abominably."

"Of course, you do. Because our families are willing to pay an exorbitant fee for you to take us off their hands."

She didn't answer that, there was no need. We all knew it was true, even if it did still sting. She chirped on about what she would put in the letter to my aunt. "And then so that she won't worry, I'll tell her that you are quite happy here. You might want to write and tell her the same."

"No, you can't say that." I sat up and shook my head. "It would be doing it up too brown. She'll never believe I'm happy. I'm not the happy sort."

"I see." She seemed to take me seriously, but I couldn't tell for certain. There was a little twist to her mouth that made me wonder. "Quite right."

She tapped the arm of the chair thoughtfully. "Then I shall tell her this: that your embroidery and sewing skills are wretched and still require considerable work, your watercolors are deplorable, and your French lessons are coming along rather slowly. But to encourage her, I will add that your nightmares appear to be less severe than they once were. I wonder if I ought to speculate that perhaps the farther you reside from Tidenham, the less the dreams seem to intrude upon your peace."

"Oh, yes, brilliant! That would do it." I stared at my teacher, amazed. Almost every word she planned to say was true, *almost*, except the part about the dreams, and yet it had nothing to do with the important facts of the matter.

"That settles that, then." She stood and shook out her stiff black skirts. "Come. I need to make haste and compose a message to Captain Grey. We'll stop by my study to write it, and then you can accompany me to the dovecote. The pigeons always behave better when you are there."

"Because I feed them."

"Hmm."

Georgie's favorite room in the house, apart from her laboratory, is Miss Stranje's study. It is my least favorite. I feel trapped here. The bookshelves tower to the ceiling and every inch is filled. Even though she has shelves lining all three walls, books are still stacked on the floor. Miss Stranje claims there is an order we cannot see to her office, and I believe her. Ask her for a book, and she knows exactly where it can be found.

Her papers, however, are a different matter. They are arranged meticulously in slots along the wall behind her and in three bins atop her desk. A cunning woman, Miss Emma Stranje, to have laid a trap so subtle that something as insignificant as a cut pen nib falling out of place would tell her that we had riffled through her papers.

She indicated a chair for me and proceeded to sit at the desk and cut a long thin strip of vellum. She possessed two inkwells, the regular variety of India ink and the invisible ink Georgiana had created. First she would compose a message in India ink and then, when that dried, she would follow with more sensitive information written in the disappearing ink.

While she worked, I fidgeted with the fringe on my chair and then started perusing the books on the shelf nearest to me. One in particular caught my attention, a collection of geographical information and maps of China, and next to it stood a book with Chinese characters etched on the spine.

Curiosity overtook me, and I interrupted her writing. "How long have you known Madame Cho?"

She didn't look up from blotting the vellum. "A great many years," she said. "She came to live with us when I was seven." She glanced up and smiled. "Cho was not much older than you are."

"How?" I blurted. "How did she come all the way from China to here?"

Miss Stranje snapped out of her reverie and frowned. "What has she told you?"

"Only that her father taught her the fighting skills she teaches us. And that she lived in a village where two rivers meet."

"Ah, yes, the Xi and the Tan." She bent again over the slender strip of paper and concentrated on making very small, careful strokes.

I scooted my chair closer and folded my arms on the edge of her wooden desk, watching her work. "Why did she come to live with you?"

"My father adopted her. We were raised as sisters."

"If she was my age, she was rather old to be adopted. How did he come by her? Did he steal her away from her home in China?"

"Good heavens, no!" She glanced up at me, astonished by my question. "Whatever gave you that idea?"

I smoothed my fingers over the soft quail feather on one of her extra quills. "It's just that Madame Cho looked excessively sad when she spoke of the place where two rivers meet. Which made me wonder why she would have left her family and a place she loved to come to England."

"What a horrid hypothesis, to think my father would do something so reprehensible. Nothing could be farther from the truth. My father was an honorable, caring man." Miss Stranje bristled at me and waved the small scrap of paper to make the ink dry faster. "You will have to ask Madame Cho. It is not my story to tell."

"You know perfectly well she won't tell me. It took almost four years before she would tell me about the two rivers." I reflected again on how closemouthed everyone was in this house.

"Probably not." Miss Stranje suppressed a sly smirk. "But you might ask if she knows any good stories about pirates."

Pirates?

I blinked, more curious than ever. And knowing full well that if Madame Cho had pirates in her history, she would keep mum about that unto death.

Miss Stranje dusted the paper with drying powder and the two of us went downstairs. I followed along behind her, heavily preoccupied with trying to figure out how in blazes pirates might fit into Madame Cho's background. We turned the corner into the first floor hallway and saw one of our two house maids, Alice, coming out of the workroom. She held a dust rag and a jar of lemon oil mixed with beeswax in one hand.

Miss Stranje hailed her. "It's awfully quiet down here, Alice. Where have they all gone off to?"

Alice bobbed a curtsey. "I'll tell you, miss, for I know exactly where they are, seein' as they've had me running in and out and to and fro. *Bring a pitcher of lemon water, Alice,* says Lady Jane. *Take that dish back to the house,* says Miss Wyndham. Where are they, miss? They're way out past the garden and beyond the roses, working with that odd gentleman from the Colonies, Mr. Sinclair. But as to what they're getting up to, I cannot say. Building something, by the looks of it. Whatever it is, more'n likely it's dangerous, because the young ladies shooed me away with strict orders to shake my rugs elsewhere. Miss Georgiana tells me I'd best take my rugs and go on over to the far side of the garden or I might get myself blown straight to kingdom come. Although what danger I could be in from that old copper tub is beyond me. Now, if anyone were to ask me, a young lady ought not—"

"Thank you, Alice. We don't mean to keep you from your work. You've been most helpful. And you needn't run any more errands for the young ladies while they are out of doors. They've legs of their own."

"Just so, miss. I have dusting and polishing to do, that's what I told them. Dusting, dusting, and more dusting." Alice glanced guiltily over her shoulder and reached back to pull the workroom door shut as if she didn't want us to notice it wasn't quite as dusted and polished as her diatribe suggested.

We left through the side door and found them, just as Alice had said, gathered together on the far side of the rose patch. All of them were there, even Lord Ravencross. He sat stretched out, sleeping in a chair. Sera perched on a bench nearby, working intently on a sketch of some kind. I suspected it was a sketch of Gabriel and experienced a twinge of jealousy. Maya was plucking a small finger harp that lay flat in her lap, while Georgie, Jane, and Mr. Sinclair huddled over some sort of tangled heap of copper and tin.

At any other country house this would have been a perfectly idyllic scene. The weather was fine. Bees hummed. Roses perfumed the air. There was even the odd butterfly fluttering about. Except at any other manor house the gentry would have been engaged in a companionable game of ninepins or shuttlecocks, whereas here at Stranje House, the young people were building a weapon.

Or a prototype for one.

Sera *was* indeed sketching Gabriel. "Must you?" I whispered. She said nothing, intent on rubbing her finger over some shading on the drawing. I strolled quietly next to Lord Ravencross and stared down at him, unable to resist thinking what an intriguing-looking man he was. The contrast of the scar against the Greek god–like perfection of his features and the strength of his jaw, well, I couldn't blame Sera for wanting to draw him. At my approach, his eyes blinked open. And whatever beauty his face contained was nothing compared to the soul-melting glory of his eyes.

"You came back," I said, swallowing my embarrassment for having been caught gawking at him.

"Thought I ought to give Sinclair a hand with his invention." He leaned up and squinted at the young inventor.

"Yes." I nodded in mock seriousness. "I see you are hard at work."

"I am." The corner of his mouth twitched ever so slightly. "I'm overseeing the work. Can't you tell?" He flopped back against the chair and closed his eyes. "Sinclair appears to have all the manual labor he needs at the moment. What's more, I have donated two skiffs to the project." He pointed at two long boats resting on the grass next to the conglomeration of copper.

"It's a catamaran design." Georgie popped up from behind the metal heap with a screwdriver in her hand. "Thank you, my lord, for the loan of your skiffs. It speeds the work along considerably not having to build the pontoons from scratch." She waved Miss Stranje and me over excitedly. "You really must come see what we're doing. It's quite brilliant."

I was not impressed. It looked as if a perfectly good tub had been cut apart with tin snips and reshaped into a small furnace. There were screws and bolts of various sizes sitting in dishes on the ground around them, and Mr. Sinclair was piercing metal sheets with a hammer and punch.

I didn't understand Georgie's enthusiasm for this pile of disassembled copper sheeting and tubing. So I turned to Jane for an explanation. "What is it?"

"A small boiler for the steam engine. Or at least the beginnings of one."

"Why are you constructing it out here in the open?" I glanced with worry toward the woods and then in the direction of Lady Pinswary's manor.

"Why wouldn't we?" Mr. Sinclair asked, still tapping the hammer against his metal punch. "Miss Stranje instructed me not to build anything explosive indoors."

"Because, Mr. Sinclair—"

"I do wish someone around here would call me by my given name." He huffed and straightened from where he'd been hunched over his work. "It's Alexander, and I confess I am lonesome to hear the sound of it and heartily tired of hearing Mr. Sinclair this and Mr. Sinclair that."

"Very well, then, Alexander," I began again. "I am concerned about you constructing it out here in the open, because there is a distinct possibility one of Lady Daneska's spies from the Iron Crown will see it."

"Oh well, then." He swatted my concerns away with the metal punch as if shooing away a gnat. "In that case, you needn't worry. There's nothing sacred about a steam engine, miss." Sinclair stretched his back and strolled closer to tower over me. "These engines have been around since before either of us were born. Why, back in 1770, a fellow in France made a steam-powered wagon for the army. Trouble was, the folks with the guillotines threatened to chop off his head because they decided science was evil and they hated progress."

Alexander gave his blond curls a brisk rub, knocking loose a shard of copper. "Interesting people, the French. On the one hand, some are smarter than a pack of hungry foxes. On the other hand, you've got a passel of 'em who are crazier than badgers in heat."

"*Badgers in . . .*" Jane exhaled loudly and rolled her gaze to the small fluffy clouds flitting across the sky. "*Please*, Mr. Sinclair. Try not to pepper your speech with bodily functions. A little civility would not go amiss."

He ignored her. "As far as I'm concerned, if someone from the Iron Crown wants to stand out here and take notes rather than torture me, I'm more than happy to let him have a go at it."

Jane leaned in and whispered in an aside to me, "When I charged him with that very same question, he told me not to worry. He says he is a *practicalist*. Whatever that might mean.

As near as I can tell, it is a philosophy held by American gentlemen who wish to find the easiest way out of a pickle."

"Ah," I said, surprised to hear Jane refer to him as a gentleman
when his manners were so atrocious.

The American gentleman had definitely captured Miss Stranje's
attention, although not for his uncouth speech. "Are you saying,
Mr. Sinclair, that this is *not* the contraption the Iron Crown is
interested in?"

He stepped back, jammed his hands in his pockets, and
glanced down nervously before answering. "That's right, miss.
This is not exactly the piece they're after."

"And what *exactly* are they after?"

"Well, you see, it's not so very difficult to build a steam engine. Not if you know what you're doing. Oh, these boilers blow
up now and again. But after you've put one or two together, it's
not as risky." He stopped and rubbed the back of his neck. "However, it is a mite trickier to make a steam engine actually do the
work you want it to perform. Like say, for instance, turn a wagon
wheel or paddle a warship."

"I see." Miss Stranje chewed her lip for a moment. "So that is
the information they wanted from you? The connections that
would make a paddlewheel turn properly."

"I think so."

"You *think* so, Mr. Sinclair?"

"Alexander," he corrected.

She waited.

"All I know, miss, is that Napoleon did some reading while
he was cooped up on Elba. He read all about my uncle's commission to build a steam-powered warship for the U.S. Navy a
couple of months ago. Why, Uncle Robert has had a steamship,
The Clermont, running up and down the Hudson since 1807.

Apparently Napoleon got letters from one of his French engineers who had a gander at our *Clermont* when we had her dry-docked in New York. So you see, they've already seen all this and more."

"Hmm," she said, tapping her forefinger nervously and waiting for him to continue.

"Turns out, even before Napoleon got back on the French throne he commissioned some of his Iron Crown engineers to secretly build a steam-powered warship like the one my uncle tried to sell him back in 1797."

Miss Stranje groaned.

"Not to worry, miss. Bonaparte should've paid Uncle Robert to build it for him back when he had a chance, because you can bet your best bonnet, Robbie won't do it now. The French went ahead and tried to copy his design. They built something, all right, but apparently it's dead in the water. A great hulking tub and no way to propel her. Seems all those French engineers can't figure out how to get the moving parts moving any faster than one of those fancy snails they like to eat so much." His eyes danced with mischief.

"I take it you do know how."

"Aye, miss, that I do." He smiled crookedly and blushed slightly as if bragging made him uncomfortable.

Miss Stranje glanced down at the note in her hands and back up at our American guest. "You must be perfectly candid with me, Alexander. No one knows better than I how brutal members of the Iron Crown can be. I must ask you again, when they questioned you, were they able to *make* you tell them anything that would help with this warship of theirs?"

His mouth quirked up and dimples formed in his cheeks. "I'm an affable fellow, miss. I told them a great many things. None of which will do them any good."

Jane studied his dimples with considerable consternation.

"Excellent." Miss Stranje's posture relaxed just a trifle. "I should like to discuss this in more depth later, Mr. Sinclair. I have the distinct impression you are holding back a few things that may be important. But for now, I beg you will excuse me. I must send this message off as soon as possible."

She glanced over her shoulder at me and then knowingly at Lord Ravencross. "I can manage the pigeons without your help, Tess. You may stay here, if you like."

Instantly, Georgie's interest shifted from tightening bolts to Miss Stranje. "You're going to send the message to Captain Grey?" She set down a ratchet and stood up, clasping the pocket watch that hung around her neck, Lord Wyatt's pocket watch. She had an unconscious habit of closing her hand around it whenever she thought of him.

"Yes." Our headmistress backed away. "But I can attend to it alone. You may go back to your work."

Georgie couldn't help herself. She trailed after Miss Stranje and so did I. Not that there was any need. It certainly wouldn't take three of us to send a pigeon. I knew why Georgie followed our headmistress, because a note to Captain Grey was a note to Lord Wyatt, and anything that had to do with him drew her like a lodestone.

I, on the other hand, came along to avoid Lord Ravencross's unsettling gaze. Even when he wasn't looking at me I could feel his thoughts curling around me. Good heavens, the man might as well stand up and wrap his arm around my shoulder. It was outrageous how, without a word or even a touch, he had a way of making me feel like an overwarm caramel, all weak, and gooey, and melted inside.

In that respect Gabriel reminded me once again of my wolf-dogs, the way they could communicate without so much as a yip between them. But Phobos and Tromos were mates. Lord Ravencross and I were definitely not mates, nor would we ever be. We were barely friends.

Miss Stranje does not keep the pigeons in a real dovecote, not like the stone turret cotes at many manors. Ours is a small, simple coop that stands across from the henhouse. Miss Stranje shooed the chickens out. The clucky hens were always invading pigeon territory. It seemed as if they liked showing off to the caged pigeons, boasting that they were allowed to roam free. Had I known how to communicate with those blustery hens, I might've pointed out that our pigeons had the glorious task of flying clear across the channel and that not a one of them would ever end up stuffed and roasted for dinner. But chickens are a thimble-headed lot.

Miss Stranje pointed to an occupied cage. "That one."

I unlatched it and lifted out a large male pigeon, stroking his purple and blue-gray plumage.

"We've only three carriers left." She sounded worried. "Two after today."

Ten pigeon coops lined the wall. On the top row, two coops were occupied by birds pecking loudly at their wooden cages. They tapped so insistently, I could almost hear them demanding to be let out so they could fly home. Each empty cage represented a message sent. On the row below, three nests held cooing pairs. Their mates had come home, carrying with them a message for us. Next to them on that same row, two lone birds sat in nests quietly awaiting their mates' return.

I felt sorry for them and opened the grain bin, tossing an extra portion of seed into their dishes. I held out my palm to allow the bird on my arm to peck up a few grains.

Georgie viewed this tableau with barely contained anxiety. "What did you tell the captain?"

Miss Stranje answered patiently, "I explained the situation, of course. Although I was mindful not to say too much lest our pigeon goes astray and lands in the wrong hands."

"Did you tell Captain Grey we suspect an invasion?"

"I'm sure he is already aware of that possibility."

"Of course." But that didn't stop Georgie from ticking off a list of things she thought ought to be included in the note. ". . . and you told them that Lady Daneska and Ghost are probably here in England. They may even be in Sussex." She stopped talking, and her eyes widened. "You don't think Daneska might be staying with her aunt, do you?"

"Absolutely not." Miss Stranje took the pigeon from me. "Daneska wouldn't be that foolish. Not after Calais. She knows we could have her arrested and that Lady Pinswary's servants can't be relied upon not to gossip."

Georgie was momentarily appeased. "Did you send my regards to Lord Wyatt? It also might be good to mention that Mr. Sinclair is respectful and that there is no danger there."

Miss Stranje looked askance at her prize student. "It is a very small piece of paper, Georgiana. There is very little room on a pigeon's leg to write long narratives about kidnappings and Mr. Sinclair's behavior in the workroom, but yes, I did my best."

"I see." Georgie looked crestfallen. "Did you at least assure them that I am all right? And that I suffered no harm in the attempted kidnapping? I wouldn't want Lord Wyatt to worry."

Miss Stranje sighed loudly. "Oh, very well." She thrust the pigeon back into my hands. "Hold him."

She opened a small inkwell kept on the shelf beside the grain bin and dipped her quill. She studiously scratched a few more words along the very edge of the narrow strip of vellum.

Georgie tried to peer over our teacher's shoulder. "Are you calling Captain Grey home?"

At this, Miss Stranje left off writing and frowned at Georgie. "*Calling him home?* Why would you say such a thing, Georgiana? He's not mine to command."

"But . . ." Stung by Miss Stranje's reprimand, Georgie lowered her eyes and kicked softly at the straw on the floor. "I thought—"

"You thought with your heart, not your head. Begging him to come home would be overstepping my bounds. I'm simply apprising him of our latest suspicions. I suggested he might be able to find proof on his side of the channel that Napoleon is building a fleet in preparation for an attack so that we could alert the admiralty. Although what Britain would do about it now challenges the imagination."

She brusquely took the pigeon from me, tucked him into the crook of her arm, and wound a folded strip of vellum around his leg. "Here." She handed me a silk thread. "Tie this on. Not too tight. That's it. Again, and now double the knot."

The bird's trepidation was obvious as we secured the message around his leg. The moment we finished, however, I felt his flutter of eagerness. He knew that soon he would be winging once more across the wide sky, homing for his nest in France.

With one finger, Miss Stranje lifted Georgie's chin. "I used your ink, Georgiana, for the more sensitive bits. And I didn't mean to be harsh with you. I understand how hard this must be for you." She sighed and glanced out the window. "I miss them, too."

Georgie left off sulking and asked, "How long will it take for the message to reach them?"

"Pigeons fly surprisingly fast." Miss Stranje gently smoothed her finger over our courier's breast feathers. "He could get there in a matter of only a few hours. Or it could take a full day. Maybe more. It depends upon the faithfulness of this little bird, how often he diverts from his path, and whether his sense of direction holds true. Then there is providence. He might meet with a storm and have to seek shelter. Or he could be shot down. Everyone is suspicious of a pigeon during war. And even if he makes it to his nest, there is the question of when, or even *if*, Captain Grey will be able to retrieve the message."

Georgie wilted under the dismal odds of our message getting through.

Miss Stranje straightened her posture and took a deep breath. "But I see no alternative, do you? If we were to dispatch a messenger, by the time he sailed the channel, and snuck across enemy lines, *if* he was able to sneak across, and located Captain Grey to deliver our message, it could be several weeks."

She held the bird tenderly for a moment longer, stroking its iridescent neck feathers. "It is all up to you, my little French friend. I envy you, in a few hours you will be home with your mate." Miss Stranje never spoke of missing Captain Grey. But her wistful sigh said what she would not.

"Fly fast and true, little one." She kissed the pigeon's head and sent him winging away.

I knew Georgie well enough to know that she watched all this and swallowed hard against the longing in her own heart. There was a catch in her voice when she said, "I'm certain when the captain learns of the danger we are in, he'll come home." Although I rather thought she was thinking of Lord Wyatt, and imagining the two men rushing home together.

"You must not hang your hopes on it." Miss Stranje gave Georgie's shoulder a sympathetic pat. "We may be best helped if they stay where they are and do the job they were assigned. They must do what is best for Britain, not what is best for those few of us at Stranje House."

Seventeen

ɢUARDIAꞃS

When we returned to the group, they were resting from their labors and discussing alternatives to Mr. Sinclair's torpedo design. Sera and Maya were especially animated. Sera was fairly bursting at the seams. "Maya's right about using a powerful crossbow and arrow. Harpoons go through the water. What if we used a harpoon with an explosive on it?"

Joining them, Georgie explained to him the mechanics of her grenade filled with Greek fire. Jane described the effects she'd witnessed in Calais, and they debated methods to house this volatile mixture and yet get it to explode on its target.

MacDougal arrived a few moments later with news that he had been successful in hiring not one but three sentinels to watch the house and sit guard over Lord Ravencross.

Gabriel met this news with surprise. "What did you do, offer them a king's ransom?"

"Nay. Told 'em yer life was in danger. Yer men were more'n willing to work for laborer's wages. Save farmer Jason's oldest boy, the lad wouldn't accept e'en a farthing for his trouble. Says he'd be pleased to come along an' watch over ye, on account of his family wishes to thank ye for the new thatch roof and milk cow ye gave 'em. More'n one man said as how neither of the other Lords o' Ravencross ever did half as much fer the tenants as do ye. They'd just as soon keep you on as lord."

Gabriel's eyes widened as MacDougal continued to describe how willing his tenants were to come and stand guard over him. He sat down listening intently, as if the idea anyone should care about his welfare were a completely fascinating turn of events.

"Fact is, m'lord, a dozen men stepped forward at the pub. I picked these three because they were accounted best able to handle a firearm."

"Remarkable." Gabriel blinked at this revelation. "My father always described them as—" He stopped and rubbed absently at the stubble on his jaw. "But I suppose he would, wouldn't he?" he said under his breath.

"Well done, Mac." Gabriel stood and, with his good arm, clapped his servant on the back. "Excellent news. Allow me to say my farewells and I'll accompany you back to the house."

I should have been relieved at the news that Gabriel would be amply protected. Except it meant my services would not be needed. There would be no late-night rendezvous in his room. No watching him sleep. No gently smoothing back his dark curls. I sighed and tried to press a smile on my face.

He could've at least had the good grace to look a little bit disappointed. Instead he stood beside the garden chair, still looking a bit dazed. When he finally did turn to me, he didn't utter a long fond farewell. No. He bowed curtly and asked if he might call the next day.

Biting back my disappointment, I asked, "Whatever for?"

"To do whatever it is gentlemen do when they call upon young ladies." He held his shoulder, and I guessed it must be aching like the very devil again.

"You needn't trouble yourself, my lord. I have no interest in entertaining callers." An apricot-colored butterfly meandered past. The ridiculous creature didn't know I was in no mood for prettiness.

"Nevertheless," Gabriel said sternly, "you are my fiancée, and as such it is my duty to make certain you are quite well—"

"*Duty?*" I said, as if the word itself had a stink.

"I misspoke." He straightened and parried with a blunt-edged tone. "It is my pleasure." He didn't sound as if it would be a pleasure. "The least I can do is make certain you are being properly cared for, after you so bravely risked your life for your friend and then valiantly conducted me home during my hour of need the other day."

I answered with a pinching frown and a forced smile. "Very prettily said, my lord, but we are *not* betrothed, as you well know. And what's more, I am quite capable of looking after myself. You're the one who needs looking after. Go home and take care of your shoulder."

He took a few steps closer to me, away from the others, flexing and unflexing his jaw before answering. "Did I say you *bravely* risked your life? Begging your pardon, I meant to say *foolishly.*"

That's better. I would much rather joust with him than have him bend his knee to me out of a sense of duty.

I cocked my head at a flirtatious angle and smiled my broadest. "The charming Mr. Chadwick had quite a differently opinion." I shamelessly batted my eyelashes.

God forgive me, I wanted to make him pay for not wishing it would be me guarding him tonight instead of some smelly old farmer. I don't know what came over me to taunt him.

He took a deep breath and moved even closer, so close that

I could smell his shaving soap and found myself staring at the cleft of his chin. His breath tickled my cheek when he spoke my name. "Tess, I worry that lump on your head is playing havoc with your memory. First our betrothal slips your mind, and then you forget it was Chadwick's father who paid you those compliments, not his sprout."

I wished I had a fan. The day had turned suddenly warm. "You know perfectly well that I could have young Chadwick eating out of my palm if I chose." I slipped away from him and crossed my arms. "You are becoming tedious, my lord. Perhaps it is time you toddled off home."

The grinding sound he made caused me to smile. But then he leaned in next to my cheek. I swallowed some of my arrogance in a breathless lump.

His lips spread in a devilish smirk. In a husky whisper, he said, "Fine talk from a young lady who claims she wants to run her lips over my scars."

My mouth flew open. I drew in a sharp breath.

How dare he mention that! *Again.* I ought to have slapped him. I seriously considered knocking that self-satisfied grin from his face. I would have, too, if it weren't for the fact that he was already in pain.

I am not good at hiding my feelings. Not good at all. And right then, standing that near to him, I could not decide between slapping him or kissing his rude lips. *Hard.*

I swallowed and stepped back, conceding the bout to him. "Scoundrel."

"I gave you fair warning about my character."

"Yes, I remember. Right before I told you that I could never marry you. I think you had best take yourself off, my lord. Before I finish the job Daneska's henchmen began."

He smiled knowing he'd gotten the upper hand and inclined his head in a nod of farewell. "Until tomorrow, Tess."

He walked off, his usual limp barely noticeable, and left me standing alone beside the roses. Breathing in their sweet fragrance, as I huffed and puffed like a dragon who had lost her fire. The stupid butterfly swooped around me in a set of drunken curling loops. *Ridiculous thing.* She was as confused as I was.

After Lord Ravencross left, I was in no mood for conversation. Dinner was a dismal affair that night. Indifferent to the discussion of gears, boiler tanks, warships, and torpedoes that dominated the evening, I ate in broody silence. I picked at my chicken pie and, during dessert, stirred my nutmeg-and-peach custard into an unrecognizable mess. I begged to be excused and went directly to bed.

I fully expected my bad temper to produce a torrent of ugly dreams. It didn't matter. I was too tired and too confused to care. I curled under my covers and found myself drifting into that same curious prison, full of comfortable silks, cushions of scarlet and amber, and a coverlet made of the finest damask.

Despite the lavishness of my surroundings, there were iron manacles on my wrists and legs. Napoleon did not carry in the silver bowl. It was Lady Daneska. I noticed odd runes worked into the silver filigree around the rim. I refused to drink. If I would not drink it for Napoleon, I most certainly would not for her. She merely laughed and plunged my face into the green witching water, holding me there until breath fled my lungs in a flurry of bubbles and I flailed for air.

Except, I didn't drown.

The mystical water flung me through the mists, and I found myself standing on the cliffs of Stranje House. Georgie, Jane, Sera, Maya, all of us were there. All of the people I cared about—Madame Cho, Miss Stranje, even Aunt Lydia, and right beside me stood Gabriel.

We all stared out to sea, fascinated by some phenomena. But what I saw there made my heart thunder and my legs turn weak—the sea tumbling and rising into a great swell. Rising higher and higher, like no wave I had ever seen, it rose until it became a great roaring wall.

"Run!" I screamed. "Run!" I turned, dragging Gabriel with me and scooping my arm around Georgie's waist to help her go faster. "Run!" I shouted to the others. But when I looked back, they were all falling behind.

Jane stumbled. Madame Cho stopped to help her up. Miss Stranje and Sera were lagging too far behind. The wave was a mountain about to tumble upon us, and I couldn't save them. I couldn't save any of them. They were all going to be dashed to pieces.

I awoke with a start, gasping for air.

Fear.

Surely there could be nothing prophetic in that dream. A wave of that proportion was too fantastical. Impossible. It must be a manifestation of my fears, as Sera had thought the day before.

"It meant nothing," I whispered. In the dark I listened to the steady breath sounds of the other girls sleeping in their beds. They were all here. Safe. My breathing settled and my heart slowed to a less frantic gallop. The dream had just been an ordinary nightmare.

Nothing. If it was nothing, why did I have this overpowering urge to sob like a foolish child?

There was only one thing to do about that. I turned back the covers and slipped into the dress I wore for running.

I left the house before dawn and tore like a charging bull along the cliffs with the wolf-dogs hard at my heels. I stopped at one point and glared at the expanse of water below. It reassured me to see the ocean behaving as it ought, the waves remaining normal sized waves, the surf crashing with dependable regularity.

I took off again, running a little less like a mad bull and a little more like a proper wolf. Phobos and Tromos seemed more content with that.

When we finally stopped, I noticed how much more swollen Tromos's belly looked. She was growing fast. I patted her and gave her a little more food that morning. I hoped this time her pups would make it. Although Phobos was bigger in size, Tromos obviously had more wolf blood in her than he did. Perhaps that had something to do with why they'd not yet had any luck producing cubs. Maybe this time.

I scratched them both behind their ears and let them wrestle with me before leaving them. Tromos gave me a farewell nudge with her nose, as if she understood the turmoil brewing in my heart. I couldn't help myself, I wrapped my arms around her for just a moment. Luckily, she tolerated my ridiculous show of affection and didn't bite me. She did shake out her fur the minute I let go, reminding me that she was a wild animal and did not like to be mauled whenever my emotions got away from me. Phobos watched all this with an amused expression dancing in his eyes.

That day, Georgie and the others worked on constructing their steam engine, and Miss Stranje and Philip set to work sealing up the secret entrances to the house. Miss Stranje settled on adding a latch that could be opened only from the inside.

It might work.

Although I couldn't imagine a latch keeping Daneska or Ghost from finding a way to sneak in once they set their minds to the task.

The best way to protect all of them, Ravencross included, would be for me to find Daneska and Ghost before they snuck into Stranje House. And when I found them, there was no other answer but that Lucien must be killed. The undertaking made prickles rise on the back of my neck every time I thought of it. I swallowed down the roiling fear. It would not be easy, but it had to be done, for Miss Stranje and the other girls' sake, for Gabriel's sake, for England's sake. My best chance of succeeding in this endeavor would be to use a long-range weapon, which meant knife, arrow, or gun. Since Miss Stranje had not yet devised a way for us to practice with firearms without alarming the neighbors, I would need to do it with either a bow or a throwing blade.

Which one?

I swallowed and decided that was a bridge I would cross when I got there. Although, I suspected that shaky proverbial bridge might be made of rotted rope and missing a few planks.

No matter. First I had to *find* the happy couple.

All morning I pored over maps, trying to deduce Daneska and Ghost's whereabouts. Assuming the henchmen had ridden out on the same morning they attacked us, I drew a circle that took in everything within a day's ride from Stranje House. Then I reasoned that they had to be hiding somewhere no more than three hours away. I narrowed my circle to a generous twenty-mile radius.

Miss Stranje stopped in the workroom. "You seem very busy. What are you working on?"

I looked up from the map. "Do you suppose you could send a note to the justice of the peace asking if they've determined from where the horses were rented?"

"I will ask, but those men could've exchanged mounts from any posting house."

"Yes, but it might give us a clue as to their direction."

"Hmm. I suppose." She traced her finger over the map. "Clever. Hunting for her before she comes to us." She tapped on one particular side of the circle. "I've given their whereabouts considerable thought as well." She drew a line across the inland part of my circle. "It seems to me they would favor a location fairly close to the shore. Someplace easy to slip in and out of, making it more convenient to communicate with their cohorts in France."

We drew smaller circles around key villages, focusing on those closest to Calais. We discussed all of the possibilities. In the end, we concluded we required more intelligence. She had two local men she could trust to investigate discreetly.

"I'll send word tomorrow, asking them to visit each of these areas to see if any strangers have taken up residence recently. They'll need to be cautious. It won't be easy. People will be reluctant to talk with them. Most of the villages in that area are deeply involved in smuggling activities."

"Precisely the kind of village they would seek out." I sat back and crossed my arms against the turmoil in my stomach. "You can only call upon *two* men? With so many places to check, and the caution they must take, it could be a week before we get word."

"I'm afraid that is all I have at my disposal at the moment." She stood and tilted her head, studying me with her sharp hawk's eyes. She sees too much. I looked away, pretending to study the maps again.

"There's something else troubling you. Are you unwell?" she asked.

I shrugged.

"When you didn't come to practice this morning, Madame Cho worried that your head must still hurt."

"No, I was practicing with the bow." My head did hurt, not from the knock the kidnappers had given it, but from thinking about the task ahead of me. "If you see her, please tell Madam Cho I will come around later and practice knife throwing."

She rested her hand on my shoulder. "Tess, obviously there's

215

something else bothering you. If it is that business with Lord Ravencross and if you would like to discuss—"

"No," I said too quickly. "I . . . I would rather not speak of it."

Any of it.

"When you're ready, then," she said, and left me.

I stared in silence at the map. It would be nearly impossible to find them this way, worse than hunting a couple of poisonous snakes in a barley field. I groaned and shoved it aside, resting my forehead in my hands.

If only I could have a dream that would help me find Daneska and Ghost. But no, I must persist in dreaming of silken prisons and Napoleon's silver bowl filled with lime green water. Of what use was that?

None at all.

Greaves intruded on my angry introspection with a nasal announcement that, true to his word, Lord Ravencross had come calling that afternoon. I sent Greaves back with a terse message that I did not wish to be disturbed.

Harsh.

Indifferent.

Well, and why not? I needed to be harsh and indifferent if I was to hunt down his brother and kill him. I shivered. And not because I was cold.

Ten minutes later, Alice came strolling through the workroom on the pretext of replenishing the oil in the lamps. She peeked over my shoulder at the maps. "My, but aren't you busy."

"Studying," I grumbled.

Alice is far too chatty to suit me. She mentioned that Lord Ravencross had indeed gone.

"A peculiar sort, that Lord Ravencross. Odd, how he lives alone in the great big house with only two servants." Alice prattled on, while I brooded silently. She flicked a rag over the lamp wiping up spilt oil. "I can tell you this, he stomped away in a great gray sulk. I almost expected a thunder cloud to appear over his head, he was so furious. Acted quite put out, he did. As if he had been sorely mistreated."

He had been.

"I doubt he'll be coming back anytime soon." There was a tinge of spite in Alice's twangy voice, and I was heartily glad when she finished filling the lamps and took herself off.

He wouldn't be coming back.

I don't know whether it was my heart or my stomach, or maybe both, but some part of me sank. Nay, part of me slid down like spilt lamp oil, dripping all the way through the floorboards, straight down into the sea churning in the caves beneath Stranje House.

Apparently I was not as indifferent as I'd boasted to myself, and not nearly cold-blooded enough to do the job ahead of me.

I reminded myself that I had no future. Not with Gabriel, or anyone. Unfortunately, the heart does not care about logic. I reasoned with myself there was no sense prolonging the pain. Gabriel was bound to abandon his chase sooner or later. It might as well be today. But as I accepted this fist of wisdom, a dull ache started in the pit of my stomach, spread to my chest, and then journeyed on a bruising path to my head.

I missed him.

Eighteen

SAINTS AND
TRAITORS

Late that night, the five of us tiptoed up the narrow passage behind the oak paneling in our dormitorium, climbing up to our secret room in the attic. I perched in the window seat, studying Ravencross Manor through our telescope. The two men MacDougal hired were traversing the grounds around the perimeter of the house. I guessed the third man, farmer Jason's son, would be sitting in the chair where MacDougal had slept the night I'd climbed through the window. I wondered if he would be able to stay awake and alert to intruders better than MacDougal had. Perhaps I might just check. If I timed my approach carefully, the guards on the grounds wouldn't see me. I could scale the wall and . . .

Sera came up beside me and whispered in my ear, "That would be an excellent way to get shot."

"Are you a mind reader now?"

"No." She grinned. "But you've trained the spyglass on his sentries' movements and tapped the seconds between their rounds with your forefinger. I've known you long enough to hazard a guess at what you were contemplating."

Sera was right. If these men were any good at their task, I could get shot. Still, it might be worth the risk.

She shook her head.

"You're happy about it, aren't you?" I reproached her quietly enough that the others couldn't hear. "Don't try to deny it. You're smiling."

Her smile vanished and she looked genuinely stricken. "I'm not. Why should I be happy about something that brings you pain?"

"Because you've always had a *tendre* for him."

"Perhaps I did once. But your happiness means more to me than any infatuations I may have foolishly woven about him. I see now that you two are more suited."

Saint Seraphina. She would be good like that. Why couldn't she be vicious and mean? I needed someone to squabble with, not someone gentle and tender and kind. And because I remembered how Mr. Chadwick made her blush, *wicked creature that I am*, I decided to point out her failings where it concerned him.

"You ought to be more careful around Mr. Chadwick. I've seen the way you look at him." I collapsed the spyglass. "He may seem cheerful and innocent, but don't let him fool you. He's a clever one, and he suspects something isn't normal here."

"I already know that. You needn't scold me. I'm scolding myself enough. I don't know why I behave so foolishly in his presence." She sat down on the opposite side of the window seat, making me scoot my feet out of the way. "Whenever I'm around him, I feel so unsettled. I lose my way. As if the world suddenly tilts sideways."

Oh, that feeling.

I looked at her with genuine empathy. "That bad?"

"No. That's not it," she protested. "I can tell what you are thinking. Nothing could be farther from the truth. I'm not attracted to him. He's nothing like Lord Ravencross."

"No one is like him," I said curtly, fuming a little. It still bothered me whenever she said things like that.

"No one is," she agreed too readily. "He's so brutish and manly."

I rolled my eyes. "*That's* what you like about him?"

"Well . . ." She glanced sheepishly at me. "That . . . and the fact that he's such a wounded soul. My heart nearly breaks every time he—"

"Stop! I don't want to hear your moonstruck fantasies about him," I blurted too loudly. The others hushed their conversation around the lamp and looked at us. "You read too many books, Sera. We all know how you've idealized Ravencross. You've painted him as some sort of Gothic hero. He's not. He's just a man with flaws and virtues. A man like any other. Your Mr. Chadwick, for instance."

"That's just it. Quinton Chadwick has no flaws." She curled her knees up and hugged them. Moonlight caught on her hair, and she looked exactly how I imagined the fairy princesses of old must've looked. "He hasn't a battle scar on him. He's led a perfect life, hasn't he? His parents are kind and understanding. They've encouraged him in his education. Hired tutors. I'm certain *he* has never been locked in a closet with only bread and water."

I shouldn't have said anything to that. It was grossly unfair how abysmally her parents had treated her. But even so, she was being far too hard on Chadwick.

"You surprise me, Sera." I shook my head softly. "Usually you are the one who notices every little speck. You see the tiniest thread out of place and deduce where someone has been and what they were doing. Except, when it comes to Mr. Chadwick—you seem to have covered your eyes." I twisted the spyglass, extending it out again. "We all fight battles within ourselves. Why can you not see his?"

Jane admonished me from her seat across the room. "Leave her be."

Sera stared at me for a moment, then laid her head atop her knees. "I admit he confuses me. One minute I would like to give him a good shake, and the next minute I find myself wanting to impress him. It's all very unnerving." She turned to stare out the window. "Even though it's not true, I tell myself I never want to see him again, and that I hope he never darkens our door—"

The shutter caught on the breeze and banged shut.

Suddenly I saw myself in the entry hall downstairs and Mr. Chadwick pounding on our door, shouting for admittance. The door flew open. Panic distorted his features, panic, terror, and pure anguish.

The vision vanished and my hands fell open with shock, the telescope rolled from my lap.

Sera lunged and caught it before it hit the floor. "Tess, what is it?"

I clung to her arm and stared into her worried face.

"You saw something, didn't you?"

I couldn't tell her. I wasn't sure what I'd seen, or what it meant. It was probably nothing. "I just got a little dizzy, that's all."

Her eyes narrowed. She knew I wasn't telling the truth.

I left the window and we joined Maya, Jane, and Georgie in the circle around our lamp. I told them of my hunt for Daneska and Ghost and about Miss Stranje's plan to send men to nearby villages and neighborhoods in search of newcomers.

But I did *not* tell them of my plan to kill Ghost.

Jane estimated our odds of finding them before they tried to breach Stranje House at roughly two hundred to one. *Bleak.*

"You can't quantify things like that," I argued. But silently, I resolved that if I couldn't find Ghost before he attacked us, I would have to settle on ending his life the minute he showed up at Stranje House.

The discussion turned to what we ought to do once we captured them. No one mentioned the obvious. Not one of them suggested we put an arrow through Ghost's treacherous heart.

Why should they? They were good and kind. Unlike me. I was ruthless and hard as stone. I kept silent and let them make their feeble, ineffectual plans.

Punch and Judy tumbled and played in my lap, chasing one another up and over my shoulder and down again. I fed them extra bread, since I wasn't certain whether or not my hunt during the next few days would take me far from home. *Perhaps forever, if I failed.* There were risks to my plan, but I couldn't allow Lucien to destroy Gabriel's life.

No matter the cost.

What was death to me? What difference would it make if it arrived now rather than a few years hence?

The moon sank low and Jane blew out our flickering oil lamp. We climbed the crumbling hidden staircase back down to bed. I laid my head on the pillow, awaiting a dream that would show me my enemy. A dream more useful than gigantic waves, or mystical green water. Sleep was slow to come. When one watches the pot, it takes forever to boil.

I closed my eyes, willing myself to dream about that traitor Daneska. Hoping for anything that might give me a clue to their whereabouts. Except, after tossing and turning for what felt like hours, dreams did not come. Only sleep. Fitful, restless, uninformative sleep. On any other night, I would've rejoiced, but I awoke in the wee hours of the morning troubled by all the peacefulness. The clock chimed four. In that drowsy state I accepted my temporary defeat and told myself to return to the comforts of slumber. No sooner had I sunk under the covers than noises downstairs roused me again. I opened my eyes, uncertain if I was in the midst of a dream or simply waking.

I heard voices. Distant and soft. They sounded real. But then, my dreams always feel real. That's the mind-snapping horror of them. The deaths I experience are not weak imitations. I sat up and walked toward the sound. Tiptoeing out of our bedroom, I saw candlelight flickering downstairs and went to the railing that overlooked the foyer.

Greaves, garbed in a wrapper and his nightcap, stood in the hall holding aloft a branch of candles. Miss Stranje looked much the same, obviously freshly disturbed from her night's rest, and yet she was greeting guests. I blinked sleep from my eyes and tried to focus on the dim scene below. A fair-haired gentleman, sea weathered and strong took Miss Stranje's hand and bowed over it. I knew him. That was Captain Grey, her childhood friend, a distant relative of some kind who has taken her father's place among the ranks of England's diplomats. A man, who on every occasion of our meeting, had earned my deepest respect and loyalty. Next to him paced a younger gentleman, tall and equal in height to the captain, but opposite in coloring and temperament. I knew instantly by the way his dark hair gleamed in the candlelight and his impatient stride that it was Captain Grey's colleague, Lord Wyatt.

They'd come home. My heart surged up happily until I spotted a third guest hanging back in the shadows. Instantly, my blood turned to fire. I could scarcely breathe. My fists molded into hot steel. I ran down the stairs heedless of the fact that I wore a nightgown.

Daneska!

She was bound and had a gag in her mouth. But there was no disguising the laughter in her eyes when she saw me. She was caught, trussed up like a rabbit for roasting, and yet Daneska still wore her usual haughty expression, as if the rest of us were simply fools placed on earth for her entertainment. Daneska's eyes are the color of winter ice. They reflect her heart. I used to think her coldness was born out of the loss of her mother, like my anger. But no. She'd been born cold, this one. A bloodless reptile.

She would murder the man I loved without a second thought. I charged straight at her, grabbed her throat, and rammed her into the oak paneling. I squeezed her perfect white neck and roared, "Where is he? Where's Lucien?"

It didn't matter that she had a gag in her mouth. Nor that I was squeezing the life out of her. She still managed to smirk at my fury.

Miss Stranje grabbed my arm and wrenched it away. *Hard.* "She can't tell us anything if she's dead."

She and Captain Grey held me back. "Calm yourself, Tess." Miss Stranje lowered her tone and spoke to me as if she were in the parlor serving tea. "I'm certain Lady Daneska will be delighted to tell you everything she has been doing, and catch you up on all the latest gossip about who has gone where, or done what, in the morning."

I had no time for Miss Stranje's headmistress nonsense. I turned to Captain Grey and begged for answers. "Ghost—he was with her. Did you catch him, too?" I bit my tongue to keep from asking, *Did you kill him? Oh, please God, let him be dead.*

The captain looked tired and worn. There was a cut on his left cheek and his knuckles were bleeding. He looked over my shoulder at Miss Stranje. There was an apology in his eyes. Regret. Shame. "He got away."

I moaned.

"Why did you bring *her* here?" I could barely keep from crying. Except these were not tears of sadness. My eyes watered with rage. "Why isn't she at London Tower with her head chopped off?" I spun back to her. "That's what they do with traitors, you know. They'll put your wicked head on a pike."

Daneska's perfect composure broke for an instant. *Only an instant.* All too quickly her cold, smug confidence returned. Like a beady-eyed albino adder.

After all, a snake does not worry that the rats might conspire against it.

Take care, Daneska, I shall be your mongoose.

One day I would put a stop to the haughtiness that burned in her eyes.

Miss Stranje spoke openly to Captain Grey just as if Satan's half sister wasn't standing right there listening. "Then you must've received our pigeon?"

"Yes." He glanced at his prisoner. "After Calais we tracked the two of them along the north coast of France into Belgium. We'd lost their trail a week ago, in Antwerp. It made perfect sense that they had snuck back into Britain to lay the groundwork for an invasion."

When he said the word "invasion," Daneska's gaze shot to him. Suddenly alert. *Alarmed.* An instant later she whipped her attention back to me. "You," she uttered around the gag.

I lifted my chin, pleased that even though her assumption wasn't true, I had partially undone her arrogance.

"We brought her here for questioning." Captain Grey set his hat on the entry table. "I thought it would be best. With her being a young lady, the government might be reluctant to question her as thoroughly as the situation warrants. I'll take her on to London in a day or two. But first, we thought it best if you were to . . . er . . ."

"House her," Lord Wyatt offered.

"Yes, of course." Miss Stranje glanced at Daneska.

"Oh, yes." I crossed my arms. "I suppose we have a moldy dungeon below stairs that ought to do for her. She won't mind the rats."

Daneska laughed. She couldn't help herself. She thinks everything is so blasted amusing.

"Tess!" Miss Stranje sounded as if she was scolding me.

Me?

When *there* stood the criminal. *There! Scold* her.

"Ungraciousness does not become you, Miss Aubreyson. Lady Daneska is a guest here at Stranje House. Royalty. As such, we will treat her with as much hospitality as she did Lord Wyatt in Calais."

A flash of panic washed over Daneska's impenetrable mask. Rightly so, for she had starved and tortured him. If we had not rescued him when we did he would be dead.

"A dungeon is too good for her." I brooded. "She can rot in her own excrement for all I care."

For some reason, that cheered Daneska up. The words were a bit muffled from beneath her gag, but I knew exactly what she'd said, "Ah, Tessie, *ma chère*. You still care."

Miss Stranje was not impressed with either of us. "Greaves, if you will please locate our irons. I believe you will find an extra set in the discipline chamber. And prepare the small guest room in the chambers below stairs."

That got Daneska's attention. Not alarm, but indignation twisted her features. She deserved better than the dungeons.

I smiled.

At the top of the stairs, a very sleepy Georgie emerged from the dormitorium, rubbing her eyes. "Who's here? I thought I heard . . ."

Lord Wyatt saw her on the landing and his face brightened, so much I thought for a moment our candles must have flared.

"Sebastian!" Georgie flew down the stairs and, completely ignoring propriety, threw her arms around his neck.

Miss Stranje ought to have scolded her. And when they kissed, she ought to have demanded a marriage proposal out of him. Instead, she looked on with a melancholy so full of soft sorrow that my own chest began to ache. Her gaze drifted to Captain Grey and immediately fluttered to the floor.

"A-hem." The captain cleared his throat.

Lord Wyatt and Georgie remembered themselves and pulled apart. Georgie stood back, shyly studying her naked toes. "Welcome home, Lord Wyatt, Captain Grey." Then she took stock of our other guest. "And Lady Daneska." She bobbed a curtsey and glanced pointedly at the ropes binding Daneska's wrists. "Lovely of you to call. I don't believe I have ever seen you in better looks."

If I had said that, Daneska would've laughed at my attempt to humble her. But because it had come from Georgie, her eyes narrowed viciously. She'd disliked Georgie from the start. But now, after having been robbed by her in Calais of two coveted prizes, the invisible ink formula and Lord Wyatt, she appeared to have formed a rather venomous hatred of our newest student.

Miss Stranje ordered the two of us upstairs to dress appropriately. "Captain Grey and Lord Wyatt have been traveling all night. I'm certain a rest is in order."

She took a firm hold of our prisoner's arm. "Come along, Lady Daneska. You may enjoy the young ladies' company after they have breakfasted."

Nineteen

PLOTTING

Daneska was here. *Here.* Everything had changed.

Long before dawn I went for my run, far too early for Georgie to come with me. Wind blew up from the sea, bringing a salty chill to the air as I traversed the cliff tops. Wispy silver clouds skirted through the dark sky, racing me. The tide was high, and every time the surf crashed against the rocks, I would burst forward as if some invisible hand pushed me faster and faster.

I loved the salt air whipping against my face and the feeling that nothing else mattered but running. The simple act of flinging one foot in front of the other and speeding past stones and cliffs and trees, all the things that had stood far longer than I had lived—that simple act washed away the turmoil in my mind in a way that a thousand baths could not.

I rounded the east side of the house and loped in long-legged strides toward the pasture and the woods, where . . . I'd killed a man.

My feet slowed as I neared the spot where I'd thrown my knife.

I saw his face. A phantom of the man I'd killed. Saw him falling. Not in a dream. Or a vision. A memory. My feet stilled completely. I saw it all again.

The first death by my hand.

I crouched, shivering, and hushed Phobos and Tromos, who wanted to keep running. I drew them close for warmth and dropped to my knees. Tromos whimpered and laid her wet nose over my shoulder.

She remembered, too.

Soon, very soon, I would have to add one more killing to my account. Would I be able to do it? Cold prickles skittered up my arms. I shuddered and looked away, burying my face in Tromos's dark fur. I should not have stopped here. I should've kept running.

I sprang up and took off at a furious pace, trying to outrun those thoughts. After exhausting myself in a ragged race around the sheep pasture, I walked back toward Stranje House. When I arrived at the gap between the two properties, I slowed down, watching the guards MacDougal had hired taking their patrols around Ravencross Manor. That ought to discourage his brother. Except I knew better. Ghost was clever and cunning . Even worse, the man was patient. He would bide his time and strike when least expected. As leader of the Iron Crown, Ghost was as relentless as Napoleon himself.

I wondered if Gabriel might try to ride out that morning, which would leave him vulnerable. Naturally, I waited. The sun peeked over the horizon and shot pink and orange streaks across the sky, and there was still no sign of him, no movement about his house and no big brown horse in the distance. So I gave up. His shoulder must not be healed well enough for riding.

Maybe tomorrow.

I dawdled walking back to the house, sighing and kicking stones along the way. Georgie sat on the garden step, waiting.

I knew it was Sebastian she was waiting for, not me. "Lord Wyatt won't be along until much later."

"I know." She sighed. "It's just that I can't bear it, knowing he's only a mile or two away, when I—"

"Yes, yes, I know. You've missed him fiercely these last weeks. Come along." I pulled her to her feet. "Sitting here won't make the time go any faster."

"As if you weren't doing the same thing. I saw you waiting near the place where Lord Ravencross usually rides." Her voice had a chastising scrape to it. "You shouldn't have turned him away yesterday. I would never send Sebastian away without seeing him."

She didn't understand. How could she? I plucked a yellowing leaf from a nearby bush and studied the pattern of veins on the underside. "It's different for you. You have an understanding with Lord Wyatt, don't you?"

She turned the color of the pink clouds in the dawning sky. "Of sorts. The life of a spy is not—" She stopped and covered her mouth briefly. "*Excuse me.* I meant to say that the life of *a man in diplomatic service* is not conducive to having a wife and children."

"But at least you have the possibility of a future."

"Perhaps." Georgie kicked at a pebble. "But only if this wretched war with Napoleon would ever end. Even then, there are no guarantees. His first allegiance is to the crown."

"The war can't last forever," I said, and instantly regretted how feeble that statement sounded. I wished I could've reassured her with more conviction, so I attempted a lighter tone. "Imagine your mother's delight at having you wed to a viscount." Her mother was keenly interested in advancing herself socially. If Georgie made an advantageous marriage she might finally win her mother's approval.

She chuckled. "I daresay she would swoon at the idea. But, I dare not look that far down the road. The future is too uncertain. That's why I intend to seize every possible moment with Sebastian."

I said nothing to that. It was different between her and Lord Wyatt. I envied her. She had a future. It might not be a perfect one, but at least they had the hope of one.

"Come." I tugged her up the stairs. "Let's find out how Lady Daneska is faring as our prisoner."

We roamed the house in search of Miss Stranje. Our elusive headmistress was nowhere to be found. Odd, how she always shows up at the most inopportune moments, and yet when one wants something, she seems to vanish entirely.

Breakfast arrived at the same hour it always did, but for me it felt as if time had ticked by slower than an old woman's cane. Georgie and I were the first ones seated. The other girls filed in shortly after, as did Mr. Sinclair, who seemed particularly buoyant at that hour of the morning. At exactly nine o'clock, Miss Stranje took her seat at the head of the table.

I frothed at the bit, waiting to find out how Miss Stranje planned to extract the information from Daneska. Except we couldn't speak of it, not yet, not with the servants and our American guest listening. So we ate in strained silence.

I contemplated various methods of interrogation in my head. Confining Daneska with only bread and water would never work. She was made of sterner stuff. I stabbed a potato drenched in rosemary and butter.

How? How could we get her to talk?

Mercifully, Mr. Sinclair broke through the tension and diverted us with his enthusiastic plans for building the small prototype of his warship engine. "We'll need to find something to serve as the piston rod. But we've nearly finished the steam cylinder. Now if I can fabricate a sturdy crank out of some-thing . . ." He twirled his fork in his fingers while he was think-ing. Judging by the look on Jane's face, I thought she might grab it straight out of his hands. But he set it down with a plunk and brightened. "Perhaps I might have one or two of your pokers?"

Miss Stranje followed his covetous gaze to the fireplace tools stored on the hearth. "You may, if that is what is necessary."

"I noticed you've other sets on most of your hearths."

"Yes." She nodded, drawing back. "But do try and leave one or two behind so that we have something with which to tend our fires."

"Yes, miss, certainly. And of course I shall need to visit a wheelwright to have a small flywheel constructed."

Her face puckered momentarily. "I do not think that wise, Mr. Sinclair—"

"Alexander."

"Very well, *Alexander*. A journey to the village puts you in too much danger. If you will make a drawing and a list of the exact dimensions, I shall send Philip to the wheelwright. It will attract far less attention if the order comes from one of us rather than a stranger."

"Excellent! In that case, we'll be whistling right along." He grabbed up his fork as if it were a shovel. "I should also like to try out Miss Barrington's and Miss Fitzwilliam's contributions to my torpedo." He smiled broadly at Georgie. "Installing Con-greve's compression trigger was pure genius. It will be sensitive enough to explode upon impact but not so sensitive that it blows up while we're loading it."

Jane gaped at him. "Egad, I should certainly hope not."

He glossed over her concerns with a cheery wave of his hand. "Don't fret. It's simply a matter of adjusting the spring pressure correctly." Jane did not look mollified. He aimed his next request at me. "Do you think Lord Ravencross might lend us his assistance in building today?"

My only answer was a shrug.

"No matter." Sinclair scooped up another helping of eggs and sausage. "I'll send a note requesting his help. I'm certain he'll oblige us. Then, if we are industrious and finish construction on the prototype tomorrow or the next day, I would like to attempt a test shot."

"A test shot?" Miss Stranje set her spoon down with a sudden and uncustomary clink. "What, *exactly*, do you propose to blow up?"

"That's the question, isn't it? To test the weapon properly, we'll need to aim at something some distance from the shore—"

Our headmistress snapped a piece of toast in half and dropped both halves on her plate. "Wouldn't it suffice to set up a wooden target out in the north pasture? There are trees there to hide the—"

"The blast. No. Wouldn't work." He shook his head, set down his fork, and blotted his mouth with the table linen. "A dry inland test proves nothing. We must see how it performs in water."

Sera spread marmalade on a muffin and mumbled, "Let us hope Mr. Chadwick is not visiting in the vicinity on the day of your test."

"Oh, yes, I see the problem. Might alarm the neighbors." He drummed his fingers briefly on the tablecloth and drank the last of his pear juice. "I have it." He set down the goblet with a plunk and grinned. "If we test it at night, it's bound to make for some picturesque fireworks. If anyone asks, we could simply say we're celebrating."

"Celebrating what?" Jane looked at him as if he was completely balmy.

"I don't know. *Anything.*" Quite jauntily, he added, "My birthday, for example."

"Is it your birthday?" she asked.

"No. I spent that day locked in a room in France. But I wouldn't say no to a delayed celebration. My mother usually bakes a spice cake for the occasion. Delicious. A thick layer of sugar icing, like so." Holding up two fingers, he showed us exactly how thick. His normally lively countenance turned melancholy for a few seconds. "Don't know when, or if, I'll ever taste it again. But no matter."

Sera looked at him quizzically. "Ordinarily, we don't make that much ado over our natal days."

"Ah. More of your English stoicism, I suppose." He studiously mopped up egg yolk with a wedge of toast, as if giving the problem some consideration. "Perhaps this once, if the question arises, you might make an exception."

Finished with the last of his eggs and sausage, he pushed back his plate. "Although it may not be necessary. You are fairly isolated here. It's quite possible no one will notice our little experiment."

"No, and why should they?" Jane spooned clotted cream on her raspberry scone and spread an equally ample serving of sarcasm over the top of her comment. "Surely no one will notice bombs bursting along the shoreline."

"Good heavens." Georgiana glanced up in alarm. "If Mrs. Pinswary sees flames, you know full well she'll march straight over here and accuse me of trying to set fire to the whole county."

We all remembered our neighbor's frantic visit shortly after Georgie first arrived at Stranje House. Miss Pinswary had received a tittle-tattle letter warning that Miss Stranje's newest student was a dangerous arsonist. It was true that Georgie had accidently set fire to her father's stables while trying to cook up an invisible ink. But her parents kept mum about the cause of the fire and when they sent her away to Stranje House, people gossiped and came to some rather unsavory conclusions. Miss Pinsway had been told Georgiana was a criminal who would murder us all in our sleep.

"Very well. A birthday celebration it is." Miss Stranje laid her spoon down carefully. "We shall simply explain to anyone who asks that you are my American cousin and it is your custom to celebrate with fireworks. Advise us when your equipment is ready to test, and we will have Cook bake a cake."

"Excellent." He beamed. "Cake and fireworks. I like the sound of that."

"I'm happy it pleases you. Now, if you would be so good as to excuse us, Mr. Sinclair. The young ladies and I have a few private business matters to discuss." Miss Stranje inclined her head, indicating the door.

"*I see*. Business matters." He rubbed his chin. "And you want me to make myself scarce." The corner of his mouth curled up mischievously. "I reckon this is your equivalent of when the gentlemen excuse themselves so they might enjoy a glass of brandy and discuss horse racing and pugilism, isn't it."

"Not at all, Mr. Sinclair." Miss Stranje smiled genially. "I assure you we won't be discussing anything so important as which horse to back at the races. Ours will simply be a dull conversation about embroidery threads, watercolor lessons, and whatnot. You know the sorts of things young ladies like to discuss in private."

He laughed then, out loud and quite heartily. Rising from his chair, he treated us all to a regal bow. "Then I shall leave you to your discussion of embroidery threads, ladies. My only request is that you do not land us all in a tangle."

He winked at Jane, who turned quite red, and chuckled to himself all the way out of the breakfast room. At a signal from

Miss Stranje, the footmen and Greaves followed him out and closed the doors, giving us our privacy at last.

Miss Stranje did not mince words. "I suppose by now you all know we are holding Lady Daneska prisoner?"

I rushed to ask, "You looked in on her this morning to make sure she hasn't escaped?"

"Yes. You may set your worries aside. She's well secured. Although it troubles me that she appears so contented with her accommodations."

I frowned at that. "Did you use the irons?"

"Of course."

"Then she's pretending. Underneath her bravado, Daneska is seething. You have my word on it." Some devilish part of me felt eager to see her wearing iron cuffs and chains instead of her customary diamonds. But first, I needed to know how best to interrogate the prisoner. "How are we going to get Ghost's whereabouts out of her?"

Sera shook her head. "If you are thinking of torture, it won't work. You know she would simply lie. Not only that, she would do it so effectively that we would be following false trails for months."

"Yes." Miss Stranje carefully sliced a strawberry into four sections and cut away the greenery. "Captain Grey and I came to the same conclusion."

"What, then?" I slammed my hand against the table, rattling the silverware. It startled even me. "Sorry." I glanced at them apologetically. "We have to find him. Before . . ." *Before he comes here and destroys his brother's life or murders him.*

"We must approach this logically." Miss Stranje meticulously wiped strawberry juice from her fingers.

I groaned. She was going to use this moment to exercise her role as our teacher. I wanted to scream *Not now,* but I bit my tongue to hold back my impatience.

"We must ask ourselves, what is it we want?"

I kept my voice level and steady, even though I felt like shaking her. "We want to know where Ghost is."

"True. Finding the leader of the Iron Crown is of vital interest. But at the moment we face a problem of even greater significance."

I stared at her, not liking the direction she was leading us.

Jane nudged me with her elbow. "Napoleon might invade."

"I haven't forgotten." I understood Napoleon's attack took precedence. Except there'd been other matters pressing on my mind. Matters such as protecting Georgie and Lord Ravencross. Except he wasn't Lord Ravencross anymore—*protecting Gabriel.* And there was only one way to do that.

Kill Ghost.

"I think we can all agree that Napoleon's impending attack is our highest priority." Miss Stranje speared one of the strawberry sections with her fork. "With Lady Daneska as our captive, we have a unique opportunity. If we can convince her to get word to Napoleon, warning him that England is prepared for his invasion and that he would be ill-advised to proceed, there is a strong likelihood he will change plans. At the very least, he might postpone his attack."

"But we aren't prepared, and Daneska would never do that." I stared at Miss Stranje, blinking, unable to comprehend her thinking. "Why would she? It's not true. And anyway, we couldn't force her to do it. Are you thinking of sending a letter in her name? I noticed last night she has her signet ring with her, so I suppose—"

"A letter would be too suspect." Miss Stranje took her time delicately consuming the last of her strawberry. "I agree with you that she would never willingly cooperate with us. And I believe I know her well enough to say she cannot be coerced."

Sera had been sitting quietly, studying our headmistress, drawing with her finger on the tablecloth. "You're thinking of misleading her, *tricking* her into carrying false information back to Napoleon."

"Exactly." Miss Stranje tilted her head respectfully at Sera. "If Daneska thinks she alone possesses critical information, she will view it as a prime opportunity to distinguish herself further in Napoleon's esteem."

Jane appeared to be deep in thought. Her crystal goblet hummed as she played the edge with her forefinger. "I daresay she might be even more motivated if she thought giving him this information would sabotage us."

"This is useless conjecture. It's impossible," I said impatiently. "How do you propose to accomplish any of this with Daneska imprisoned here in our—" I stopped, suddenly afraid of Miss Stranje's answer. "You wouldn't."

Miss Stranje clasped her hands in a tight fold.

"Escape!" I turned to the others. "She's suggesting we let Daneska escape." I could see Jane and Sera had already tumbled to this idea. Maya, too. But Georgie looked as horrified as I felt.

"No, you can't." Trembling, I grabbed the edge of the table to steady myself and pleaded. "Have you forgotten she tortured Lord Wyatt? Her betrayal? The secrets she's given our enemies? She's too dangerous. She's a traitor. She's . . ."

My enemy.

All the air seemed to have left the room.

My arguments paled to a silent frozen whisper.

I hated that Miss Stranje waited patiently for me to calm down. I hated the sad expression on her face as if she understood my agony. Most of all, I hated that she was right.

Jane gently laid her hand on my arm, and I finally drew a breath. "It might not be so bad," she said somberly. "It's possible we'll catch two birds with this one dreadful stinking stone. Think, Tess. She'll probably go straight to *him* as soon as she escapes. This way, she'll carry false information to Napoleon and, at the same time, she might lead us to Ghost."

She might. Still, it turned my stomach sour to think of letting our betrayer go.

Miss Stranje spoke in an oddly subdued tone. "We must proceed cautiously or she will see through our plan. We all know how exceptionally clever she is. If this is to work, Lady Daneska must believe that she gleaned this information from us. Not that we fed it to her."

My hand shook as I reached for my glass of lemon water.

Georgie suggested that we *accidentally* let her see us constructing the warship.

"Yes, brilliant." Jane set down her fork. "And it should be fairly easy to make certain she observes Mr. Sinclair's fireworks on test night. At the very least she'll hear the noise from the explosions."

Sera cleared her throat, trying to get our attention. "Perhaps Lord Ravencross might be persuaded to increase the guard around his house. That way Lady Daneska might catch a glimpse of what appears to be an army building up."

"I'm not so sure." Jane turned to Sera. "Local farmers make a rather ramshackle looking army, wouldn't you say?"

Sera acknowledged Jane's criticism with a quick nod and charged bravely forward. "Perhaps, but if we were to bring Mr. Chadwick and his father into our confidence, we might be able to convince them to call out the local militia and post them at either Stranje House or Ravencross Manor."

"Splendid idea, my dear." Miss Stranje leaned forward, with eagerness practically shooting out of her fingertips. "The sound of troops training might be the perfect ploy to convince her that England knows of the threat and is preparing." She sat back. "Although I would prefer we did not bring the Chadwicks *all the way* into our confidence."

By this she meant she didn't want them to know that she was coordinating a spy ring from her girls' school.

"And how do you expect us to do that?" Lady Jane sniffed, carefully setting her silverware at exact angles across her plate. "The younger Mr. Chadwick will not be easily duped."

"He need not be duped at all." Maya's gaze floated gracefully around the table to each of our astonished faces. "Tell him the truth, with a few minor adjustments, and his curiosity will be appeased. Indeed, if he believes he is doing it to save England it will place him in the position of a hero. Something, I daresay, he would rejoice in."

"Minor adjustments?" Miss Stranje's eyes glittered with intrigue.

Maya rolled her palm to me. "Tess might recall something her abductors said about murdering Lord Ravencross so that a French landing party could be housed at Ravencross Manor. Perhaps she now remembers hearing Napoleon's name mentioned." Maya tilted her head and spoke directly to me. "All of Britain is afraid of invasion. If Tess were to deliver this news with sufficient terror, as if she had just awakened to these suppressed memories . . ."

"He would believe her." Sera finished.

Maya smiled. "Just so."

"Excellent." Miss Stranje all but clapped. "Well done, Maya."

Jane set her plate away from her. "A pity Mr. Chadwick must be used so falsely by us."

"Nonsense," Miss Stranje corrected her sharply. "There is

nothing false in it. He may well be saving his country. At least, we must all hope and pray that this tactic will stave off invasion for the next month."

Sera stared at her water glass, turning the stem. "He will like the thought of being a hero."

"Exactly," agreed Miss Stranje. "I shall send an urgent note this very morning."

I shook my head. This was not what I had in mind. *None of it.*

The pulse in my neck throbbed. "Even if we accomplish all this, how will you let Daneska escape? If you make it too easy, she won't believe it. She'll know she's being set up."

Miss Stranje's features softened, and she leaned toward me.

I backed away. Her expression frightened me. I'd a thousand times rather she came at me with her hard, disapproving frown. Not this. Not this caring look, drenched with worry. This one made me want to run.

"Your question brings me to the most difficult part."

I swallowed. *More* difficult than it already was? She leveled that statement at me and I'd rather she'd aimed a knife at me. I could dodge a knife.

"It is my considered opinion that it will be more believable if one of you helps her escape."

"None of us would do that. She'd never believe it," Georgie protested before I'd even fully absorbed Miss Stranje's words.

Miss Stranje stared at me, dripping with reluctance. And yet she pressed forward, coming at me like a surgeon who must hack off the leg of an unlucky soldier. "There is only one of you that she was close enough to believe would help her."

The food in my belly turned to jagged stones. My arms fell to my sides, suddenly heavier than lead weights. "Me? You can't mean me."

Except she did.

"No!" I gasped. "I won't do it. I can't."

Yet even as I said it, I knew that I had to. *I must.*

I swallowed against the bitter taste of bile in my mouth. I could hardly breathe. If she had asked me to beat a confession out of Daneska—I would've gladly done that. If she'd ordered me to ride out and keep riding until I found the real Lord Raven-cross, and then thrust a sword into his heart—I could've done that, too. But not this. She expected me to pretend I cared about Daneska, enough to help her escape.

"It won't work." I shook my head. "I'm no good at lying."

"No, you're not." She took a deep breath and launched into a sermon. "It's quite possible this task will prove beneficial for you as well."

Impossible.

She wanted me to ask how. But I didn't. Because I knew what she was suggesting and it was impossible.

Undaunted she pressed on. "It is not healthy for you to harbor ill will toward another human being."

I drew back, indignant. *Make no mistake about it, I do not harbor ill will. My ship of ill will rides boldly across a sea of anger in glorious billowing full sail.*

"Forgiveness can bring peace."

Peace?

Me?

I almost laughed. Didn't she know? I was not made for peace. I was made for unrest, for sleepless nights, for dreams of unspeakable terror. I was made for madness, not peace.

"I know Lady Daneska hurt you. She betrayed all of us, you most of all, because you were closest to her. But she knows what we all know deep inside . . ." Miss Stranje waited for me to meet her gaze. Waited to see if I was actually absorbing any of her sermon.

She reached for me, but my arms stayed where they were, wrapped tight around my middle, too busy holding me together.

She silently pleaded with me to listen. "Hatred and anger are not the opposites of love, Tess. They are backsides of the same playing cards. It is easier to flip hostile feelings over and find the love and forgiveness that have been hidden there all along, aching to be found, than it is to produce new feelings."

Through gritted teeth, I shot a question at her. "Then what is the opposite of love?" *Because whatever that is, that's what I feel for Daneska.*

"Indifference."

One word. One word that hit me in the gut so hard I almost doubled over. Because I didn't feel indifferent toward Dani. I couldn't.

Miss Stranje pitied me then. I could see it. So I closed my eyes.

"Do you see why you're the only one here who Daneska would believe could soften her heart enough to help her escape?"

I sank back. Curling into the chair. Massaging my forehead. Scarcely able to keep down breakfast.

It was too much. I covered my face with my hands. I had only just accepted the fact that I must become a murderer and kill Ghost. Now Miss Stranje was demanding I forgive my greatest enemy and become her friend, so that ultimately I could betray her.

I wondered briefly which of these two—murder or forgiveness—would prove more treacherous to my soul.

Miss Stranje broke into my whirling thoughts. "Will you do it?"

"No." Sera stood abruptly. "We can't ask this of Tess. Look at her. This is too painful for her. I'll do it."

"She'd never believe it of you, Sera." Jane sounded mournful. "Remember how she used to call you a useless mouse. She never really liked the two of us. Only Tess." Jane reached for my shoulder; her touch was gentle, but her pity pressed more weight atop it. "I'm sorry," she said. "You know I'd take your place if I could."

I stared at my plate.

"I might be able to help you," Maya said in a soothing, lyrical voice.

Surprised, I looked up. "How? What do you propose to do? Mesmerize me into not hating Daneska?" I hadn't meant for it to sound as biting as it did.

"Not exactly. Although music and meditation might help you forget some of the anger you feel toward her."

Did I want to do that? Forget Daneska's betrayal? No.

Georgie sat across from me, watching my every move with worried eyes. "We'll *all* help you."

"Good," I said, with more enthusiasm than I felt. "Help me by strangling her."

"As to that," Miss Stranje said cryptically, drawing our attention. "We will need to make genuine attempts to get information from her. I'm afraid we must use some rather . . . er . . . persuasive methods, even though we know they won't work. If we don't, Daneska won't believe it when Tess helps her escape."

Sera kept staring at me, her brow squeezed up in worry. "This is going to be very difficult for you. Perhaps I should try. She disliked me, but she might believe I am weak enough to feel sorry for her, and—"

Dear sweet Sera, she was kind, but not weak. Never that. And not even Lady Daneska, in all her cynicism, would believe Seraphina Wyndham could be disloyal.

"No. Jane's right. Daneska and I were like sisters before you came." I pushed away from the table and stood. Somehow, I would have to find a way to stop hating her. "God help me, it will have to be me."

Twenty

DECEPTION

Scarcely a half hour went by after Miss Stranje sent the note before Mr. Chadwick and his father rushed into Stranje House in a state of great alarm. They were shown again into the blue parlor, where Miss Stranje laid the groundwork. I was some moments later ushered in, after having pinched my face almost to the point of bruising it and drizzling salt water down my cheeks. I did my best to produce tears, but after so many years of resisting them, the ruddy things wouldn't come. I relied upon an attitude of utter panic to carry my part.

"Oh, sirs! Thank goodness you've come." I collapsed into a chair and feigned such wide-eyed distress that both men drew back nervously. When I clutched at the elder Mr. Chadwick's hand, and told him my dreadful tidings and begged him to do something, his weathered pallor whitened.

"Good heavens, child."

"If only I'd remembered this horrible news sooner. The very name Napoleon fills me with terror. That must be why I forgot.

And to think that those awful men were sent to kill Lord Raven-cross so that they might clear the way for Napoleon to launch his attack."

He rubbed his chin, deep in thought. "Makes sense. No fortresses nearby to contend with like there are at Dover or Chatham, and it's a straight road from here to London."

How this speech was supposed to comfort me I could not tell. "So you can understand why I am speechless with fear. Please, sir, tell me you can do something, I beg of you."

"Yes, my dear. Rest assured, we will do something." He patted my hand, huffled and puffled, floundering for speech. "These are bad times. Bad times, indeed." He glanced desperately about the room.

"I'm not entirely sure how these things work." Miss Stranje spoke with an innocent hesitancy that did not come naturally to her. "But since you are the magistrate, can you not call up our local militia?"

At this, he leapt up and began to pace with great agitation. "No, miss. That would be our Lord Lieutenant, a good friend, and the very man who appointed me magistrate. My son and I shall ride with all haste to his estate, where we will explain the situation. He will immediately do all that is required to protect our country, of that you can be certain."

"Thank you," I answered quietly.

The younger Mr. Chadwick bowed elegantly to me as they were taking their leave. "Is there anything more you would like to tell us, Miss Aubreyson?"

There was such genuineness about him that I almost faltered. In a hushed voice he asked, "If there is something else—"

Miss Stranje rushed to my aid and put her arms about my shoulders. "I'm afraid this whole experience has overtaxed her, Mr. Chadwick. We are so very grateful to you for handling these dreadful matters for us. I confess we were beside ourselves trying to figure out what ought to be done."

"Course you were," boomed his father. "Far too grievous a situation for the weaker sex to manage. You need a man about the place, Miss Stranje. You did right sending for us. Now we must be off to advise the Lord Lieutenant of these grievous circumstances. I've no doubt but what he will muster up the militia as quickly as can be done. You and the young ladies will have protection, Miss Stranje, even if I have to load up my musket and come guard the place m'self. Come along, Quinton."

Miss Stranje seated herself in the chair beside me. "Sharp eyes, that young man. I shall have to watch him." I wasn't sure what she meant by that, whether to watch out for him or to put him to work in her little family of spies.

"You performed admirably, my dear."

"I feel guilty."

"I see no reason why you should. Everything we told them is dangerously close to the truth. England is in peril at the moment. You and I are simply trying to preserve the country we love the best way we know how." She leaned back in the chair and sighed. "I sent word by courier to Lord Castlereagh's office. But with the wars stretching our military to the breaking point, the political climate shifting, and French sympathizers in the House of Lords making so much noise, unless an attack actually occurs on British soil, I fear the foreign secretary's hands are tied."

I liked climbing walls and throwing knives, but just then I didn't like the other parts of being a spy or, as Miss Stranje preferred to call us, diplomatic aides.

"You know what must be done now?"

I must face Lady Daneska. More deception.

I nodded.

"I think you should hand me your dagger for safekeeping."

"You're afraid I'll use it on her."

"Hmm." She held out her palm. I lifted my skirts and unsheathed my newest weapon and handed it over. "Shall we be going?"

Miss Stranje decreed that I should be the one to bring Daneska her food. Something about how food softens the heart. If she planned to soften Daneska's heart, she was going to have to offer better fare than gruel and crusty bread. She led the way downstairs to the underbelly of Stranje House, giving me a few instructions along the way, but most of the time we walked in awkward silence. When we reached the bottommost floor, she pressed a large brass key into my hand and whispered, "Thank you for your bravery, Tess. I wish I could spare you this task."

I folded my fingers around the key. "She can no longer hurt me."

Even though we both knew it was a lie, she didn't argue with me. She simply brushed my arm sadly and pointed the way. "The cell is down this hallway. Turn to your right after you pass the discipline chamber. It is the door at the far end." She stepped into the shadows. "I shall wait for you here."

Stranje House had dungeons left over from the Tudor years when there were enemies around every corner. Even back then, Miss Stranje's ancestors were involved in political intrigues. But as dungeons go, this one wasn't as bad as one might imagine. There were no dead rats or skeletons. Not yet, anyway. I unlocked the heavy oaken door, and the hinges groaned as it creaked open.

The small chamber was shadowy but not as dim as the hallway. At the top of the wall there was a small window, about the size of a cutlery box, providing some light. The glass was crusted with a salt glaze from the moist sea air, which made it difficult to see through. The gray stone walls held in the damp and cold even though it was summer. Mold crept through cracks, and a slow, dark sludgelike moisture seeped through, leaving black trails to the floor. Greaves had laid a pallet on the stones along with a woolen blanket.

"So the noble Countess Valdikauf is reduced to sleeping on the floor."

She sat up atop the pallet looking as regal as possible considering there was no throne and she was chained to the wall. Although they had given her a generously long leash. I'd have much rather seen her arms stretched between two iron rings. Instead, she had ample chain and looked altogether too comfortable.

Gruel sloshed in the bowl and the crust of dry bread tumbled about the tray as I carried it into her cell. I wrinkled my nose. Her chamber pot stunk, but I wasn't about to empty it for her.

Despite the stench, she smiled up at me, still as confident as if we were meeting in a grand parlor. "I'm surprised Miss Stranje trusted you to be alone with me."

I stood by the door with that stupid tray and didn't know what to say. "What makes you think she did?"

She smirked. "Because I'm not already dead."

I laughed at that. I don't know why. It seemed enormously funny to me. Funny that Daneska knew how murderous I felt toward her and yet Miss Stranje supposed I could turn this relationship around and convince the bloodless Countess Valdikauf that we were such dear close friends that I would help her escape.

In that moment I realized how utterly absurd this plan was. I decided to stop pretending, because it was useless. "Maybe I poisoned your food." I glanced menacingly at the gruel. "You never know."

"Oh, but I do know, my dear Tessika. Poison is not your style."

"Don't call me that," I snapped.

She shrugged. "You are most assuredly the knife type. If you decided to kill me, you would use that lovely blade you have strapped to your leg." She pointed to my calf. "That isn't to say that you wouldn't strangle me given enough provocation."

"True. About the strangling, I mean." I glanced down at where the sheath was hidden beneath my dress. "But Miss Stranje made me remove my dagger."

"*Mon Dieu.*" She clucked her tongue. "Tessie without her blade." She chuckled at this. "Do you think our Miss Stranje was afraid I might grab your leg and seize your trusty knife?" She shook her head, golden curls dancing. "Surely she knows you would best me in a fight. Especially because I am forced to wear these charming bracelets." She held out her wrists, admiring the iron manacles as if they were encrusted with jewels. "No. I believe she confiscated it so you would not run me through when I irritated you sufficiently."

"You've already irritated me sufficiently. Do you want this food or not?"

"That is a silly question. How could I possibly *want* that?" she sneered coldly at the meager offering on the tray, all the amusement gone. "But I suppose this swill is all she will give me." She waved her hand and turned away. "Leave it. Set it down. Unless you plan to stay and feed me by hand."

"Hardly." I plunked it on the floor beside her, spilling some of the weak gruel. "I rather thought I'd dump it over your head. But only if you said you wanted it."

"Tessie, Tessie." She grinned and reached for the porridge. "You haven't changed a bit."

"That's where you're wrong." I gripped the key tight in my fist. "I've changed a great deal. I know better than to trust the likes of you."

Having been denied the luxury of a spoon, Daneska drank

watery porridge and peered at me over the lip of the bowl. "Why must you always take things so personally? You had nothing to do with the decisions I made."

She didn't look so haughty now with gruel smeared on her upper lip. "That's just it," I said. "You didn't care about anyone else's feelings when you made those decisions."

"*C'est la vie.*" She shrugged. "I did what was necessary. The Germans, they have a saying, *In der Not frisst der Teufel Fliegen.* In times of trouble, even the devil eats flies. One must do what one must do."

"Perfect. Then you should be very comfortable down here so close to hell. Although I'm not sure how many flies you'll be able to catch with no windows."

It had always annoyed me that she mixed her languages so readily, but now it made sense. Daneska felt no allegiance to any particular country.

"*Touché.* See, you haven't changed." She wiped her mouth on her sleeve. "I've missed you. We must catch up. Tell me, how are your dreams these days?"

I grimaced and turned away so she wouldn't see. "You have no right to ask about something so private." Never mind that she already knew more about my dreams than most people did. I'd been a fool to trust her so easily back then.

"Oh, but Tessika, I like talking about your dreams."

"Well, I don't."

"I told him about you, you know."

"What?" I spun around.

"You heard me. Yes, I told Emperor Napoleon himself about you—that you see the future in your dark dreams. He was most intrigued."

I shivered. "Why would you do that?"

"Ah, well, you see, the emperor, he is quite fascinated with dreams. He showed me one of his prized possessions, his Oraculum. A most interesting little book that he found in the tombs of Egypt or somewhere or other. Red leather, about so big, with celestial symbols etched across the cover. He calls it his *Book of Fates* and told me it allows him to interpret dreams."

"How can a book do that?"

With a casual lift of her shoulder, she feigned ignorance. "It contained a great many charts and numbers, and a list of symbols. Very complex and scientific. *Naturallement*, he would be able to explain it to you much better than I."

"Hmm. But since that will never happen—"

"It could." She sat up much straighter, like a snake rearing up because it sees a mouse within striking distance. "It could happen. He is most desirous of meeting you. And I have always known you were bound for greatness."

"Greatness?" I scoffed. "Madness, yes. Greatness, no." Bound for hell, judging by the way my fingers itched to grab her neck. "Flattering me is pointless. You are just trying to get me to help you escape."

"I would not flatter you, *mon amie*. We know each other too well for that." She tore off a piece of bread and held it up, contemplating it. "Me, I do not need visions to know the future. I have eyes and a mind. These dreams of yours, they come for a purpose. It must surely mean there is something of consequence you must do."

I had a purpose, all right. It was to stop her and Ghost. But I bit my tongue and aimed for sarcasm—always a safe place to hide one's feelings. "And the great Emperor Napoleon, I suppose he told you to invite me to court."

"*Brava.* Brilliant guess." Her chains clinked as she raised her hands in mock applause. "He did! He invited you to his palace."

"You jest."

"No. I am quite serious." The mockery melted from her face. She was telling the truth.

Still, I found it impossible to comprehend. "My dreams are filled with nothing but inscrutable horrors. Why would he have any interest in those?"

"Ah, but that is the very reason you must come with me to Paris, so Napoleon can help you interpret them."

"I hate my dreams," I muttered, shaking my head. She had to be lying.

"*Hush*, you must not say this. Why would you despise such a gift? Napoleon says our dreams teach us that which we must know. It is for us to discover what the fates wish us to learn."

I crossed my arms, refusing to take secondhand instruction from a pompous despot like Napoleon. "If his fates serve him so well, why did he fail so miserably in Russia? How come he was defeated and exiled on Elba? No, you and your emperor can keep these fate-spawned dreams, if that's what these are. It is no gift to close my eyes at night and watch men die."

"Perhaps, you will change your mind," she said softly, as if she planned to do the changing for me.

I wasn't sure how all this fit into Miss Stranje's scheme to help Daneska escape. I may have played my part incorrectly. I suppose I ought to have capitalized on her offer, but the thought sickened me. Especially when I considered the silver bowl and swirling green water from my dreams.

So I said nothing. The silence thickened and hung heavy between us until her gaze darted to the small window. "I hear hammering and the sound of metal being pounded. What are they building?"

"Nothing." I made a show of trying to distract her from the window by shoving her tray with the toe of my shoe. "Eat your food or I'll take it away."

She sopped the bread in her remaining gruel. "You need not be so ill-mannered. That temper of yours will spoil your pretty face."

"And why shouldn't I be angry? Your henchmen almost killed me."

She shrugged. "*Idiots.* They were sent to do a simple task and botched it completely."

"A simple task? By that you mean you sent them to abduct Georgie and kill Lord Ravencross."

I intentionally used Gabriel's title, and she flinched.

I leaned against the heavy wood of the door, which was the cleanest part of the chamber. "I understand why you wanted Georgie, for the ink. But why kill Lord Ravencross?"

"Don't call him that."

"Why not? He is the rightful Lord of Ravencross."

"Don't play coy, Tess. You know he is not."

I baited her further. "Even so, why do you hate him so much that you would have him murdered?"

" 'Hate' is too strong a word, *mon amie.* It is more that he is an irritation, like a gnat at a picnic. The troublesome kind, that buzzes and buzzes and no matter how often you swat it, it keeps coming back and annoying everyone."

How dare she liken him to a gnat? I wanted to swat *her.* "I suppose it is like the rats that crawl through these dungeons at night. Running every which way, snapping and nibbling on fingers no matter how many traps we set."

Daneska hated rats. She'd abhorred Punch and Judy when I discovered them as babies in a nest and took them to raise as pets. She'd tried on several occasions to feed them to the stable cats.

"You can go." She tried to dismiss me, shooing me away with a wave of her hand, but her clinking chains spoiled the effect.

"I'm supposed to stay and take the tray when you are done. Miss Stranje doesn't want you fashioning a weapon with it."

She chuckled at that, even with a mouthful of bread. She ate with her fingers and somehow managed to make it look elegant. "And I suppose she gives me only this scratchy wool blanket and denies me soft sheets because she is worried I might wind them together and make a rope with which to hang myself."

I scoffed at that. "We all know you would never do anything so convenient as hang yourself."

Her face pinched together in a rare frown, but she quickly banished it. "No more fussing. Come, Tessika, sit beside me. You must tell me all about your life here since I left." She patted the pallet, but I remained standing. "You have fallen in love, I think. *Oui?*"

I couldn't help it—I drew in too quick a breath.

She tittered, her fake laugh, the one that sounded like breaking glass. "So you like him, this young pretender who lives at Ravencross." She would not call him lord.

I refused to let her pull me in to her web.

"There's no sense denying it," she teased. "I see it on your face."

"How? It's so dark in here, you can't see anything clearly." I walked to the window and stretched up on my tiptoes, attempting to clean off a spot. The grime of several years wouldn't give way easily, but I was able to rub off enough that it provided a filmy portal.

There was that jingling laugh again. "I can see you well enough to know."

"Hand me the tray. You've had enough."

"Why him, Tessie?" She snatched the last of the bread and set it in her lap. "You are beautiful. You could have other suitors. Better ones." I'd forgotten how sincere she sounded when she tried. In a soft, caring voice, she lamented, "Why him?"

"It doesn't matter." I grabbed the tray from her.

"Doesn't it?"

"No." It had the horrible ring of truth, because it *didn't* matter why I liked him, or even why I loved him. Gabriel and I had no future.

"It's just as well." She sounded oddly subdued. Relieved. Almost as if my feelings truly did matter to her.

Impossible.

Nothing ever mattered to Daneska beyond her own desires. She studied the vastly uninteresting floor, and I guessed she was contemplating the fact that Ghost planned to kill his younger brother.

"You're not going to kill Gabriel. Neither of you are. I won't let you."

I left the dungeon, and Miss Stranje waited exactly where I'd left her. We climbed the stairs in silence. Not until we stepped out on the main floor did she speak. "Well?"

"It's done. I cleaned the window as well as I could without being obvious, but I only managed to clear a small circle." I heaved a sigh and shook my head. "It's so high. She'll have to climb the wall. If her chains don't reach, she'll have to jump if she's to see anything at all. Even then it will be very little."

"She's resourceful. She'll think of something." Miss Stranje stopped to adjust a painting hanging on the wall of the back gallery. "Do you think she suspected anything?"

"No. But I did nothing for her to suspect. We bickered mostly."

"Good." She picked up the pace. The soles of her shoes clicked decisively against the floorboards. "Exactly as I expected."

"*Good?*" I caught her arm, and one of her ancestors glared down at me from a painting. I let go. "Don't you see? Resurrecting our friendship could take a very long time. *Ages.* If ever."

"Of course. These things take time." She continued down the hall with me tagging alongside.

"*Time,* yes. But we don't have forever to work with here." How long *did* we have, I wondered.

"Very well, I see your point. Tell me exactly what the two of you said. If you are right, we may need to change plans. Unfortunately, we have very few options."

I walked beside her, telling her all that had transpired between Daneska and me. Most of it, anyway. I left out the part where Dani accused me of being in love with Ravencross.

I was so absorbed in the telling of it, I hadn't realized she'd led us to the side door that opens onto the garden. She stopped with her hand on the knob.

"Nothing you've told me makes me think we should abandon hope. On the contrary, it went much better than I'd anticipated. Well done." She clapped my shoulder. "I will leave you here. They're all out there, working on the ballista. The day is quite fine. After that dreary dungeon, perhaps you ought to enjoy some sunshine."

She was up to something. I could tell. What's more, she knew I could tell. She tilted her head, indicating what lay beyond the door. "Go on, then. He won't bite."

Gabriel. She meant Gabriel. I swallowed. Me, I'm not afraid of anything. I've leapt from a pier to catch a moving ship. I've stood, knife drawn, in a field facing a gang of murderers. In London, I fought hand to hand with Daneska's henchmen. But the thought of meeting Gabriel made my legs weak.

I've listened to the other girls talk enough to know this wasn't the silly weakness love produces. It couldn't be. I thought of a hundred excuses for my nerves. The strain of having dealt with Daneska. The part I had to play with the Chadwicks. Yes, there were a myriad of other reasons. But the pure and simple truth was I didn't trust myself to not want to run to him and wrap my arms around his neck as I'd seen Georgie do to Lord Wyatt.

It was unfair that Miss Stranje should foist this situation on me. I lifted one eyebrow, intentionally trying to appear severe. "I'm surprised at you, Miss Stranje. What kind of girls' school are you running where the gentlemen are allowed to run tame among your students?"

"Wicked child." The corner of her mouth turned up in a half smile and she turned the handle, leaving me standing there with the door swinging open in full view of the horde of people out in our garden.

The day was fine and it might have been lovely in the garden, except all the sawing and hammering and pounding of metal somewhat spoiled the effect. Ravencross looked up at me, and my foolish knees melted.

I told myself I would simply speak with him to make certain he was healing properly. That's all. Except someone needed to convince him to hire more men. I could do that. I ought to find out if farmer Jason's son was able to stay alert through the night. Oh, yes, these were dandy excuses. Perfect reasons to stand next to him and watch his mouth move as he answered. First-rate deceptions every one of them.

Truth was, I wanted to be near him.

What harm would there be in just being near him? So long as I remembered it was only in passing. A fleeting moment of pleasure. Why not eat, drink, and be merry, for tomorrow we die? If only there wasn't the die part. My heart dropped. It felt as if the darn thing tumbled down the steep stairs of Stranje House and sank past Daneska's cell, past hope, into a dark, bottomless dungeon.

He stared at me and his face was glorious to behold. I had no idea—No, that's not true. I'd always thought he would be that beautiful when he smiled, *really smiled*. Except it was more than that. He looked like his angelic namesake, a glorious heavenly being who had no business loving the likes of me.

I've always said I don't cry. And I don't. Heavens above, I'd just tried my hardest when the Chadwicks were here and couldn't produce a tear to save my life. So this wasn't crying. It's possible a droplet of water leaked out of the corner of one stupid eye, because I felt the salty wetness burning a trail down the side of my cheek and dashed it away.

The breeze lifted his dark locks as he walked toward me. All I could do was watch, envious that the wind could run her fingers through his hair and I could not. He had the good grace not to bow. Instead, he tilted his head and watched me descend the garden stairs.

I tripped on the third step. Tripped. *Me*, who could dance better than anyone else here, could run without falling across sheep pastures riddled with obstacles, and perform Madame Cho's defensive movements flawlessly.

I stumbled.

He reached for me, clasped my hand to keep me safe, and suddenly I felt grateful for my graceless moment. I held his hand until I reached the last stair.

"Will you walk with me?" he asked.

Would I walk with him? Tongue-tied and stupidly shy for no reason at all, I nodded. Except I didn't want to walk here in the park, not where they would all be watching us. And especially not if Lady Daneska had found a way to peek through her dungeon portal and spy on the goings-on in the yard.

He must have noticed my reluctance, because he offered an alternative. "The day is warm. We might take the path along cliffs."

Twenty-one

SYMBOLS

I liked walking with him. I liked the even rhythm of our steps as we crossed the gravel drive, and the easy way we navigated rangy mounds of green thistles and clumps of sea grasses waving gently along the cliffs overlooking the sea. The tide was in, splashing hard against the rocks below, sending cool spray up every third or fourth wave. Yes, I liked walking with Ravencross. Except he wasn't Ravencross.

"What was your name before you became Lord of Ravencross?"

"Helmsford." He scooped up a handful of small stones and threw one of them, side-armed, out into the ocean. "Simple, uncomplicated Gabriel Helmsford. And I'd give a considerable sum to go back to it."

I bit my tongue, holding back the secret that wanted to come rushing out. I steered the subject to a less volatile topic. "I suppose you know that Lord Wyatt and Captain Grey captured Lady Daneska. We're holding her at Stranje House."

"So I heard." He sent another stone soaring out over the water. "Why wouldn't you see me yesterday?"

"I was working," I said defensively. "Trying to figure out where Daneska had set up her lair. Trying to keep you safe."

He turned to me, gripping the last of his stones in his fist. "When are you going to stop this absurd quest to protect me?"

"When I'm convinced you're out of danger."

"It's a dangerous world. None of us are ever safe." He threw the last stone, sent it sailing so far out that neither of us would be able to see it fall into the sea. "It's foolishness, Tess. Tilting at windmills. As far as I'm concerned, there are worse things than death."

"Not to me."

"Anyway, they caught Lady Daneska, so you wasted your time." He stepped in front of me, bringing me to a halt. "Time you might better have spent with me."

A decision I'd regretted, but I had my reasons. Perfectly sound reasons. "I told you—"

"I know what you said. You can't marry me because there's only death ahead of you." He leaned over me, frowning. "That makes every minute we have even more valuable, wouldn't you say?"

Even though his nearness warmed me to my toes, I backed up. Afraid I'd selfishly forget how loving me would destroy him. "You don't understand."

"No, I don't." He pressed forward. "Enlighten me."

The ocean lapped in and out, crashing against my frantic thoughts. I didn't want to tell him about the madness that awaited me. I couldn't bear to think of him pitying me. The thought of him viewing me as a broken creature to be locked in an attic sickened me. But he deserved at least some of the truth.

"My mother died." It sounded vague and flat, but it felt raw and naked.

I gathered the fabric of my neckline, clutching it, looking up at him, uncertain. His brown eyes held a tenderness that warmed me like morning cocoa. His hair hung loose by his cheek. So near. Mere inches from my hand. I could almost reach up and—

"Tell me about her," he said.

My lips parted in surprise. No one had ever asked that of me. People had asked how she died, and about her dreams. Sad details. No one had ever asked me about *her*.

A thousand scattered memories of her rushed to mind—good, happy, wondrous moments. My mother was more than her madness. Salt stung my eyes. Yes, that was it, not tears, it was the salt air. I blinked the stinging away.

"She . . . she was kind and gentle. Loving. Not like me. I'm more like my father. Mama was small and delicate. She reminded me of a wood sprite." I caught my lip and looked away, at the grass blowing along the cliffs, embarrassed at having exposed such a childish thought.

"Mama loved the forest . . . and animals. Especially animals. I remember her teaching me to recognize the high-pitched cry of a baby hedgehog and showing me where the foxes hid their kits. She understood the language of trees and grasses. Songs, she called them. All creatures, even the insects and butterflies, sang songs. She taught me to recognize the songs of the woods, and so I did. The tune the wind plays through the leaves when a storm is coming. The ripple of the brook drumming on stones, and how it roars just before a flash flood."

I felt a flush of excitement as I told him these things, things I'd kept buried for years.

"She used to tell me how the vales and forests were our true home." I stopped talking. My chest began to squeeze too hard. I swallowed and bit down on my lip.

I miss her.

A tendril of hair blew across my eyes, and he tucked it behind my ear. "What about your father?"

I fought the urge to lean my cheek into his hand. "They'd known each other since they were children. When he died, I thought her heart would remain broken forever. Maybe it did. Her dreams got worse after that. Except it's hard to know, Napoleon's conquests grew worse then, too. During the Peninsular War, she would wake up sweating and gasping for air."

I had to tell him the rest of it then, the ugly part. "The dreams drove her mad. She ran crying into the woods and fell to her death in a ravine."

A blast of sea spray sent the two of us dashing away from the edge of the cliffs.

"You may as well know the whole thing. Dreams killed my grandmother, too. They terrified her so much that one night her heart stopped. My grandfather grieved all the rest of his days. Then when my mother . . . " I pressed my face into my hands. "Gabriel, this curse . . . I refuse to burden you with it. I won't."

He gently pulled my hands down and forced me to look at him. "You *are* like your mother. You have her passion for nature and living things." He ran his fingers down the side of my face. "Tess, there's a warmth about you. It's as if you radiate love. It's almost unexplainable. Whenever I'm with you, my pain lessens."

"In your shoulder?"

He shook his head. "Not just there." He laid a fist over his heart. "Don't you see, your curse is loving too much. You try to hide it. You cloak it beneath a flimsy veil of anger. But the truth is you care so deeply it puts the rest of us to shame."

I pulled from the comfort of his hand and looked away, feeling even more naked than before. My thoughts fluttered in a hundred confusing directions.

He caught my shoulder, not allowing me to escape. "I've seen it time and time again. Like the day you risked stealing my horse to help Georgie. And in London, the way you fought Daneska's men to protect her. You would've willingly died to save her. I saw it then, and even that time you dared me—the day we kissed. Do you remember?"

I would remember that day until my last breath.

"I knew what you were doing. Some people might've thought you were brazen. I knew better. You were so brave, the way you tried to break through to me. I saw even then, how deeply you cared. Although why you chose to care about me, I cannot fathom." He let go of my hand. "There are far worse curses, Tess. We all live under one kind or another."

He raked a hand through his hair and turned to stare at the churning sea. "My father . . . Dear God, if you'd known him, you'd understand. Just being his son was a curse. Your mother cared too much. Whereas my father beat us for being too soft. Nothing we did was ever good enough. Sometimes he thrashed us just to ensure we would harden up."

He glanced back at me, shame distorting his features. "We were to be lords, you see. *Rulers.* And rulers must be feared if they're to maintain order. They must be relentless in administering justice. Poachers must be hanged. Rents must be paid on time, regardless of the harvest. Never let the tenants think you're soft, or they'll take advantage."

I saw then, in his haunted eyes, the lost forlorn boy.

"My brother, Lucien, suffered even more than I. He was the heir. Father never let him forget it. He insisted Lucien must be forged of iron if he intended to take his place as Lord of Ravencross. God, how I hated that title. It stood for cruelty."

I wished desperately I could take his agony away. But how could I save him from these things that had already happened? He was Gabriel, my beautiful, scarred Gabriel, in spite of or maybe because of all those wretched things that had happened to him.

He pointed at Ravencross Manor. "Those men . . ." He bowed his head. "Tess, do you know why those men have come to stand guard?"

I shook my head, waiting for him to tell me the answer.

"It's not because of the coin I offered to pay. No, my tenants heard rumors that I was in danger and they are sending their old men and young boys, anyone they can spare from the fields, to protect me. I've had to send dozens of them away with my thanks and a loaf of bread for their trouble. But do you know why they come? It's because I am *not* my father. They are terrified that whoever inherits the estate after me will be as unyielding as my brother was, or my father, and his father was before him."

Gabriel's shoulders sagged, his head bowed in shame. "All my life I tried to please him. A tyrant." He looked up then, rage sparking like flint in his brown eyes. "My brother and I learned to bear his whippings without flinching, and yet Father still thought I was too weak. 'It's not good enough to have muscle on the outside,' he would say. 'One must have steel on the inside.' The army was his idea. He thought battle would toughen me up, bought a commission for me and sent me packing." A sad, caustic laugh jarred Gabriel's shoulders. "Battle was a reprieve as far as I was concerned. Until . . ."

The familiar remorse twisted his features, and I knew he was thinking of that day with his brother.

I felt sorry for Lucien, too, knowing that the monster he'd become was not entirely of his own making. I ached to tell

Gabriel the truth, knowing it might ease some of his pain, but knowing also it would generate new anguish.

There must be right words somewhere in the world to comfort him, but I couldn't find them. Even the old language deserted me. Empty, I had nothing to give but myself. So I wrapped my arms around him and pressed my cheek against his chest.

His heart pounded and crashed as violently as the surf. When he finally surrendered and rested his arms around me, I felt him ease. Warmth washed through me. And *peace*.

He held me and I felt his lips kiss my hair. He asked, "Do you understand now?"

I nodded. Wishing this small miraculous moment of peace would last longer. I had so few. But it couldn't. It mustn't. "I understand," I whispered, sadly letting go. "Even so, I could never let you suffer through my madness. You don't know what it's like."

He held me away from him, gripping my shoulders, and frowned. "You would rather make me suffer without you?"

Peace evaporated like the ocean spray and left me dry, lonely, and hurting.

I lowered my eyes, unable to answer his question, and so I dodged it with a query of my own. "About those extra men your farmers wanted to send . . ."

I laid out our plan to trick Lady Daneska, and he agreed to begin drilling a small troop on the grounds at Ravencross. We stopped and stared out at the sea. It was fair and calm today, no ominous swells rising from her balmy blue depths. The breeze was light and gently blew through our hair. I could've stood there relishing that moment for a great long while except for a bee that buzzed annoyingly close to my head.

Bees and wasps have never bothered me in the past. I've never been stung. Indeed, they've been known to crawl on my hand and leave me as unscathed as a rose petal. That's why it surprised me to have one flit so menacingly close. A large bee, too. Larger than most. Light glinted off its wings, and the bee shimmered gold.

I stared openmouthed. It was actually made of gold. An entirely golden bee, both wings and body. A moment later another shining bee appeared. Then there was not two bees, but five, then ten, and all of them angrily darting to and fro about my head. I waved my arms, trying to shoo them away.

Gabriel frowned. "What is it? What's wrong?"

"The bees," I said, swatting to defend myself as one of them buzzed toward my mouth.

Ten bees turned into twenty and then a swarm. I ran, calling to Gabriel that we must run for shelter. I worried when I heard no answer and didn't see him running alongside me. Through the swarm of golden bees encircling me, I saw Gabriel still back on the cliffs.

He was kneeling over me holding my unconscious body. Calling my name. Trying to rouse me.

"I hate these dreams," I said and ceased running. *Why should I try to escape the inescapable?*

I allowed the golden bees to batter and sting me. They swarmed over me, crawling into my nose and up my skirts, a great stinging, suffocating blanket.

Twenty-two

DAYDREAMS

I awoke to find Gabriel holding me, his fingers stroking my cheek. Relief washed the distress from his features. He hugged me close and sighed. "You're back."

Not dead?

At least, not dead yet. I grimaced. My skin burned from where the golden bees had stung me over and over again. I rubbed my arm but did not feel the welts I'd expected. I inhaled fresh air and let go of the scorching heat that had filled my lungs. As I did, the searing pain began to fade.

Renewed worry furrowed his brow. "What's wrong?" he begged. "Tell me."

This was the very thing I meant to spare him. Waking dreams. Mad visions. I couldn't talk about it, not yet. Wisps of sunlight shone like a halo around his dark curls.

I looked away, unable to bear his anxious expression, and saw Miss Stranje and Captain Grey running toward us. She must've been using her spyglass again.

Breathless, they reached us and Gabriel answered their questioning gazes. "I don't know what's wrong. We were talking and all of a sudden she collapsed. I think she's in pain."

Miss Stranje knelt beside me and brushed my hair away from my forehead. "What was it, Tess? What did you see?"

"Nothing. Pure lunacy. Bees. Not even real bees. They were made of gold. A swarm of them attacking me for no reason."

What would she make of that?

Gabriel tightened his grip on me. "She's not well."

Captain Grey placed his hand on Miss Stranje's arm. Exchanging grim glances, they came to some sort of silent conclusion.

Captain Grey took charge. "We will discuss this later, Miss Aubreyson. For now, I think it would be best to take you back to the house so you can rest. Do you think you can walk?"

"I'll carry her." Gabriel started to lift me.

"And rip your stitches? Thank you very much, but I think not." I felt stronger with every passing minute. "I can manage on my own." I struggled to sit up, but Gabriel glowered, stubbornly holding me in place with his good arm.

"Oh, for pity's sake. I'm much better. *Truly.*" I smiled to reassure him. He didn't believe me. "Kindly stop frowning at me and help me up. *Please?*"

Grumbling, he released his viselike hold on me. He and Captain Grey helped me to my feet, and with my arms draped over their shoulders, as if I were a cripple instead of a madwoman, we made our way back to Stranje House. They set me down on the divan in the blue parlor.

Gabriel immediately began to pace, his limp more pronounced than normal. "Tell me what happened out there. One minute you were swatting at something in the air, and the next . . ." He shook his head. "You fainted."

Miss Stranje sat on the chair nearest me. "We're all still learning how her dreams take hold."

"*That's* what that was?" Gabriel stopped and raked his fingers into his hair. "A dream?"

"I warned you." I closed my eyes, hiding, feeling utterly exposed and humiliated. "You didn't know what the madness was like. Now that you've had a taste of it, perhaps you will finally understand why I can't—" I couldn't say the rest of it, not with Miss Stranje and the captain leaning on every word. "Why we don't have a future."

"I've already explained how I feel," Gabriel blurted. "Why won't you listen to me?"

"Because I have lived through it with my mother and my grandmother. You haven't."

"I'll not have you thinking that way, Tess." Miss Stranje sounded irritated. "These are dreams. Not madness."

"It's a painfully small leap from one to the other." I fiddled with a loose thread on the fabric of the divan.

And then a short hop to death.

"No." Miss Stranje leaned in, wearing her sternest teacher face. "Dreams and visions are merely that, dreams and visions. Madness lies only in how one reacts to them."

I massaged my forehead, which throbbed as if there were still bees banging around inside it. "I don't expect you to understand. How could you?"

"It doesn't matter." Gabriel stopped pacing and crossed his arms. "Madness. Dreams. Visions. Whatever they are, whether they are a gift or a curse, I don't care. They make no difference to me." So these were his words of love? A cloaked pledge of his undying affection, delivered with all the gentleness and affection of a great scowling brown bear.

"Well, it should matter," I snapped. "Attacked by golden bees. That's madness pure and simple."

Captain Grey clapped Gabriel on the shoulder. He meant it as a comforting *man-to-man-I-know-how-difficult-women-can-be* gesture, except it startled Gabriel. Surprise whipped across his features. I wondered if such claps on the shoulder had meant something entirely different when his father had delivered them.

The captain noticed it, too, and removed his hand. He went to stand next to Miss Stranje's chair and addressed me in soldier-like tones. "Perhaps not, Miss Aubreyson. Napoleon's royal crest bears a liberal application of golden bees. Even the flag he commissioned during his exile on Elba displayed golden bees across every field. They are considered a symbol of resurrection and immortality. So you can see why they are of particular significance to him. Your dream could very well be a warning of things to come."

I glanced with uncertainty at Gabriel. "Very well. But what were they doing attacking me?"

"That I'm afraid is a bit of a mystery. But I think it is safe to say that your dream is linked to Napoleon somehow."

I turned my head and studied the silk painting hanging on the far wall, a pair of long-legged storks standing beside a placid pond. Right now, I felt anything but placid. I risked a sideways glance at Miss Stranje.

She scrutinized me with pursed lips. "There's something more. What aren't you telling us?"

"Something Daneska said today. It's all flummery, of course."

"And yet it troubles you."

I took a deep breath and told them everything she'd said. *Almost.* "Apparently Napoleon is quite superstitious about dreams. Daneska told him about mine. The emperor showed her his Oraculum, a prized tome he calls his *Book of Fate*, which he uses to interpret dreams and guide his decisions. Daneska said it appeared to be very scientific with numbers, and charts, and interpretations of dream symbols . . ."

"*And?*" she pressed.

Gabriel paced while he listened, his limp worsening with each turn around the divan.

I sank back as far as I could against the cushions, wondering if it would be better to keep it to myself. Finally, I conceded to her searing scrutinization. "If you must know, Napoleon told her to invite me to his palace to, um, discuss dreams with him."

Miss Stranje leaned very close, not so hawkish this time. No, now she peered at me with the ferocity of an eagle homing in on a helpless rabbit. I will admit to feeling just a little bit afraid. "You mean Napoleon asked you to come and dream *for* him."

When Gabriel heard what Miss Stranje said, he came to a sudden halt and stood very still at the end of the divan. "What did you tell her?"

Some perverse part of me wanted to point out the advantages. "Perhaps it would be the best place for me. Locked in a room where I can't hurt anyone"—*that someone being Gabriel*—"and with Emperor Napoleon eager to interpret these maddening dreams of mine."

"Don't be a fool," snapped Ravencross.

"I'm not a fool." I huffed. "There are far worse situations in the world than being housed in a palace."

I thought his glare might be hot enough to blind me.

Miss Stranje sat back and crossed her arms, wearing a smug half smile. "You needn't concern yourself, my lord. She told Lady Daneska no."

"Of course, I did."

Gabriel's shoulders relaxed. "Well, why didn't you say so?"

Miss Stranje answered for me. "I should think it was to get a reaction from you, my lord." She turned to me and patted my shoulder. "At least now we know what the dream with the silver bowl meant."

"Still doesn't explain the confounded bees." Captain Grey rubbed at the stubble on his jaw and stared out the window.

That night I couldn't face going to see Daneska in the dungeon. My encounter with the bees still had me too flustered. She was bound to sense my agitation, and knowing Lady Daneska, she would needle me until I accidently gave something away, or broke her arrogant nose with my fist. Either way, I simply couldn't take the risk. For those reasons Miss Stranje assigned Jane the task of bringing our prisoner her supper, but not before I discussed with them an idea that might assist with our current dubious plan.

After much debate, we chose to implement both ideas simultaneously.

The next morning, I brought Daneska her breakfast. The hunk of dry bread looked crustier, and the porridge much thicker than it had been yesterday.

"More wine, I see." She flicked her finger against a glass of dark red port. "I had wondered why Lady Jane brought such a generous portion last night. *To help you sleep,* she said. But now, here is an equally generous portion with my breakfast."

"Be grateful it isn't gin." I set the tray down, not caring that some of the wine splattered her.

"*Merci.*" She did a mock curtsey without getting up from her pallet. "I am most appreciative that you are using a wine, albeit an inferior one, to induce a drunken stupor rather than gutter swill." She laughed at her own quip. "But if you suppose I will tell you where Ghost hides, you must try harder than this." She clucked her tongue and turned away from the tray in disgust. "As if one cup of wine would loosen my tongue."

"I told them as much." That wasn't true, but I hoped flattery might lull her into overconfidence. The wine had been entirely my idea. I knew from experience how Dani relaxed and became far more talkative after a glass or two of liquor.

"At least *you* knew better." She lifted the glass and turned it, until the slender rays of light that shone through her window caught on the ruby liquid. "There's nothing else in it?"

"You're worried about poison?" I asked.

"No, silly. Laudanum. One stupor to make a prisoner talkative is as good as another, *non?*"

"Thank you for the suggestion. Sadly, we don't have your expertise when it comes to extracting information. This is merely wine."

"How disappointing." She stared into the cup. "This is because Miss Stranje, despite the rack and whips she has for show in her elaborate discipline chamber, does not have the stomach for torture." She took a swig of the wine. "I would not have thought her so soft."

"She's not soft," I shot back. "Far from it. She wouldn't have any qualms about clamping you on the rack and giving it a good crank. And I'd have helped her, too. No, you have Seraphina to thank for this. It was she who objected."

"That one." Daneska exhaled with disgust. "Seraphina, little mouse, she was always so weak." I noticed she slurred the word "always."

"Shut your mouth, Dani. Better yet, drink up or put some food in it. I don't have all day to watch you eat." I crossed my arms and leaned against the door, brooding. "And anyway, you're wrong. Sera's not weak. Shy, perhaps, but she's not weak at all."

Daneska nipped at her stale bread crust, ignoring me.

Irritated, I blurted, "That girl is more intelligent than you, or *anyone* else I know. In fact, it was Sera who convinced us that no matter what we did to you, you would simply lie and send us on wild-goose chases. She was right."

"*Oui*, but I was so looking forward to it." She pretended to pout. "Cursed little white mouse, I should've stepped on her when I had a chance." She ripped the hunk of bread in half. "But you are wrong, Tessie, *ma chère*. Intelligence and strength—these two have nothing to do with each other. How do you say . . ." Daneska's speech lurched awkwardly, and despite her affected French, I noticed her Slavic accent becoming far more dominant.

"Oh, yes, now I remember. These two are not bedfellows." The chains on her cuffs clinked as she raised both hands, weighing each attribute. "It is possible to be clever without having courage." The manacles rattled and she winced.

I grabbed her arm and inspected it. "Blast. These irons are cutting into your wrists."

She jerked out of my hold. "Why do you care? You said it yourself: my head will soon be on a pike. What are a few scrapes on the wrist compared to that?"

"I *don't* care. I shouldn't. You've done the same to others. And much worse." I tore a strip of cloth from my underskirt and stuffed it between the rough iron edges on the inside of her wrist. "I saw Sebastian after you were done with him, and I've seen Mr. Sinclair's scars—" I flinched, having let his name slip out.

"Ah! The young protégé of Monsieur Fulton." She brightened, all of a sudden too keen, too sharp. "So you are hiding him here. That explains all the hammering and sawing I hear. He is building something, a weapon perhaps?"

I dropped her wrist. "It explains nothing."

She twittered, a high plinking sound that plucked at my

nerves. "Oh, but it does, *mon amie*. It explains all." She leaned back against the wall. The wine relaxed her guard at least that much. "So your young Ravencross, is he helping with this project, as well?"

"Enough talk about my friends." I brushed my hands off, trying to remove the grime of her blood and the rusting irons. "You haven't told me anything about *your* illustrious paramour. How fares Ghost?"

She smirked. "What you really want to ask is *where* fares Ghost."

I frowned. She was not nearly drunk enough.

Dani crooked her finger and leaned forward, pretending to tell me a secret. I knew better than to go along with her.

"Come," she cajoled. "I shall tell you where he is." When I didn't fall for her gambit, she threw her hands into the air in a noisy clatter of chains and another brief grimace. "Here. There. *Everywhere*. He is a Ghost, *n'est-ce pas?*"

This was all a grand lark to her.

Miss Stranje had forgotten to confiscate my knife this morning. I whipped out my dagger and lunged at Daneska. Yanking her to her feet, I growled, "This is not a joke, Dani. If the wine doesn't loosen your tongue, perhaps this will."

I aimed the tip of the blade directly at her eye. She quivered in my grasp. For an instant, she looked afraid. Then fear vanished and, once again, Lady Daneska cared for nothing. "Put down your blade, Tessika. I will tell you the truth."

Even though her voice had lost its malicious pitch, I didn't lower my knife. I inched it closer.

"Before you cut my eyes out, look into them and see if I am telling you the truth." She didn't even blink. "I have no reason to lie, Tess. I don't know where he is." She didn't, I could see it.

"But you do know where he *might* be," I said.

"*Ja*, a thousand different places. Enough to keep you running to and fro for the next century. But I can tell you this . . . I know where he *will* be." She continued to meet my gaze, steady and unflinching. "He will come for me. *Soon*."

I let go.

She leaned against the wall a moment longer. "Whether it is to kill me, or set me free, *that* I cannot tell you." She slid down the wall and sat stiff-backed on her pallet. "He will not allow me to remain here. It is too dangerous for him. And for our emperor." She shrugged and put her Countess of Deceit mask back on. "It is possible I may know a few things of interest to Lord Wyatt and his persuasive friends in the British government. One way or another *Le Fantôme*, Ghost, he will never let them take me to London."

"Lucien wouldn't kill you. He's your lover, your paramour for more than two years. He wouldn't."

"Ah, but he would." She chuckled quietly. "Ghost weighs all things against what must be done. There is no room in his world for idle sentiment."

I sheathed my knife and sank onto the pallet beside her. "If that's true, how can you love him?"

Her perfect brow pinched. She turned up her nose at me as if I had the plague. "Who said anything about love?"

"But . . ."

"Oh. I see your confusion. You thought I went away with him out of some foolish romantic notion. *Love*." She spat the word. "Fah! It weakens the mind. Poor Tessie, you are so hungry for the stuff. Me, I would rather eat this gruel."

And she did. She picked up the bowl and let the thick gray paste run into her mouth, like a snake swallowing a rat whole.

I stood, needing to get away from her. "I don't believe you. I remember all those nights, how happy you were when you talked about him. How desperate you were to sneak out and rendezvous with him."

She blotted her mouth on a corner of her skirt. "How else was I to convince you to help me, and him to make me part of—" She suddenly realized what she was about to admit aloud.

As if I didn't already know. "The Iron Crown," I said flatly.

"*Bon,*" she answered with a slight lift of her brow. "Then you understand. Love has nothing to do with it. I do not believe in such paltry nonsense."

Love, paltry?

"How sad for you," I said, and meant it. What a barren existence life would be without love. I'd seen love transform my mother's face, her love for my father, for our forests, for me, and in those moments graced by that *paltry* sentiment, she'd found freedom from the horrors of her visions. I'd witnessed the joy in Gabriel's face when he'd looked up at me in the garden. Nothing would ever take that shining glimpse of love away from me. Not even death.

"No." She sneered. "Stop! Get that hideous look off your face. You will not pity me." She slammed her fist against the dungeon wall, and through gritted teeth roared, "Don't you dare feel sorry for me."

I turned away, staring at the window, any place but at her. Because I couldn't stop pitying her.

I reminded myself how cruel she was, what a vicious liar, a traitor, even a murderer, and yet all I could see was how broken she was.

Daneska calmed her anger, as if a cooling breeze wafted through the stifling air of her cell. She took a long swig of her wine. "My dear, gullible Tessika. It is *I* who feels sorry for *you.* This feeble thing you call love, reality burns it off as the sun does the morning fog." She lifted the wineglass, silently toasting the walls of her cell. "Love weakens you. It impairs your judgment. And worst of all, it forces you to sacrifice things you should not sacrifice."

Daneska tapped her forehead. "If you must love something, love yourself. Trust in your own wits, not a man. You and your wits, these two things can be counted on not to betray you."

I sighed. "And they won't kill you in the night."

"*Exactement*," she whispered, and grabbed what remained of her crusty bread, turning it round and round in her fingers. "They will not kill you in the night."

She sat very still, still enough that I heard her shallow breaths, and a drip of moisture slide from a blackened crack and plunk on the floor. "*C'est la vie.* He must do what is necessary."

"Will you fight him?"

She met my gaze, sober as a hanging judge. "But of course."

"Truly? You would kill him, your lover, the Grand Knight of Napoleon's Iron Crown?"

"I don't understand this question." She tilted her head, squinting at me, sincerely confused. It wasn't the wine. That simple question had truly baffled her "But of course I would. What else is there? I do what I must to survive."

She would. I saw Daneska differently then, like a strange mythical beast I didn't understand. Dangerous, treacherous, but she also looked fragile, friendless, and so utterly alone.

"Then I will help you."

She scoffed at me. "And how would you do that?"

"I could kill Ghost."

"Impossible. You are good, *ma chère*, but not good enough to best him." She shook her head. "Besides, there is still the chance he may decide to help me escape."

She looked down, studying the bread she had now torn into bits in her lap. Hesitation didn't sit comfortably on her features, the muscles and pathways for it had never fully developed. "He might."

"*Might*. Which do you think it will be?" I asked.

She masked her uncertainty with sangfroid and weighed the two invisible answers in each hand, chains clanging as the scales tipped one way and then the other. "It is too difficult to guess. I would not place a wager on either one."

I planted my hands on my hips and smirked. "I know you better than that. More than likely you would place bets on both."

"Ah. *Très bien*. So I would." She laughed, not her high, fake ear-shattering titter. She laughed honestly, and the sound nearly broke my heart.

Time to leave.

I picked up the tray. "Decide, Dani. Which shall it be? Do you want me to help you kill him? Or are you going to take a chance that he will help you escape?"

Twenty-three

TRESPASSERS

Jane and Miss Stranje waited for me around the corner from the discipline chamber. I handed Jane the tray, and confessed to Miss Stranje, "You were right. About the two sides of the same card, I mean. I don't hate her anymore."

I didn't. I felt sorry for her.

"I'm sorry." Miss Stranje sighed, and then she did something she rarely does. She hugged me.

I pulled away in surprise. "I don't understand. I've forgiven Dani. I thought that's what you wanted me to do. Why are you sorry that I still care about my friend?"

"I'm not sad about that, Tess. I'm sorry that the love you have for your friend still causes you so much pain. And that it will most assuredly continue to do so."

True, Daneska could hurt me now. Now that I cared about her again, I was vulnerable. But then I realized that whatever bad thing Daneska might do in the future would hurt whether I forgave her or not.

And I could certainly count on her to do something bad.

We walked up the stairs without speaking, until Jane asked, "Did Lady Daneska say anything of use?"

"Yes, she swears Ghost will come for her. *Here.*" I pressed my hand against the wall to steady myself, suddenly unnerved as I remembered the dream of Lucien in these very passages. It made my chest burn to think how vulnerable Stranje House was. If Daneska was right, he might show up any day.

Any moment.

"She's convinced he won't allow her to be taken to London for questioning," I explained. "I believe her. She also said it is just as likely that he'll kill her as rescue her."

"Good heavens." Jane rubbed a chill from her arm as if the shadow of Ghost were already upon us. "And this is the man she ruined herself for."

Miss Stranje continued up the stairs, slower than before, as if contemplating one fact on each step. "Daneska has a point. Ghost will need to solve the problem one way or the other. Regrettably, killing her may prove more expedient than rescuing her."

"We can't let that happen," Jane blurted. "Not here. I don't like Daneska any more than you do, but we can't let him murder her under our very noses."

"We won't." I didn't tell Jane that if it came down to it, I would help Dani kill Lucien.

"How? Stranje House isn't fortified well enough." Jane squeezed forward, pressing up beside us on the narrow stairs. "Yes, we've put latches on the secret entrances, but there are any number of windows. And Tess is proof, they are often the easiest access points. We can hardly post a guard at every window."

"Calm down, Jane." Miss Stranje opened the door out into the gallery. "We will arrange her escape before he comes. We should be able to manage that before much longer. Did you let it slip that Mr. Sinclair is here?"

"Yes. She tumbled straightaway to the idea that he's helping us build a weapon of some kind."

"Wait." Jane grabbed my arm. "If she knows he's here, doesn't that put him in danger? Ghost will want him out of the way, too, or recaptured."

Miss Stranje answered for me. "It's a risk we have to take. It was the perfect opportunity to plant a clue that Britain is preparing defenses against Napoleon."

Jane rushed out in front of us, set the tray on a side table, and stopped us with her arms out wide. "But don't you see, if Ghost could slip in here to murder Daneska, he could do the same to Alexander, I mean, to Mr. Sinclair."

Unaffected, Miss Stranje passed around her and kept walking. "That's highly unlikely, Lady Jane. He has protection. He's almost always accompanied by one or the other of you."

"What good is that?" She followed after her. "Tess is the only one of us with enough skills to do anything to save him if he should be confronted by Ghost or one of his hired thugs."

"And whose fault is that?" Miss Stranje scolded. "I suggest you pay more attention in defensive arts class in the future."

"Tess, wait." Jane turned to me. "You have to protect him. Anything could happen. And then . . . then he wouldn't be able to finish his warship. We've got to keep him alive. Don't you see, he has ideas for other things, too. Steam-powered plows. All kinds of marvels. Think what a loss it would be to England—the world." She grabbed my sleeve. "You have to keep him safe."

"I thought you didn't like him."

"I don't. It's *progress* I'm thinking of, you know, the general well-being of mankind."

"Oh, yes, I see. In that case, since you love *mankind* so dearly, you play nursemaid to Mr. Sinclair. I've other things to do."

That evening at dinner, Mr. Sinclair announced that his miniature warship was ready for a test voyage. "To see how the pontoons perform and if she's seaworthy."

"Or if she sinks like a stone?" Jane asked innocently.

"She won't. But if she does, let's hope it's not too far from shore, for I'll need a crew aboard, to shovel coal and tend the furnace while I steer." He looked directly at her.

"Me?" Jane's hand fluttered to her breast. "Shovel coal? I think not."

"I'll do it. Glad to be aboard." Lord Wyatt saluted as if Sinclair were the ship's captain, which I suppose he ought to be by rights.

"I'm coming, too." Georgie grinned.

"I'm not so certain that's wise." Lord Wyatt looked genuinely concerned. "I remember your last excursion in these waters. You absconded with our row boat and nearly drowned."

That had been Georgie's first night at Stranje House. "I thought I needed to escape." She cast an apologetic look at Miss Stranje.

"Yes, and not only did you wreck a perfectly good row boat but you nearly dashed yourself to pieces on the rocks."

"Oh fiddle faddle. I shall buy you another boat some day." She waved his protests away. "Anyway, Phobos and Tromos saved me and all that is behind us now. Tess has been showing me how to swim. Not that I'll need to, but I'm fully prepared if the need should arise. Although I'm certain it won't. I worked on those pontoons myself, and the mechanism that turns the paddle wheel is pure genius."

I interrupted before she could wax poetic about flywheels and crankshafts. "You're not fully prepared. Showing you how to swim is a far cry from actually practicing in the water. There is a great deal of difference."

"Perhaps, we might—" Sera tried to squeeze a word in, but her soft voice was easily overlooked.

Maya tinked her finger against her glass goblet ever so slightly, and for some reason the sound caught our attention. "I think Sera has an idea."

Sera blushed when everyone hushed and turned to look at her. "I, uh, thought you might bring something aboard that floats, so that in case of an emergency, those who don't know how to swim might cling to in the water." She swallowed, because we all continued to stare. "Just in case."

"Excellent idea." Miss Stranje raised her glass to Sera.

Georgie rubbed her chin thoughtfully. "Something like a pig's bladder filled with air. Only that wouldn't be large enough to keep a whole person afloat. Perhaps several pigs' bladders, strung together—"

"Egad, Georgie. You're getting as bad as he is." Lady Jane shot a scolding look at Mr. Sinclair. "You're making me quite nauseous with all this talk of entrails."

Captain Grey cleared his throat. "I've heard stories of sailors surviving shipwrecks owing to a barrel that floated by. Any sort of buoyant wood ought to serve."

"I believe I have some waterproof kegs in the cellar. Would that do?" Miss Stranje asked. "Cook will object, but I'm sure we can borrow two or three of her pickling barrels with the promise of returning them to her the next day or two."

"First-rate plan. Pickling barrels with the air sealed inside will work splendidly. That's settled, then." Mr. Sinclair rubbed his hands together eagerly. "Although they should be entirely unnecessary, as we won't be that far from shore in the first place."

Jane carefully set her fork on her plate. "Well, I like the idea of a contingency plan, since I'll need to come along to navigate."

Mr. Sinclair straightened and turned in surprise to Lady Jane. "You will? I had thought Captain Grey would most likely handle that task."

"Oh. Well, naturally, I must defer to Captain Grey's expertise." She sniffed. "But I did work rather hard on the building of this monstrosity. I should like to be aboard her maiden voyage in some capacity."

"I see." He laid two fingers over his lips, suppressing a grin. "What do you think, Captain? Might you require someone to assist you with the telescope?"

Captain Grey nodded gravely. "I believe there will be plenty of room for an assistant, Mr. Sinclair."

"There you are, Lady Jane. You will be our chief telescope holder." Mr. Sinclair pronounced this as if she'd just been given the post of the Queen's lady-in-waiting.

Jane cast her gaze to the ceiling. "I'm honored, to be sure."

Mr. Sinclair skimmed through the rest of his plan. "While we are out in the water, I would very much like to test Miss Barrington's ballista. I've just about got the cranks ready to be installed. Miss Fitzwilliam's modification to my torpedo has me frothing at the bit to see if it works. The resourcefulness all of you demonstrate still has me in awe. I would never have thought of using a grenade filled with Greek fire in combination with Congreve's compression switch."

Georgie beamed with pride at his proclamation.

Mr. Sinclair rubbed his palms together excitedly. "So during the HMS *Mary Isabella*'s maiden voyage I believe we are ready to make those test shots we discussed a few days ago, the ones involving fireworks and cake." His eyebrows lifted, as if cake were the most exciting part.

Miss Stranje's shoulders drooped ever so slightly and she shared an apprehensive exchange with Captain Grey. "Yes, of course, the test shot."

"*Mary Isabella?*" Jane sat up, her spine suddenly rigid, and she was so piqued she nearly came out of her chair altogether. "You named *our* boat after *your* sweetheart back in the Colonies?"

"Ship, Lady Jane. She's a ship, not a boat. I will admit she's small, and naught but a prototype to be sure. But she's a pint-sized warship sure as anything, and a fine one at that. As to the name, my lady . . ." He blushed and ran a finger around his collar. "Well, I would've named her after my Uncle Robert, but I didn't think it fitting, she isn't quite grand enough to carry his name. So I named her in honor of my mother, Mary, and my grandmother, Isabella. Two fine, strong women. Both of them small in stature, but feisty and with more endurance and fight in them than ten men."

"Oh." Jane sank back against her chair. "I see." She remained fairly quiet throughout the rest of dinner.

There was a lengthy debate about whether it would be better to experiment with the explosives during the day or the night. Captain Grey pointed out that at night most of our neighbors would be fast asleep and far less alert to any noises or bombs bursting in the sky. Lord Wyatt and Mr. Sinclair insisted that it would be impossible to site their test targets properly in the dark. At length we decided to set lamps on floating wood, which would allow the more explosive portion of Mr. Sinclair's birthday celebration to take place in the early evening, before it became pitch-black. Afterward we would hold a late supper and feast upon the much anticipated cake. That way, the *fireworks* display would occur while most of the inhabitants of Fairstone Meade had settled inside for their evening meals.

Normally after dinner, Lady Jane would've taken herself off

to the library to read until bedtime, or to work on the estate account books, or draw out her crop rotation plans. But tonight she traipsed after me to the ballroom and asked if I would help her practice actually throwing someone over her shoulder, rather than just bragging about it. Jane doesn't admit to anything so humbling as having bragged, nor does she ask for help very often, so I couldn't very well say no.

Madame Cho joined us on the mats, assisting Jane with the correct moves. After several tries, Jane managed to heave me over onto the mat, but then she immediately leaned over me to make certain I was all right.

"Jane," I grumped at her, "you're supposed to lift your foot above my neck and prepare to stomp my throat if I move."

She dropped to her knees on the mat beside me. "I'm not sure I could do that."

"Then you'll be dead," I said flatly. "And whoever you're trying to protect will be dead, too."

Madame Cho thumped her bamboo staff on the floor and barked, "Again."

After four more attempts, Jane's shoulders sagged and she plopped down in the center of the mat. "This is hopeless. Let's try something else." She brightened. "We could work on my knife throwing."

I exhaled loudly and sat beside her. "I watched two days ago, when nine times out of ten you missed the target altogether. That target is twice as broad as a man. If you can't even strike the straw, Jane, you won't be able to hit an attacker. Not without a great deal of practice."

"What about swords?"

I almost laughed, it was hard not to, so I simply shook my head. She threw up her hands. "Then what am I to do?"

Madame Cho and I exchanged worried glances. I crossed my

arms and stared at the wall of knives. "What about close combat with a dagger?"

Madame Cho nodded.

Excited that we might have found a protection that would work for her, I tried to explain the thinking behind it. "It's all about trickery. Like this . . ." Madam Cho and I demonstrated. "You must make your attacker think you plan to move in this direction, but at the last minute you spin to the side and thrust. Do you see? Surprise is our greatest defense."

Lady Jane nodded eagerly. "Except that seems rather more like an offense than a defense."

I ignored her argument, not wishing to get pulled into a debate about definitions. "For instance, you could pretend to be helpless, and when the attacker gets close enough, you could pull a blade out of your pocket, like so."

She clapped. "I like that idea. I could do that. Teach me more. Tomorrow I'll cut holes into the pockets of my day gowns, and I'll wear a knife strapped to my waist. I can reach in and *voilà!*" She aimed an invisible dagger at me.

I laughed. It was difficult to picture Lady Jane as dangerous; most of the time she reminded me of a prim and proper governess with a biting sense of humor. But I have to admit, she took to close combat like a baby duck to water. By the end of the night, she had successfully mastered three close combat moves.

She bent to catch her breath and I clapped her on the shoulder. "You're a natural."

"Won't Mr. Sinclair be surprised." She planted her hands on her hips and glistened with hard-earned pride.

"Poor fellow." I rubbed my side where she'd jabbed me with a wooden knife. "You're not planning to use these moves on him, are you?"

"No, silly. When I save his life."

Twenty-four

FAIRLY TRICKY

The next morning I ran in the early dawn. The horizon promised a clear day, but low-lying mists snaked across the grass and fields, and all the world was still iron gray. I wished it would hurry up and turn light, because I couldn't shake the dream I'd had that night.

No silver bowl or silks. No green water or golden bees. I dreamed of thrashing in the cold sea, struggling to keep from drowning. The water had been dark and gray like the charcoal sky was now, and I saw only split seconds of their faces, but Daneska was there, and Gabriel. Through the dark I'd seen his hair drenched in seawater and his mouth open, clamoring for air, as he came up from a wave.

I'd awakened thrashing in my tangled sheets. So I did what I always do. I got up and tried to outrun the terror.

The wolf-dogs didn't join me that morning. Sometimes they preferred to prowl the woods hunting. After that horrid dream I found the solitude oddly comforting. I wanted to run so hard I couldn't think of anyone or anything else.

Spent, after having raced across the field like the very devil chased me, I slowed when I neared the edge of the sheep paddock and came to a stop near a raspberry bush tucked in the hedgerow. In the dim light, I plucked one. But I knew, by the way it didn't let go of the stem, that it wasn't yet ripe. None of the berries were. As useless as my dreams, they held the promise of fruit, but in reality there was nothing to bite into except sour, inedible stones.

Maybe I did need Napoleon to interpret my dreams.

I shook the thought away. Napoleon's interest would not be in helping me. No, he would be concerned only about dreams that bespoke his future victories. I also knew that being locked in a room with a silver bowl would drive me to madness faster than living with these inscrutable nightmares.

And one more reason I couldn't go to France . . .

I would not want to be that far away from Gabriel. I looked across the paddock, and there, as if I'd conjured him, rode Ravencross. Zeus cantered with proud, high steps as if he carried a duke or the Prince. I watched him ride as unerringly as an arrow, straight toward my heart.

He rode up beside me and doffed an imaginary hat. Gabriel is not inclined to wearing hats, even though he ought to do so for propriety's sake, and to keep his head warm, and to cover all those lovely errant curls of his. But I said nothing. I had no right to scold. I seldom wear a bonnet, preferring not to have my vision restricted like a dray horse wearing blinders. Not only that, but I'm quite fond of the feel of the wind on my cheeks.

Zeus pranced prettily beside me as I walked down the pasture toward the house.

"I'm surprised to see you are riding, my lord. Are you sure that is a good idea? Your stitches cannot be healed."

"It all comes down to a matter of choices, Miss Aubreyson."

He sounded so very formal. "Surely you have noticed the tents encamped on my lawn?"

I wasn't sure what one thing had to do with the other, but I played along. "I did. I presume some members of the militia have already arrived."

"Yes. They began arriving yesterday carrying letters from the Lord Lieutenant saying that I was to give them succor and see to their training. There are men bivouacked inside the house as well. Mrs. Evans has been bounding about the halls like a great flapping goose, opening rooms and trying to prepare enough food. It would appear the manor is being turned into a make-shift fort. Hence, you can see the necessity of my riding out."

"To escape all the commotion?"

"No." Gabriel looked down at me quizzically and Zeus side-stepped. "Of course not. I wouldn't have argued with the doctor so bitterly if that were the reason."

"Why, then?" I fancied he might say it was because he missed me, or because he longed to see me, or that he yearned for these few stolen moments we had together.

Instead, he chided me as if I were a dim-witted child. "I should think it is perfectly obvious. There are at least a dozen men encamped on my lawn. You should not be out here alone and unchaperoned."

I may have sputtered. I know some sort of unladylike noise blew through my lips. "Don't be ridiculous, my lord. I can take care of myself. You should've listened to your physician and stayed in bed."

He grumbled something I could not quite hear because Zeus danced forward. He reined in his horse and groused, "I detest lying in bed. It is even more intolerable if I imagine you out here, running by yourself, at the mercy of any one of these randy jackanapes who might decide you are fair game."

Hands on hips, I frowned hard enough that it should've toppled him from his saddle. "Now you're just gammoning me. You know perfectly well there's not a man among them who could outrun me."

He relented under my ferocious stare. "Very well, there may be something to that. Nevertheless, you are a fairly fine-looking female and far more vulnerable than you think."

Fairly?

If he'd been standing on the ground instead of sitting all pompous and arrogant atop his big horse, I would've socked him square in his sore shoulder. "Fairly?"

He twitched in his seat and gave me a rascally smirk. "Yes, *fairly*. Didn't I just say so?"

"I'm overcome by your flattery, my lord Silver-Tongue."

"Yes, well, I worried you might be, so I kept it to a minimum. Wouldn't want to spoil you."

Zeus had the audacity to whinny and toss his head at that very moment, as if he thought his master's gibe was particularly amusing.

"Oh, no, we wouldn't want that." I sulked and glared at Zeus, too, the mangy traitor. "And now why don't you and your snickering horse take yourselves off home. As you can see, I am unaccosted. Apart from that, except for the sentries, your troops are all sound asleep at this hour."

He ignored my request that he leave. "Fortunately for you, I gave those sentries orders not to shoot my fleet-footed neighbor. I don't mind telling you, Tess, it is fairly ticklish trying to explain to these soldiers why there is a young lady running up and down these fields in the wee hours of the morning."

"*Fairly.*" I brooded at hearing the word again.

"Yes, but it had to be done. Otherwise I worried you might end up with a bullet lodged in your lovely person."

Lovely?

I stopped walking away from him quite so fast. "Thank you for asking them to hold their fire. I hadn't thought of the fact that I might look like a shadow running between the trees."

He dismounted then and fell into step beside me, both of us silent. Zeus stopped to graze on an inviting tuft of grass, and as we waited Gabriel broke the uneasy silence between us. "The militia will begin training today. MacDougal was a sergeant in my battalion and, as such, he has agreed to run the men through their drills. He is in high spirits at the prospect. I hired him away when I sold my commission, because I knew I could count on Mac, but I believe he misses the military."

It made sense, now, Gabriel's gruff Scottish man-of-all-work. "He seems quite devoted to you, my lord."

"A good man, Mac. Loyal as the day is long." He paused, and I wondered if he was thinking about his brother, who was so wretchedly disloyal. "I've instructed the men to practice on the grounds nearest Stranje House, which means they'll be marching and practicing their drills and formations as close to Lady Daneska's prison cell as is possible."

"Excellent," I said, and skimmed my hand over Zeus's sleek neck.

"Aye, now if I could just settle Mrs. Evans." He rubbed his neck. "I hired two girls from the village to help her in the kitchens and yet she still carries on as if I've asked her to feed Wellington's entire army. I shall have to hire two more girls or I won't hear the end of it."

"Serving girls?" I turned to him in alarm. "And village maids at that. Then it is you who needs guarding, my lord, not I."

He chuckled, and I wasn't sure in that light, but I thought he might have turned a bit pink. "No, Tess. You're the only lass with enough courage to look at me squarely. The two girls she hired cower like mice against the wall if I so much as walk down a hall. With these scars and this confounded limp"—he swatted at his thigh—"most women find me as frightening as one of those beasts in the Grimm brothers' tales."

Frighteningly beautiful.

My beast.

"Just as well," I muttered. "See that they don't find out exactly how beautiful you are, because if one of those cheeky girls dares flirt with you, I will march straight over and throttle her."

I quite liked it when Gabriel smiled. It was a magnificent thing, not unlike the sun dawning. Which it did just then, in brilliant pink and orange streaks that chased away the gray.

"I must be going in now," I said quietly. "Miss Stranje's rules."

"I'm serious about being circumspect while the troops are here." He tucked my hair behind my ear, letting his fingers graze my cheeks a few moments longer than needed. "Promise you'll guard yourself around them, so that I needn't worry?"

I wanted to tease him, but he looked so very earnest that I couldn't bring myself to do it. I couldn't, not with his fingers barely touching my cheek, just enough to completely muddle my senses and melt my wits down to the wick. All I could do was nod.

After breakfast that morning, Stranje House was as noisy and busy as the troops drilling next door at Ravencross Manor. Fortunately, Lord Ravencross lent us four of his strongest men to help carry the bits and pieces of Mr. Sinclair's warship down to the beach, where the remainder of the construction would take place. Our shoreline is particularly rocky, especially near the caves, so we had to traverse some distance to a sandy outcropping beyond the rocks.

The hike up and down the cliffs was too narrow to carry anything bulkier than one of Lord Ravencross's skiffs, which had been made over into pontoons. They would've been bulky enough if they'd still been skiffs with open hulls. But the mouths of each of these long boats had been tacked over with oilcloth and covered with pitch. Each boat had become a gigantic drum. It took two men, Captain Grey and Lord Wyatt, walking in careful alignment to carry down each pontoon.

Gabriel's men carried down the boiler and the furnace in two pieces. Sinclair and Georgie planned to connect them later. There were several stacks of lumber, that Jane explained would be used to construct a deck across the top of the two pontoons, three long crankshafts, a basket of gears, two flywheels, and the entire conglomeration had to be hauled down a narrow winding path.

Georgie, Lord Wyatt, the captain, and Mr. Sinclair started right away on construction while Lady Jane and Sera took careful notes. I carried down the last of their copper piping and one of the pickling barrels we'd pilfered from our cook, Magda, to use as floats in case the ship sank.

Georgie was ecstatic that our miniature warship so closely resembled Robert Fulton's pontoon warship, the *Demologos*. "Except our steam engine won't fit belowdecks as it will on his, but ours will sit quite tidily suspended between the pontoons where the paddle wheel can turn unimpeded."

"And we have no cannons," observed Jane dryly.

Georgie did not like anyone criticizing their creation, not even Jane. "Naturally, our prototype is too small to bear the weight of a cannon. But we have our ballista."

"Hardly comparable to the thirty-two guns Fulton's ship will hold," Lord Wyatt teased.

Mr. Sinclair sprang to Georgie's defense. "Last I heard, the

Demologos won't bear up under the weight of those two hundred-pounders he intended to mount fore and aft. Had to leave 'em off." He twirled a screwdriver, pensively gazing off in the distance. "Still, with thirty guns she'll be a beauty."

"I like ours," muttered Georgie, tightening a fitting.

Unbeknownst to Georgie, Lord Wyatt smiled fondly at the back of her head. "Aye, she's a beauty all right."

I took my leave, as it was well past time to bring Lady Daneska her breakfast.

Cook filled Daneska's bowl of gruel while I poured the wine for her, and I hurried to carry it down the stone steps to the dungeon. When I opened the door, she seemed startled to see me and quickly pulled the blanket up to her neck. Mercurial as ever, her surprise changed to a pout. "I thought you weren't coming."

"I'm late, I know. But look, I've brought you a peace offering. A dried plum. I had to slip it out of the pantry without Cook noticing. You know how she watches over every grain of rice."

Daneska's iron bracelets rattled when she snatched it from the tray and tore it in half with her teeth, chewing the leathery fruit while she sneered at me. "I suppose you expect me to thank you for this one measly prune."

"No. I merely felt bad for my long delay in bringing your food."

"Oh, yes, you are so very concerned for my welfare." She held out her manacled wrists. "If that is true, unlock these and let me go."

I said nothing, but backed away and leaned against the wall.

"But no, you would rather let Ghost slit my throat, *n'est-ce pas?*" She gulped down half the wine and wiped her mouth with her sleeve. "*Voilà*, no more trouble from the Lady Daneska. All of you will rejoice." She lifted her goblet in a toast.

"I offered to help."

She rolled her eyes at me and guzzled the rest of the wine.

"Tell me where he is and I will end him."

"You?" She slammed the cup down. "*Fah.* He is not your straw mannequin that he may be so easily slain." She took the hunk of bread and shoved the tray with the bowl of gruel untouched back to me. The pewter goblet clinked onto its side. "Take it and go."

"As you wish."

"Wait." She leaned and grabbed the edge of the tray, smiling slyly up at me as if she had a secret she wished to share. "Did you think about what I said? Did you think about Napoleon's offer? We could escape, together, you and I. I know where there is a boat. We could return to Paris. Think, Tessika, you would be a national treasure, feted and cosseted. Fine wines. Divine food, not this bland English fare, and—"

I knew what she would say next. "The richest silks . . ."

"Yes, of course." She leaned back, realizing that somehow she'd gone too far. She didn't wait for my answer and she shoved the tray again, this time with her foot, sending it slopping across the floor.

"The rats will like that."

"Go away. I have a headache. All that shouting and thump-thump-thumping of soldiers' feet, that is your doing, I suppose?" she snarled.

"I had nothing to do with that. The Lord Lieutenant called out the militia, not I."

"But you tricked him into doing it, didn't you?"

"You had more to do with it than I did," I snapped. "We know why you're here—to prepare the way for Napoleon to attack Britain. Did you think the government wouldn't do anything about it? Of course, they called out the militia. Here, and all along the coast."

I snatched up the tray and left her cell before she could tell that I was lying.

The next morning, I refused to speak to her. I delivered her tray and said nothing.

"I don't hear any more hammering in the yard," she said almost cheerfully. When I didn't answer, she conjectured on her own. "Perhaps they have finished work on Mr. Sinclair's project?"

I crossed my arms and pressed my lips together.

"How very clever you all are to help him. What is it? I wonder." She ate very daintily that morning, dabbing her mouth when it needed to be wiped and, instead of gulping everything down as if it were her last meal, she dawdled. "Could it be his uncle's famous underwater boat . . . what is it they called it?"

I kept mum and stared at the window, wondering just how much she had seen of Sinclair's warship.

Daneska took her sweet time sipping the wine and soaking little hunks of bread in it. "Or perhaps it is just a copy of one of his uncle's gunships, the one that runs on steam."

"Are you quite finished?" I snapped up the tray and jerked the cup from her hand.

The next day was worse.

I trudged down the dark stairs into the chilly bowels of Stranje House carrying Daneska her food, thinking I would have to agree to go with her if, according to our plan, I was ever going to help her escape. When I unlocked the door, she didn't look up. She sat holding her knees, staring glumly at the wall across from her. She didn't greet me, didn't say anything, no clever insults, no biting remarks, not even so much as a sneer when I set the tray down.

"Are you ill?" I asked.

"No." Daneska's listless response was devoid of her normally vibrant accent. Straightway she reached for the port and gulped down half the glass. "I am as good as dead."

"Don't be silly," I said. Even though she was my enemy, I hated seeing her like this. "I told you, I won't let Lucien kill you. We've posted a guard. One of us stands watch in the corridor at all times."

"*Oh, yes, my guards,*" she scoffed. "Ha! Ten men couldn't stop him, let alone one little girl. No, I am doomed." She slammed down the empty glass and shoved the gruel across the tray. "Take it away. I haven't the stomach for it today."

"At least keep the bread. You may feel hungry later."

"What does it matter?" She rested her head on her knees. "I will die soon. I know because I saw him last night."

"You can't have." Incredulous, I looked about the cell as if he might still be here. "Ghost? Here? How? We saw no one coming or going."

Without making an effort to move her arms, she turned her head and pointed a finger. "There, at the window."

"It can't be. You must've dreamed it."

She smiled as if I'd said something funny, but she didn't have the strength to bother laughing. "I'm not like you, Tessika. I have no dreams. Besides, did I imagine that new streak on my little peephole to the world?"

"You're only saying that to trick me into believing you."

Except the window did look different. I hurried to the wall and hoisted myself up to have a closer look. "You put that there."

"To what end?"

"How should I know? Another of your schemes." I inspected the new mark and saw right away it wasn't a smear at all.

"Think what you will." She leaned her head on her knees again. "It's on the outside."

With my palm, I scrubbed a wider opening, which proved that someone had indeed cleaned off a small circle on the glass outside. The circle was just large enough to see into her dungeon. I let go of the sill and dropped to the floor.

"I told you," she said without looking at me.

"Did he say anything?"

At least that won a sneer out of her. "Don't be daft. How could he?"

"Lovers have many ways of communicating. His eyes. A hand gesture. *Something.* He must have given you an indication of his plans."

She just shook her head.

I slapped my hand against the wall. "What do you think his intentions are?"

"The same as they were yesterday."

I roared with frustration. "For once, Dani, I wish you would give me a straight answer."

"I have no answer to give." It was just plaintive enough to be the truth.

"Then at least tell me what you decided about my offer to help you. Together we might be able to kill him."

A *shrug.*

"That's it?" I wanted to shake her.

She didn't look at me. She swept her hand over the woolen blanket on her pallet, smoothing out the small lumps and ripples.

"Very well, have it your way." I snatched up her tray and tossed the bread in her lap. "I've decided without you. In fact, I decided a long time ago. You may stop worrying. I'm going to kill Lucien."

I tromped out, slamming the heavy door with a deafening clunk, and locked her in. Chains clattered as she got to her feet.

"No, Tessika. Wait! You don't understand what you're up against. You cannot do this."

I wheeled around and stared at her through the bars. "Watch me."

"He's clever. And strong. Almost inhumanly so. He'll kill you, Tessika. Mark my words. Don't go after him, or you'll die."

I ignored her and took off down the hall, charging upstairs ahead of Sera and Miss Stranje.

They pattered up behind me. "What happened? What's wrong?"

"Ghost. He's been here." *At Stranje House.* I took the risers two at a time. "He knows she's here."

And he'd violated my sanctuary.

I rushed into the gallery, plopped the tray on a side table, ran the length of the hall, and burst out the garden door. I dashed to the side of the house that held the dungeon, to the spot where Lucien had trespassed.

Breathing in short heaves like a furious wolf, I stared at the narrow rectangle of glass that looked in on Daneska's dungeon. Sera ran up beside me.

"Dani said she saw him out here." I pointed at the smeared glass and started to walk toward it. "Maybe she lied."

There was a chance.

Daneska was the daughter of lies.

And just this once, I hoped she remained true to her birthright.

Please be a lie.

Sera caught my arm and yanked me back. "Look." She pointed at the ground and I saw I was about to trample a footprint. "And the grass has been flattened here, where he knelt and wiped the window to see her more clearly."

"Then it's true."

"Yes. I'm afraid so." She scoured the ground for more hints.

I wondered—nay, I hoped—was this only a bad dream?

"I'm sorry, Tess, but this is most definitely a man's boot print."

"How did he know she was here?"

"It's possible he followed Captain Grey and Lord Wyatt after they captured her. Or one of his men may have followed them." Sera wandered to some nearby bushes and found a broken branch. She searched the ground beneath it, following what few scattered prints she could find. "Or he may have simply guessed this is where the captain and Lord Wyatt would bring her."

"What of Phobos and Tromos? Why didn't they raise an alarm?"

She glanced sympathetically at me. "He lived across from Stranje House. He's familiar with the dogs. Not only that, he would've dealt with them in the past when he and Dani had their assignations. I'm sure he had a simple solution." Sera searched through nearby bushes and lifted out a soiled oilcloth. She sniffed it. "And here it is. He came prepared. Meat."

"Those traitors!" I spun around, looking for my shadow dogs. "I'd wondered where they'd gotten off to this morning. They weren't there for my run. They've feasted on his bribery and now they're hiding from me. As well they should."

Miss Stranje had caught up to us. "You mustn't be so severe on them. They're loyal, you know they are. If they realized we were being threatened, they would protect us with their lives. But I'm afraid when it comes to fresh meat, they're easily distracted."

Sera found more signs that had seemed completely invisible to me until she pointed them out. She spotted another partial boot imprint here, an overturned stone there, and another broken twig. "It is too bad we haven't had rain," she mumbled. "It would be much easier to follow his trail."

We tracked him to the secluded side of the house that hid

our knife-throwing targets and the panel I used to slip in and out of Stranje House. She stopped and spent several minutes checking the ground around it and the edges of the small opening.

At length Sera stood and turned to me, her brow puckered and her lips pursed. "Do you think it's possible that when Lady Daneska lived here, she showed Ghost our secret passages?"

"Yes." I swore silently. My fists flexed open and shut. "And for all we know, he could still be in there now."

Miss Stranje's hand flew to her temple and she rubbed it as if in pain.

"Surely he wouldn't be that bold," Sera said.

Miss Stranje glanced at me, her expression grim. "Bold? Yes. I wouldn't put it past him. He would take pleasure in the audacity of hiding here in the bosom of his enemy. But he's not stupid, and this may be too risky, even for him."

"One way to find out." I lunged for the panel.

She grabbed my arm. "That would be suicide."

"Not with this." I yanked my dagger out of the sheath.

"Even with that." She gave my arm a shake. "Think, Tess. He'd hear you coming. There are too many crevices and corners for him to hide in those dark passages. That little knife is hardly enough to protect you against the likes of him."

I clamped my teeth together. That was the second time today someone predicted I'd lose against him. I gritted my teeth and ground out, "But he might be in there . . . in my . . . my *places*." *My fortress. He has invaded my refuge.* I wanted to howl my anger.

"*Our* places." She held my shoulders firmly. "And if he *isn't* in there, you will waste a lifetime trying to prowl all those passages alone. No, we must approach this sensibly. Methodically. Rationally."

She gripped my shoulders tighter and leaned close, bearing down on me with her fierce hawk face. "Mark me, Tess. I'll not have you dead. Do you hear me? I will not."

I yielded with a nod and she let go.

"Have it your way." I whistled for the wolf-dogs. "They'll run him down." When they didn't come, I whistled again. "Where are those two beggars?"

Normally Phobos would have galloped to me in less than a heartbeat. But that morning he came around the corner at a weak trot, much slower than usual. He stepped sideways and lurched slightly, almost stumbling. Tromos followed behind him at a dragging pace, head down, and her tail drooping at half-mast.

My heart slowed almost to a stop. "No," I whispered and knelt to greet them. Their glassy eyes confirmed my suspicions. "The bastard drugged them."

"Good heavens." Miss Stranje stooped beside me, stroking Tromos's neck. "It's a mercy he didn't give them enough poison to kill them."

"He may have thought he did."

"Poor Tromos." She felt Tromos's nose for moisture and heat. "I hope her pups weren't harmed. Poor girl. She's lost so many litters. I'd hoped this time her pups would make it."

"Sera, hand me that meat cloth. Let's see if they can find him." I held the soiled wrapping up to Phobos's nose. He jerked away, recognizing the scent of the meat that had made him sick. "Find him," I commanded. But Phobos sat down. I raised the bloody cloth to Tromos's nose, hoping she would understand. "Hunt?" I asked.

Tromos tilted her head and sniffed the cloth again.

"That's right. Good girl. *Helfeydd*. Hunt." I used the old language. Her ears perked. "Find him. *Darganfydd*." I pointed toward the secret panel.

She put her nose to the ground, scanning from right to left, and followed the trail back to Daneska's cell window. She yipped and pawed the glass. Phobos joined her then, and the two of them went to work sniffing Ghost's path through our grounds.

They increased speed and followed the scent away from the house and into the park. My heart clenched when both dogs seemed particularly interested in the tall brush next to where the trees gapped between Stranje House and Ravencross Manor.

"There are more boot prints here." Sera pointed to the soil next to the tall underbrush. "These impressions are fairly deep. He must've stood here for a long while."

I crossed my arms and pressed them tight against my middle, knowing exactly what Lucien had done. "He hid from this vantage point and yet he had a clear view of the guards making their rounds at Ravencross Manor." I pictured him standing here, calculating when he might best sneak in and murder his brother. "I should go and see if Gabriel is all right."

"There's no need." Miss Stranje laid her hand on my forearm. "We'd have heard if he wasn't. He'll be arriving here in an hour or so. You must learn to trust him."

"It's not him I don't trust. It's his brother."

"I understand. But do remember, Gabriel defeated Lucien once. He can do it again if the need arises."

Maybe.

"Defeated him? They nearly killed each other. If he sees Ghost, the shock of seeing his brother alive might very well unnerve him. Lucien would not hesitate to use that advantage."

"Don't underestimate Gabriel. Besides, you cannot worry every time he is out of your sight. Life is fraught with peril. The mind can conjecture any number of deadly scenarios. What if he should fall down the stairs, or his horse throws him, or his ship sinks? Such speculations do you no good. We must deal with trouble when it comes. Not before."

I turned away, realizing that every time Captain Grey left her, Miss Stranje didn't know if he would return or not. She tugged me away from the spot where Lucien had skulked. "Come, the dogs are heading toward the road. It looks as though Ghost left and returned to whatever hole he is hiding in."

Phobos and Tromos stood at the gate, barking, wanting to get out and finish running him down. I patted them and assured them they'd done an excellent job. "You shall have extra bones today. And plenty of water to wash the poison away. I will see to it." I scratched Tromos's favorite spot behind her ears. "The bad man is gone."

But he'll be back.

Twenty-five

TRAPS

Miss Stranje spoke as if she read my mind. "We must carry on with our plan as if everything is normal. This may be our chance to trap him." She hurried off to tell Captain Grey what had transpired.

The rest of the day we worked on preparations for that evening's celebration. Some of us labored on the warship, while others helped Cook prepare for the birthday feast. Jane insisted the cake be done to Mr. Sinclair's specifications, and she made the frosting herself.

That afternoon, after I'd taken my turn at guarding the corridors outside Daneska's cell, Miss Stranje sent me to cut some roses for the table. Lord Ravencross insisted it was his duty to assist me in this onerous task.

We strolled out to the roses and he watched the militia running through their drills. He chuckled at one point and shook his head. "They're a motley bunch. Mac is on the verge of pulling his hair out trying to get them into shape. He's determined to run them through twice as many practice formations as they did yesterday."

I studied him as he spoke and wondered if it wouldn't be better for him to know the truth about his brother. Perhaps he could be persuaded to keep it a secret and go on as if he didn't know. Except that would be dishonest. Gabriel would never keep the title knowing it still belonged to his brother. If he told the House of Lords the truth, he would be forced to surrender his lands and home, his tenants would be in peril of a new overseer, and Gabriel's own loyalties might come into question. There could be a trial . . . and then his life would unravel.

I sighed. Trapped by the truth on both sides.

He carried the basket while I cut blooms from Miss Stranje's towering rosebushes.

"Smell." He lifted a perfect white blossom to my nose.

"Lovely," I said, trying to look pleased.

"You're being awfully quiet. Are you well?" He stroked the soft petals against my cheek.

I turned away to clip another rose. I'd asked Daneska that same question this morning. As it turned out, the same shadow hung over both of us. "Quite well, my lord. Worried, that's all. So much lives or dies on today's venture being a success."

"You worry too much," he said flippantly.

"Perhaps in this instance you are worrying too little."

He laid the rose in the basket. "How can I worry when I'm happier than I've ever been?"

I caught my lip, unwilling to snatch that happiness away from him even though his brother could appear at any moment and shatter his joy to pieces.

Eat, drink, and be merry, for tomorrow we . . .

I hated the end of that blasted expression. So I refused to be merry, as if that might stave off death.

A little too viciously, I cut another stem, ending another rose's life. I consoled myself that even if I hadn't cut it, the blossom would've died soon.

"Tess." He stilled my hand. "We're alone. They've all gone inside."

I glanced around. The garden was empty. The militia had marched across to the far side of the field. "And what does that signify?"

He set down the basket of roses. "I've had this idea that I can't seem to escape. It's the darnedest thing. I keep imagining you kissing me."

"I? Kiss you? Shouldn't it be the other way round?"

"Last time that's how it was. I kissed you." He came closer, trapping me between him and the rosebush.

I jutted my chin. "Yes, and rather roughly as I recall."

"Exactly. I made a mess of it."

I wouldn't say that. I was quite fond of that kiss.

Heat flooded my cheeks. Unable to meet his gaze, I studied the weave of his linen shirt.

"Now it's your turn."

"Oh, but I already kissed you, a few days ago. Don't tell me you have forgotten?"

"I remember, on the cheek, after that stunning declaration. But I've been thinking about lips."

"You may think about them all you want, my lord," I said, shaking my head and looking down. Afraid to meet his gaze. "I don't think it would be wise."

"Wisdom is for old men." I felt his breath on my forehead, warm and inviting.

"But this isn't the time. Nor the place. I'm quite certain Miss Stranje is up there with her telescope at this very minute, and she'll have it trained directly . . ."

He tilted my chin up, and when I met his gaze, my excuses faded. Gabriel's eyes are soul-soothing brown, and his lips make me long for him in ways I should not. The sweet smell of summer roses wrapped us in a honeyed cloak of euphoria.

"It will be all right," he said, his voice husky with the promise of bliss.

If only that were true.

"But tomorrow, or the next day, or maybe the next, it won't be all right," I argued, trying to break free of his spell. "Any day Napoleon may . . ."

He brushed his palm across my cheek, melting the last of my defenses. "I don't know what the next day will bring, but so long as I have breath, I'll not waste another minute without you. Tess, I—"

I didn't need to hear his professions of love. What good were words? I read the language of his soul and knew what he was about to say better than he did. I leaned up and pressed my lips against his.

Gabriel pulled me to his chest and covered my mouth with his. He kissed me back, gently at first, but then his kiss deepened, filled with the hunger of a lifetime without affection. And that same devastating force that bends mighty trees in a hurricane and sparks lightning in the storm surged through us.

I have never felt so weak as I did in that moment he held my mouth captive.

Nor as powerful.

When he let go, my legs wobbled and I clung to his arm.

"Good Lord," he said.

At least he could speak. I could only smile.

And I never smile.

. . .

Very late in the afternoon we all gathered down on the shore and prepared to launch the *Mary Isabella*. It turned out that Jane was needed to navigate after all, because it was decided that Captain Grey should row out ahead of them to place the targets for the bombs that Mr. Sinclair, Maya, and Georgie had designed.

We stood onshore rehearsing who was to go aboard the *Mary Isabella* and who was to stay ashore. Lord Ravencross stood beside me, drumming with excitement. "This has the air of a momentous occasion. I believe I would like to sail out with them."

The dream I'd had of him drowning in dark gray water flashed before my eyes. "No!" I gulped down some of my fear and in a calmer voice advised him against it. "My lord, you must believe me, there are very good reasons why you must not go out on the water. Not tonight. In fact, we should both stay ashore. Both of us."

It must've been the desperation behind my plea because he looked askance at me and then relented. "Ah." He pursed his lips and nodded gravely. "I wondered why you didn't insist on going with them." Then he had a sudden thought. "But the others, will they be all right?"

I sighed and shifted uncomfortably, digging the toe of my shoe into the sand. "I don't know. I told you these dreams are next to useless. I only know for certain that you and I did not fare well in the water at night."

There was no more time to discuss it. Mr. Sinclair gave the order, and we helped shove the *Mary Isabella* into the sea. The tide carried her out a short way from shore, and Lord Wyatt lit the furnace. At the first puff of smoke, we all cheered. A few moments later and the piston rod lurched into action, and the paddle wheel began to turn.

"Huzzah!" The shout went up, both aboard ship and onshore.

The wheel turned as if by magic, slapping the water with a

soothing rhythm as it carried them farther from the beach. Georgie jumped up and down, clapping. Lord Wyatt tried to nudge her a little farther from the edge of the flat deck while she jumped. Maya waved merrily at us.

Even Miss Stranje looked quite pleased. I couldn't help but dance a little myself. Gabriel was right: if it weren't for the terror of that dream, I would've very much liked to have been on that ship.

Sera and I hugged each other with delight and waved back to the sailors aboard our very own little warship.

"Come." Sera tugged my arm. "From up on the cliffs we'll be able to see when they fire the bombs at the targets."

The three of us dashed up the trail to the top of the cliffs overlooking the ocean. I pulled our telescope out of my pocket and trained it on the *Mary Isabella*, watching her chug out to sea.

The evening was fine and fair as the sun lowered to the horizon, kissing a few scattered clouds with brilliant halos. Before the launch, Miss Stranje had instructed the servants to carry a table to the bluffs. Maya had spread a cloth over it, and the rest of us laid out plates of cheese and bread, bowls of early strawberries, and glasses for the wine Lord Ravencross contributed. Everything was perfectly assembled, so that we looked very much like a group of friends gathered for a perfectly innocent seaside picnic.

One of Gabriel's soldiers helped Captain Grey row out several furlongs, where they placed two buoyant slabs of wood. Then they lit two large Chinese lanterns, which lifted like glowing kites, and tethered them to the floating wood. Lanterns had been Madame Cho's idea. She helped us construct them and told us how, when she was a child, she and her brothers used to make them out of papers dyed bright colors. Our white silken globes looked beautiful floating just above the waves. They glowed like giant fireflies in the early evening sky and created a perfect target for Miss Stranje to aim Sinclair's bomb harpoon, as I'd taken to calling the ballista they built to fire their spears with explosive tips.

Through the glass I watched Mr. Sinclair carefully lift from the munitions rack a spear rigged with the bomb he and Georgiana had constructed. They hadn't been certain how volatile the bombs might be and had thought that for this test voyage, it would be prudent to bring aboard only two of the four bombs they'd constructed. I could tell from here Jane was nervous as she watched him carry it.

He motioned with his head for her to move back. "Farther." I saw him gesture. He steadied himself on the rocking ship and made each step with all the caution of a father holding a sleeping infant he was terrified of awakening. Not until he cradled the spears in the groove running down the center of the ballista did he step back and take a deep breath.

"He's loaded the arrow," I told the Sera and Gabriel.

"Let me see." Gabriel wanted a turn with the spyglass, and I could tell by the way Sera strained up on her toes to see, so did she. He took a look and then handed the glass to her. "That ship is a marvel."

Lord Ravencross had dressed with care for the occasion, in a proper coat and everything. The effect on me was rather embarrassing. I could not keep from looking at him. He turned and caught me staring at him. I blushed and looked away, unable push from my thoughts the way he had kissed me. So I busied myself slicing cheddar, and if the ruddy knife would've stopped shaking I might've done a half-decent job of it.

He strolled over and placed his hand atop mine. "I fear for the cheese."

I couldn't help it, I laughed. Something I'm not accustomed to doing. Fortunately, just then a flock of curlews flew overhead. Their odd rippling song always sounded as if they were injured.

Lucky for me, it covered the even more awkward bark of my laughter.

"They're getting ready to shoot the first one," Sera shouted.

Maya stood on the starboard deck holding aloft a large red swallowtail signal flag, waving it back and forth to let Captain Grey know they were ready. Captain Grey replied by waving a white striped flag, giving them the go-ahead to discharge the explosives.

"Miss Stranje is sighting the ballista." Sera gave me a turn with the spyglass, and I focused it on our headmistress lining up the giant bow.

Miss Stranje had insisted that she be the one to handle the weapon. "If Captain Grey is anywhere in the vicinity of your targets, I simply will not allow anyone but me to aim that thing. It's too dangerous." She'd taken several practice shots from shore using unarmed spears but ruminated on the fact that the weight of the bomb would have considerable effect on the trajectory.

Captain Grey and the soldier were rowing mightily to get as far away from the target as possible. I swung the glass back to the *Mary Isabella*. Georgie was bouncing up and down on her toes. Lord Wyatt appeared to be leaning over Miss Stranje, giving her additional instructions. She shooed him away. Mr. Sinclair seemed to be concentrating on steering the rudder. And I knew from experience that in the middle of all that chaos, Maya would be humming softly to herself.

With a snap and jolt, the arrow whizzed across the horizon. It raced across the sky faster than any gull, and when it dipped to go underwater, the sound of the explosion made me jump. We didn't need the telescope to see the burst of flames as the bomb exploded and sent a fountain splashing up in the ocean.

Gabriel whistled and took the telescope dangling from my fingertips. He adjusted it. "She missed the target. It won't run through the water like we thought it might. That compression switch is too sensitive."

Gabriel put down the telescope. "Sinclair is reloading," he apprised us. "I expect now they won't try for a shot through the water."

Maya waved the red flag and Captain Grey responded with the all-clear signal. We were so preoccupied with the first explosion and anxious about the next test arrow that we failed to notice the gentleman walking out to join us on the cliffs until he hailed us.

"Good evening!" Mr. Chadwick called.

We all turned. All except Lord Ravencross, who was busy staring through the telescope.

"Good evening." Sera turned quite red. Or perhaps it was only the sun's reflection as it changed to rose and gold on the horizon.

"There it is," Gabriel reported. "She's fired the second one. It's headed straight for the Chinese lantern."

"I say!" Mr. Chadwick took off his hat and shaded his eyes with it, watching our spear's progress. The trajectory was promising. The arc looked nearly perfect. It hit the lantern and exploded in a burst of fire and sparks.

"Magnificent!" Gabriel lowered the spyglass.

"Fireworks?" asked our justice of the peace's son, still holding his hat and staring at the smoke fading from the explosion. "And what sort of craft is that they're firing from?" He pointed at the smoke puffing from our steamship.

Sera, Gabriel, and I looked at each other, uncertain how to respond. It was Sera who turned to him with an unusually broad smile. "Aren't the fireworks splendid, Mr. Chadwick? You must join us for our celebration."

"Celebration?" He looked confused and tucked some of his cherubic curls back behind his ear. "Lord Ravencross's men mentioned you were having some sort of festivities. Is it a royal jubilee of some kind? I hadn't heard."

"Oh, no, nothing quite as grand as that." She told him about Miss Stranje's cousin from America and how he liked to celebrate his birthday with explosives.

Mr. Chadwick bowed cordially to her. "I didn't mean to intrude. I'd called on Lord Ravencross on a business matter and his men told me I might find him here." He turned briefly to Gabriel. "The militia appears to be getting into fighting order, my lord. Your man MacDougal is doing a superb job of it."

Gabriel muttered his agreement and turned back to watch the last of the explosion burn out.

"You must join us for supper, Mr. Chadwick," I said, thinking that his company might be good for Sera, and besides it would've been boorish not to ask him to dine with us. "We'll have a grand supper and there will be cake to follow, cake with frosting. Or so I'm told. The more the merrier." I directed him to the table. "You must be parched after your ride over. A glass of wine, perhaps?"

Sera stood beside the table, fidgeting with the cloth. She attempted to keep our guest distracted from looking at the steamship puffing back to shore. "Do you enjoy fireworks, Mr. Chadwick?"

"I suppose everyone must. How can one not?" Mr. Chadwick kept trying to glance over his shoulder toward the sea. "My father took me to London to see the fireworks display at Vauxhall Gardens. But those produced a different sort of explosion than yours do."

"These are a special type," Lord Ravencross assured him.

Mr. Chadwick nodded genially to me. "A pleasure to see you again, Miss Aubreyson. I see you are getting along better with Lord Ravencross."

I have no idea why, but my cheeks warmed foolishly at his comment. "I . . . He . . ."

Mr. Chadwick rocked on his heels. "And have you consented to be his wife?"

"Heavens no." I gaped at him. "What I mean to say is, there has been a misunderstanding—"

"That's a tactless question, Mr. Chadwick." Gabriel pushed himself between me and Mr. Chadwick.

"Begging your pardon, my lord. I had thought that you announced . . . but she . . ." He realized the pickle he'd gotten himself into and backed away, turning to look for Sera. There was little chance then of our keeping the warship a secret, for when he turned he had a first-rate view of the steamship puffing merrily toward the shore. "By the stars! It's a steamship."

"So it is, Mr. Chadwick, so it is," said Sera quietly. "We call her the *Mary Isabella*."

The setting sun cast a mellow orange glow over everything, while the sky above us darkened to a deep Spanish blue.

"I'm going to go help pull her ashore." I dashed away from them, taking the path down the cliffs. Gabriel wasn't far behind.

Our sailors waved at us as they landed on the shore. "Did you see it?" Jane shouted to me. "Wasn't it glorious?"

"It was," I shouted back, racing along the beach to meet them.

Mr. Sinclair grabbed Jane by the waist and gleefully spun her around. She swatted at his shoulders. "Put me down this instant, Mr. Sinclair. Do try to be civilized."

"I can't help myself, Lady Jane. I'm just so blamed happy I feel as if I might burst." He set her down, still grinning broadly. "But then, what do you expect? After all, I am a heathen from the Colonies."

Lord Wyatt jumped onto the beach. Gabriel and I helped him tug the craft as far onshore as possible, and then he tied the docking line around a sturdy boulder.

"Well done, everyone." Miss Stranje applauded. "Well done."

Lord Wyatt slapped Sinclair genially on the back. "First rate, Sinclair. Your uncle would be proud."

I warned them that Mr. Chadwick had surprised us with a visit and that he would be along shortly with Sera. A few moments later the two of them walked up the beach toward us.

Mr. Chadwick's eyes were enormous, and for once he seemed at a loss for words.

Sera turned to him. "What do you think?"

"It's a marvel." He twisted his hat in his hands and smiled hesitantly, as if he wasn't quite sure what he'd stumbled upon.

"Yes, well, that it is. But now I confess, I'm famished." Miss Stranje tugged him away from our prototype. "Shall we all adjourn to the house for some supper and cake?" She looped her arm through Mr. Chadwick's, towing him away from our ship, but he continued trying to peek over his shoulder.

Mr. Sinclair had the same problem. He couldn't stop fussing over his ship, inspecting the pontoons for damage and smoothing his hand over the connecting rods and the flywheel.

"Come along, Mr. Sinclair," Jane called to him. "The furnace is out and your beautiful *Mary Isabella* is snug and secure in the cove."

He walked up the beach beside Jane, turning around and walking backward every once in a while to gaze at the *Mary Isabella*. "She's a beauty, isn't she?"

"Indubitably." Jane caught him before he tripped on a rock.

We had all climbed up to the bluffs. Miss Stranje crooked her finger at Sera. "Miss Wyndham, perhaps you would like to show Mr. Chadwick to the house. He must be positively famished after his long ride over here."

"It's not so very long a ride," Mr. Chadwick assured her. "We're only a few miles up the coast."

"I'm well aware of the distance." Miss Stranje patted his arm as if he was ten years old instead of twenty. "I've been to your estate and had tea with your lovely mother on several occasions. An extraordinary woman, your mother. I'm fortunate to count her a friend. That is all the more reason why you must join us for a bite of supper and cake. I wouldn't dream of sending you home hungry at this hour."

"I oughtn't impose. Although I do have some news for Lord Ravencross, about the incident." He turned in search of his subject. "My lord, the coroner has concluded his investigation. He and my father are convinced the men who made an attempt on your life were indeed hired assassins. I'm not as certain we've come upon the complete answer yet. I don't suppose you have any French relatives who might want to do you in?"

"None." Gabriel's answer was flat and didn't invite speculation.

"It is so very perplexing. I find it particularly puzzling that these same men would also attempt to abduct the young ladies. My father and the coroner have closed the matter, but we are still left with a great many unanswered questions."

Miss Stranje clicked her tongue in a mild scold. "Come, Mr. Chadwick, we must not speak of such distressing matters tonight." She handed him off to Sera. "This is a birthday celebration. We shall be happy for Mr. Sinclair's sake. He is a very long way from home."

"My apologies. I promise to set the mystery aside for the evening." Mr. Chadwick bowed. "But if I'm to stay, you must all call me Quinton. Please, I insist upon it."

He was a nuisance, an obstacle to be sure, and altogether too curious about everything, but I have to admit it was difficult not to like Quinton Chadwick.

"Are you a fifth child, Mr. Chadwick?" Sera asked as he strolled with us back to Stranje House.

"Oh, you mean because my name is Quinton." He smiled at her. "No, my mother named me after her father. He was the fifth child. I, on the other hand, am an only child."

"Of course you are." Sera sighed. "No wonder they doted upon you."

"They did," he agreed cheerily. "I am most fortunate."

"You are. I envy you." Sera quietly admitted the sad truth. She said it so softly I doubt anyone but me paid any heed.

Mr. Chadwick regaled us the rest of the way with stories of how his intrepid mother taught him to ride and jump hedges as a youngster, and how his father taught him to play chess at six, but when at seven he bested his father, their chess-playing days came to a close.

We entered the dining room and all of us murmured approval at the sight. Greaves instructed the footmen to set an extra place at the table. The spectacle of the dining room was all very grand and elegant. The silver shone in the candlelight, the crystal goblets glistened, and my roses graced the center of the table in a large vase.

I could scarcely look at them. Even the fragrance of those blossoms reminded me of Gabriel's heated kiss in the garden and caused my cheeks to burn. Gabriel, on the other hand, stared at them quite steadily and with a jovial curl of his lips. It was not like him to be jovial.

Cook had prepared a feast for us. Of course, most of us had assisted in the preparations. That is, when we weren't busy mixing gunpowder or building bomb casings. The result was a banquet suitable for a duke's birthday and, we hoped, passable for our American. He praised Miss Stranje and seemed genuinely delighted. We took our seats around the table and were treated to a first course of white soup. After which Greaves and our footman paraded in carrying platters of roast chicken, new potatoes and creamed peas, crab soufflé, mutton roasted with turnips and carrots, and steaming freshly baked rolls slathered in butter.

Best of all, throughout the entire meal, the biggest, most splendid cake I have ever seen sat on the sideboard tantalizing us.

Cake.

I'd heard stories of such cakes served at the Prince Regent's palace in Brighton and at great homes in London, but I'd never seen one in person. Cook had outdone herself. Not only that, but our cake was coated with a thick, glistening sugar icing.

After tucking away a hearty portion of mutton, several slices of chicken, and a generous helping of crab soufflé, Mr. Sinclair set down his knife and blotted his mouth, looking quite satisfied. "I must say, that cake looks extraordinary."

How he would have room for it strained the imagination.

"It's twice as big as any my mother ever baked. I thank you, Miss Stranje. This is a perfect end to a perfect day."

Lady Jane smiled to herself.

Georgie leaned over and confided to me, "Jane made the icing. Boiled butter and sugar mixed with egg whites. Cook fussed at her, saying it was a sin to cover up such a fine moist spice cake with a crust of sugar. But Jane convinced her with a tale of woe about how our poor Mr. Sinclair is such a long way from home and he would be terribly disappointed without it."

Poor Mr. Sinclair raised his cup, not in a toast but in a proposal. "What would you say to inviting all the servants in to share a piece of it with us? That's what we do at home on our birthdays." He lowered his glass. "Do you suppose your Madame Cho would like to eat cake with us? It might help her warm up to me a mite. I'm afraid we got off to a bad start when I first arrived . . ."

I didn't hear a word he said after that.

Twenty-six

COUNTERTRAPS

An intense uneasiness came upon me. Not as in a dream, or a day vision; it was as if I'd misplaced something of monumental proportion. I rose with a start. "I'll take Madame Cho a plate." She was standing guard downstairs, but I couldn't very well remind them of that with Mr. Chadwick sitting at the table.

Miss Stranje squinted at me as if trying to figure out what I was up to. "Philip will take her a plate."

But the footman was busy serving the fruit and cheese, and Greaves was pouring wine.

"I would like to do it. I haven't seen her much today." More to the point, my insides were gnawing on themselves. I couldn't possibly sit another minute until I checked on her and Daneska myself. I filled a plate and promised to return to carry cake to her, or perhaps I would relieve her of her duties elsewhere so that she might come and enjoy cake with Mr. Sinclair in person.

Ravencross studied me with an uneasy expression. "I'll come with you."

"No, thank you, my lord. I would rather go alone."

His features shuttered closed. He suspected I was up to something. But I couldn't very well allow him into the dungeons and passages lurking beneath Stranje House.

I forced myself to walk with calculated calm until I left the dining room and turned the corner. Then I flew through the hall and raced down the stairway to the dungeons and cellars. They were dark, darker than they should be. The lamps had sputtered out, or else someone had put them out. I held the plate of food with a trembling hand and pulled my dagger from its sheath. I slowed my steps, not wanting careless footfalls to alert anyone to my presence. The closer I got to those cold underground corridors, the more I felt certain something was very wrong.

There was one lamp at the end by Daneska's cell. That would be Madame Cho's lamp, a thin oily amber light that flickered and shivered off the gray stone walls, creating shadows that unnerved me as they moved beside me like phantoms. I peeked around the corner and drew back. Cho was not at her post and Daneska's cell door hung partially open.

I set the plate down and crept forward, inching toward the door with my dagger poised to strike. The heavy oak creaked as I pushed it open. Daneska was hunched over Cho.

Daneska spun around. "There you are! I've been waiting for you."

"Get away from her." I charged in with my dagger.

But Daneska jerked Cho's limp body in front of her and held a knife at Madame's throat. I recognized the blade. It was Madame Cho's own knife. She'd been disarmed. I couldn't understand it. "How?"

Daneska pressed the knife tighter against Madame Cho's throat. "Drop your dagger. Now, if you please."

I let my blade clatter to the floor.

"Kick it over here. That's right."

Cho's head was bleeding heavily. "What have you done to her?"

"It's nothing. A little bump on the head, that is all." She swung one of her manacles in a circle, as if it were a mace. "At least these bracelets came in handy for something."

This was all too incomprehensible. If I didn't know better I would've thought it was a dream. "How did you get them off?"

Daneska pursed her lips as if I was being foolish. "Did you really think I couldn't pick the lock on these old things? *Phfft.* I've had them off since the second day."

"But your wrists, I saw—"

"Oh, yes, that was so very affecting, or perhaps the word is affectionate, when you ripped your own dress to cushion my poor torn skin." She was mocking me. "Really, Tessika, didn't you wonder why I hadn't torn my own underskirt to do that for myself?"

"How did you ever get the better of Cho? She's faster than you are."

"Fast isn't everything. Birds are fast. Haven't you ever thrown a rock to kill a morning dove? Did you know Madame Cho is the only one who ever empties my slops? Oh, but this is not done out of kindness. No. She never even looks in my direction when she does it. Cho hates me too much. And yet she does what none of the rest of you will do. She didn't know I'd had my chains off. She toddled in to change my piss pot a few minutes ago. One hard swing from the corner, and she went down like a good little dove."

"You wretch."

"The hardest part was slipping those irritating things back on every time one of you came down to visit me."

I started for Madam Cho, but Daneska yanked her in tighter

with the knife. "*Tsk, tsk.* Stay back or I'll cut her throat." Her eyebrows danced up as if the thought excited her. "I may do it anyway unless you talk sweetly to me."

"What do you want, Daneska?"

She exhaled with irritation. "I have been perfectly clear from the first day."

When I shrugged, she snapped at me, "You."

She wasn't making sense. "Go ahead, run away. Escape. But leave Madam Cho alone. She's bleeding. Let me take care of her. I promise I won't stop you. Go," I pleaded.

"Why are you being thick?" She frowned at me. Daneska doesn't frown very often. She doesn't want to ruin her pretty face. At least that's what she told me once. I think it is more likely that she is quite happy being wicked.

"You are coming with us, Tessika. You are the prize I will bring to Napoleon. And now you must hold very still because Ghost, he is not so fond of you as I am."

He stepped through the doorway with a pistol pointed straight at my head. A pistol I had seen before in a dream.

Lucien.

Ghost. I sucked back a gasp. He looked so much like Gabriel, and yet not. He was taller than his brother, and as improbable as it seemed, he was even more handsome. But a wintery hardness radiated off him that put the cold stones around us to shame. His father would've been pleased. Lucien had, indeed, turned to steel. He moved toward me, cornering me, every step deliberate and efficient.

Maybe if I was very, very good he would disappear as he had in that dream.

"Ah, *très bien.* I see you remembered the rope." Daneska smiled at him. "Tie her hands. Mind you, she is a tricky one. Use a very good knot."

He said nothing, as if he need not trouble himself responding to Daneska.

"Now, Tessika," Daneska began to chide me with unsettling cheerfulness. "If you make one tiny move that I don't like while the real Lord of Ravencross secures your hands, I will cut Cho. And just to prove I mean what I say, I will start right here by her chin." Daneska etched a thin line of blood along the underside of Madame Cho's chin.

No!

My shoulders lurched to attention, and I tried to hold in the unbidden noises screaming up my throat—a war cry, a wounded moan. Either sound would betray me and testify to Daneska the hold she had over me. For Madame Cho's sake, I arched my neck, and choked it back down my gullet.

She saw through me and scoffed. "You always were too fond of this old woman." She waggled the bloody knife at me. "If I kill her, I'll be doing you a favor. I tried to warn you, love makes you weak."

A low, guttural rumble came from Ghost. It was a sound achingly familiar to me, having heard his brother utter it. But when it came from Lucien, it sounded twisted and indecipherable. I couldn't tell if what Daneska had said pleased him or annoyed him, or both.

He slammed me against the wall and studied me closely. Too closely. His icy gaze seared down the curve of my neck and over the rise of my breasts. Then he glowered at me, taking the measure of my soul. Where Gabriel's eyes are a warm melting brown, Lucien's are dark, like soil found at the bottom of a deep pit. There was no light in them.

He watched my face steadily as he twisted my wrists and bound them with a rough hemp rope, cinching the knot so tight I couldn't keep from grimacing. My wince drew the faintest suggestion of a smile to his lips, but it quickly vanished.

"Did you get the drawings?" Daneska asked him.

Lucien pulled some folded papers out of his coat. "They were right where they were supposed to be." He shook them open. The first was a detailed drawing Sera had made of Sinclair's warship.

The second pleased Daneska enormously. "Notes. A list of parts and materials. It's all here."

Jane's notes.

I grimaced. "You've got what you want, just go."

She grinned and folded up the papers. "Oh, no, my dear, you are coming with us. You're to be the emperor's new toy."

"You can't make me dream for him."

"Oh, but I can, my dear Tessika." She laughed and ripped a strip of cloth from the hem of her filthy underdress. "I can."

The silver bowl.

Of course! The green water was probably absinthe laced with laudanum. The two were often mixed together. Once they got me to the palace, they intended to keep me in a drugged stupor, trapped in the madness of my dreams.

Better I die here.

She twisted the torn cloth and held it out to Lucien. "Gag her."

The instant he turned, I kicked out as hard as I could, aiming a crippling blow at his knee. In one stunningly smooth motion, Ghost dodged it, grabbed my foot, and flipped me to the floor. My head hit the stones, and for a second I thought the lantern had flickered out.

Daneska laughed, looking quite gleeful as she knelt over me and tied the gag in place. "I told you, you are no match for him."

Ghost jerked me to my feet.

Madame Cho was still unconscious and bleeding when they locked her in the cell. I prayed someone would come for her soon.

Like a lamb being led to slaughter, Daneska and Ghost led me out of the dungeon and down into the secret passage that wound beneath Stranje House to the sea cave. We were so far beneath the house that even if I could scream, no one would hear me.

Their sloop was tied to the dock in the cave. We passed the skeleton that had frightened Georgie so badly her first night at Stranje House. On a lark, Jane and I had dressed those old bones in a pink gown. I thought to myself that the gown was getting a little faded and if I ever came back to Stranje House I might fix that. Odd, the mundane thoughts that tumble through the mind when everything else has turned impossibly dark and hopeless.

They tugged me into the boat and tied my lead line to a cleat on the gunwale. The thing about the sea cave is that it is rather tricky to navigate. It's not hard to row into the cavern, especially if the tide is with you. No, it's the rowing *out* that's difficult.

Ghost, who up until this time remained frighteningly quiet, began to curse. "You're going to have to help, Daneska."

"Must I?" She grimaced at the long oars. "I bet we could make her do it."

"With her hands tied? Don't be daft. Row."

And so Daneska did her best, and while they struggled, trying to keep from bashing into the cave walls, I worked on loosening my knot. Neither of us made rapid headway. By the time they managed to row out of the cave, my progress on the knot had taken a disheartening turn. Amid all the sloshing, the rope had gotten wet and the hemp began to swell.

Once a boat clears the mouth of that cave, the sea is determined to push it back in. Especially at high tide, which it was that night. And if that doesn't do the job, there are always the rocks. The waves tend to smash unwary sailors against the rocky shore.

"I'm tired." Daneska slumped over her oars.

"Stop complaining and put your back into it."

Unfortunately, Daneska did a much better job than I thought she would. Soon we were moving farther from the coast and my chances of escape were lessening by the second. I picked furiously at Ghost's knot, but between the hemp swelling and my fingers turning numb from lack of circulation, I'd managed to loosen only one loop.

My heart sank when Lucien said, "You can stop now. We're far enough away that we can hoist the sail."

It was a clear night and I could see the lights of Stranje House atop the cliff. Surely by now they knew what had happened. I hoped above all that they'd found Madame Cho and were tending to her injuries.

At this point I knew I had little chance of escaping alive. The fading silhouette of Ravencross Manor drew my gaze and filled me with regrets. I wished I'd kissed Gabriel one more time. I wish I hadn't fretted about not having a future. I should've been happier when I had the chance.

Still, I picked at the rope. *Habit,* I suppose. Miss Stranje required us to do timed practices of getting ourselves untied. Normally I excelled at it, but Ghost tied an exceptionally good knot, and the wet rope made it nearly impossible to loosen. Frustrated, I growled and bit down on the gag in my mouth, working it with my teeth.

They were hauling up the sail when I caught a faint sound that made me start picking at my ropes faster. The *slap, slap, slap* of a paddle wheel. It was far-away, and if you didn't know what it was you might think it was just the lapping of the waves in the distance or the beat of a sail catching the wind. Except this sound was too regular. Mechanically regular. Even with that filthy gag in my mouth, my lips spread in a wide smile. It was so blessedly wonderfully regular. Quite possibly the most beautiful sound I'd ever heard.

They would see the sloop's white sail, I told myself. *Please God, let them see that white sail shining in the moonlight.* The sound got louder by the minute, and I picked at my bonds faster. Finally, I could see the outline of the ship and the puff of smoke rising from her stack.

"Do you hear that?" Daneska asked.

"Hear what?" Ghost asked.

I tried to make a noise despite the gag in my mouth. It drew her attention for a moment. "Hush. Be grateful I didn't make you row. I daresay, I shall have blisters for a week. Whereas you could've rowed and spared me—"

She squinted in the direction of the sound and stood up.

"Sit down, Dani," Ghost snarled. "If the sail comes about, it will knock you overboard. I'm in no mood to stop and fish your carcass out of the water. Although you could do with a bath."

"Do you not hear that? It's the oddest noise and it's getting louder." Then she saw it. "What is that?" She pointed.

"I'll not tell you again, Daneska. Sit down or I will knock you overboard myself." He held the tiller with one hand and with the other reached over to adjust the boom line.

She plopped back down on the rowing thwart, and jabbed her finger in the direction of the steamship. "For pity's sake, look!"

He turned with deliberate slowness in the direction she pointed. Straightened. Stood and looked harder. "Damnation."

Ghost tied off the tiller and ran to the bow. He drew out the flintlock he'd pointed at me earlier, aimed, and fired. The blast nearly deafened me. But I thought I heard a distant *ping*. His bullet must've hit metal. *Please let that be all it hit. Let it be a hole in their smokestack, not in something that would sink them, and not in someone's body.*

I couldn't bear it if one of them got hurt trying to save me. I was the one who was supposed to do the saving. Not them. They had too much at risk.

The sail trapped a cloud of acrid gun smoke in the boat. Dani coughed. Ghost primed his gun and fired again. My heart clenched tighter than the knot Lucien had tied around my hands.

The warship steamed straight for us. I heard a soft whistling sound. Through the dark I saw moonlight catch on the silver tip of a spear speeding straight for the bow of our sloop. Ghost dove out of the way, just as the spear hit where he'd been standing and exploded in a burst of flame.

The impact rocked the sloop, and flames crackled to life on the bow.

They were trying to shoot us down. *Even with me aboard the ship.* It stung. But a split second later I realized they'd chosen rightly. Daneska and Ghost had to be stopped at any cost.

Good!

As things stood, I'd planned to attack Ghost once I got these ropes off. I'd intended to sink the ship, along with Ghost, Daneska, and the stolen warship plans. I would much rather die out here under the stars and the wide-open sky than trapped in Napoleon's silken prison.

But as I considered where the spear struck, I suspected Jane had the spyglass to her eye and knew exactly which end of the sloop I was sitting in. Either way, shooting us down was my best chance of escape.

"Bucket!" Ghost shouted from where he had fallen amidships. But Dani grabbed a wool blanket from beneath the thwart and began beating the flames. It didn't work. There is oil in a Greek fire bomb and that oil spreads and latches on rather handily to things like woolen blankets.

"Wet it!" Ghost yelled at her as he grabbed a bucket. She

dipped the blanket in the sea. He hung over the side and scooped water onto the flame, spreading the oil in blazing rivulets along the bow. He cursed.

Daneska grumbled that it was all my fault as she beat out flames. Then she changed her tune and swore that as soon as she could get her hands on Georgiana Fitzwilliam, she would ring her worthless neck.

"This is that smart-mouthed little redhead's doing." She made sure I was paying attention to her rant. "Mark me. I'll have her freckled hide for this."

I quietly slipped off my shoes and hoped she hadn't noticed that I'd finally freed myself from Ghost's confounded knot.

Waves lapped against the side of the boat. This was my chance. Soon the fire would be out and Daneska would have the presence of mind to tie me more securely. I heard the constant chug of the steam engine getting closer. The quarter-moon cast little light that night. It glimmered soft as doves' wings on the rolling swells. I slipped out of my gag and silently set the ropes aside.

The *Mary Isabella*'s silhouette was black and distinct against the charcoal gray of night. The pinprick glow of a lantern twinkled on her starboard bow like a guiding star—a very tiny needle in this vast watery haystack. I marked her direction and, gauging the moonlit ripples of the sea, noted that I would need to cut across the current.

The fire crackled quieter. Daneska beat at the flames less furiously. It was time.

I did not mean to make a splash, but flinging oneself out into the sea tends to have that effect. When I surfaced, I heard Daneska scream, "She jumped!"

Dani cursed me in one of her many languages, or maybe several. Then she tried to reason with me. "Would you rather drown than serve the man who will one day rule the world? Are you that big a fool?"

I am.

My petticoats quickly waterlogged and weighed me down. I chided myself for not ripping them off before I'd jumped. The ocean was cold and salt burned my eyes. I'd expected that. What I hadn't expected was the strength of the current pulling me off course.

Despite the sloshing in my ears, I heard Daneska's frantic plea. "Lucien, do something. She's getting away."

"What would you have me do? Our ship is afire."

"She was supposed to be my gift to Napoleon. If she's going to be obstinate, shoot her. Kill her!" Dani always was the sort who would rather rip something up than share it.

"Don't be a fool. Help me get this fire out. Let her go. She'll drown before they get to her anyway."

"Not her. She's not the drowning sort. Give me your gun. I'll do it." Daneska usually remains calm. Nothing ruffles her scales. She never screeches. Why would she screech when she found cooing so much more effective? And yet, that night, she shrieked at Ghost, as if the clawing pitch of her voice might force him to comply. "Change sail. Bring us around."

I didn't look back. I swam. Swam for all I was worth. The current fought me. My waterlogged gowns kept pulling me under. Still I swam.

"Give me your gun," she screamed.

The first shot seemed to echo across the waves. It sounded louder than a flintlock on land. The blast seemed to ripple through the massive sea and stir the waves. With a splash, the musket ball plunged into the water next to my shoulder.

I would be lying if I said I wasn't afraid. I was. But I raced against terror almost every night in my dreams. Terror and I were old friends.

The galloping of my heart only made my arms and legs pump faster. I dove under the waves, thinking if she couldn't see me, she couldn't hit me. But I couldn't tell direction from under the waves, and underwater the current seemed to blow me sideways as if I were nothing but a feather. I burst through the surface gasping and lost.

Still, I pulled myself forward through the sea, spitting out salt water and flinging seaweed out of my eyes and mouth, trying to cross the current to where I'd last seen the *Mary Isabella*. Desperate for air and unable to see between the swells, I kicked my hardest and lifted my head as high as I could above the waves. When a swell carried me up, I spotted her lantern shining in the distance and I dove for it.

Just as I dove forward into the sea, another shot rang over my head. The ball whizzed past and sliced through the water not more than an arm's length in front of me. I prayed she would be slow at reloading.

The warship chugged toward me, coming closer and closer. Not much farther, I told myself. How could I make them see me? They wouldn't even know I was in the water. If I tried to wave or shout, it would give away my position to Daneska. Except then I realized Georgie would know. She would hear the shooting and guess I had jumped. Jane would know, too. And Gabriel. When I thought about it, I realized everyone aboard that warship, with the exception of Mr. Sinclair, would be absolutely certain that I'd jumped.

I flung my arms ahead, pulling and grabbing at the water as if it were a fallen ladder and I was crawling across it to save my life. Sloshing and churning across the waves, my arms burned and I'd gulped down near as much water as I had air. I stuck my head up and through bleary eyes I thought I saw that there were not one but two lamps on the bow.

If I could see the *Mary Isabella,* so could Daneska. And she would know where to follow me. Another gunshot cracked through the air. This one struck mere inches from my head. I swam under the waves, spreading my wings through the water like a bird. A very weary bird. When I emerged for breath, I heard Gabriel. His voice echoed like a church bell over the water. "There! She's in the water. There."

"They're shooting at her. Fire another arrow!" That sounded like Georgie. I heard the panic and wanted to call out to her and tell her to not be afraid. But every ounce of my strength was needed for forcing one arm in front of the other.

Another shot shook the night. This one came from in front of me. They were firing at Daneska.

"This will scare them off." It sounded like Lord Wyatt. I heard the twang and sharp snap of a spear firing. An instant later, an explosion ruptured the sky.

No! I wanted to shout. *Don't frighten them away. Chase them down.* They must be captured or sunk to the bottom of the sea. Our warship was faster than their crippled sloop, or it would be if they didn't stop to rescue me.

But I was tiring out, gagging on brine, and sinking lower with every floundering stroke. I would never make it to shore. Even reaching the *Mary Isabella* seemed an impossible feat. At least Daneska had stopped shooting at me. Ghost was right; she needn't have wasted her ammunition. His prediction that I would become fish food was proving true.

Bitterly chilled, my arms felt wooden and numb. My fingers were so cold I couldn't feel them. I'd swallowed so much salt water

I needed to retch. I hadn't taken a full breath for far too long. Still, I flopped one hand forward and tried to drag myself through the waves as best I could.

"I think I see her," someone shouted. But I could no longer discern voices. They sounded so very faint and far away, as if echoing to me from across a great valley. I heaved up water. There was no strength left. *None.* Not even an ounce. My arms relaxed and floated wide. I bobbed on a swell. My gown felt so very heavy. It tugged at me, luring me down into the blissful deep.

I vaguely heard shouts—arguing. "Ravencross, no! Don't. You'll never find her in those waves. Good Lord, not in your boots, man. You'll drown. "

Somewhere in front of me I heard a splash. But the water around me was not stirred.

They shouted his name, hollering for him to come back. In the feeble meanderings of my air-starved mind, it dawned on me that Gabriel had jumped in after me.

The thought spiked through me like a fiery dagger.

No!

With the same certainty that Georgie and Jane would've known I jumped, I knew Gabriel had dived in to come get me.

I moaned. Gabriel had a chest full of stitches. These waves would tear them out as sure as night follows day.

For his sake, I rolled to my side, belched out seawater, and flung my arm out, grabbing at the water in a desperate stroke forward. And then another. And another. A terrifying thought drove me to move faster. I remembered hearing of men who drowned because their boots filled with water and, like lead weights, dragged them under.

Where was he?

I swept seaweed out of my eyes and thought I saw him. At

least I saw *something* splashing in the water toward me. It could've been dolphin or a sea serpent for all I knew. But I aimed for it, fighting to keep afloat.

When next I chanced to look, I saw him fling one arm out of the water, grasping for purchase in the rolling waves. He was headed in my direction, doing his best to come to me. But when it was his other arm, his wounded arm's turn to carry him forward, he sank.

My scream was cut short by a surge of salt water slapping my face. I spewed it out and pushed toward where I saw him go under.

He burst up, several yards in front of me, flailing with one arm to stay up, his mouth open, gasping for precious air, just as he'd done in my wretched dream.

Mr. Sinclair shouted, "Good Lord, he's going under again. Ravencross, grab the barrel. It's right behind you."

He wouldn't.

I was in front of him. He wouldn't turn back. He wouldn't go anywhere but straight ahead.

To me.

Someone aboard the warship held a lantern down closer to the water. Just enough light for me to see Gabriel pitch forward and sink.

Before that night I had thought myself merely a competent swimmer, not nearly as good at it as I am at running. But the thought of him sinking under the waves set me to paddling harder than Mr. Sinclair's steam engine.

Right there in the frigid waters of the Atlantic I decided I wanted to live. I wanted to live very much. And the reason I wanted to live was drowning, right there, a few yards in front of my face. So I swam, and I thrashed my way through those swells with every last ounce of fire I had left in my furnace.

We nearly collided.

Sputtering, gulping, and spitting salt water, he cast his good arm out, trying to pull one-sided through a wave. I grabbed him and shoved him high enough that he could get a clean breath. Then I bobbed up from under the wave that enveloped us. In fits and starts he tried to talk. "Should've . . . taken off . . . m' boots," says he.

My shoulders shook at his proclamation. I kicked with all my might toward Cook's pickling barrel, dragging him along, wishing to heaven I could grab enough air so I could laugh, or cry. I wasn't sure which. We slapped our hands on the pickle barrel, gasping.

Someone tossed us a rope, and as I turned to snatch the end out of the water, I caught a glimpse of Daneska's sloop sailing away. *Escaping.* I coiled the rope around my wrist and Ravencross wrapped his good arm around my waist. Lord Wyatt and Captain Grey quickly pulled us to the warship. But when we reached the side of the craft, Gabriel kept hold of the barrel and insisted they lift me onto the boat first.

Captain Grey and Georgie hauled me out of the water. They no sooner pulled me onto the flat deck of the *Mary Isabella* than my stomach lurched. I crawled to the side and coughed up seawater while Georgie pulled back my hair and held my shoulders. Captain Grey warmed his coat on the furnace, and as soon as I finished my indelicate business and managed to right myself to a sitting position, he wrapped the warmed coat around my shoulders.

Jane and Lord Wyatt were tugging Gabriel aboard. I grabbed hold of the captain's arm. "You must go after them." He said nothing but patted my shoulders and went to help Lord Wyatt, who shouted that Gabe's ruddy boots weighed more than an anchor.

Georgie wrapped an arm around my shoulders. I pointed at the sloop's sail skating farther and farther away from us. "Go after them," I gasped. "They stole the plans."

Jane squatted down beside us. "No, Tess. Those were red herrings."

"A bit of misdirection," said Mr. Sinclair from the rudder.

Was I understanding her? "Red herrings?" I asked.

"Yes. Fakes." Jane's face brightened with mischief. "My idea."

I blinked. She'd kept another secret from me. But we could talk about that later. "What of Madame Cho?" I choked. "Is she—"

Georgie rubbed my arms, trying to warm away my shivers. "Miss Stranje, Sera, and Maya are with her. They sent for the doctor. We think she'll be all right." Georgie patted me. "Let's go home and see."

At last they pulled Gabriel aboard. Jane jumped aside as he sloshed up onto the *Mary Isabella* beside me.

"Your poor chest." I rested my hand on his shoulder, trying to see if there was blood mixed in with the muck from the ocean. "You've probably torn out every single stitch."

He was still grappling for breath and coughing up seawater. He shook his head and reached for my face, his fingers skimming the side of my cheek. I imagined he wanted to say something profoundly romantic, like *I love you so much I would rather have died a thousand deaths than lose you.* Instead he rolled to the side and let loose with more salt water.

Even in that light I could see the purplish bloom spreading across his chest. "Jane! He's bleeding. What do we do?"

But it was Captain Grey who sprang to Gabriel's aid. "For starters, we need to cut him out of that wet shirt."

Lord Wyatt threw another shovel full of coal into the furnace, slammed it shut, and rushed to kneel beside us. He drew a knife out of his boot.

"No need." Gabriel tried to object. He got as far as saying,

"I—I can take it off," before he retched again. I smoothed his wet hair back from his face. All he could do was nod.

Lord Wyatt slit the cambric so that Gabriel's shirt slid down his arms. "Gabe, turn so we can see the wound."

Gabriel nodded and flopped over. He swiped at his mouth and sat up, leaning back against me for support.

"Georgie, hold the lamp a bit lower, if you would." Sebastian produced a handkerchief and blotted gingerly at the wound. "You've torn it, and we've no alcohol to clean it out with." He stood and whipped off his coat, and after warming it as Captain Grey had done, he tucked it over Ravencross. "Keep him as warm as possible."

Captain Grey called out the order, "Make haste to shore, Mr. Sinclair."

"Aye." Mr. Sinclair saluted. "Lady Jane, consult your telescope to check our direction, if you please. Point us straight for the beach. Toss in more coal, my lord, and we'll see what she can do."

Moonlight illuminated the sail of Daneska's sloop, a tiny white wedge disappearing on the horizon.

I softly kissed the top of Gabriel's sodden head as he lay against me. It pleased me that he reached for my hand and wound his fingers in mine.

Twenty-seven

ᏀHE ᏉOW

Captain Grey offered to carry me up to the house, but I assured him that would not be necessary. "I rather think walking might put a stop to this infernal rocking and sloshing going on in my head."

"Ah." He nodded as if he'd experienced the feeling. "It might at that."

It was Gabriel I worried about. He was so tall and broad, how would we haul him up the cliffs?

He grumbled at me for even suggesting the idea. "My chest is torn open, Tess, not my legs. I am perfectly capable of making it up those cliffs."

All the same, Captain Grey and Lord Wyatt insisted that Gabriel walk between them on the hike up to the bluffs. We finally straggled to the top and were making our way to the house when Miss Stranje came running out, flapping toward us like a raven in the night. She carried a blanket, and the minute she reached me she wrapped it around me.

The fact that she carried a blanket surprised me. "You knew I'd jump."

"Oh, my dear sweet girl, of course I did." She pressed a kiss to my forehead. "I knew you would get away." She turned with a grateful smile to Captain Grey. "And that they would find you."

"Ravencross needs this more than I." I handed the blanket back. "Without him I would've drowned. His stitches are torn out, and he—"

She was already rushing to his aid.

Sera raced up, her elfin features twisted with worry. She clasped me as if I had returned from the dead. Although she is slight and weighs no more than air, she hugged me fiercely and didn't let go. A rush of feelings flowed from her and warmed me better than Miss Stranje's blanket. Sera's shoulders quaked and, in strangled fits and starts, she managed to say, "I was afraid we'd lost you."

If she were my little sister I couldn't have loved her one ounce more. I didn't know what to say or how to comfort her. So I teased her with false bravado. "You needn't have been afraid. It would take a great deal more than Lady Daneska to do me in."

"Indeed." She swiped away the tears on her cheek and grinned at that, shining brighter in that dark night than even the moon.

"Madame Cho?" I asked. "How is she?"

She caught her lip pensively. "Her chin required a few sutures but it will mend. But the injury to her head was quite severe." Sera guided me into the house.

Miss Stranje caught up to us. "When Madame Cho regained consciousness, her first words were asking after you. You can go see her as soon as we get you out of those wet clothes."

"But Gabriel—"

She tugged me aside as Lord Wyatt and Captain Grey helped Gabriel up the stairs. "The doctor is here and the men will see to changing his clothes. There's nothing you can do for him until after the doctor has examined him and taken care of what must be done."

I was dismissed. She followed the men up, issuing directions as to which spare room to put Lord Ravencross in, and sending Philip to fetch the doctor from Madame Cho's room.

"Come." Sera urged me up the stairs.

"What of Mr. Chadwick?" I asked, worried he might still be lurking about.

"We sent him home as soon as Miss Stranje realized you weren't coming back to the dining room. She guessed something was wrong. I saw her check the clock on the mantel at least three times. Not fifteen minutes passed before she feigned a severe headache and sent him packing." Sera's eyebrows lifted as if she found some private joke amusing. "Of course he knew she was pretending. Poor Mr. Chadwick, his curiosity about us is nearly driving him mad. Fortunately, I suspect he is far too polite to do anything about it."

"I wouldn't be too sure."

Sera helped me change and we slipped into Madam Cho's room.

Maya sat in a chair by the bed. She rose immediately when she saw me and hugged me gently, kissing each of my cheeks. "I knew you would escape."

"I wish I could've been so certain." I smiled awkwardly, unaccustomed to so much affection. "How is she?"

The three of us turned to look at our teacher. Madame Cho's head was bandaged awkwardly, leaving tufts of her dark hair sticking out around the edges. "She looks so very pale."

Maya squeezed my hand. "The doctor dosed her with laudanum. Our main concern is that she holds steady through the night."

"May I sit with her for a while?"

She nodded, and I took her chair. They stood beside me for a bit longer, watching the rise and fall of our patient's chest. "They've situated Lord Ravencross in the guest bedroom," I explained quietly to Maya. "But they won't let me see him. He tore open the old wound. Will you two please see if you can find out anything?"

Maya rested her hand on my shoulder for a moment. "We will. But you must not worry. He is very strong."

"Even strong men die of infection," I said.

Maya swept a lock of hair back and tucked it behind my ear. "Fear will not keep infection away."

I nodded, too weary to argue. They left and I leaned forward, resting my head on the bed beside Madame Cho. The sound of her breathing comforted me. When I'd been younger and alone in the house, she would sometimes come to the dormitorium and sleep in the bed across from mine, especially after I'd had a bout of bad dreams. The sound of her even breathing was like a soothing lullaby.

Ours was a wordless kinship. We shared the joy of strength and movement. I relished sparring with her, whether with sword, knife, or staff. She always challenged me to fight harder, smarter, faster. She'd given me a deep appreciation for a perfectly timed throw and taught me to anticipate movements in a fight as easily one does a partner's dance steps.

And we both understood the relentless instruction of pain.

I glanced up when her breathing faltered. "Fight," I whispered the words she'd urged me on with so often. "You must fight."

A moment or two later she fell back into the familiar breathing pattern and I laid my head down again, too exhausted to hold it up.

I don't know how much time passed before I felt Cho's hand

stroke my hair. I grabbed her hand and kissed her palm. "You're awake."

"Water," she rasped.

I helped her sip from a cup rigged with one of Georgie's slender glass tubes. She finished drinking and issued an order in a gravelly voice. "You look terrible. Go rest."

"Thank you for the pretty compliment." I stroked her hand. "But I'm staying right here."

"You need not stay. I have no fear of death, child." She breathed heavily and closed her eyes.

"Exactly," I whispered, not sure if she still heard me. "Which is why I must stay here and make certain you don't give up on life too easily."

"Why should I not?" Her old eyes flashed open, shining black in that dim light, hard and sharp, like two dagger points of obsidian. "You do."

"Not anymore." I clutched her hand and kissed it, and a tear slipped free and burned down my cheek, and then another. *Never again would I give up without a fight.* "Never again."

Madame Cho's lips spread in a contented smile. "Good." Her eyes closed and she drifted back to sleep.

A half hour later, Maya and Sera came back and delivered their report.

"We listened at the door," Maya confessed, as if the activity compromised her dignity.

"They must've dumped a great deal of alcohol on the wound because we could smell it from outside the door." Sera looked worried. "Not only that, but I heard Lord Ravencross grumble about it being a waste of perfectly good whiskey."

Maya hesitated and then said, "The doctor asked for Miss Stranje to hand him his scalpel and the sulfur powder, and to thread his needle."

Sera shifted uncomfortably. "So they must've cut away the damaged flesh and taken more stitches. After that it was just, you know . . ."

"Groans," I said.

They both nodded.

I left Madame Cho in their care and took off down the hall, where I paced up and down in front of Gabriel's room. My frustration boiled up and was ready to bubble over. I raised my hand, ready to pound on the door, when Miss Stranje opened it and stepped out into the hall.

"He's asleep now. We've given him laudanum. There's no sign of infection. Not yet. The doctor will sit with him through the night to make certain he doesn't become feverish."

I let out the breath I'd been holding.

"You, young lady, must get some rest. We will need a full accounting of events from you in the morning. Be at breakfast. We've plans to make."

I stared at her. Did she actually expect me to sleep while he was in pain? Apparently she did, because she shooed me down the hall as if I were a goose rooting around in her garden.

I fully intended to sneak into his room during the wee hours of the morning. But I am ashamed to say I drowsed and fell fast asleep. My only excuse was that I was exhausted. I awoke to find the sun was already up and it was time to go down to breakfast.

Miss Stranje caught up to me in the hallway outside the breakfast room. "Madame Cho is much improved this morning. Seeing you last night must've been a tonic."

"Wonderful." I smiled, greatly relieved. "Since I am such a tonic, when can I see Gabriel?"

Her back straightened and she turned very stiff and formal.

"The doctor left orders this morning that Lord Ravencross is to be confined to bed for a few days until we can be sure the new stitches will hold. I certainly can't allow you to visit a gentleman's bedroom. That would not only bring shame to my establishment, it would put you in complete disgrace."

"But I have already visited in his—"

"Hush." She held up one finger. "Regardless of what you may or may not have done in the past, in my house you will behave within the bounds of propriety."

We strolled into her sunny yellow breakfast room, but it might as well have been painted a dismal storm gray, for such was my temperament.

In terse sentences I related the events of the previous evening. When I explained that Lady Daneska had been free of her manacles since the second day of her imprisonment here, Captain Grey set down his fork and stared out the window.

"I wondered why she had been so easy to capture in Rye." He spoke softly, as if it pained him to admit it.

At this Lord Wyatt added, "It did seem a bit too easy." He and Georgie exchanged worried glances.

Miss Stranje tilted her head, studying the captain. "Then Lady Daneska wanted to be our prisoner all along. Knowing Rye was closer to Stranje House than to London, she would be fairly certain you would bring her here for questioning rather than London."

Captain Grey set his fork on his plate and sat back stiff shouldered. "I'm afraid we played straight into her hands."

"No matter." Mr. Sinclair finished a bite of his blueberry scone and dusted off his fingers. "It all turned up right in the end. They found the dummy plans, so at least they won't be hunting me for the time being."

Captain Grey agreed. "Yes, and the sooner we get you, the

real plans, and the prototype to London so Lord Castlereagh and the foreign office can have a look at it, the better."

"How soon will you be going?" Jane very carefully set down her glass, as if the lemon water were so precious it must not incur even the smallest ripple.

Captain Grey answered, "Tomorrow, or the next day, as soon as the craft is ready for travel and the plans and notes are ready."

To this she merely swallowed and stared at her plate for a moment. "Sera and I have finished the drawings and notes. They are ready." She said this in a flat, listless tone. "But are you sure it's safe to transport everything so soon? We have yet to determine who let Ghost into the house to steal the false plans."

It was as if we were back on the ship and just dropped over a huge wave. The scone slipped out of my fingers and fell on the plate. "Someone let Ghost in?"

Sera, who had been aimlessly pushing bits of a kipper around her plate, answered without looking up. "I checked everything. All the windows were locked tight, even in the kitchen and servants' quarters. There were no signs indicating he forced his way in."

I remembered something Ghost had said. "They knew," I blurted. "They *knew* where the plans would be. Ghost said, *They were right where they were supposed to be.* As if he and Daneska had been told where to look." I turned to Jane and Sera. "How did you know to make the misleading documents?"

Jane pursed her lips. Sera looked down at the demolished kipper on her plate.

"Sera and Jane suspected we might have another traitor in the house." Miss Stranje slowly turned the stem of her water glass. "They came to me and we discussed making the falsified drawings and notes. It was done in secret because we were concerned about whom to trust."

"You didn't trust even me?" I asked.

"Of course we trust you. But have you forgotten the original plan?" Jane acted as if I'd insulted her loyalty and not the other way around. "The plan was that the two of you would escape. If Lady Daneska had turned on you, we didn't want you to have to hide any more information than necessary."

I gripped the edge of the table to steady myself. "Do you know who did it? It can't be one of us. We were all at the celebration. Can it?" Inside I was screaming, we can't have another traitor. Not again. *Not again.*

Miss Stranje gave a quick shake of her head. "We don't know. Not yet. We will discuss the matter at another time."

The thought that someone in the house had betrayed us made my head hurt and my breakfast churn almost as badly as it had after swallowing all that salt water the night before.

The remainder of morning was taken up with planning the trip to London. Mr. Sinclair, the captain, and Lord Wyatt would sail the *Mary Isabella* east, then through the channel and straight up the Thames.

I begged to be excused, saying I needed to lie down for a nap. They were all very solicitous of my health. But I assured them I simply required a short rest.

Miss Stranje had forbidden me from seeing Lord Ravencross, but the doctor was gone and I knew a secret passage that led to that guest room. So I took myself off to the dormitorium and went directly to the panel on the back wall. One quick push and I was tiptoeing down a flight of rickety old stairs and around a corner with Punch and Judy scampering alongside me. I tossed them some bread to keep them from scurrying through into his room with me. The door was a narrow panel that opened up just beyond a small bureau to the side of his bed.

He wouldn't be able to see me from where he lay facing the

door. I crept ever so quietly so as not to disturb him. He lay perfectly still, his dark curls framing his Grecian features against the white pillow. He looked paler that normal.

"What took you so long?" He didn't even open his eyes.

"*Wretch.* How did you know it was me?"

"It was either a gigantic rodent climbing through the wall, or it was you. I made a lucky guess."

"You've such a way with words, my lord. Terribly flattering to be compared a giant rodent." I pretended to sulk.

He ignored that. "Where have you been? I thought I would go mad wondering how you are." At last he opened his eyes, and I couldn't help but smile at the warmth in them. So unlike his brother's.

"You are the one at risk for fever, not I." I laid my hand on his forehead, checking. "Gabriel, about your brother . . ."

He grabbed my hand and pulled it to his lips. "I know why you didn't tell me. Georgie explained."

I breathed out with relief.

His voice turned hard. "If I'd lost you because of him, I swear I would've hunted him down and finished the job."

"No, you wouldn't. You're not that kind of man. But what do you intend to do about him being alive?"

"I don't know." He closed his eyes and rubbed my fingers lightly against the rough stubble of his cheek. "At the moment, nothing."

He still looked dreadfully weary. "What were you thinking to jump in after me?"

He let go of my hand. His eyes blinked open and set my soul humming like a bee to molasses. "I was thinking that I'd rather be dead than live without you."

I swallowed and placed my hand on his bedside table to steady myself. "Well, that was rather foolish."

"I agree. Completely insane. Someone should knock some sense into me. But by all the stars, I would do it again."

I smiled. By now I was becoming quite accustomed to the muscles required to do so. "Then you may as well know, I made a vow to myself. When it looked as if I might never have the chance to kiss you again, I was filled with regret. So I vowed to do it more often."

"You made a vow?" His eyebrow lifted with curiosity.

"Yes."

"A sacred vow?"

"Don't be ridiculous. It was just a vow, like any other old vow."

"To kiss me more often?"

"I did say something to that effect."

"You did, and yet here I am still unkissed."

"You are a rather mercenary fellow, aren't you?"

"I warned you about my character defects. But in this case, I am merely trying to help you keep your vow. I've been told breaking such things can be perilous to one's soul, and since I wouldn't want you to suffer in the fires of—"

"Oh, very well, if you insist."

"No." He pressed back against the pillows and winced with pain for his trouble. "I shan't force you to do something that makes you unhappy."

No he wouldn't, would he?

"That's just the thing, Gabriel. It makes me quite happy, deliriously happy." I bent slowly to his mouth, and as I did, the light shifted, the smell of whiskey-soaked bandages and fresh linen vanished, the room shimmered away, and I seemed to fall through time and space.

I felt the most glorious sensation in my palm.

A small hand tucked inside mine.

I looked down and saw the achingly beautiful face of a little girl.

I knew immediately she was my daughter because I recognized some of my distinctive features reflected back in her dear little face. And even though she looked somewhat like me, it was obvious who her father must be. She had Gabriel's soft brown eyes.

What an adorable dress she wore, shaped like a little velvet bell. A bonnet framed her perfect features and I saw the gift in her. One day my daughter would have dreams. Even so, I wasn't afraid. Because I would be there to guide her.

I, too, wore peculiar fashions, a great round skirt nipped in at the waist, with absurdly huge sleeves. And yet I still sported daggers strapped to each calf, and . . . oh, yes! Inside my absurd sleeves, I had tucked a third knife sheath.

We stood on the cliffs of Stranje House. I'd untied my bonnet so I could feel the ocean breeze blow through my hair. On the other side of my little daughter stood her father, his face free of anger and pain. He stared out at a calm sea and a brilliant sky adorned with a few fluffy clouds. I soaked in the wonder of that moment, and joy whirled through my chest and flew all the way through my fingertips.

My daughter looked at her hand as if the sensation startled her. "Mama?"

All I could say was, "Yes, darling. Yes."

Anything else would've come out in a rush of tears.

For once I loved dreaming.

I didn't know if this was a vision of things to come, or simply a wishful daydream. It didn't matter. Dreams are really nothing more than possibilities. And this possibility filled me with hope.

"Tess?" Gabriel patted my cheek. "Tess, are you all right?"

"Yes," I answered weakly. "Yes, I am more than all right, my lord."

I finished what I'd begun and kissed him with all the sweetness and promise welling up inside me.

The door flew open. Miss Stranje looked in, alarmed. "Tess!

Stop that this instant, or I will force this make-believe betrothal of yours to become a reality. Good heavens!" Then she echoed the question I'd put to her a few days earlier. "What sort of girls' school do you think I am running?"

I smiled as I passed through the doorway. "A most unusual sort."

In answer, she swatted me on the behind, and Lord Ravencross laughed.

He never laughs.

AFTERWORD

D ear Reader,
    As you may have noticed, there is a significant depar-
ture from history in this story. Napoleon, even after his escape
from Elba, did not succeed as well as depicted in this story.
The Stranje House novels present an alternate history based
on events that happened in *A School for Unusual Girls*. We are
speculating on what might have happened if Louis XVIII had
been assassinated and Napoleon garnered the full backing of the
people of France.

Other background elements in the story are factual.

Napoleon's fascination with fate and interpreting dreams is
historically accurate. His Oraculum was left behind in his "Cab-
inet of Curiosities" when he fled Leipzig. He did indeed call it
his *Book of Fates*, and we still have copies of it today.

Mr. Sinclair, Robert Fulton's nephew, is a fictional character.
Although after reading Fulton's letters and several historical

commentaries on his character, I feel certain that if Fulton had a nephew interested in engineering, he would've taken that young man under his wing. He was that sort of man. Fulton was extremely generous to his widowed mother and sisters, and even purchased a farm for his mother.

All of Fulton's inventions mentioned in this story are real. He actually did build a submarine for Napoleon, the *Nautilus*. As you might have guessed, Jules Verne named his fictional submarine in honor of Fulton. In 1804, after having been frustrated by Napoleon's rejection of his work, Fulton offered those same ideas to Britain. The prime minister, William Pitt, commissioned him to build a submarine for England and also considered buying his steam-powered gunship. But shortly thereafter Admiral Nelson soundly defeated the French navy at Trafalgar, and Fulton's projects were no longer needed.

Robert Fulton returned home and built a warship for the United States, the famed *Demologos*. The warship described in this story is based on that design.

In my letter at the end of *A School for Unusual Girls* I mentioned the *domino effect*. One act, by one person, can have global impact. Consider altering one person in history, and follow the ripples through time. For example, what if Abraham Lincoln had died before he became president of the United States? Or George Washington. How would life be different?

Those two men were center stage. It's easy to see how different our lives would be without them. But there are other people working off stage who change life for millions of people; for instance Jonas Salk, who discovered a vaccine for polio. Or Robert Fulton. What about your family doctor? Your teacher? Or your best friend?

And you.

You make a difference in the lives of the people around you, and be certain, there is a ripple effect around the globe.

Kathleen Baldwin loves hearing from readers. You can contact her through her Web site, and also find other goodies there: book club guides, a Regency glossary, excerpts, and historical extras.

KathleenBaldwin.com.

Turn the page for a sneak peek at Jane's story,
to be told in Refuge for Masterminds,
Book 3 of the Stranje House series.

REFUGE FOR MASTERMINDS

Lady Jane Moore has a secret. A secret that must be kept buried. For if anyone discovered the truth, her life at Stranje House would crumble. And with Napoleon Bonaparte's invasion of England underway, everyone at Stranje House is already in danger. *Mortal danger.*

Jane knows it. She may not be like Tess, who has the advantage of prophetic dreams. Nor is she like Sera, who notices every detail no matter how miniscule and draws conclusions based on the smallest thread of evidence. She doesn't possess Maya's ability to soothe the tempers around her with a few well-spoken words. Neither is she a brilliant scientist like Georgie. According to Miss Stranje, Lady Jane Moore is a mastermind.

Jane doesn't consider herself a mastermind. Quite the contrary, she believes herself to be an ordinary young lady. It's just that she has a rather excessive bent toward the practical. She tends to grasp the facts of a situation quickly, and by so doing, she's able to devise and implement a sensible course of action.

But that's all there is to it. Well, there is the fact that she also organizes the players in her plans with quiet efficiency. So much so, that occasionally Lady Jane's friends tease her for being a bit managing.

Do they expect her to sit back and do nothing when trouble is brewing? *Not likely.* Not when the people she cares about are at risk. Call it being a mastermind if you must, it is a trait that comes in rather handy in a world full of spies, sabotage, and double-dealing. Especially now that Jane and Sera have rooted out the truth: *There is a traitor at Stranje House.*

Someone is sneaking information to Lady Daneska and Ghost, Napoleon's spies. Jane is determined to find out who it is before the bonds of friendship at Stranje House are ripped apart by suspicions. Her desperate hunt for the traitor ensnares Alexander Sinclair, the brash American inventor, in an ambush that puts his life in danger. Sinclair may well be the most maddening man in all of Christendom, a wicked-tongued rascal with boorish manners, but for some reason, Lady Jane cannot bear the thought of the golden-haired genius being harmed.

Is Jane enough of a mastermind to save Alexander, her friends at Stranje House, and possibly England itself?

Find out in *Refuge for Masterminds,* coming soon from Tor Teen.

TOR TEEN
READING AND ACTIVITY GUIDE TO

EXILE FOR DREAMERS

A Stranje House Novel

by Kathleen Baldwin

Ages 13–17; Grades 8–12

ABOUT THIS GUIDE

The Common Core State Standards–aligned questions and activities that follow are intended to enhance your reading of *Exile for Dreamers*. Please feel free to adapt this content to suit the needs and interests of your students or reading group participants.

Pre-reading Activities

1. *Exile for Dreamers* is told from the viewpoint of Tess, who sometimes feels more connected to the animal and natural world than human society. Ask students to think of a pet or favorite outdoor spot and write a 2–3 paragraph essay describing this animal or location, explaining how it makes them feel and, perhaps, when they feel drawn to this creature or place.

2. Much of the action of the novel takes place within the walls of Stranje House, a boarding school for "difficult" young women. Ask students to list other stories they have read which feature boarding school settings, such as the Harry Potter series, and to discuss any boarding school experiences they, friends, or family members may have had.

Have your group create a brainstorm list of their expectations for a story set in a boarding school.

Supports Common Core State Standards: W.8.3, W.9-10.3, W.11-12.3; and SL.8.1, SL.9-10.1, SL.11-12.1

DEVELOPING READING AND DISCUSSION SKILLS

1. As the novel begins, readers meet narrator Tess running. What reason does she give for her action? What other unusual qualities do readers discover about Tess in the opening pages of the novel? What information does Tess share about Stranje House and about her running companion, Georgiana?

2. At the end of chapter one and continuing in chapter two, Tess is the victim of what kind of violence? What violence does she herself wreak? What chain of events does this set in place with local law enforcement?

3. Describe Tess's feelings toward Lord Gabriel Ravencross as the story begins. Why does she feel that their relationship can have no future?

4. Describe the appearance and background of Jane, Sera, Maya, and Georgiana, Tess's fellow students at Miss Stranje's school. What special talents does each girl possess?

5. Consider the novel's title. What are at least three ways the notion of "exile" is at play in the story? Who do you think are the dreamers to which the title refers?

6. Whom do Miss Stranje and her students believe to be responsible for the attempted kidnapping of Georgiana and the attack on Lord Ravencross? What is this villain's relationship to Stranje House?

7. How does the arrival of Mr. Sinclair change the situation at Stranje House? Whom does Sinclair claim as his uncle? What does he propose to build while hiding at Stranje House? Do you think the girls are right to offer him their help? Explain your answer.

8. Who is Madam Cho? What role does she play at Stranje House? What is special about her relationship to Tess? What is special about Tess's relationships to Punch and Judy, and to Phobos and Tromos? How do all of these friendships impact your understanding of Tess's character?

9. What is unusual about Tess's dreams? How do Miss Stranje and the other students react to her dreams? What value do they believe the dreams hold? Does Tess feel the same way about her dreams as others do? Why or why not?

10. In chapter nine, what terrible truth do Tess's classmates admit to her? How does this relate to the dream that begins the chapter? What is Tess persuaded to do with this new information? How does this relate to the group's suspicions about Daneska's evil plans?

11. What is the Iron Crown? How does it pose a danger to England? What seems to be the relationship between Daneska, Ghost, and Napoleon?

12. In chapters ten and eleven, Tess reveals a great deal about her past to readers. Does this change your understanding of Tess's character or of the way she refuses Gabriel's proposal? Had you been a classmate of Tess, what advice might you have offered her?

13. As the novel progresses, the relationships between Jane and Sinclair, and between Sera and the younger Mr. Chadwick, become increasingly complex. How might these complications affect the students' perceptions of these men? Do you

think it makes them vulnerable? Cite examples from the novel to support your positions.

14. Describe the strange dream Tess has in chapter seventeen. Do you think this dream is prophetic or does is symbolize Tess's fear? If not her fear what else might it represent? What secret plan does this dream lead her to make? Do you think she will be able to follow through on this plan? Why or why not?

15. Explain the interface between the Stranje House group's plans to aid Mr. Sinclair, to deceive Mr. Chadwick, and to hunt down Daneska. What secrets must be kept (and from whom) to see each plan through?

16. What three individuals arrive at Stranje House in chapter eighteen? How does this change the group's understanding of Daneska and Ghost's plans? How does it affect their strategies at home?

17. On page 244, Miss Stranje tells Tess, "Hatred and anger are not the opposites of love. They are backsides of the same playing cards. It is easier to flip hostile feelings over and find the love and forgiveness that have been hidden there all along, aching to be found, than it is to produce new feelings." Do you agree? Can you think of examples from other books, movies, or your own life that prove or disprove Miss Stranje's advice?

18. Tess comes to learn that neither she nor Gabriel had an easy childhood. How might their childhood experiences have contributed to the bond the two now feel for each other?

19. Are Mr. Sinclair and the girls successful in building their prototype? What are the next steps for their invention? What horrible event occurs as they are celebrating the successful launch at Stranje House?

20. On page 333, Tess contrasts what she sees in Lucien's eyes with what she sees in Gabriel's. How does this harken back to her ability to understand animals?

21. What is finally revealed to be Daneska's plan for Tess? How does this revelation make Tess's dreams make sense?

22. How would you explain Tess's deep attachment to Stranje House? Why might she feel more connected to the place than the other students? How might this relate to her final future-facing dream near the novel's end?

23. From her curiosity about Madame Cho's childhood to her fear that her own life will end in madness, Tess is a character driven by the notion that the past and family define who we are and who we can become. How might this notion be applied to other characters in the story? Could this novel be read as a broader explanation of this notion? Explain your answer, citing quotes from the book.

Supports Common Core State Standards: RL.8.1-4, 9-10.1-4, 11-12.1-4; and SL.8.1, 3, 4; SL.9-10.1, 3, 4; SL.11-12.1, 3, 4

DEVELOPING RESEARCH AND WRITING SKILLS

People and Places

1. If you completed pre-reading activity #2, revisit it now. With friends or classmates, discuss the following questions: Were your expectations for a boarding-school story met? If so, in what ways? If not, what elements of this novel did you find most surprising?

2. Several outsiders arrive at Stranje House in the course of the story, and Miss Stranje and the girls struggle to keep them from knowing the truth about the place. In the character of

Mr. Sinclair or the younger Mr. Chadwick, write a series of journal entries describing your arrival at Stranje House, your first impressions of its mistress and students, and your thoughts about what is really being taught within the school's walls.

3. Daneska was once Tess's good friend at Stranje House. Create a chart comparing and contrasting these two characters in terms of their ability to love, their senses of duty and loyalty, their relationships to Stranje House, and their dreams for the future.

Regency and Romance

4. *Exile for Dreamers* is set in Regency England. Go to the library or online to learn more about this time in history. Make a timeline of key historical events of the period, paying particular attention to those involving Napoleon.

5. "Alternate history" is a literary genre in which recognizable historical figures have experiences different than those recorded in history books, and notable events end differently and lead to different futures. Based on your research in exercise 4, above, write a short essay explaining the historical events which have been changed to make *Exile for Dreamers* an "alternate history." Read your essay aloud to friends or classmates.

6. Overlapping the Regency Period is the Romantic Era. Go to the library or online to learn how people of the Romantic Era viewed art, literature, and nature. Who were some key literary and artistic figures of the era? What elements of Romanticism can be found in the language and characterizations in *Exile for Dreamers*? Create a multimedia-style presentation based on your research to share with friends or classmates.

7. With friends or classmates, role-play dialogues between Miss Stranje and Captain Grey, Georgiana and Lord Wyatt, and Tess and Gabriel. Have each couple discuss their sense of responsibility to England and their feelings of devotion to each other. Begin each role-play with one character saying, "Unfortunately, the heart does not care about logic" (page 217).

Dreams and Dreamers

8. The real Napoleon was fascinated by dreams. Go to the library or online to learn about dream theories of the nineteenth century and today. Create an information poster based on your research.

9. As the novel ends, it remains unclear how Ghost gained entry into Stranje House and what "insider" helped Daneska escape. Who do you think is the traitor? In the character of this person, write a confession to mail to Stranje House from your new place of exile.

10. In the afterward, author Kathleen Baldwin notes that "one act, by one person, can have global impact." With friends or classmates, discuss what this might mean for people in today's world. Could you act in a way that would affect many others? Perhaps you dream of curing a disease, negotiating peace, teaching kids, or coaching a team in an innovative way. Create a poem, set of song lyrics, or a visual art composition reflecting on the "one act" you dream of making and what you hope its impact will be.

Supports Common Core State Standards: RL.8.1-4, RL.9-10.1-4, RL.11-12.1-4; W.8.2-4, W.9-10.2-4, W.11-12.2-4; W.8.7-8, W.9-10.6-8, W.11-12.6-8; and SL.8.1, SL.8.4-5; SL.9-10.1-5; SL.11-12.1-5